A Basic Classical and Operatic Recordings Collection for Libraries

by
KENYON C. ROSENBERG

The Scarecrow Press, Inc.
Metuchen, N.J., & London
1987

Library of Congress Cataloging-in-Publication Data

Rosenberg, Kenyon C.
   A basic classical and operatic recordings
collection for libraries.

   1. Music--Discography. 2. Operas--Discography.
I. Title.
ML156.2.R7 1987   016.7899'12   87-12747
ISBN 0-8108-2041-2

Dedicated to Herman Quick With Respect,

Indebtedness and Affection

A BASIC CLASSICAL AND OPERATIC RECORDINGS COLLECTION

FOR LIBRARIES

PREFACE

It is the author's hope and intention to provide school, public and academic librarians (other than those whose libraries must support the programs of music schools or conservatories) with the means for either creating or augmenting a nuclear classical and operatic recordings collection. Nuclear is here taken to mean not only the usual representative group of well-known works by easily recognized composers (e.g., the Beethoven 5th, Tchaikovsky 4th, and Brahms 1st Symphonies), but also those works of quality by, perhaps, lesser known composers which are capable of either sustaining the interests, or satisfying the curiosity of intelligent audiences. Obviously, given the constraint of space, and the expressed aim of this work, not every composer will be represented.

For example, many of those of the rank following Rachmaninoff or Dvořák or Elgar are, for the most part, excluded. This means that the likes of Bottesini, Cage or Quantz will be absent. Exceptions are those odd composers who have one or more compositions which are sufficiently familiar or popular that their exclusion would cause audible eyebrow raisings. Examples of these latter would be Mouret (for his "Masterpiece Theater" fanfare) and Pachelbel, for his ubiquitous Canon. To the admirers of those worthies not herein represented, apologies, but ars longa, vita (et spatium) brevis.

The arrangement of this listing is alphabetical by composer's surname (spellings follow Schwann (i.e., the "Super" Schwann, as it now

iii

styles itself) for those names which require transliteration to the Rom
alphabet). Within that primary alphabet, works are alphabetical by gene
type (i.e., Ballet, Chamber, Choral, Concerted, Instrumental, Operat
Orchestral, Symphonic and Vocal); then alphabetical (and possi
numerical) by genre or form (or by opus or catalog number, e.g., t
Schmieder Thematisch–systematisches Verzeichnis.... for J.S. Bach
works). In the case of J.S. Bach specifically, I have chosen to use t
general type (e.g., Chamber, Choral, etc.), and then list the works
Schmieder number. I have done this because of the profusion of Bac
works, and the fact that most persons can readily identify a work wi
only the Schmieder number, if necessary. I believe this should ma
finding individual works of this composer somewhat simpler. Where mc
than one performance is given, the arrangement is, again, alphabetical
performer or ensemble. Availability in the U.S. was determined by usi
the Winter 1987 issue of the "Super" Schwann catalog.

SYMBOLS USED HEREIN:

"A"   Required in every library

"B"   Useful in medium and large public
       and academic libraries

"C"   Recommended only for large public
       and academic libraries

"*"   Best budget priced stereo version

"$"   Best regular stereo version, but more
       expensive than "*" (occasionally "$"
       may be used to denote a monophonic
       version which the manufacturer has
       scheduled at "regular" stereo price)

"$$"   The best and, probably, the most costly
       version, usually a digital or direct

recording, in other words: incomparable

"!" Monophonic version (usually budget priced) which offers a magnificent (or unique) performance, but sonic qualities less than any of the above

"🄱" Cassette version

A few words about interpreting the above:

1. In all cases of anthological recordings (i.e., where, in addition to the work recommended, there are additional, not necessarily recommended, pieces), the author has included in his selection criteria the intrinsic value of the collateral works, plus, of course, their performances and sonic qualities.

2. If your library already owns a copy of a work rated "A" and the version owned is one rated "*" or "$," you may wish to add a copy of one of the other recommended versions, particularly one rated either "!" or "$$." One of these may well satisfy your most discerning (or demanding) listeners (i.e., those who seek either historically interesting performances or "state-of-the-art" recordings).

3. When only one version of a work is listed (usually "*" or "$"), it is because both the performance and the sound quality are, in combination, the best possible, and anything more costly would be mere extravagance.

4. Upper and lower case letters are used herein to indicate the major and minor keys, respectively (e.g., "C" indicates the key of C major, "g" the key of g minor, etc.). Keys are not provided for works which contain more than ten separate items.

5. For those ballets (and other such works) which, in the original, are long and from which short, and usually popular, suites have been created, the author has frequently recommended the entire work. Often,

v

however, when a suite is more popular than the original work in toto, either the suite, or both the latter and the full work, may be recommended. Whatever the options, these recommendations were made with as little caprice as is within the author's meagre grasp, and are the result of considered judgement.

6. Recordings of the Musical Heritage Society are not listed in Schwann. They may be ordered from the Musical Heritage Society, 1 Park Road, Tinton Falls, New Jersey 07724. Membership in the Society gratis, and its catalog is available on request (and will be sent, for modest fee to new members at the time membership is requested). Occasionally, recordings on the Hungaroton, Qualiton or Supraphon labels may be difficult to obtain (and not all their items are listed in Schwann). Ordering information and catalogs may be gotten from Qualiton Imports Ltd., 39-28 Crescent Street, Long Island City, New York 11101.

7. The author has not attempted to judge performance on the basis of: the taking of repeats; minor augmentations of the score; or, solely, on the use of "authentic" (a most infelicitous term used to mean "contemporary with the composer") instruments. To have done so would have increased the space required for this tome, and would have been of primary interest to schools of music rather than to the audience intended. Where possible, however, the composers of cadenzas employed in concert are indicated.

8. Instead of prices for recordings, price ranges are indicated by symbols, which symbols are described below.

9. I extend, in advance, my apologies both for any errors (which, of necessity, I must own), and to those readers who do not find their favorite composers, works or performances listed between these covers. For these lacunae only the author is culpable. These choices are based on my own experience and the assistance of informed colleagues. It is hoped that those who employ this listing will find it useful as a selection tool for their libraries: on this be assured of my sincerity.

Although many librarians have recording vendors with whose prices and services they are pleased, the following listing is offered for those seeking new or additional reputable establishments which provide either unique services or discounts, or both (for _Schwann_ catalog subscriptions, address orders to "Super" Schwann, Dept. A0001, P.O. Box 41094, Nashville, TN 37204):

Liberty Music Shop
417 East Liberty Street
Ann Arbor, MI 48104
Phone: 313-662-0675
Offers discounts ranging from 25% to 50% discount on LPs, compact discs and tapes to _bona fide_ libraries (discount varies with size and frequency of orders, etc.). Particularly good for special ordering those European (and other foreign) labels which may be either not available or difficult to find in the U.S. Special orders accrue no discount.

Rose Records
214 South Wabash Avenue
Chicago, IL 60604
Phone: 312-987-9044

Offers minimum of 20% off "list price" for almost anything listed in Schwann (except for "cutouts," which are already discounted, and compact discs, which are discounted at 10% off "list:" exceptions are noted in the Rose Catalog, which may be had on request) to schools and libraries with open accounts. Orders over $50.00 require no postage or handling fee ($2.40 additional for each order, otherwise).

Serenade Records
1713 G Street, NW
Washington, DC 20006
Attention Mail Order Department
Phone: 202-638-5580

Like Rose Records, Serenade Records carries a very large stock of recordings. In addition, though, I have found the staff assigned to the classical recordings department to be the most knowledgeable I have encountered anywhere. Further, they are extremely service oriented. Serenade offers a variety of discounts depending on availability of the recordings, multiple copies, etc. Generally, however, their discounts do not exceed 30%.

THE CARE, HANDLING AND CLEANING OF RECORDINGS, ETC.

To protect recordings from the multifarious ills which may plague them, there are a few things which, if not only remembered, but also practiced, will extend their useful lives considerably. Here, then, some somber recommendations:

1. Don't put your grubby fingers on the playing surfaces. However meticulous you may be in your personal habits, unless you have just finished soaking them in aqua regia, your fingers are covered by a thin film of oil (and amino ACIDS) which will be transferred to the disc's surface. These "little" fingerprints will make for audible distortion and even worse, will tend to cause dust to adhere to those portions of the disc where they are to be found. If, before reading this, you have, in your blissful state, already gotten fingergoop on your precious recordings, all may not be lost. Try washing the disc by placing about a half gallon or so of tepid (please, NOT HOT!!!) water in a container large enough for the disc to lie in. Add about three or four drops of ordinary dish-washing liquid (e.g., Ivory, Lux, etc.). Stir the solution until you're satisfied that it really is a "solution," then place the disc into it, holding it (as you always should) by its edges with your palms. Move the disc about (up and down is best) within the solution for about 30 to 40 seconds. Remove the disc and, once more holding it properly (palms, remember?), rinse it thoroughly under gently running tepid water, then shake off as much water as you can. Stand the disc upright on a towel (yes, paper will do as well as cloth) and support it by leaning its upper edge (the ungrooved part

gainst some object so that it stands almost upright. Allow it so to stand until it is completely dry. For a truly unsanitarily dirty disc, after removing it from its bath try wiping its playing surfaces <u>GENTLY!!</u> with a very soft, lint-free cloth or paper before rinsing or drying it. If things have gotten this bad, though, shame on you! You probably mistreat small animals, too.

2. Don't store recordings near heat nor in direct sunlight. Unlike tropical fish or plants, recordings thrive best in a moderate temperature (a range of 65° to 75° F) and low relative humidity (less than 55%). Higher temperature will eventually probably cause warping, about which more later. Higher humidity may cause the formation of mold on the disc, or the jacket or the inner sleeve, or all three.

3. Don't leave recordings lying around. Aside from the clutter (of which your better friends will silently disapprove), your discs will probably become dusty, warped, or both. Place them vertically on shelves, and be sure that the opening of the inner sleeve faces up: this helps prevent dust from getting onto the disc, and tends to make removing the disc from its outer liner (or "jacket") neater since your fingers are prevented from contacting the disc's surface.

4. To help prevent a disc from warping: one of the principal causes of this phenomenon is storing discs in their "shrink wrap." By all and any means, remove and dispose of this non-biodegradable stuff immediately after receiving recordings. "Shrink-wrap" does tend to shrink as it ages (don't we all?) and will, ultimately, shape the disc rather like Quasimodo.

5. Since you can't keep your discs hermetically sealed, especially when playing them, try a little preventive maintenance to keep them clean. Do close the dust-cover of the turntable while the disc is on the platter (assuming the turntable will so allow—if the dust-cover will not properly close with a disc on the platter, obviously ignore my injunction—one must, after all, reason some things out for oneself). Also, several companies make devices which are rather like tone-arms, and which

contain some kind of brush and plush roller arrangement which will cle
the disc just before the stylus does its awesome task. There are seve
such devices, and I recommend their use. Better ones come with
conductive (graphite) brush and grounding cable arrangement which he
relieve the disc of its static charge (and thus allows dust to be remov
more easily). Whatever type of disc cleaner you elect to employ, if it
supplied with a fluid which is somehow to be used with the system,
recommend dumping the liquid and using plain distilled water instead
Some of the other liquids may cause chemical damage to your discs.
nifty gadget is the "rolling" record cleaner manufactured by Nagac
(priced about $20.00). It has a tacky surface which does not deposit a
residue on the disc's surface, but removes loose surface debris. T
Nagaoka is also easily cleaned and stored.

6. Not only is it important to clean your discs, it is equa
important to clean your stylus. After removing the head-shell from t
tone-arm, you may dip a fine, thin, soft artist's brush in distilled wat
and lightly (VERY lightly) "paint" the stylus from back to front. Bett
yet, buy a stylus cleaning kit. They are inexpensive, easy to use (a
usually come with explicit instructions or illustrations), and most of the
are good. Ask a reputable audio equipment dealer to recommend one.

7. What is true for phonograph discs is essentially true for casset
tapes, also. They are best kept in the same environmental temperatu
and humidity as discs, and they are best stored vertically in the
containers.

8. Cassette tapes should be kept stored in the "play" or "recor
wind modes rather than the "fast-forward" or "rewind" modes. The
latter two tend to wind the tapes unevenly and erratically. If you dor
believe me, look at one tape rewound in "play" and one in "fast-forward
notice that the tape in the first is very smooth along the miniature spo
while the second is "ragged" and sloppy in its appearance.

9. Keep cassette tapes away from magnetic fields (e.g., electr

x

ons, loudspeakers, telephones, or any device which has <or induces> a
agnetic field). The magnetism of such devices may erase portions of the
pes, or change a Beethoven 5th Symphony to a work by Stravinsky.

10. Clean and demagnetize the heads in your tape recorder/player
ith the appropriate head cleaning tapes (there are several on the market,
st get one made by a "name" manufacturer) and use a demagnetizing
assette (again, made by a recognizably reputable manufacturer).

A few words about any errors encountered herein: I fall back on
ie ingenious statement of Melville's (in _Typee_): "No one can be more
ensible than the author of his deficiencies in this and many other respects
.. he hopes the reader will charitably pass over his shortcomings...."

K. C. Rosenberg
Alexandria, Virginia
February, 1987

ADAM, ADOLOPHE—CHARLES
1803–1856

A composer of numerous once popular operas and ballets, Paris-born Adam's fame now rests solely on his score for the ballet <u>Giselle</u>.

Ballet

B <u>Giselle</u> (1841)

$ London Symphony Orchestra; Anatole Fistoulari, conductor; Mercury 2-77003 (2 discs).

ALBÉNIZ, ISAAC
1860–1909

Albéniz was a Spanish Nationalistic composer whose suite of piano pieces, called <u>Iberia</u>, is very popular and much recorded.

Instrumental

B <u>Iberia</u> (19) Nos.1–12

* Alicia De Larrocha, piano; Turnabout 34750–34751 (2 discs), ▣ CT–4750–4751.

ALBINONI, TOMASO
1671–1750

Composer of well over 40 operas, many concerti, cantatas, etc., Albinoni was also a famous violinist. He was sufficiently well thought of by Johann Sebastian Bach that the latter composed two fugues on some of Albinoni's themes. Ironically, Albinoni is now known almost exclusively for his Adagio (which was fleshed out from an Albinoni fragment in this century by one Remo Giazotto) and for his Concerti for Oboe.

Orchestral

A Adagio, in g

* Toulouse Chamber Orchestra; Louis Auriacombe, conductor; Seraphim S-60271, ▣ 4XG-60271. Includes Corelli's Concerto grosso ("Christmas"), Op.6 No.8, in g; Mozart's Serenade ("Eine kleine Nachtmusik") for Strings, in G, K.525 and Pachelbel's <u>Kanon</u>, all also rated A.

C Concerti for Oboe and Orchestra, Op.9, Nos.1-12

$ Heinz Holliger, oboe; I Musici; Philips ⓢ 7313012. Includes Nos.2, in d; 5, in C; 8, in g and 11, in B flat.

ALFVÉN, HUGO
1872-1960

Swedish Nationalistic composer Hugo Alfvén's only truly popular work is the Swedish Rhapsody No.1, often called Midsommarvarka (literally "Midsummer Vigil").

Orchestral

B Swedish Rhapsody No.1 (1904)

$ Philadelphia Orchestra; Eugene Ormandy, conductor; Columbia MS-7674. Includes Sibelius' Finlandia, Op.26, rated A and Karelia Suite, Op.11, rated B; also Grieg's Norwegian Dance Op.35 No.2, rated B, "Homage March" from the Sigurd Jorsalfar Suite, Op.22 and the "Norwegian Rustic March" from the Lyric Suite, Op.56. With the exception of the Alfvén work the performances are lackluster.

ALKAN, CHARLES VALENTIN
1813-1888

Alkan (real name Charles-Henri Valentin Morhange) has to be one of the most eccentric yet most original Early Romantic composers of the third rank (his eccentricity even extended to his modus morendi: Alkan was a Talmudic scholar who was "pressed" to death when reaching for a volume, ostensibly one of the Talmud, which reposed on one of the top shelves of a bookcase; the bookcase and its contents fell upon him, thus ending his life at age seventy-four). Although he was born twenty years before Brahms and forty-nine before Debussy, Alkan's piano music presages that of both in its use of advanced (and often bizarre) chromatic harmonies. Also bizarre are some of his titles: Marche funèbre d'un Papagallo ("Funeral March for a Parrot"), Le Frisson ("The Shiver"), etc. Much of his piano music is of great technical difficulty and is often very evocative of things natural (e.g., the wind, sea, etc.). His importance as a composer was only really recognized in the mid-1950s. It would appear that Alkan also had some difficulty with his own music since, after retiring from concertizing (at age sixty), he would privately play the music of any composer except that written by himself.

Instrumental

C Études for Piano, Op.39 (12), No.1-7 and 12: all in minor keys (No.1,"Comme le vent;" No.2, "En rhythme molosique;" No.3 "Scherzo diabolico;" Nos.4-7, "Sinfonie" <"Allegro assai;" "Adagio;" "Allegretto alla barbaresca;" "Ouverture"> and No.12, "Le Festin d'Ésope")

* Michael Ponti, piano; Candide 31045.

C <u>Grande Sonate</u>, Op.33
\$ Ronald Smith, piano; Arabesque 8140, 8140.

ARENSKY, ANTON
1861-1906

Anton Stepanovich Arensky was born in Novgorod (Russia) and studied composition for three years with Rimsky-Korsakov at the St. Petersburg Conservatory. Following his graduation in 1882, he was appointed professor of harmony and counterpoint at the Moscow Conservatory. The volume of work produced by Arensky is not very great, but his compositions are marked by a stylistic similarity to Tchaikovsky: affecting melodies and colorful orchestration. Although Arensky did not possess a genius of Tchaikovsky's magnitude, he is relatively well-known for a few lovely and touching pieces. Arensky succumbed to tuberculosis in a sanitarium in Terijoki, Finland (where he had been a patient for many years).

Chamber

C Trio for Violin, 'Cello and Piano, Op.32, in d

\$ Jascha Heifetz, violin; Gregor Piatigorsky, 'cello; Leonard Pennario, piano. RCA LSC-2867. Includes Martinu's Duo for Violin and 'Cello (1927) and Vivaldi's Concerto for Violin, 'Cello, String Orchestra and Continuo (with Malcolm Hamilton, harpsichord).

BACH, CARL PHILIPP EMANUEL
1714-1788

C.P.E. Bach (sometimes called the "Berlin" or "Hamburg" Bach) was the second son of Johann Sebastian Bach (by his first wife, Maria). He received his second and third forenames from those of his godparents: Georg Philipp Telemann a major composer, and friend and contemporary of the elder Bach's; and Adam Emanuel Weltzig (a court musician at Weissenfels). C.P.E. was well known for his prowess as a keyboard performer (he is generally considered the founder of the "expressive" style of keyboard writing). He was equally well known for his compositions (wherein he is noted for his Empfindsamkeit, or "expressiveness") which, in retrospect, serve as a bridge between the contrapuntal marvels of his father (C.P.E. thought little of counterpoint) and the great classicism exemplified by Haydn at his height. The "W" listing for his works are from the Wotquenne Catalogue thématique des oeuvres de C. Ph. E. Bach.

Concerted

C Concerti for 'Cello and Strings, W.171-172 (2), Nos.1-2: in B flat and A

$ Csaba Onczay, 'cello; Liszt Chamber Orchestra; János Rolla, conductor; Hungaroton 12229.

Instrumental

C Sonatas for Harpsichord, W.48 ("Prussian") (6), Nos.1-6

$ Louis Bagger, harpsichord; Musical Heritage Society 1885Y.

BACH, JOHANN CHRISTIAN
1735-1782

Known as the "English" or "London" Bach (for having lived the last twenty-five years of his life in London), Johann Christian was the youngest son of Johann Sebastian and that notable's second wife, Anna Magdalena. According to contemporary reports he was not a particularly good keyboard performer. However, under the influence of his elder brother, C.P.E., he gained sufficient repute as a composer that no less than Mozart mourned his passing and the subsequent "loss to the musical world." J.C. Bach's compositional style was somewhat Italianate and less "formal" than that of most of his predecessors. His way with charming melodies and his essays into the early symphonic form make him a most easily accessible and comprehensible composer for today's listeners.

Symphonic

4

B Symphonies, Op.6 (6), Nos.1–6: in G, D, E flat, B flat and g

$ Academy of St. Martin-in-the-Fields; Sir Neville Marriner, conductor; Philips 9502001.

BACH, JOHANN SEBASTIAN
1685–1750

One of the four or five giants of Western music, Johann Sebastian Bach was undoubtedly the greatest Baroque exponent of counterpoint, though the frequent apparent ease of his works belies their complexity. He was also well known, even during his lifetime, as one of the greatest of all organists. As a composer, however, his greatest fame came posthumously, and the revival of his works was in large part due to the efforts of Mendelssohn. Bach was married twice (first to his cousin: Maria Barbara Bach, who died in 1720; then to Anna Magdalena Wülken) and was the father of 20 children (7 with Maria, 13 with Anna Magdalena), several of whom became notable musicians in their own rights. Another example of his prodigiousness is the number and variety of his compositions: about 300 cantatas for the Lutheran Church; Passions for each of the four Gospelists; a large number of secular vocal works, four "suites" for orchestra (the introductory movements are actually rudimentary symphonies); a vast number of chamber pieces (many of them for solo keyboard, violin, 'cello, etc.); numerous concerti (including the famous six "Brandenburg" Concerti); and a massive number of oeuvres for solo organ. The Schmieder Thematisch-systematisches Verzeichnis.... of J.S. Bach's works (by means of which numbers Bach's compositions are arranged herein) lists over one thousand separate items by this incomparable genius.

Chamber

C S.1014–1019, Sonatas for Violin and Harpsichord (6), Nos.1–6: in b, A, E, c, f and G

$ Alice Harnoncourt, violin; Nikolaus Harnoncourt, viola da gamba; Herbert Tachezi, harpsichord; Teldec 2635310 (2 discs).

* Josef Suk, violin; Zuzana Ružičková, harpsichord; Quintessence 2703 (2 discs), ♭ 2703.

C S.1030–1035, Sonatas for Flute and Harpsichord (6), Nos.1–6: in b, E, A, c, e and E

* Jean-Pierre Rampal, flute; Robert Veyron-Lacroix, harpsichord; Odyssey Y2-31925 (2 discs).

B S.1079, <u>Musikalische</u> <u>Opfer</u> ("Musical Offering")
$ Vienna Concentus Musicus; Nikolaus Harnoncourt, conductor; Teldec 641124, ⊟ 441124.

A S.1080, <u>Kunst</u> <u>der</u> <u>Fuge</u> ("Art of the Fugue")
$$ Cologne Musica Antiqua; DG ARC-413728-1 AH2 (2 discs), ⊟ 413728-4 AH2.

$ Herbert Tachezi, organ; Teldec 2635373 (2 discs).

Choral (A. Cantatas)

B S.51, <u>Jauchzet</u> <u>Gott</u> <u>in</u> <u>allen</u> <u>Landen</u> ("Praise God in all Lands")
$ Teresa Stich-Randall, soprano; Saar Chamber Orchestra; Karl Ristenpart, conductor; Nonesuch 71011, ⊟ N5-71011. Includes the same composer's Magnificat, S.243, in D (with Bianca Maria Casoni, contralto; Pietro Botazzo, tenor and György Littasy, bass), also rated B.

A S.80, <u>Ein</u> <u>feste</u> <u>Burg</u> <u>ist</u> <u>unser</u> <u>Gott</u> ("A Mighty Fortress is Our God")
$ Edith Mathis, soprano; Trudeliese Schmidt, soprano; Dietrich Fischer-Dieskau, baritone; Munich Bach Orchestra; Karl Richter, conductor; DG ARC-2533459. Includes Bach's Cantata, S.140 (with Peter Schreier, tenor), <u>Wachet</u> <u>auf</u>! ("Sleepers Awake"), which is also rated A.

A S.140, <u>Wachet</u> <u>auf</u>! ("Sleepers Awake")--see entry for Cantata S.80, <u>Ein</u> <u>feste</u> <u>Burg</u> <u>ist</u> <u>unser</u> <u>Gott</u> ("A Mighty Fortress is Our God"), immediately <u>supra</u>.

B S.147, <u>Herz</u> <u>und</u> <u>Mund</u> <u>und</u> <u>Tat</u> <u>und</u> <u>Leben</u> ("Heart and Mouth and Deed and Life")
$ Elly Ameling, soprano; Dame Janet Baker, mezzo-soprano; Ian Partridge, tenor; John Shirley-Quirk, baritone; King's College Chapel Choir, Cambridge; Academy of St. Martin-in-the-Fields; Sir David Willcocks, conductor; Angel S-36804. This Cantata is justly famous for the exquisite aria "Jesu, Joy of Man's Desiring." Includes the same composer's

Motets, S.226, <u>Der Geist Hilft</u> ("The Spirit Helps"); S.228, <u>Fürchte dich</u> <u>nicht</u> ("Fear Not") and S.230, <u>Loben den Herrn</u> ("Praise the Lord").

C S.202, <u>Weichet nur</u> ("Just Depart") (Known as The "Wedding Cantata")

* Elly Ameling, soprano; Collegium Aureum; Quintessence 2704 (2 discs), ⓑ 2704. Includes Bach's Cantatas S.209, <u>Non sa che sia dolore</u> ("He Who Knows Not Sadness"); S.S.211, <u>Schweiget stille, plaudert nicht</u> ("Be Still!, Don't Chatter!") (Known as The "Coffee Cantata"), rated C and S.212, <u>Mer hahn en neue Oberkeet</u> ("We Have a New Squire") (Known as The "Peasant Cantata"), rated C.

A S.208, <u>Was mir behagt</u> ("What Pleases Me") (Known as The "Hunt Cantata")

\$ Arleen Augér, soprano; Edith Mathis, soprano; Peter Schreier, tenor; Theo Adam, bass; Berlin Chamber Orchestra; Peter Schreier, conductor; DG ARC-2533364. This work contains the lovely soprano aria known as "That the Sheep May Safely Graze."

C S.211, <u>Schweiget stille, plaudert nicht</u> ("Be Still! Don't Chatter!") (Known as The "Coffee Cantata")--see entry for S.202, <u>Weichet nur</u> ("Just Depart") (Known as The "Wedding Cantata"), <u>supra</u>.

C S.212, <u>Mer hahn en neue Oberkeet</u> ("We Have a New Squire") (Known as The "Peasant Cantata")--see entry for S.202, <u>Weichet nur</u> ("Just Depart") (Known as The "Wedding Cantata"), <u>supra</u>.
Choral (B. Magnificat)

B S.243, in D--see entry for S.51, <u>Jauchzet Gott in allen Landen</u> ("Praise God in All Lands") under Choral (A. Cantatas), <u>supra</u>.
Choral (C. Mass)

A S.232, in b

\$ Rotraud Hansmann, soprano; Emiko Liyama, soprano; Helen Watts, contralto; Kurt Equiluz, tenor; Max van Egmond, bass; Vienna Concentus Musicus; Nikolaus Harnoncourt, conductor; Teldec 48233 (2 discs).
Choral (D. Oratorios)

A S.248, <u>Christmas</u>

$ Paul Esswood, counter-tenor; Kurt Equiluz, tenor; Siegmund Nimsgern, bass; Wiener Sängerknaben Chor; Chorus Viennensis; Vienna Concentus Musicus; Nikolaus Harnoncourt, conductor; Teldec 3635022 (3 discs), ▣ 3435022.

* Agnes Giebel, soprano; Marga Höffgen. contralto; Josef Traxel, tenor; Dietrich Fischer-Dieskau, baritone; Leipzig Gewandhaus Chorus and Orchestra; Kurt Thomas, conductor; Seraphim S-6040 (3 discs).

C S.249, Easter

* Helen Donath, soprano; Anna Reynolds, mezzo-soprano; Ernst Haefliger, tenor; Martti Talvela, bass; RIAS Chamber Chorus; Berlin Radio Symphony Orchestra; Lorin Maazel, conductor; Philips Sequenza ▣ 7311084.

Choral (E. Passions)

A S.244, St. Matthew

$ James Bowman, counter-tenor; Paul Esswood, counter-tenor; Tom Sutlicffe, counter-tenor; Kurt Equiluz, tenor; Max van Egmond, bass; Karl Ridderbusch, bass; King's College Chapel Choir, Cambridge; Vienna Concentus Musicus; Nikolaus Harnoncourt, conductor; Teldec 4635047 (4 discs).

$ Edith Mathis, soprano; Dame Janet Baker, mezzo-soprano; Peter Schreier, tenor; Dietrich Fischer-Dieskau, baritone; Matti Salminen, bass; Regensburger Domspatzen; Bach Chorus and Orchestra, Munich; Karl Richter, conductor; DG ARC-2712005 (4 discs), ▣ 3376016.

C S.245, St. John

* Kurt Equiluz, tenor; Bert Van t'Hoff, tenor; Max van Egmond, bass; Siegfried Schneeweiss, bass; Jacques Villisech, bass; Wiener Sängerknaben Chor; Chorus Viennensis; Nikolaus Harnoncourt, conductor; Teldec 48232 (2 discs).

C S.246, St. Luke

$ Vienna State Opera Chamber Chorus and Orchestra; George Barati, conductor; Lyrichord 7110 (3 discs).

Concerted

A S.1041-1042, Concerti (2) for Violin and Orchestra, Nos.1-2: in a and E. S.1042 is a transcription, by Bach, of his S.1058, Concerto for Harpsichord and Strings, in D, rated A.

$ Alice Harnoncourt, violin; Walter Pfeiffer, violin; Vienna Concentus Musicus; Nikolaus Harnoncourt, conductor; Teldec 641227, ▣ 441227. Includes Bach's S.1043, Concerto for 2 Violins and Orchestra, in d (with Walter Pfeiffer, violin): arranged, by Bach, from his S.1062, Concerto for 2 Harpsichords and Strings, also rated A.

A S.1043, Concerto for 2 Violins and Orchestra, in d, this is a transcription, by Bach, of his S.1062, Concerto for 2 Harpsichords and Strings--see entries for S.1041-1042, Concerti (2) for Violin and Orchestra, Nos.1-2: in a and E. S.1042 is a transcription, by Bach, of his S.1058, Concerto for Harpsichord and Strings, in D, immediately supra.

A S.1046-1051, ("Brandenburg") Concerti (6) for Various Instrumental Combinations and Orchestra, Nos.1-6: in F, F, G, G, D and B flat
   $ English Concert; Trevor Pinnock, conductor; DG ARC-2742003 (2 discs), ▣ 3383003.
   * Jean-François Paillard Chamber Orchestra; Jean-François Paillard, conductor; RCA AGL2-5289 (2 discs), ▣ AGL2-5289.

A S.1052-1065, Concerti (14) for 1, 2, 3 or 4 Harpsichords and Strings
   $ Gustav Leonhardt, harpsichord; Leonhardt Consort and Vienna Concentus Musicus; Gustav Leonhardt, conductor; Teldec 5635049 (5 discs). Includes S.1052-1058, Concerti (7) for Solo Harpsichord and Strings; S.1059, Concerto for Harpsichord, Oboe and Strings, rated B; S.1060-1062, Concerti (3) for 2 Harpsichords and Strings; S.1063-1064, Concerti (2) for 3 Harpsichords and Strings and S.1065, Concerto for 4 Harpsichords and Strings. Additional soloists are Herbert Tachezi, harpsichord; Alice Harnoncourt, violin and Jürg Schaftlein, oboe.

A S.1052, Concerto for Harpsichord and Strings, in d
   * Glenn Gould, piano; Columbia Symphony Orchestra; Vladimir Golschmann, conductor; Columbia MY-38524, ▣ MYT-38524. Includes Bach's S.1053, Concerto for Harpsichord and Strings, in E and S.1056, Concerto for Harpsichord and Strings, in f, both also rated A.
   $ Herbert Tachezi, harpsichord; Vienna Concentus Musicus; Nikolaus Harnoncourt, conductor; Teldec 641121, ▣ 441121. Includes a very nice

performance of S.1060, Concerto for Violin and Oboe, in c: arranged by Bach from his Concerto for 2 Harpsichords and Strings, in c (same Schmieder number), which is also rated A, and featuring soloists Alice Harnoncourt, violin; Jürg Schaftlein, oboe.

Also--see entries for S.1052-1065, Concerti (14) for 1, 2, 3 or 4 Harpsichords and Strings, immediately supra.

A S.1053, Concerto for Harpsichord and Strings, in E

$ Glenn Gould, piano; Columbia Symphony Orchestra; Vladimir Golschmann, conductor; Columbia MS-7294. Includes Bach's S.1055, Concerto for Harpsichord and Strings, in A, also rated A.

Also--see entries for S.1052-1065, Concerti (14) for 1, 2, 3 or 4 Harpsichords and Strings.

A S.1054, Concerto for Harpsichord and Strings, in D

$ Glenn Gould, piano; Columbia Symphony Orchestra; Vladimir Golschmann, conductor; Columbia MS-7001. Includes S.1056 and S.1058, Concerti for Harpsichord and Strings, in f and g, both also rated A.

Also--see entry for S.1052-1065, Concerti (14) for 1, 2, 3 or 4 Harpsichords and Strings, supra.

A S.1055, Concerto for Harpsichord and Strings, in A--see entries for S.1053, Concerto for Harpsichord and Strings, in E, and S.1052-1065, Concerti (14) for 1, 2, 3 or 4 Harpsichords and Strings, both supra.

A S.1056, Concerto for Harpsichord and Strings, in f--see entries for Harpsichord and Strings, in D, S.1054, Concerto for Harpsichord and Strings, in D and S.1052-1065, Concerti (14) for 1, 2, 3 or 4 Harpsichords and Strings, all supra.

A S.1058, Concerto for Harpsichord and Strings, in g--see entries for S.1054, Concerto for Harpsichord and Strings, in D, and S.1052-1065, Concerti (14) for 1, 2, 3 or 4 Harpsichords and Strings, both supra.

B S.1059, Concerto for Harpsichord, Oboe and Strings, in d--see entry for S.1052-1065, Concerti (14) for 1, 2, 3 or 4 Harpsichords and Strings, supra.

A S.1060, Concerto for Violin, Oboe and Strings, in c,--see entries for S.1052-1065, Concerti (14) for 1, 2, 3 or 4 Harpsichords and Strings and under Marcello, Concerted, Concerto for Oboe and Strings, in d (1716), infra.

A S.1062, Concerto for 2 Harpsichords and Strings, in c--see entries S.1052-1065, Concerti (14) for 1, 2, 3 or 4 Harpsichords and Strings, supra.

A S.1063, Concerto for 3 Harpsichords and Strings, in d
* Robert Cassadesus, piano; Gaby Cassadesus, piano; Jean Cassadesus, piano; Philadelphia Orchestra; Eugene Ormandy, conductor; Odyssey Y-31531. Includes Bach's S.971, Concerto ("Italian"), in F, also rated A, and Mozart's Concerto for 3 Pianos, in F, K.242, rated C.
Instrumental (A. Solo 'Cello)
B S.1007-1012, Suites (6), Nos.1-6: in g, a, c, b, d and E
$ Lynn Harrell, 'cello; London 414163-1 LH2 (2 discs), ♭ 414163-4 LH2.
$ János Starker, 'cello; Mercury 77002 (3 discs).
Instrumental (B. Solo Harpsichord)
B S.772-801, Two-Part Inventions (15); Three-Part Inventions ("Symphonies") (15)
$ Glenn Gould, piano; Columbia D3S-754 (3 discs).   Includes S.825-830, Partitas (6), Nos.1-6: in B flat, c, a, D, G and e, also rated B.
* George Malcolm, harpsichord; Nonesuch 71144.   (Two-Part Inventions only).

B S.806-811, Suites ("English") (6), Nos.1-6: in A, a, g, F, e and d
$ Alan Curtis, harpsichord; Teldec 4635452 (4 discs).   Includes S.812-817, Suites ("French") (6), Nos.1-6: in d, c, b, E flat G and E, rated C.
$ Glenn Gould, piano; Columbia M2-34578 (2 discs).

C S.812-817, Suites ("French") (6), Nos.1-6: in d, c, b, E flat, G and E

$$ Christopher Hogwood, harpsichord; L'Oiseau Lyre 411811-1 OH2 (2 discs), ⌑ 411811-4 OH2.

Also--see entry for S.806-811, Suites ("English") (6), Nos.1-6: in A, a, g, F, e and d, immediately _supra_.

B S.825-830, Partitas (6), Nos.1-6: in B flat, c, a, D, G and e--see entry for S.772-801, Two-Part Inventions (15); Three-Part Inventions ("Symphonies") (15), _supra_.

A S.846-893, Wohltempierte Klavier ("Well-tempered Clavier"), (48 Preludes and Fugues <one for each Major and minor key>, sometimes called "The Mighty 48;" the work is in 2 Books, each of 24 selections)
$ Glenn Gould, piano; Columbia M4-42042 (4 discs), ⌑ M4-42042.

B S.906, Fantasia, in c
$ Trevor Pinnock, harpsichord; DG ARC-410706-1 AX2 (2 discs), ⌑ 410707-4 AX. Includes the same composer's S.894, Preludium, Fugue and Allegro, in a; S.903, Chromatic Fantasy and Fugue, in d and S.910 and S.912, Toccatas for Harpsichord (2) (from S.910-916, Toccatas and Fugues for Harpsichord <7>), in f sharp and D.

A S.971, Concerto ("Italian"), in F--see entry for S.1052, Concerto for Harpsichord and Strings, in d, under Concerted, _supra_.

A S.988, Variations ("Goldberg") (Aria with 30 Variations)
$ Glenn Gould, piano, Columbia IM-37779, ⌑ IMT-37779.
* Gustav Leonhardt, harpsichord; Quintessence 7151, ⌑ 7151.
$ Trevor Pinnock, harpsichord; DG ARC-2533425, ⌑ 3310425.
Instrumental (C. Solo Organ)
B S.542, Fantasy and Fugue, in g (The "Great")
$ E. Power Biggs, organ; Columbia M-31424, ⌑ MT-31424. Includes S.544, Prelude and Fugue in b; S.545, Prelude and Fugue, in C; S.572, Fantasy in G; S.680, Chorale Prelude, "Wir glauben all' an einen Gott, Schöpfer" ("We All Believe in One God, the Creator") and S.753, "Jesu, meine Freude" ("Jesus, My Joy"), from the Clavierbüchlein vor Wilhelm Friedemann Bach ("Little Clavier Book for Wilhelm Friedemann Bach"), written by J.S. for his eldest son.

A S.543, Prelude and Fugue, in a

$ E. Power Biggs, organ; Columbia MS-6748. Includes S.540, Toccata, in F; S.552, Prelude and Fugue, in E flat ("St. Anne"), also rated A; S.590, Pastorale, in F and S.654, Chorale Prelude, "Schmücke dich, o liebe Seele" ("Adorn Thyself, Oh Beloved Soul").

B S.552, Prelude and Fugue, in E flat ("St. Anne")--see entry for S.543, Prelude and Fugue, in a (The "Great"), immediately supra.

A S.564, Toccata, Adagio and Fugue, in C--see entry for S.565, Toccata and Fugue, in d, immediately infra.

A S.565, Toccata and Fugue, in d

$ E. Power Biggs, organ; Columbia MS-6261. Includes Bach's S.564, Toccata, Adagio and Fugue, in C; S.577, Fugue, in G (The "Jig"); S.578, Fugue, in g (The "Little") and S.582, Passacaglia and Fugue, in c, all also rated A. These are among the most powerful and thoughtful Bach organ performances recorded, and Biggs plays even the most difficult passages with great ease and intelligence.

* Symphony Orchestra, Leopold Stokowski, conductor; Seraphim B 4XG-60235. Includes Stokowski's impressive orchestral transcriptions of not only the S.565, but also S.80, Ein feste Burg ist unser Gott ("A Mighty Fortress is Our God") (Chorale only), full entry rated A; S.248, Christmas Oratorio, (Shepherd's Song, only), full entry rated A; S.478, Aria, Komm Süsser Tod ("Come, Sweet Death"), rated A; S.582, Passacaglia and Fugue, in c, rated A and S.1002, Partita No.1, in b, for Solo Violin (Sarabande only), full entry rated A.

A S.577, Fugue, in G (The "Jig")--see entry for S.565, Toccata and Fugue, in d, immediately supra.

A S.578, Fugue, in g (The "Little")--see entry for S.565, Toccata and Fugue, in d, supra.

A S.582, Passacaglia and Fugue, in c--see entry for S.565, Toccata and Fugue, in d, supra.

C S.599–644, Orgelbüchlein, ("Little Organ Book"), 46 Chorale Preludes for Organ

$ Robert Noehren, organ; Orion 75200–75201 (2 discs), ♭ 625.

B S.645–650, Chorale Preludes ("Schübler") (6) Nos.1–6

$ Marie-Claire Alain, organ; Musical Heritage Society 0551W. Includes Bach's Organ Sonatas ("Trios") S.529, in C and 530, in G.

Instrumental (D. Solo Violin)

A S.1001, 1003 and 1005, Sonatas (3), Nos.1–3: in g, a and C and S.1002, 1004 and 1006, Partitas (3), Nos.1–3: in b, d and E

$ Jascha Heifetz, violin; RCA LM–6105 (3 discs). Although monophonic, this wonderful old set carries a regular price.

$ Nathan Milstein, violin; DG 2709047 (3 discs).

Orchestral

A S.1006–1069, Suites (4) for Orchestra, Nos.1–4: in C, b, D and D

* Collegium Aureum; Quintessence 2702 (2 discs), ♭ 2702.

$ Jean-François Paillard Chamber Orchestra; Jean-François Paillard, conductor, RCA ARL2–2800 (2 discs). Includes the Orchestral Suite S.1070, in g, attributed to Bach.

A S.1067, Suite No.2, in b, for Flute and Strings--see entry for S.1066–1069, Suites (4) for Orchestra, Nos.1–4: in C, b, D and D, immediately supra.

BARBER, SAMUEL
1910–1981

American Neo-Romantic composer Samuel Barber is undoubtedly best known for his hauntingly tragic Adagio for Strings (second movement from his Quartet, Op.11), often played for state funerals. Although he was a skillful writer for orchestra and voice, his three operas have never been as well received as they ought. Still, Barber's place among the more important American-born composers seems quite secure: he was a thorough craftsman who invested his works with intellect, passion and, often, a sense of futility and power.

Chamber

B String Quartet, Op.11

  * Concord Quartet; Leslie Guinn, baritone; Nonesuch 78017, ♮ 78017. Includes Barber's Dover Beach (for Voice and String Quartet) (1931), rated C, and David Rochberg's Quartet No.7 (with Baritone). The second movement of the Barber work is the basis for the famous "Adagio for Strings" (when orchestrated for string orchestra).

Concerted

B Concerto for 'Cello and Orchestra, Op.22

  $ Raphael Wallfisch, 'cello; English Chamber Orchestra; Geoffrey Simon, conductor; Chandos ABRD-1085. Includes Shostakovich's Concerto for 'Cello, Op.107, in E flat, rated C.

C Concerto for Piano and Orchestra, Op.38

  $ John Browning, piano; Cleveland Orchestra; George Szell, conductor; Columbia MP-39070, ♮ MP-39070. Includes Barber's Concerto for Violin and Orchestra, Op.14, rated B. The performers in the Concerto for Violin are Isaac Stern, violin and the New York Philharmonic Orchestra conducted by Leonard Bernstein.

B Concerto for Violin and Orchestra, Op.14--see entry for Concerto for Piano and Orchestra, Op.38, immediately supra.

Operatic

C Vanessa (1958)

  $ Eleanor Steber, soprano; Rosalind Elias, mezzo-soprano; Regina Resnik, mezzo-soprano; Nicolai Gedda, tenor; Giorgio Tozzi, bass; Metropolitan Opera Orchestra; Dimitri Mitropoulos, conductor; RCA ARL2-2094 (2 discs).

Orchestral

A Adagio for Strings (Second Movement from String Quartet, Op.11, Orchestrated by the Composer)

  $ Eastman-Rochester Orchestra; Howard Hanson, conductor; Mercury 75012E. Includes Barber's Medea's Meditation and Dance of Vengeance (1946), rated C; The School for Scandal Overture (1932), rated B and Symphony No.1 (in One Movement), Op.9, rated B.

15

C <u>Medea's Meditation and Dance of Vengeance</u> (1946)--see entry for Adagio for Strings (Second Movement from String Quartet, Op.11, Orchestratd by the Composer), immediately <u>supra</u>.

B <u>The School for Scandal</u> Overture (1932)--see entry for Adagio for Strings (Second Movement from String Quartet, Op.11, Orchestrated by the Composer), <u>supra</u>.

Symphonic

B Symphony No.1 (in One Movement), Op.9--see entry for Adagio for Strings (Second Movement from String Quartet, Op.11, Orchestrated by the Composer) under Orchestral, <u>supra</u>.

Vocal

C <u>Dover Beach</u> (for Voice and String Quartet) (1931)--see entry for String Quartet, Op.11 under Chamber, <u>supra</u>.

BARTÓK, BÉLA
1881-1945

Often classified as an expressionist or Neo-Classical composer, Bartók defies categorization. He was an eclectic creator of music, but one whose own imprint on his works is always unmistakable. The corpus of his compositions is not huge, but its influence on those who came after him is pervasive, particularly his Quartets and the Concerto for Orchestra. He and his friend and colleague, Zoltán Kodály, spent a fair amount of their time collecting Hungarian and Roumanian folk songs, which they published in 1906. Perforce this experience, Bartók employed the speech patterns of his native Hungary in many of his pieces, as he also used Hungarian folk rhythms (and occasional elements of Hungarian and Roumanian folk melodies). Bartók's works are demanding of careful attention and are often extremely difficult to perform--even for the best executants. For many listeners, Bartók is a sufficiently formidable composer as to be considered off-putting. Still, he is one of the truly great composers of this century and every library must have him represented by at least two of his works.

Ballet

B <u>Miraculous Mandarin</u> Suite, Op.19

* Minnesota Orchestra; Stanislaw Skrowaczewski, conductor; Candide 31097, ⓑ CT-2196. Includes Bartók's Wooden Prince Suite, Op.13, also rated B.

B Wooden Prince Suite, Op.13--see entry for Miraculous Mandarin Suite, Op.19, immediately supra.

Chamber

B Divertimento for String Orchestra (1939)

$ Hungarian State Orchestra; Antal Doráti; conductor; Hungaroton 11437. Includes Bartók's Concerto for Orchestra (1943), rated A.

A String Quartets (6), Nos.1-6: Op.7, in a; Op.17, in a; (1927); (1928), in C; Op.102, in B flat and Op.114, in D

$ Tátrai Quartet; Hungaroton 1294-1296 (3 discs).

Concerted

C Concerto for Piano No.2, in G (1931)

$ Vladimir Ashkenazy, piano; Chicago Symphony Orchestra; Sir George Solti, conductor; London 7167, ⓑ 5-7167. Includes the same composer's Concerto for Piano No.3, in E (1945), rated B.

B Concerto for Piano No.3, in E (1945)

* Gyorgy Sandor, piano; Vienna Pro Musica Orchestra; Michael Gielen, conductor; Turnabout 34036. Includes Bartók's Concerto for Viola (1945) (Unfinished, Completed and Orchestration by Tibor Serly), rated C. The violist is Ulrich Koch, and he is accompanied by the Luxembourg Radio Orchestra conducted by Alois Springer.

Also--see entry for Concerto for Piano No.2, in G (1931), immediately supra.

C Concerto for Viola (1945) (Unfinished, Completed and Orchestration by Tibor Serly)--see entry for Concerto for Piano No.3, in E (1945), immediately supra.

B Concerto for Violin No.2, in b (1938)

* André Gertler, violin; Czech Philharmonic Orchestra; Karel Ančerl, conductor; Mercury 75002.

Instrumental

17

C <u>Mikrokosmos</u> (153 Graded Short Pieces for Piano, in 6 Books) (1926-1937)

$ Deszö Ránki, piano; Teldec 3635369 (3 discs).

Operatic

B <u>Bluebeard's Castle</u>, Op.11

$ Christa Ludwig, mezzo-soprano; Walter Berry, baritone; London Symphony Orchestra; István Kertész, conductor; London 414167-1 LE, ▯ 414167-4 LE.

Orchestral

A Concerto for Orchestra (1943)

* Czech Philharmonic Orchestra; Karel Ančerl, conductor; Quintessence 7152, ▯ 7152.

Also--see entry for Divertimento for String Orchestra (1939) under Chamber, <u>supra</u>.

BEETHOVEN, LUDWIG VAN
1770-1827

In that self-same musical pantheon which includes Bach, Haydn, Mozart and Brahms, the name of Beethoven must also be inscribed. No composer coming after him has been able to gainsay Beethoven's influence. That influence was so great that no less a one than Brahms delayed for about two decades the writing of his Symphony No.1 because he felt "...uncomfortably haunted by the shadow of Beethoven." Of the approximately 250 opus-numbered works of Beethoven, a remarkable number are extremely popular. His much-discussed deafness (the onset of which took place in his 28th year and which was probably caused by syphilis--the disease which ultimately took his life and which he probably contracted in 1796) did nothing to diminish either his creativity or his greatness: this despite the famous "Heiligenstadt Testament" of October 6, 1802, in which he hinted at imminent suicide--a step never taken and, probably, ultimately abhorred by him as cowardly. It is in Beethoven, beginning with the Symphony No.3 ("Eroica"), that the Romantic movement in music came into full flower. Beethoven's life was beset by a variety of adversities, a goodly number of which were of his own making. He was a lifelong bachelor who tended to idealize women and to fall in and out of "love" with admirable ease. His music is characterized by innovation within existing forms and by a sense of triumphant individualism. One of the aspects of Beethoven's music which is seldom noted is the freshness of his use of orchestral color. More often remarked upon is his increasing the size of the orchestra but, as with everything of musical concern to Beethoven, this expansion was primarily to enlarge the spectrum of sound with which he might work, and not simply an egocentric adventure. Few composers have ever equalled his ability to convey his unique sense of "man's will supreme." The Symphony No.5, with its insistent 4 note rhythmic motif ("three dots and a dash"—the Morse code for the letter "v," which has nothing whatever to do with Beethoven), is probably the most famous symphonic work ever penned. Beethoven's last four Quartets are usually placed alongside the most profound artistic statements in the western world. Curiously, John Ruskin (a personage usually revered for his artistic sensibilities and discrimination) could write to John Brown (in a letter dated February 6, 1881) that "Beethoven always sounds to me like the upsetting of bags of nails, with here and there an also dropped hammer...": this of the composer whose fecundity and genius brought the forms of the symphony, instrumental quartet, sonata and concerto to their full modern development. The "K" numbers for some Beethoven works identify those cataloged in the Kinsky thematic catalog of Beethoven's works; "WoO" numbers translate to "Werk ohne Opuszahl" ("work without opus number").

Chamber

C Septet for Strings and Winds, Op.20, in E flat

* Boston Symphony Chamber Players; Nonesuch 78015, ◘78015.

A Sonatas for 'Cello and Piano (5), Nos.1–5: Op.5, Nos.1–2, in F and g; Op.69, in A and Op.102 Nos.1–2, in C and D

$ Lynn Harrell, 'cello; James Levine, piano; RCA ARL–32060 (2 discs).

A Sonatas for Violin and Piano (10), Nos.1–10: Op.12 Nos.1–3, in D, A and E flat; Op.23, in a; Op.24, in F ("Spring"); Op.30 Nos.1–3, in A, c and G; Op.47, in A ("Kreutzer") and Op.96, in G

$ Henryk Szeryng, violin; Ingrid Haebler, piano; Philips 67690114 (5 discs).

$ Jascha Heifetz, violin; Emanuel Bay, piano; RCA LM–6707 (5 discs). This is a monophonic set at full price.

B String Quartets (16): Op.18 (6) Nos.1–6, in F, G, D, c, A and B flat; Nos.7–16: Op.59 (3) Nos.1–3, in F ("Rasumovsky"), e and C; Op.74, in E flat (The "Harp"); Op.95, in f; Op.130, in B flat; Op.131, in c sharp; Op.132, in a; Op.133, in B flat (fragment in one movement, called "Grosse Fuge") and Op.135, in F

$ Talich Quartet; Calliope 1631–1640 (10 discs).

For orchestral version of Op.133, in B flat (fragment in one movement, called "Grosse Fuge")--see entry under Symphonic, Symphony No.3 ("Eroica"), Op.55, in E flat, infra.

A Trios for Piano, Violin and 'Cello (11), Nos.1–10: Op.1 Nos.1–3, in E flat, G and C; Op.11, in B flat; Op.44, 14 Variations on an Original Theme, in E flat; Op.70 Nos.1–2, in D and E flat; Op.97, in B flat ("Archduke"); Op.121a (Adagio, 10 Variations on "Ich bin der Schneider Kakadu" and Rondo, in G) and K.10, in B flat, Opus Posthumous

$ Eugene Istomin, piano; Isaac Stern, violin; Leonard Rose, 'cello; Columbia M5–30065 (5 discs).

B Trios for Violin, Viola and 'Cello (5), Nos.1–5: Op.3, in E flat; Op.8, in D ("Serenade") and Op.9 Nos.1–3, in G, D and c

* Grumiaux Trio; Philips Festivo 6770159 (3 discs).   Includes Beethoven's Serenade for Flute, Violin and Viola, Op.25, in D.

Choral

A Missa solemnis, Op.123, in D

$$ Margaret Price, soprano; Christa Ludwig; mezzo–soprano; Wieslaw Ochman, tenor; Martti Talvela, bass; Vienna State Opera Chorus; Vienna Philharmonic Orchestra; Karl Böhm, conductor; DG 413191–1 GX–2 (2 discs), ♭ 413191–4 GX–2.

Concerted

A Concerto for Piano No.1, Op.15, in C

$ Maurizio Pollini, piano; Vienna Philharmonic Orchestra; Eugen Jochum, conductor; DG 2532103, ♭ 3302103.

Also--see entry for Concerto for Piano No.4, Op.58, in G, infra.

B Concerto for Piano No.2, Op.19, in B flat

$$ Maurizio Pollini, piano; Vienna Philharmonic Orchestra; Eugen Jochum, conductor; DG 413445-1, ◙413445-4 GH.   Includes Beethoven's Concerto for Piano, No.4, Op.58, in G, rated A.

! Solomon, piano; Philharmonia Orchestra; Issay Dobrowen, conductor; Turnabout THS-65071, ◙ CT-2234.

A Concerto for Piano No.3, Op.37, in c

* Emil Gilels, piano; Cleveland Orchestra; George Szell, conductor; Angel AE-34434, ◙ AE-34434.

$ Maurizio Pollini, piano; Vienna Philharmonic Orchestra; Karl Böhm, conductor; DG 2531057, ◙ 3301057.

A Concerto for Piano No.4, Op.58, in G

* Robert Casadesus, piano; Amsterdam Concertgebouw Orchestra; Eduard van Beinum, conductor; Odyssey 32160056.   Includes Beethoven's Concerto for Piano No.1, Op.15, in C, also rated A.

$ Maurizio Pollini, piano; Vienna Philharmonic Orchestra; Karl Böhm, conductor; DG 2530791.

A Concerto for Piano No.5 ("Emperor"), Op.73, in E flat

$ Alfred Brendel, piano; London Philharmonic Orchestra; Bernard Haitink, conductor; Philips 412917-1 PM, ◙ 412917-4 PM.

$ Sir Clifford Curzon, piano; Vienna Philharmonic Orchestra; Hans Knappertsbusch, conductor; London 41020, ◙ 41020.

! Walter Gieseking, piano; Philharmonia Orchestra; Herbert von Karajan, conductor; Odyssey 32160029.

! Vladimir Horowitz, piano; RCA Symphony Orchestra; Fritz Reiner, conductor; RCA ARM1-3690.

! Solomon, piano; Philharmonia Orchestra; Sir Herbert Menges, conductor; Seraphim ◙ 4XG-60298.   This, like the Gieseking recording, supra, is also a monophonic recording, but a masterful performance.

A Concerto for Violin, Op.61, in D

$ Jascha Heifetz, violin; Boston Symphony Orchestra; Charles Munch, conductor; RCA LSC-1992, ◙ RK-1045. First movement cadenza by

Leopold Auer (modified by Heifetz), second and third movement cadenzas by Joseph Joachim.

* Josef Suk, violin; Czech Philharmonic Orchestra; Franz Konwitschny, conductor; Quintessence 7213, ♮ 7213.

Also--see entry for Romances for Violin and Orchestra, Nos.1-2: Op.40, in G and Op.50, in F, immediately infra.

C Romances for Violin and Orchestra, Nos.1-2: Op.40, in G and Op.50, in F

$ Pinchas Zukerman, violin; London Philharmonic Orchestra; Daniel Barenboim, conductor; DG 2543520, ♮ 3343520. Includes the same composer's Concerto for Violin, Op.61, in D, rated A.

Instrumental

C Albumblatt ("Für Elise"), K.59, in a

* Hans Boepple, piano; Orion ♮ 668. Includes Beethoven's Bagatelles for Piano (27), Nos.1-27: Op.33, Op.119 and Op.126 and Bagatelles for Piano (2), K.52-53, in c and C, all rated C.

C Bagatelles for Piano (27), Nos.1-27: Op.33, Op.119 and Op.126

* Alfred Brendel, piano; Turnabout 34077, ♮ CT-4077.

Also--see entry for Albumblatt ("Für Elise"), K.59, in a, immediately supra.

A Sonatas for Piano (32), Nos.1-32: Op.2 Nos.1-3, in f, A and C; Op.7, in E flat; Op.10 Nos.1-3, in c, F and D; Op.13 ("Pathétique"), in c; Op.14 Nos.1-2, in E and G; Op.22, in B flat; Op. 26 ("Funeral March"), in A flat; Op.27 Nos.1-2, in E flat and ("Moonlight") in c sharp; Op.28 ("Pastoral"), in D; Op.31 Nos.1-3, in G, ("Tempest"), in d and E flat; Op.49 Nos.1-2, in g and G; Op.53 ("Waldstein"), in C; Op.54, in F; Op.57 ("Appassionata"), in f; Op.78, in F sharp; Op.79, in G; Op.81a ("Les Adieux"), in E flat; Op.90, in e; Op.101, in A; Op.106 ("Hammerklavier"), in B flat; Op.109, in E; Op.110, in A flat and Op.111, in c

$ Vladimir Ashkenazy, piano; London CSP-11 (12 discs).

A Sonata for Piano No.8 ("Pathétique"), Op.13, in c

$ Wilhelm Backhaus, piano; London 41013, ♮ 41013. Includes Beethoven's Sonatas for Piano Nos.14 and 23, Op.27 No.2 ("Moonlight"), in c sharp and Op.57 ("Appassionata"), in f, both rated A.

$ Vladimir Horowitz, piano; Columbia M-34509, ♮ MT-34509. Includes the same works as the Backhaus version, immediately supra.

! Solomon, piano; Seraphim 4XG-60286. Includes the same works as the Backhaus version, supra.

Also--see entry for Sonatas for Piano (32), Nos.1-32: Op.2 Nos.1-3, in f, A and C; Op.7, in E flat; Op.10 Nos.1-3, in c, F and D; Op.13 ("Pathétique"), in c; Op.14 Nos.1-2, in E and G; Op.22, in B flat; Op. 26 ("Funeral March"), in A flat; Op.27 Nos.1-2, in E flat and ("Moonlight") in c sharp; Op.28 ("Pastoral"), in D; Op.31 Nos.1-3, in G, ("Tempest"), in d and E flat; Op.49 Nos.1-2, in g and G; Op.53 ("Waldstein"), in C; Op.54, in F; Op.57 ("Appassionata"), in f; Op.78, in F sharp; Op.79, in G; Op.81a ("Les Adieux"), in E flat; Op.90, in e; Op.101, in A; Op.106 ("Hammerklavier"), in B flat; Op.109, in E; Op.110, in A flat and Op.111, in c, immediately supra.

A Sonata for Piano No.14, Op.27 No.2 ("Moonlight"), in c sharp--see entries for Sonata for Piano No.8 ("Pathétique"), Op.13, in c, immediately supra and Sonatas for Piano (32), Nos.1-32: Op.2 Nos.1-3, in f, A and C; Op.7, in E flat; Op.10 Nos.1-3, in c, F and D; Op.13 ("Pathétique"), in c; Op.14 Nos.1-2, in E and G; Op.22, in B flat; Op. 26 ("Funeral March"), in A flat; Op.27 Nos.1-2, in E flat and ("Moonlight") in c sharp; Op.28 ("Pastoral"), in D; Op.31 Nos.1-3, in G, ("Tempest"), in d and E flat; Op.49 Nos.1-2, in g and G; Op.53 ("Waldstein"), in C; Op.54, in F; Op.57 ("Appassionata"), in f; Op.78, in F sharp; Op.79, in G; Op.81a ("Les Adieux"), in E flat; Op.90, in e; Op.101, in A; Op.106 ("Hammerklavier"), in B flat; Op.109, in E; Op.110, in A flat and Op.111, in c, supra.

A Sonata for Piano No.21 ("Waldstein"), Op.53, in C

$ Emanuel Ax, piano; RCA ARL1-2083, ♮ ARK1-2083. Includes Beethoven's Variations and Fugue ("Eroica"), Op.35, in E flat, rated B.

$ Vladimir Horowitz, piano; Columbia M-31371, ♮ M-31371. Includes Beethoven's Sonata for Piano No.23, ("Appassionata"), Op.57, in f, also rated A.

Also--see entry for Sonatas for Piano (32), Nos.1-32: Op.2 Nos.1-3, in f, A and C; Op.7, in E flat; Op.10 Nos.1-3, in c, F and D; Op.13 ("Pathétique"), in c; Op.14 Nos.1-2, in E and G; Op.22, in B flat; Op. 26 ("Funeral March"), in A flat; Op.27 Nos.1-2, in E flat and ("Moonlight") in c sharp; Op.28 ("Pastoral"), in D; Op.31 Nos.1-3, in G, ("Tempest"), in d and E flat; Op.49 Nos.1-2, in g and G; Op.53 ("Waldstein"), in C; Op.54, in F; Op.57 ("Appassionata"), in f; Op.78, in F sharp; Op.79, in G; Op.81a ("Les Adieux"), in E flat; Op.90, in e; Op.101, in A; Op.106 ("Hammerklavier"), in B flat; Op.109, in E; Op.110, in A flat and Op.111, in c, supra.

A Sonata for Piano No.23 ("Appassionata"), Op.57, in f--see entries for Sonatas for Piano (32), Nos.1-32: Op.2 Nos.1-3, in f, A and C; Op.7, in E flat; Op.10 Nos.1-3, in c, F and D; Op.13 ("Pathétique"), in c; Op.14 Nos.1-2, in E and G; Op.22, in B flat; Op. 26 ("Funeral March"), in A flat; Op.27 Nos.1-2, in E flat and ("Moonlight") in c sharp; Op.28 ("Pastoral"), in D; Op.31 Nos.1-3, in G, ("Tempest"), in d and E flat; Op.49 Nos.1-2, in g and G; Op.53 ("Waldstein"), in C; Op.54, in F; Op.57 ("Appassionata"), in f; Op.78, in F sharp; Op.79, in G; Op.81a ("Les Adieux"), in E flat; Op.90, in e; Op.101, in A; Op.106 ("Hammerklavier"), in B flat; Op.109, in E; Op.110, in A flat and Op.111, in c, and   for Sonatas for Piano Nos.8 ("Pathétique"), Op.13, in c and 21 ("Waldstein"), Op.53, in C, supra, and for Sonata for Piano No.21 ("Waldstein"), Op.53, in C, supra.

B Variations (17) and Fugue for Piano ("Eroica"), Op.35, in E flat

* Sviatoslav Richter, piano; Quintessence 7210, ♭ 7210.   Includes Beethoven's Variations for Piano (6) on an Original Theme, Op.34, in F and Variations for Piano (6), Op.76, in D, both rated C.

Also--see entry for Sonata for Piano No.21 ("Waldstein"), Op.53, in C, supra.

C Variations for Piano (6) on an Original Theme, Op.34, in F--see entry for Variations (17) and Fugue for Piano ("Eroica"), Op.35, in E flat, immediately supra.

C Variations for Piano (6), Op.76, in D--see entry for Variations (17) and Fugue for Piano ("Eroica"), Op.35, in E flat, supra.

A Variations for Piano (33) on a Waltz by Diabelli, Op.120

$ Friedrich Gulda, piano; Harmonia Mundi 5127.

Operatic

A Fidelio, Op.72

$ Christa Ludwig, mezzo-soprano; Jon Vickers, tenor; Walter Berry, baritone; Gottlob Frick, bass; Philharmonia Chorus and Orchestra; Otto Klemperer, conductor; Angel S-3625 (3 discs).

Orchestral

A Overtures: Coriolan, Op.62; Egmont, Op.84; Fidelio, Op.72; Leonore, No.3, Op.72a and Prometheus, Op.43

$$ London Philharmonic Orchestra; Klaus Tennstedt, conductor; Angel DS-38045, ♮ 4DS-38045.

B Overtures: Consecration of the House, Op.124; Coriolan, Op.62; Egmont, Op.84; King Stephen, Op.117; Prometheus, Op.43; Ruins of Athens, Op.113

* Minnesota Orchestra; Stanislaw Skrowaczewski, conductor; Turnabout ♮ CT-2316.

Symphonic

A Symphonies (9), Nos.1-9: Op.21, in C; Op.36, in D; Op.55 ("Eroica"), in E flat; Op.60, in B flat; Op.67, in c; Op.68 ("Pastorale"), in F; Op.92, in A; Op.93, in F and Op.125 ("Choral"), in d

* Columbia Symphony Orchestra; Bruno Walter, conductor; Odyssey Y7-30051 (7 discs). In the last movement of the Symphony No.9, the forces include the Westminster Choir; Emilia Cundari, soprano; Nell Rankin, mezzo-soprano; Albert Da Costa, tenor, William Wilderman, baritone, and the New York Philharmonic Orchestra (the last of these is not noted in the program notes).

A Symphony No.1, Op.21, in C

$$ Berlin Philharmonic Orchestra; Herbert von Karajan, conductor; DG 415505-1, ♮ 415505-4 GH. Includes Beethoven's Symphony No.2, Op.36, in D, also rated A.

* Vienna Philharmonic Orchestra; Pierre Monteux, conductor; London ♮ STS5-15238. Includes Beethoven's Symphony No.8, Op.93, in F, also rated A.

Also--see entry for Symphonies (9), Nos.1-9: Op.21, in C; Op.36, in D; Op.55 ("Eroica"), in E flat; Op.60, in B flat; Op.67, in c; Op.68

("Pastorale"), in F; Op.92, in A; Op.93, in F and Op.125 ("Choral"), in d, immediately supra.

A Symphony No.2, Op.36, in D--see entry for Symphony No.1, Op.21, in C, immediately supra.

Also--see entry for Symphonies (9), Nos.1-9: Op.21, in C; Op.36, in D; Op.55 ("Eroica"), in E flat; Op.60, in B flat; Op.67, in c; Op.68 ("Pastorale"), in F; Op.92, in A; Op.93, in F and Op.125 ("Choral"), in d, supra.

A Symphony No.3 ("Eroica"), Op.55, in E flat

! Berlin Philharmonic Orchestra; Wilhelm Furtwängler, conductor; Turnabout THS-65020.

* Columbia Symphony Orchestra; Bruno Walter, conductor; Odyssey 𝕭 YT-33925.

* Philharmonia Orchestra; Otto Klemperer, conductor; Angel AE-34424, 𝕭 4AE-34424. Includes an orchestral version of the String Quartet, Op.133, in B flat (fragment in one movement, called "Grosse Fuge"), rated B.

For original version of String Quartet, Op.133, in B flat (fragment in one movement, called "Grosse Fuge")--see entry under Chamber, String Quartets (16): Op.18 (6) Nos.1-6, in F, G, D, c, A and B flat; Nos.7-16: Op.59 (3) Nos.1-3, in F ("Rasumovsky"), e and C; Op.74, in E flat (The "Harp"); Op.95, in f; Op.130, in B flat; Op.131, in c sharp; Op.132, in a; Op.133, in B flat (fragment in one movement, called "Grosse Fuge") and Op.135, in F, supra.

Also--see entry for Symphonies (9), Nos.1-9: Op.21, in C; Op.36, in D; Op.55 ("Eroica"), in E flat; Op.60, in B flat; Op.67, in c; Op.68 ("Pastorale"), in F; Op.92, in A; Op.93, in F and Op.125 ("Choral"), in d, supra.

A Symphony No.4, Op.60, in B flat

* Cleveland Orchestra; George Szell, conductor; Odyssey Y-34600, 𝕭 YT-34600. Includes Beethoven's Symphony No.5, Op.67, in c, also rated A.

Also--see entry for Symphonies (9), Nos.1-9: Op.21, in C; Op.36, in D; Op.55 ("Eroica"), in E flat; Op.60, in B flat; Op.67, in c; Op.68

("Pastorale"), in F; Op.92, in A; Op.93, in F and Op.125 ("Choral"), in d, supra.

A Symphony No.5, Op.67, in c

$ Vienna Philharmonic Orchestra; Carlos Kleiber, conductor; DG 2530516, ♮ 330472.

Also--see entries for Symphony No.4, Op.60, in B flat, immediately supra and for Symphonies (9), Nos.1-9: Op.21, in C; Op.36, in D; Op.55 ("Eroica"), in E flat; Op.60, in B flat; Op.67, in c; Op.68 ("Pastorale"), in F; Op.92, in A; Op.93, in F and Op.125 ("Choral"), in d, supra.

A Symphony No.6 ("Pastorale"), Op.68, in F

* Columbia Symphony Orchestra; Bruno Walter, conductor; Columbia MY-36720, ♮ MY-36720.

Also--see entry for Symphonies (9), Nos.1-9: Op.21, in C; Op.36, in D; Op.55 ("Eroica"), in E flat; Op.60, in B flat; Op.67, in c; Op.68 ("Pastorale"), in F; Op.92, in A; Op.93, in F and Op.125 ("Choral"), in d, supra.

A Symphony No.7, Op.92, in A

$$ Collegium Aureum; Pro Arte PAD-123, ♮ PCD-123.

Also--see entry for Symphonies (9), Nos.1-9: Op.21, in C; Op.36, in D; Op.55 ("Eroica"), in E flat; Op.60, in B flat; Op.67, in c; Op.68 ("Pastorale"), in F; Op.92, in A; Op.93, in F and Op.125 ("Choral"), in d, supra.

A Symphony No.8, Op.93, in F--see entry for Symphony No.1, Op.21, in C, supra.

Also--see entry for Symphonies (9), Nos.1-9: Op.21, in C; Op.36, in D; Op.55 ("Eroica"), in E flat; Op.60, in B flat; Op.67, in c; Op.68 ("Pastorale"), in F; Op.92, in A; Op.93, in F and Op.125 ("Choral"), in d, supra.

A Symphony No.9 ("Choral"), Op.125, in d

$ Elisabeth Schwarzkopf, soprano; Elisabeth Höngen, contralto; Hans Hopf, tenor; Otto Edelmann, bass-baritone; Bayreuth (1951) Festival Chorus and Orchestra; Wilhelm Furtwängler, conductor; Angel CDC-47081.

This is a monophonic recording and it is also one of the greatest live performances of any work ever recorded.

$ Dame Joan Sutherland, soprano; Marilyn Horne, mezzo-soprano; James King, tenor; Martti Talvela, bass; Vienna Philharmonic Chorus and Orchestra; Hans Schmidt-Isserstedt, conductor; London 41004, ♮ 41004. This, I believe, is the greatest modern (i.e., stereo) recording of this work.

Also—see entry for Symphonies (9), Nos.1-9: Op.21, in C; Op.36, in D; Op.55 ("Eroica"), in E flat; Op.60, in B flat; Op.67, in c; Op.68 ("Pastorale"), in F; Op.92, in A; Op.93, in F and Op.125 ("Choral"), in d, supra.

Vocal

B An die ferne Geliebte ("To the Distant Loved One"), 6 Songs, Op.98

$ Dietrich Fischer-Dieskau, baritone; Jörg Demus, piano; DG 139197. Includes Adelaide, Op.46; Als die Geliebte sich trennen wollte, WoO.132; An die Geliebte, WoO.140; Andeken, WoO.136; Das Glück der Freundschaft, Op.88; In questa tomba oscura, WoO.133; Lieder (4), Op.82; Ruf vom Berge, WoO.147; Schilderung eines Mädchens, WoO.107; Sehnsucht, WoO.146 and Zärtliche Liebe, WoO.123.

BELLINI, VINCENZO
1801-1835

Italian bel canto opera composer Bellini is particularly well regarded for his three masterpieces: Norma; I Puritani ("The Puritans") and La Sonnambula ("The Sleep-Walking Woman"). His musical talent found expression in lyricism and the fruits of that talent demanded great vocal agility from his singers. Bellini's operas are considered to be vocal tours de force and are not frequently essayed (nor ought to be) except by the finest and most technically accomplished singers.

Operatic

A Norma (1831)

$ Dame Joan Sutherland, soprano; Marilyn Horne, mezzo-soprano; John Alexander, tenor; Richard Cross, bass-baritone; London Symphony Chorus and Orchestra; Sir Richard Bonynge, conductor; London 1394 (3 discs), ♮ 5-1394.

C I Puritani ("The Puritans") (1835)

$ Dame Joan Sutherland, soprano; Luciano Pavarotti, tenor; Piero Cappuccilli, baritone; Nicolai Ghiaurov, bass; Covent Garden Chorus; London Symphony Orchestra; Sir Richard Bonynge, conductor; London 13111 (3 discs), ₿ 5-13111.

C La Sonnambula ("The Sleep-Walking Woman") (1831)

$$ Dame Joan Sutherland, soprano; Luciano Pavarotti, tenor; Nicolai Ghiaurov, bass; London Opera Chorus; National Philharmonic Orchestra, London; Sir Richard Bonynge, conductor; London LDR-73004 (3 discs), ₿ LDR-73004.

BERG, ALBAN
1885-1935

Alban Berg was a student of Arnold Schoenberg's and was, therefore, essentially an atonal dodecaphonist (what an epithet) despite his obvious lyrical gift. Further, many of Berg's works are characterized by being so condensed that they pass before the ears almost before they have begun (and to many listeners this is considered a mercy). Despite his brief life (he succumbed to blood poisoning brought on by an insect bite--no penicillin then, don't you know) and rather small body of works, Berg produced some profoundly important ones. Berg's works are characteristic of his powerful musical intellect and, on occasion (e.g., Wozzeck and Concerto for Violin), by intense emotional content. The Berg Concerto for Violin (1935), by the way, was dedicated to "the memory of an angel": the then recently deceased 18-year-old Manon Gropius, daughter of the notorious Alma Mahler-Werfel-Gropius. His music is not easily accessible for most listeners, and it often requires repeated hearing and great attention.

Chamber

C Chamber Concerto for Violin, Piano and 13 Winds (1925)

* Prague Chamber Harmony; Libor Pešek, conductor; Quintessence 7179, ₿ 7179. Includes Berg's Concerto for Violin (1935) with Josef Suk, violin, rated A.

B Lyric Suite for String Quartet (1926)

29

$ Berg Quartet; Teldec 641301. Includes Berg's String Quartet, Op.3, rated C.

C String Quartet, Op.3--see entry for Lyric Suite for String Quartet (1926), immediately supra.

Concerted

A Concerto for Violin (1935)--see entry for Chamber Concerto for Violin, Piano and 13 Winds (1925) under Chamber, supra.

Operatic

B Lulu (1928-1934)

$ Teresa Stratas, soprano; Yvonne Minton, mezzo-soprano; Kenneth Riegel, tenor; Franz Mazura, baritone; Paris Opéra Orchestra; Pierre Boulez, conductor; DG 2711024 (4 discs). The last act of this performance, which was left unfinished by Berg, was completed by Friedrich Cerha.

A Wozzeck (1915-1921)

$ Evelyn Lear, soprano; Fritz Wunderlich, tenor; Dietrich Fischer-Dieskau, baritone; Schöneberger Boys' Choir; Berlin State Opera Orchestra; Karl Böhm, conductor; DG 2707023 (2 discs).

Orchestral

A Three Pieces for Orchestra, Op.6

$ London Symphony Orchestra; Claudio Abbado, conductor; DG 2543804. Includes Berg's Altenberg Lieder and Lulu Suite (both with Margaret Price, soprano).

BERLIOZ, HECTOR
1803-1869

Berlioz (born Louis Hector Berlioz) is accounted both the first great theoretician and practitioner of orchestration (on which subject he wrote a highly respected treatise) despite his proficiency on but one instrument: the guitar. He is also considered to be the prototype of the "Romantic," or Byronic, artist or composer. To the latter his Mémoires attest and make for enjoyable reading (if taken somewhat in the same vein as Cellini's Autobiography, on which, interestingly, Berlioz based an opera--indicative of his acknowledgement of their intellectual and emotional kinship). Berlioz was a composer whose music is suffused with color, sensibility, immediacy, inventiveness, passion (often verging on abandon), and a love of, and flair for, the dramatic: his own life is often mirrored in his work. Although extremely intelligent, he was temperamentally unsuited to work within the confines of accepted form, unlike Beethoven or Bach. Rather, his works are, although well structured, not entirely formal, and he left little impress on any given form (as did, say, Haydn on the symphony). Yet Berlioz, via his conception and use of the idée fixe, presaged the use of "motto themes" by such eminences as Liszt and Wagner (with his Leitmotivs). Further, his influence is evident in Liszt's tone poems, which harken back to the Berlioz of such works as the "concert" overtures Carnaval romain ("Roman Carnival") and Le Corsaire. Berlioz' Symphonie fantastique is one of the most popular works in the symphonic repertoire, and is a splendid display piece (both for orchestras and sound systems). One item of some moment to librarians: to supplement his income as a composer and music critic, Berlioz was the Librarian of the Conservatoire de Paris from 1852 until his death.

Choral

A Grande Messe des Morts (Requiem Mass), Op.5

$ Stuart Burrows, tenor; French National Radio Chorus; French National Radio Orchestra; French Radio Philharmonic Orchestra; Leonard Bernstein, conductor; Columbia M2-34202 (2 discs), ▤ MT-34202.

Concerted

A Harold in Italy, for Viola and Orchestra, Op.16

! William Primrose, viola; Royal Philharmonic Orchestra; Sir Thomas Beecham, conductor; Odyssey Y-33286.

* Josef Suk, viola; Czech Philharmonic Orchestra; Dietrich Fischer-Dieskau, conductor; Quintessence 7103, ▤ 7103.

Operatic

C Béatrice et Bénédict (1862)

$ Christiane Eda-Pierre, soprano; Dame Janet Baker, mezzo-soprano; Helen Watts, contralto; Robert Tear, tenor; Thomas Allen, baritone; Jules Bastin, bass; Robert Lloyd, bass; John Alldis Choir; London Symphony Orchestra; Sir Colin Davis, conductor; Philips 6700121 (2 discs).

A La Damnation de Faust ("The Damnation of Faust," After Goethe): Cantata, Op.24

$ Josephine Veasey, mezzo–soprano; Nicolai Gedda, tenor; Jules Bastin, bass; London Symphony Chorus and Orchestra; Sir Colin Davis, conductor; Philips 6703042 (3 discs).

B Roméo et Juliette: Dramatic Symphony, Op.17

$ Brigitte Fassbaender, mezzo–soprano; Nicolai Gedda, tenor; John Shirley–Quirk, baritone; Vienna State Opera Chorus; ORF Orchestra; Lamberto Gardelli, conductor; Orfeo S–087842H (2 discs), ♫ C–087842H.

C Les Troyens ("The Trojans") (1856–1859)

$ Berit Lindholm, soprano; Josephine Veasey, mezzo–soprano; Jon Vickers, tenor; Peter Glossop, baritone; Roger Soyer, baritone; Wandsworth School Boys' Choir; London Symphony Chorus and Orchestra; Sir Colin Davis, conductor; Philips 6709002 3 (5 discs), ♫ 7699142.

Orchestral

A Overtures: Béatrice et Bénédict (1862); Benvenuto Cellini (1838); Carnaval romain ("Roman Carnival"), Op.9 and Corsaire, Op.21.

* Boston Symphony Orchestra; Charles Munch, conductor; RCA Victrola ♫ ALK1–4474.

A Overtures: Béatrice et Bénédict (1862); Carnaval romain ("Roman Carnival"), Op.9; Corsaire, Op.21; King Lear, Op.4; Rob Roy (1832)

$ Scottish National Orchestra; Sir Alexander Gibson, conductor; Chandos 1067.

A Roméo et Juliette: Suite of Excerpts, Op.17

* Chicago Symphony Orchestra; Carlo Maria Giulini, conductor; Angel AE–34467, ♫ AE–34467.

Symphonic

A Symphonie fantastique ("Fantastic Symphony"), Op.14

* Chicago Symphony Orchestra; Sir George Solti, conductor; London 414307–1 LJ, ♫ 414207–4 LJ.

$ Montreal Symphony Orchestra; Charles Dutoit, conductor; London 414203–1 LH, ♫ 414203–4 LH.

* Vienna Philharmonic Orchestra; Pierre Monteux, conductor; London ♫ STS5-15423.

Vocal

C Nuits d'été ("Summer Nights"): Song Cycle, Op.7

$ Dame Kiri Te Kanawa, soprano; Paris Orchestra; Daniel Barenboim, conductor; DG 2532047, ♫ 3302047. Includes Berlioz' La Mort de Cléopâtre: Cantata (1829) (with soprano Jessye Norman).

BERNSTEIN, LEONARD
1918–

Although best known for his Broadway musical West Side Story (1960) (and yes, it has been that long), Bernstein has written some "serious" works of enduring quality. His music is marked by jazz influences and a keen sense of rhythm.

Choral

C Chichester Psalms, for Chorus and Orchestra (1965)

$ Camerata Singers; New York Philharmonic Orchestra; Leonard Bernstein, conductor; Columbia MS-6792. Includes Bernstein's Ballet Facsimile (1947).

Orchestral

B Candide Overture (1956)

$ Boston Pops Orchestra; Arthur Fiedler, conductor; RCA LSC-2789, ♫ RK-1033. Includes Grofé's Grand Canyon Suite (1931) in a rousing and colorful performance, rated A.

BIZET, GEORGES
1838–1875

Baptized Georges, Bizet's "registered" name was Alexandre-César-Léopold Bizet. Georges is best known as the composer of the most popular and performed opera ever: Carmen, a work almost as perfect as it is entertaining (this despite its initial failure—the composer not living to see its eventual success). Only a few other of Bizet's works are still popular, even though he completed about 7 other operas, numerous choral works, a good deal of solo piano music, several dozen songs, etc.

Operatic

A <u>Carmen</u> (Based on a Novella by Prosper Mérimée) (1873–1874)

$ Adriana Maliponte, soprano; Marilyn Horne, mezzo–soprano; James McCracken, tenor; Tom Krause, baritone; Manhattan Opera Chorus; Metropolitan Opera Children's Chorus and Orchestra; Leonard Bernstein, conductor; DG 413279–1 GX3 (3 discs), ♭ 413279–4 GX2.

$ Victoria De Los Angeles, soprano; Janine Micheau, soprano; Nicolai Gedda, tenor; Ernest Blanc, baritone; French National Radio Orchestra and Chorus; Sir Thomas Beecham, conductor; Angel S–3613 (3 discs).

Orchestral

A <u>L'Arlésienne</u> Suites Nos.1–2 (1872) (Incidental Music for a Play by Alphonse Daudet)

$ National Philharmonic Orchestra, London; Leopold Stokowski, conductor; Columbia CBS MY–37260, ♭ MY–37260. Includes Bizet's <u>Carmen</u> Suites Nos.1–2 (1873–1874), also rated A.

Also––see entry under Offenbach, Ballet, Gaîté Parisienne (Arranged by Manuel Rosenthal) (1938), <u>infra.</u>

A <u>Carmen</u> Suites Nos.1–2 (1873–1874)––see entry for <u>L'Arlésienne</u> Suites Nos.1–2 (1872) (Incidental Music for a Play by Alphonse Daudet), immediately <u>supra.</u>

B <u>Jeux d'enfants</u> ("Children's Games") (Orchestrated by Bizet from his Work for Piano, 4 Hands, Same Opus), Op.22

$ Orchestre National de la Radio et Television Française; Jean Martinon, conductor; DG 415913–1 GMF, ♭ 415913–4 GMF. Includes Bizet's <u>La Jolie Fille de Perth</u> Suite (After a Work by Sir Walter Scott) (1867), rated C and Symphony No.1, in C (1855), rated B.

Also––see entry under Dukas, Orchestral, <u>L'Apprenti sorcier</u> ("The Sorcerer's Apprentice") (1897), <u>infra.</u>

C <u>La Jolie Fille de Perth</u> Suite (After a Work by Sir Walter Scott) (1867)––see entry for <u>Jeux d'enfants</u> ("Children's Games") (Orchestrated by Bizet from his Work for Piano, 4 Hands, Same Opus), Op.22, immediately <u>supra.</u>

Symphonic

34

B Symphony No.1, in C (1855)—see entry for <u>Jeux</u> <u>d'enfants</u> ("Children's Games") (Orchestrated by Bizet from his Work for Piano, 4 Hands, Same Opus), Op.22 under Orchestral, <u>supra</u>.

BLOCH, ERNEST
1880-1959

Several of Swiss-born (and American-naturalized) Ernest Bloch's compositions are Judaic in inspiration, for example, his famous <u>Schelomo</u> and <u>Baal</u> <u>Shem</u> <u>Tov</u>. Bloch was a fine composer in the forefront of the third rank (i.e., after the likes of Grieg and Rachmaninoff).

Chamber

C <u>Baal</u> <u>Shem</u> <u>Tov</u>, ("Master of the Good Word") for Violin and Piano (1923)

* Isaac Stern, violin; Alexander Zakin, piano; Columbia CSP AMS-6717. Includes Bloch's Sonata No.1 for Violin and Piano (1920).

Concerted

B <u>Schelomo</u> ("Solomon"): Rhapsody for 'Cello and Orchestra (1915)

$ János Starker, 'cello; Israel Philharmonic Orchestra; Zubin Mehta, conductor; London 414166-1 LE, ♭ 414166-4 LE. Includes Bloch's <u>Voice in the Wilderness</u> for Orchestra and 'Cello Obbligato (1936).

BOCCHERINI, LUIGI
1743-1805

Born in Italy, Boccherini spent several years in Spain, where he found favor for many of those years. He was known both as a composer and as a very accomplished 'cellist (he wrote 4 Concerti for that instrument). His output was very large, including 20 Symphonies, 125 String Quintets (from one of which comes the famous "Boccherini Minuet"), 48 String Trios, etc. Boccherini's music is nicely melodic and does not make too many demands on the listener's intellect: not a bad epitaph, all in all.

Chamber

B Quintet for Strings, Op.11 No.5, in E (Occasionally misnumbered as "Op.13 No.5")

* Alexander Schneider, violin; Felix Galimir, violin; Michael Tree, viola; David Soyer, 'cello; Lynn Harrell, 'cello; Vanguard S-291, ⊞ HM-43. Includes Boccherini's Quintet for Guitar and Strings, Op.50 No.2, in C (with guitarist Alirio Diaz). The Op.11 is famous for its "Boccherini Minuet."

BOITO, ARRIGO
1842-1918

Boito (baptized not Arrigo, but Enrico) was acknowledged not only as a very fine poet and librettist (he did the libretti for Verdi's masterpieces: <u>Otello</u> and <u>Falstaff</u>), but also as a more than competent composer of the Italian Late-Romantic school. Boito's must enduring work is the opera <u>Mefistofele</u> ("Mephistopheles"), based on Goethe's <u>Faust</u>.

Operatic

C <u>Mefistofele</u> ("Mephistopheles") (After Goethe's <u>Faust</u>) (1868-1875)

$ Montserrat Caballé, soprano; Mirella Freni, soprano; Luciano Pavarotti, tenor; Nicolai Ghiaurov, bass; Trinity Boys' Choir; National Philharmonic Orchestra, London; Oliviero de Fabritiis, conductor; London LDR-73010 LH3 (3 discs), ⊞ LDR5-73010 LH3.

BORODIN, ALEXANDER
1833-1887

The illegitimate son of Imeretian Prince Gedeanishvili and the wife of an army doctor (Avdotia Konstantinovna Kleinecke, née Antonova), Borodin was listed (as was the practice then) as the lawful son of one of his father's serfs—one Porfiry Borodin. Hence, his full name was Alexander Porfirevich Borodin. Borodin became a physician whose specialties were chemistry and pathology. His first fame came with the publication of several papers in chemistry, but Borodin's affinity for music showed itself early by virtue of several compositions, many yet extant. It should be remembered that Borodin was essentially a musical autodidact. Borodin became friends with Mily Balakirev and Modest Mussorgsky, both of whom influenced his musical development. With them, and also César Cui and Nikolai Rimsky-Korsakov, Borodin became part of the group known as "The Five" (or "Mighty Fist" when nearly literally translated from the Russian appellation coined by the Russian art critic and historian, Vladimir Stassov). "The Five" were influential for their Nationalistic music, their colorful orchestrations, their employment of lush melodic themes, and their use of exotic or historical settings for their works. Borodin is somewhat physical sciences in Russia, a good indication of his egalitarian views in a time when such were exceedingly uncommon. It remains unfortunate that Borodin is best remembered in this country for those of his melodies which found their way into the Broadway musical, Kismet. O tempus....

Chamber

B String Quartet No.2, in D (1881–1885)

$ Fitzwilliam Quartet; London 7239. Includes Borodin's String Quartet No.1 (1875–1979), in A. The second movement of the Quartet No.2 is popularly known as, ugh, "Baubles, Bangles and Beads" whilst the third (in this case, slow) movement is oft heard as "This is My Beloved:" "If Borodin were alive today he'd be spinning in his grave"––spuriously attributed to Samuel Goldwyn.

Orchestral

B In the Steppes of Central Asia (1880)

$ USSR Symphony Orchestra; Yevgeny Svetlanov, conductor; Quintessence 7165, ♮ 7165. Includes Borodin's Symphony No.2, in b (1876), also rated B.

A Prince Igor: Overture and "Polovtsian Dances" (1890)

$$ London Symphony Chorus and Orchestra; Sir George Solti, conductor; Mobile Fidelity 517. Includes Glinka's Overture to Russlan and Ludmilla (1838–1841), rated A; Mussorgsky's Night on Bald Mountain (Orchestrated by Rimsky-Korsakov) (1860–1866), rated A and Khovanshchina: Introduction and "Dance of the Persian Slaves" (1872–1880), rated C. One of the dances from Prince Igor is popularly known as "Stranger in Paradise."

Symphonic

B Symphony No.2, in b (1876)––see entry for In the Steppes of Central Asia (1880) under Orchestral, supra.

BRAHMS, JOHANNES
1833–1897

37

Brahms is the only composer of the first rank not to have composed either any operas or true program music. With the exception of his songs and choral works, he wrote nothing but absolute music for both symphonic and chamber ensembles, and for solo instrument. He was born in Hamburg but spent the last three and a half decades of his life in Vienna, which fact directed his creative impulses towards greater outwardness and larger forms. His works are usually imbued with extraordinary craftsmanship and display a master's handling of the Baroque and Classical forms. Yet, throughout his works Brahms conveys a feeling of warmth, affection and understanding unlike any other composer. Certainly he was thoughtful about his work: he did not complete his Symphony No.1 until his 43rd year (because, he indicated, he felt the nearness of Beethoven and was intimidated by Beethoven's work in the symphonic form). Even so, after a performance of the Symphony No.1, a member of the audience noted the similarity between the last movement of Brahms' Symphony No.1 and that of Beethoven's Symphony No.9, to which he rejoined, "Certainly, but the wonder is that it is so apparent to any ass." It is interesting to observe that George Bernard Shaw, in 1893, only 4 years before Brahms' death, wrote that "Brahms is just like Tennyson, an extraordinary musician, with the brains of a third-rate village policeman." Shaw, however, had the grace to excuse himself later and apologize on the grounds that Brahms' "idiom" was unfamiliar to him and compared his own feuilleton to Beethoven's denunciation of Weber's Overture to <u>Euryanthe</u> as a "...string of diminished sevenths." Brahms held closely to his motto, "Frei, aber froh" ("single, but happy;" based on the motto of his friend, the violinist Joseph Joachim, whose own precept was "Frei, aber einsam"-- "single, but lonely") and musically employed the first three letters of it (i.e., FAF) as the notes for several of his works (e.g., opening of the Symphony No.3, etc.). He remained unmarried (and, one assumes, "froh") to his death. With Bach and Beethoven, Brahms is the last of what Hans von Bülow called the "three Bs of music."

Chamber

A Quartets for Piano and Strings (3), Nos.1–3: Op.25, in g; Op.26, in A and Op.60, in c

$ Beaux Arts Trio; Walter Trampler, viola; Philips 6747068 (3 discs).

B Quintet for Clarinet and Strings, Op.115, in b
$ Cleveland Quartet; Richard Stoltzman, clarinet; RCA ARL1-1993, ⚱ ARL1-1993.

B Quintet for Piano and Strings, Op.34, in f
* Juilliard Quartet; Leon Fleisher, piano; Odyssey Y-35211, ⚱ YT-35211.
$ Quartetto Italiano; Maurizio Pollini, piano; DG 2531197.

A Sonatas for 'Cello and Piano (2), Nos.1-2: Op.38, in e and Op.99, in F
$ Vladimir Ashkenazy, piano; Lynn Harrell, 'cello; London 7208, ⚱ 7208.

C Sonatas for Clarinet (or Viola) and Piano (2), Nos.1-2: Op.120 No.1-2, in f and E flat
$ Richard Goode, piano; Richard Stoltzman, clarinet; RCA ARC1-4246, ⚱ ARC1-4246.

A Sonatas for Violin and Piano (3), Nos.1-3: Op.78, in G; Op.100, in A and Op.108, in d
$ Pinchas Zukerman, violin; Daniel Barenboim, piano; DG 415003-1 GX2 (2 discs), ⚱ 415003-4 GX2.

A String Quartet No.1, Op.51, in c
$ Cleveland Quartet; RCA VCS-7102 (2 discs). Includes Brahms' other String Quartets: Nos.2-3: Op.51 No.2, in a and Op.67, in B flat, both rated B.

B String Quartet No.2, Op.51 No.2, in a--see entry for String Quartet No.1, Op.51 No.1, in c, immediately supra.

B String Quartet No.3, Op.67, in B flat--see entry for String Quartet No.1, Op.51 No.1, in c, supra.

B Trio for Clarinet (or Viola), 'Cello and Piano, Op.114, in a flat

$ Peter Schmidl, clarinet; Friedrich Dolezal, 'cello; András Schiff, piano; London 410114-1, ♮ 410114-4. Includes the same composer's Trio for Horn, Violin and Piano, Op.40, in E flat, rated A. In this latter the pianist is also Schiff, but the hornist is Gunther Högner, and Helmut Binder is the violinist.

A Trio for Horn, Violin and Piano, Op.40, in E flat
$ Vladimir Ashkenazy, piano; Itzhak Perlman, violin; Barry Tuckwell, horn; London 6628. Includes Franck's Sonata for Violin and Piano, in A (1886), also rated A.

Also—see entry for Trio for Clarinet (or Viola), 'Cello and Piano, Op.114, in a flat, immediately supra.

A Trios for Piano, Violin and 'Cello (3), Nos.1-3: Op.8, in B; Op.87, in C and Op.101, in c
$ Isaac Stern, violin; Leonard Rose, 'cello; Eugene Istomin, piano; Columbia M2S-760 (2 discs).

Choral
A Ein Deutsches Requiem ("A German Requiem"), Op.45
$ Elisabeth Schwarzkopf, soprano; Dietrich Fischer-Dieskau, baritone; Philharmonia Chorus and Orchestra; Otto Klemperer, conductor; Angel S-3624 (2 discs), ♮ 4X2S—3624.

Concerted
A Concerto for Piano No.1, Op.15, in d
* Sir Clifford Curzon, piano; London Symphony Orchestra; George Szell, conductor; London 411579-1 LJ, ♮ 411579-4 LJ.

* Leon Fleisher, piano; Cleveland Orchestra; George Szell, conductor; Odyssey ♮ YT-31273.

A Concerto for Piano No.2, Op.83, in B flat
* Leon Fleisher, piano; Cleveland Orchestra; George Szell, conductor; Odyssey ♮ YT-32222.

$ Maurizio Pollini, piano; Vienna Philharmonic Orchestra; Claudio Abbado, conductor; DG 2530790, ♮ 3300790.

A Concerto for Violin, Op.77, in D

$ Jascha Heifetz, violin; Chicago Symphony Orchestra; Fritz Reiner, conductor; RCA AGL1-4909. Cadenzas by Heifetz.

A Concerto for Violin and 'Cello ("Double Concerto"), Op.102, in a
$ David Oistrakh, violin; Mstislav Rostropovich, 'cello; Cleveland Orchestra; George Szell, conductor; Angel S-36032, ♫ S-36032.

* Josef Suk, violin; André Navarra, 'cello; Czech Philharmonic Orchestra; Karel Ančerl, conductor; Quintessence 7203, ♫ 7203. Includes the same composer's Academic Festival Overture, Op.80, also rated A.

Instrumental

B Hungarian Dances (21), Nos.1-21: for Piano, Four Hands (1868, 1880)
$ Katia and Marielle Labeque, piano; Philips 6514107, ♫ 7337107.

Also--for orchestral version of same entry, see under Orchestral, infra, and for violin and orchestra version of No.7, in A (1868), see entry under Saint-Saëns, Concerted, Havanaise for Violin and Orchestra, Op.83, infra.

C Variations and Fugue on a Theme by Handel, Op.24
* Julius Katchen, piano; London ♫ STS-15150. Includes the same composer's Variations on a Theme by Paganini, Op.35, rated B.

B Variations on a Theme by Paganini, Op.35--see entry for Variations and Fugue on a Theme by Handel, Op.24, immediately supra.

Orchestral

A Academic Festival Overture, Op.80
$ Cleveland Orchestra; George Szell, conductor; Columbia MS-6965. Includes Brahms' Tragic Overture, Op.81 and Variations on a Theme by Haydn, Op.56a, both also rated A.

* Columbia Symphony Orchestra; Bruno Walter, conductor; Odyssey ♫ YT-30851. Includes the same works as the Szell recording, immediately supra.

Also--see entry under Concerted, Concerto for Violin and 'Cello ("Double Concerto"), Op.102, in a, supra.

A Hungarian Dances (21), Nos.1-21: for Orchestra (1868, 1880)

$ Ferenc Liszt Chamber Orchestra; János Rolla, conductor; Erato STU-71411, ♮ STU-71411.

Also--for piano version of same entry, see under Instrumental, supra, and for violin and orchestra version of No.7, in A (1868), see entry under Saint-Saëns, Concerted, Havanaise for Violin and Orchestra, Op.83, infra.

B Serenade No.1, Op.11, in D

$ Amsterdam Concertgebouw Orchestra; Bernard Haitink, conductor; Philips 9500322.

A Tragic Overture, Op.81--see entry for Academic Festival Overture, Op.80, supra.

A Variations on a Theme by Haydn, Op.56a--see entry for Academic Festival Overture, Op.80, supra.

Symphonic

A Symphonies (4), Nos.1-4: Op.68, in c; Op.73, in D; Op.90, in F and Op.98 in e

$ Chicago Symphony Orchestra; James Levine, conductor; RCA CRL4-3425 (4 discs).

! New York Philharmonic Orchestra; Bruno Walter, conductor; Odyssey 32360007 (3 discs).

Vocal

B Rhapsody for Alto, Chorus and Orchestra, Op.53

$ Brigitte Fassbaender, mezzo-soprano; Prague Philharmonic Chorus; Czech Philharmonic Orchestra; Giuseppe Sinopoli, conductor; DG 410864-1 GH, ♮ 410864-4 GH. Includes Brahms' Nänie for Chorus and Orchestra, Op.82 and Triumphlied for Chorus and Orchestra, Op.55.

C Liebeslieder ("Love Songs") Waltzes, Op.52 and Neue Liebeslieder ("New Love Songs") Waltzes, Op.65: Waltzes for Vocal Quartet and Piano, Four Hands

$ Edith Mathis, soprano; Brigitte Fassbaender, mezzo-soprano; Peter Schreier, tenor; Dietrich Fischer-Dieskau, baritone; Karl Engel and Wolfgang Sawallisch, piano, four hands; DG 2532094, ♮ 3302094. Includes

Brahms' Vocal Quartets, Op.64 Nos.1-3 (An die Heimat ("To the Homeland"), Der Abend ("The Evening") and Fragen ("Questions").

B Vier Ernste Gesänge ("Four Serious Songs"), Op.121

$ Dame Janet Baker, mezzo-soprano; Cecil Aronowitz, viola; André Previn, piano; EMI 065 03279 (must be special ordered). Includes Brahms' Lieder: Op.59 No.4; Op.84 No.4; Op.91; Op.94 No.4; Op.95 No.4; Op.105 Nos.1 and 4 and Op.106 No.1

$ Kurt Moll, bass; Cord Garben, piano; Acanta 4023525. Includes Brahms' Lieder: Op.86 Nos.4-6; Op.94 Nos.1-3, and 6; Op.96 No.1; Op.105 Nos.4-5.

BRITTEN, BENJAMIN, LORD
1913-1976

Raised to the peerage (the first composer ever so honored) shortly before his death, Britten's full name and title were Edward Benjamin Britten, Baron of Aldeburgh. Britten studied with Frank Bridge (whom he considered his most influential teacher), John Ireland and Arthur Benjamin. Britten is generally recognized as indisputably the most important English composer since Sir Edward Elgar, and possibly since Henry Purcell (and that goes back a bit--to the 17th century). There seems little doubt that, without any national limitation, Britten is certainly the greatest composer for voice of this century. Although his instrumental and orchestral music is often imbued with charm, wit, intelligence, etc., it appears that words were the primary stimuli to his finest creations. For many listeners, much of Britten's music is rather like skydiving: a rarefied and acquired taste. To them he often sounds précieux, and more's the pity, since, in fact, there is an uncommon strength to Britten's work (e.g., Serenade for Tenor, Horn and Strings, Peter Grimes, etc.). Since one often encounters the name of the late Sir Peter Pears, the famous English tenor and "consort" of Britten's, and since Pears' name is often mispronounced, I offer the following verse published in Punch a couple of decades ago:
"There's no need for Peter Pears
To give himself airs:
He has them written
By Benjamin Britten."

Choral

A Ceremony of Carols, Op.28

* King's College Chapel Choir, Cambridge; Sir David Willcocks, conductor; Seraphim S-60217. Includes Britten's Hymn to St. Cecilia, Op.27 and Missa brevis, Op.63, in D, both rated C.

C Hymn to St. Cecilia, Op.27—see entry for Ceremony of Carols, Op.28, immediately supra.

C Missa brevis, Op.63, in D—see entry for Ceremony of Carols, Op.28, supra.

B War Requiem, Op.66

$ Galina Vishnevskaya, soprano; Sir Peter Pears, tenor; Dietrich Fischer-Dieskau, baritone; London Symphony Chorus and Orchestra; Benjamin, Lord Britten, conductor; London 1255 (2 discs), ⑤ 5-1255.

Operatic

C Billy Budd (After Melville) (1951)

$ Sir Peter Pears, tenor; Peter Glossop, baritone; John Shirley-Quirk, baritone; Michael Langdon, bass; Ambrosian Singers; London Symphony Orchestra; Benjamin, Lord Britten, conductor; London 1390 (3 discs).

B Peter Grimes (After George Crabbe) (1945)

$ Heather Harper, soprano; Jon Vickers, tenor; Jonathan Summers, baritone; Covent Garden Opera Chorus and Orchestra; Sir Colin Davis, conductor; Philips 6769014 (3 discs), ⑤ 7699089.

Orchestral

B Matinées musicales (After Rossini), Op.24

$ National Philharmonic Orchestra, London; Sir Richard Bonynge, conductor; London LDR-71039. Includes Britten's Soirées musicales (After Rossini), Op.9, also rated B and Respighi's La Boutique fantasque ("The Fantastic Toyshop") (After Rossini) (1919), rated A.

B Soirées musicales (After Rossini), Op.9—see entry for Matinées musicales (After Rossini), Op.2, immediately supra.

C Variations on a Theme of Frank Bridge, Op.10--see entry for Young Person's Guide to the Orchestra, Op.34, immediately infra.

A Young Person's Guide to the Orchestra, Op.34

$ Boston Symphony Orchestra; Seiji Ozawa, conductor; RCA 🄱 ALK1-9537. Includes Mussorgsky's Pictures at an Exhibition (Orchestrated by Ravel) (1874), also rated A.

$ London Symphony Orchestra; Benjamin, Lord Britten, conductor; London 6671. Includes Britten's Variations on a Theme of Frank Bridge, Op.10, rated C.

Vocal

C Les Illuminations, for Solo Voice and Orchestra (After Rimbaud), Op.18

$ Robert Tear, tenor; Philharmonia Orchestra; Carlo Maria Giulini, conductor; DG 2531199 PSI. Includes Britten's Serenade for Tenor, Horn and Strings, Op.31 (the horn soloist is Dale Clevenger), rated B.

B Serenade for Tenor, Horn and Strings, Op.31--see entry for Les Illuminations for Solo Voice and Orchestra (After Rimbaud), Op.18, immediately supra.

BRUCH, MAX
1838-1920

Bruch was a Late-Romantic German composer known, essentially, for but three pieces (the ones listed below). Bruch fits nicely into the middle portion of the third rank of composers (which rank is too large by half) somewhere after Rachmaninoff.

Concerted

B Concerto for Violin No.1, Op.26, in g

$ Itzhak Perlman, violin; London Symphony Orchestra; André Previn, conductor; Angel S-36963, 🄱 4XS-36963. Includes Mendelssohn's Concerto for Violin, Op.64, in e, rated A.

C Kol Nidrei for 'Cello and Orchestra, Op.47

$ Lynn Harrell, 'cello; Philharmonia Orchestra; Vladimir Ashkenazy, conductor; London LDR-71108 LH, ⊟ LDR5-71108 LH. Includes Dvořák's Concerto for 'Cello, Op.104, in b, rated A.

C Scottish Fantasy for Violin and Orchestra, Op.46

$ Jascha Heifetz, violin; New Symphony Orchestra of London; Sir Malcolm Sargent, conductor; RCA AGL1-4896. Includes Vieuxtemps' Concerto for Violin No.5, Op.37, in a, also rated C.

BRUCKNER, ANTON
1824-1896

Bruckner was a late-blooming Late-Romantic (or, for those pedantically inclined, Neo-Romantic) German composer who was an ardent fancier of Wagner (on meeting Wagner the first time, Bruckner is said to have knelt before the august Richard and to have kissed the hem of his coat: such are the things of which legends are made). Bruckner has come into fashion as a composer of elephantine works (built of anti-climaxes heaped one upon another) only since the 1960s. A portion of a review of his Symphony No.3, published in Keynote (New York), December 12, 1885, eloquently expresses this author's view: "A hearing of the work induces a feeling of surprise that any sane publisher should have accorded the score the dignity of print, that is only equalled by a natural wonderment on the part of the listener that anyone should punish an inoffensive audience by the infliction of its performance, for anything more inane and wearisome cannot well be conceived than this olla podrida of miscellaneous rubbish...." Still, for some reason, known only to sadomasochists, Bruckner's music enjoys a popularity sufficient to entitle him to space here.

Choral

B Te Deum, in C (1884)

$ Jessye Norman, soprano; Yvonnne Minton, mezzo-soprano; David Rendall, tenor; Samuel Ramey, bass; Chicago Symphony Chorus and Orchestra; Daniel Barenboim, conductor; ⊟ DG 415616-4 GW. Includes Bruckner's Symphony No.4 ("Romantic"), in E flat (1880), rated A.

Symphonic

C Symphony No.1, in c (1891)

$ Berlin Philharmonic Orchestra; Herbert von Karajan, conductor; DG 2532062, ♮ 3302062.

C Symphony No.2, in c (1891?)
* Amsterdam Concertgebouw Orchestra; Bernard Haitink, conductor; Philips Sequenza 6527183, ♮ 7311183.

C Symphony No.3, in d (1889)
$ Berlin Radio Symphony Orchestra; Riccardo Chailly, conductor; London 417093-1 LH, ♮ 417093-4 LH.

A Symphony No.4 ("Romantic"), in E flat (1880)
$ Columbia Symphony Orchestra; Bruno Walter, conductor; Columbia MP-39026, ♮ MPT-39026.
Also--see entry for Te Deum, in C (1884), under Choral, supra.

B Symphony No.6, in A (1881)
$$ Bavarian State Orchestra; Wolfgang Sawallisch, conductor; Orfeo S-024821.

A Symphony No.7, in E (1883)
* Philharmonia Orchestra; Otto Klemperer, conductor; Angel AE-34420, ♮ AE-34420.

A Symphony No.8, in c (1887)
$ Dresden State Orchestra; Eugen Jochum, conductor; Angel S-3893 (2 discs).

A Symphony No.9, in d (1896)
$ Columbia Symphony Orchestra; Bruno Walter, conductor; Columbia MP-39129, ♮ MPT-39129.

CANTELOUBE, JOSEPH
1879-1957

Born in France as Marie-Joseph Canteloube, this composer added "de Malaret" to his name later, but is always referred to as "Canteloube."

Canteloube is now represented almost solely by his <u>Chants</u> <u>d'Auvergne</u> ("Songs of the Auvergne"). There are 27 such songs, collected and provided with both lovely piano, or gorgeous orchestral, accompaniments (it is the accepted practice for a singer to be accompanied, at any given time, by one or the other, not both simultaneously, nor alternating between the two), by Canteloube.

Vocal

C <u>Chants</u> <u>d'Auvergne</u> ("Songs of the Auvergne") Complete (Five Books comprising Nos.1–27) (1923–1940)

$ Frederica von Stade, mezzo-soprano; Royal Philharmonic Orchestra; Antonio de Almeida, conductor; volume 1: Columbia IM–37299, ▣ IMT–37299; volume 2: Columbia IM–37837, ▣ IMT–37837.

C <u>Chants</u> <u>d'Auvergne</u> ("Songs of the Auvergne") Selections (1923–1940)

$ Anna Moffo, soprano; American Symphony Orchestra; Leopold Stokowski, conductor; RCA AGL1–4877. Contains the most popular of the <u>Chants</u>: "L'Antouèno," "Pastourelle," "L'Aïo dè Rotso," "Malurous Qu'o uno Fenno," "Baïlèro," "Passo pel Prat" and "Brezairola." Also includes Villa-Lobos' <u>Bachianas</u> <u>Brasileiras</u> No.5 for Soprano and 8 'Celli (1938–1945), rated C and Rachmaninoff's <u>Vocalise</u>, Op.34 No.14, rated B.

CASTELNUOVO—TEDESCO, MARIO
1895–1968

Born in Florence, Castelnuovo-Tedesco settled in the U.S. in 1939. He had studied with Pizetti and he produced a wealth of music, most notably (if only for sheer volume) a setting for every song to be found in the works of Shakespeare, and some distinguished film scores. His Concerto for Guitar now holds the principal place among his works.

Concerted

C Concerto for Guitar No.1, Op.99, in D (1939)

$ John Williams, guitar; Philadelphia Orchestra; Eugene Ormandy, conductor; Columbia MS–6834. Includes Rodrigo's <u>Concierto</u> <u>de</u> <u>Aranjuez</u> for Guitar and Orchestra (1939), rated A.

CHABRIER, EMMANUEL

1841-1894

Chabrier (full name Alexis-Emmanuel Chabrier) was an attorney (due to family pressures), and later a bureaucrat in the French Ministry of the Interior. He ultimately overcame these disadvantages to become a composer. His works are distinguished by a typically Gallic exuberance, particularly through colorful orchestration and charmingly tricky rhythms. Among Chabrier's friends were the painter Manet and the poet Verlaine. Satie and Ravel both acknowledged the influence of Chabrier's works on their own compositions.

Orchestral

A España Rhapsody (1883)

$ L'Orchestre de la Suisse Romande; Ernest Ansermet, conductor; Decca 6.43.265 AH (must be specially ordered—don't settle for any other recording). Includes Chabrier's Pastorale Suite (1880), rated C; "Danse Slave" and "Fête Polonaise" from Le Roi malgré lui ("The King in Spite of Himself") (1887), the "Danse" rated C and the "Polonaise" rated B, and the Joyeuse Marche (1888), rated B.

Also—see entry under Ibert, Orchestral, Escales ("Ports of Call") (1922), infra.

C "Danse Slave" from Le Roi malgré lui ("The King in Spite of Himself") (1887)—see entry for España Rhapsody (1883), immediately supra.

B "Fête Polonaise" from Le Roi malgré lui ("The King in Spite of Himself") (1887)—see entry for España Rhapsody (1883), supra.

B Joyeuse Marche (1888)—see entries for España Rhapsody (1883), supra and under Dukas, Orchestral, L'Apprenti sorcier ("The Sorcerer's Apprentice") (1897), infra.

C Pastorale Suite (1880)—see entry for España Rhapsody (1883), supra.

CHAUSSON, ERNEST
1855-1899

49

Paris–born Ernest–Amédée Chausson studied with Massenet and Franck. His works bear the impress of Franck, yet not that composer's sense of construction. Chausson's music tends to be somewhat given to that peculiar melancholy of some of the Late–Romantics (e.g., Rachmaninoff, etc.), but his works also bear an individuality quite specially that of Chausson (verstehen wir?). Perhaps Chausson's melancholia was a premonition of his early and peculiar death: he accidentally bicycled down a hill into a rather stout wall (one assumes brake failure).

Concerted

B Poème for Violin and Orchestra, Op.25

! Jascha Heifetz, violin; RCA Victor Symphony Orchestra; Izler Solomon, conductor; RCA AGM1-4924. Includes Conus' Concerto for Violin, in e (1897); Saint-Saëns' Introduction and Rondo Capriccioso for Violin and Orchestra, Op.28, rated B and Sarasate's Zigeunerweisen ("Gypsy Airs") for Violin and Orchestra, Op.20 No.1, rated B. The accompanying orchestra and conductor for Heifetz in the Saint-Saëns and Sarasate works are the London Philharmonic Orchestra under Sir John Barbirolli.

Also––see entry under Saint-Saëns, Concerted, Havanaise for Violin and Orchestra, Op.83, infra.

CHERUBINI, LUIGI
1760-1842

Although Cherubini (full name Maria Luigi Carlo Zenobio Salvatore Cherubini) was born in Florence, he lived in Paris essentially from 1788 until his death. He was head of the Conservatoire de Paris from 1821 until 1841. He met Beethoven (who admired his music) and was in charge of the Conservatoire while Berlioz was a student there (in his Mémoires, Berlioz humorously, but somewhat inventively, recounts his first meeting with Cherubini, which ostensibly ended with Cherubini chasing Berlioz around the library of the Conservatoire in an attempt to evict him from the premises. According to Berlioz' own account, he had mistakenly entered the building through the "women's" entrance, a practice equated with apostasy by Cherubini). Cherubini was an admirer of Gluck (for the purity of Gluck's instrumentation) and was considered conservative in his musical style. Cherubini was primarily concerned with the subjugation of "beauty," etc., to the importance of the "idea" which the music was to convey. Cherubini wrote masterfully and beautifully for the voice. He was also a fine exponent of counterpoint. Mendelssohn and Beethoven were among his many admirers, and Cherubini's music represents itself very well today: more than can be said for those whose popularity occluded Cherubini's during his lifetime: Boieldieu and Auber (and if those gentlemen are not to be found in this volume, how ever could they possibly be of any musical merit?).

Operatic

B Médée ("Medea") (1797)

$ Sylvia Sass, soprano; Magda Kalmár, soprano; Klára Tákacs, mezzo-soprano; Veriano Luchetti, tenor; Kolos Kovats, bass; Hungarian Radio Chorus; Budapest Symphony Orchestra; Lamberto Gardelli, conductor; Hungaroton 11904-11906 (3 discs).

CHOPIN, FRÉDÉRIC
1810-1849

Chopin was born near Warsaw (and christened Fryderyk Franciszek Chopin, the first and middle names he later Gallicized to Frédéric François). His father came of purely French stock. It is no surprise, then, that Frédéric went to Paris (in 1787) to advance his career. Further, except for his excursions back to Poland and also to Germany and England (and, in the company of his inamorata: George Sand, to Majorca and the Spanish mainland), Chopin resided in France, wherein he became acculturated and accepted as essentially French in his compositional style. This latter is somewhat simplistic, since Chopin's Polish heritage ran too deeply within him ever to have been truly forsaken. With the exception of his Sonata for 'Cello and Piano and 2 Concerti for Piano (and a few other works written for solo piano and later expanded, or piano with orchestral accompaniment), all of Chopin's works are for solo piano. In this realm he is remarkably alone: sensitive, subtle, innovative, brilliant and requiring the greatest interpretive ability possible--he explored virtually every aspect of his chosen instrument. It was to introduce Chopin to the public that Robert Schumann began a critique of Chopin's Variations, Op.2 with the famous "Hats off gentlemen, a genius!" Only the Sonatas for Piano of Beethoven make for apt comparison to the range and expressiveness of Chopin's music for solo piano.

Concerted

B <u>Andante spianato et Grande Polonaise</u>, Op.22

* Peter Frankl, piano; Innsbruck Symphony Orchestra; Robert Wagner, conductor; Turnabout 34473. Includes Chopin's Concerto for Piano No.1, Op.11, in e, also rated B.

Also—for solo piano version of same entry, see Impromptus (4), Nos.1-4: Op.29, in A flat; Op.36, in F sharp; Op.51,in G flat and Op.66, in c sharp ("Fantasie Impromptu") and same entry, both under Instrumental, <u>infra</u>.

B Concerto for Piano No.1, Op.11, in e

\$ Artur Rubinstein, piano; New Symphony Orchestra, London; Stanislaw Skrowaczewski, conductor; RCA LSC-2575, ∄ RK-1004.

Also—see entry for <u>Andante spianato et Grande Polonaise</u>, Op.22, immediately <u>supra</u>.

B Concerto for Piano No.2, Op.21, in f

\$ Claudio Arrau, piano; London Philharmonic Orchestra; Eliahu Inbal, conductor; Philips 7300110. Includes Chopin's <u>Krakowiak</u>, Concert Rondo for Piano and Orchestra, Op.14, rated C.

C <u>Krakowiak</u>, Concert Rondo for Piano and Orchestra, Op.14—see entry for Concerto for Piano No.2, Op.21, in f, immediately <u>supra</u>.

Instrumental

A <u>Andante spianato et Grande Polonaise</u>, Op.22

\$ Vladimir Horowitz, piano; RCA ARM1-2953, ∄ ARM1-2953. Includes Chopin's Ballades (4), Nos.1-4: Op.23, in g; Op.38, in F; Op.47, in A flat and Op.52, in f, rated A; Barcarolle, Op.60, in F sharp, rated B and "Polonaise-Fantasie," Op.61 (No.7 of 16 Polonaises), rated C. This is a monophonic disc at regular price.

Also—see entry for Impromptus (4), Nos.1-4: Op.29, in A flat; Op.36, in F sharp; Op.51, in G flat and Op.66, in c sharp ("Fantasie Impromptu"), <u>infra</u>.

A Ballades (4), Nos.1-4: Op.23, in g; Op.38, in F; Op.47, in A flat and Op.52, in f

* Vladimir Ashkenazy, piano; ♩ London 410275-4. Includes the same composer's Barcarolle, Op.60, in F sharp, rated B; Nouvelles Études, Op.25 Nos.25-27 (Opus Posthumous), rated A and Scherzo No.2, Op.31, in b flat, rated B.

$ Artur Rubinstein, piano; RCA LSC-2370.

Also--see entry for <u>Andante spianato et Grande Polonaise</u>, Op.22, immediately <u>supra</u>.

B Barcarolle, Op.60, in F sharp--see entries for Ballades (4), Nos.1-4: Op.23, in g; Op.38, in F; Op.47, in A flat and Op.52, in f, immediately <u>supra</u> and <u>Andante spianato et Grande Polonaise</u>, Op.22, <u>supra</u>.

A Études (27), Nos.1-24: Op.10 Nos.1-12 and Op.25 Nos.1-12

$ Maurizio Pollini, piano; DG 2530291, ♩ 3300287.

B Impromptus (4), Nos.1-4: Op.29, in A flat; Op.36, in F sharp; Op.51, in G flat and Op.66, in c sharp ("Fantasie Impromptu")

$ Artur Rubinstein, piano; RCA LSC-7037 (2 discs). Includes Chopin's <u>Andante spianato et Grande Polonaise</u>, Op.22, rated A and Polonaises (16), Nos.1-6: Op.26 Nos.1-2, in c sharp and e flat; Op.140 Nos.1-2, in a and c; Op.44, in f sharp and Op.53, in A flat, rated A.

A Mazurkas (51), Nos.1-51

$ Artur Rubinstein, piano; RCA ARL3-5171 (3 discs), ♩ CRK-2-5171.

B Nocturnes (21), Nos.1-21

$ Daniel Barenboim, piano; DG 2741012 (2 discs), ♩ 3382012.

A Nouvelles Études, Op.25 Nos.25-27 (Opus Posthumous)--see entries for <u>Andante spianato et Grande Polonaise</u>, Op.22, <u>supra</u> and Ballades (4), Nos.1-4: Op.23, in g; Op.38, in F; Op.47, in A flat and Op.52, in f, <u>supra</u>.

C "Polonaise-Fantasie," Op.61 (No.7 of 16 Polonaises)--see entry for <u>Andante spianato et Grande Polonaise</u>, Op.22, <u>supra</u>.

A Polonaises (16), Nos.1-6: Op.26, Nos.1-2, in c sharp and e flat; Op.140 Nos.1-2, in a and c; Op.44, in f sharp and Op.53, in A flat--see entry for Impromptus (4), Nos.1-4: Op.29, in A flat; Op.36, in F sharp; Op.51, in G flat and Op.66, in c sharp ("Fantasie Impromptu"), supra.

B Préludes, Op.28 (24), Nos.1-24
$ Maurizio Pollini, piano; DG 2530550.

B Scherzi (4), Nos.1-4: Op.20, in b; Op.31, in b flat; Op.39, in c sharp and Op.54, in E
$ Artur Rubinstein, piano; RCA LSC-2368.
Also--for Scherzo No.2, Op.31, in b flat, see entry for Ballades (4), Nos.1-4: Op.23, in g; Op.38, in F; Op.47, in A flat and Op.52, in f, supra.

A Sonata for Piano No.2, Op.35, in b flat
$ Artur Rubinstein, piano; RCA LSC-3194. Includes Chopin's Sonata for Piano No.3, Op.58, in b, rated C. The Sonata for Piano No.2 is famous for its "Funeral March" slow movement.
* Abbey Simon, piano; Turnabout 34272, 🎵 CT-2235. Includes Chopin's Sonata for Piano No.3, Op.58, in b, rated C.

C Sonata for Piano No.3, Op.58, in b--see entry for Sonata for Piano No.2, Op.35, in b flat, immediately supra.

A Waltzes (19), Nos.1-19
$ Claudio Arrau, piano; Philips 9500739, 🎵 7300824.
* Abbey Simon, piano; Turnabout 34580, 🎵 CT-2102.

CIMAROSA, DOMENICO
1749-1801

Born in Aversa, near Naples, Cimarosa succeeded Antonio Salieri (he of recent fame occasioned by the play and film Amadeus) as Kapellmeister to the Austrian court of Leopold II. At the death of Leopold, Cimarosa's fortunes (based largely on his opera Il matrimonio segreto <"The Secret Marriage"\>) waned, and he died en route to St.

Petersburg, having accepted a court post there. Cimarosa was a fine comic opera craftsman, and Percy Scholes dubs him "...the Italian Mozart." Albeit his talent was excellent, especially the manner in which he handled voices (and vocal ensembles), the comparison to Mozart, "Italian" qualified or not, is rather hyperbolic.

Concerted

B Concerto for Oboe and Strings (Arranged from Melodies of Cimarosa by Arthur Benjamin)

$ André Lardrot, oboe; Vienna State Symphony Orchestra; Felix Prohaska, conductor; Vanguard 2036. Includes Albinoni's Concerto for Oboe, Op.7 No.3; Handel's Concerti for Oboe (1740), Nos.1-2, both in B flat, rated B, Haydn's Concerto for Oboe, in C, H.VIIgC1 (Attributed), rated A and Salieri's Concerto for Flute and Oboe, in C, rated B.

COPLAND, AARON
1900–

Born in Brooklyn, New York, Copland studied with Rubin Goldmark and the redoubtable (and late) Nadia Boulanger. His early ballets are thought to characterize the American musical idiom: jazz harmonies (although Copland always seemed to have handfuls of triads handy with which to lard his earlier works), vital rhythms, and "American speech patterns." His later works tend towards the absolute (as opposed to the programmatic) and, in some of them, he toys with polytonality, polyrhythms, dodecaphony and atonalism, but never, however, completely eschewing that American quality peculiar to the likes of Gershwin (i.e., brassy independence without a soupçon of sentimentality).

Ballet

A Appalachian Spring Suite (1944)

$ New York Philharmonic Orchestra; Leonard Bernstein, conductor; Columbia MG-30071 (2 discs), ⧈ MGT-30071. Includes the same composer's Billy the Kid Suite (1938), rated C; Rodeo Suite (1942), rated B and El Salón México (1936), rated B.

C Billy the Kid Suite (1938)--see entry for Appalachian SPring Suite (1944), immediately supra.

B <u>Rodeo</u> Suite (1942)—see entry for <u>Appalachian</u> <u>Spring</u> Suite (1944) <u>supra</u>.

Orchestral

B <u>Fanfare for the Common Man</u> (1944)

$ Philadelphia Orchestra; Eugene Ormandy, conductor; Columbia MS-6684. Includes Copland's <u>Lincoln Portrait</u> (1942) narrated by Adlai E. Stevenson, rated C, and Ives' <u>Three Places in New England</u> (1903-1914), rated A.

C <u>Lincoln Portrait</u> (1942)—see entry for <u>Fanfare for the Common Man</u> (1944), immediately <u>supra</u>.

B <u>El Salón México</u> (1936)—see entry for <u>Appalachian Spring</u> Suite (1944) under Ballet, <u>supra</u>.

Symphonic

C <u>Dance</u> Symphony (1925)

$ London Symphony Orchestra; Aaron Copland, conductor; Columbia MS-7223. Includes Copland's <u>Short</u> Symphony (1931-1933).

CORELLI, ARCANGELO
1653-1713

I doubt that anyone could dislike a 17th century Italian violinist and composer whose first name was "Arcangelo," especially one who was known for the amiability of his disposition. Corelli was among the first of the real violin virtuosi, extending the capability of his instrument to include double stops (although the technique and instrument of his day tended to preclude playing much above the third position). He was also an entrepreneur who, through publishing (including his own compositions), performing and teaching, amassed a considerable fortune (in addition to a highly valued collection of paintings). Handel ostensibly said of Corelli's frugality that "He likes nothing better than seeing pictures without paying for it, and saving money." It was largely through Corelli's extension of the concerto grosso form that the modern symphony (both the form and the orchestra) came closer into being. His music is insightful, lucid, melodic, and encompasses a variety of feeling and character. In fine, he remains an estimable composer.

Orchestral

B Concerti Grossi, Op.6 (12), Nos.1–12

* Cantilena; Adrian Shepherd, conductor; Chandos 3002 (3 discs).
Number 8, in g ("Christmas"), is among the most popular pieces penned by
Corelli.

Also—for Concerto Grosso, Op.6 No.8 ("Christmas"), in g, see entry
under Albinoni, Orchestral, Adagio, in g, supra.

COUPERIN, FRANÇOIS
1668–1733

Sometimes called "Couperin le Grand" to distinguish him from the
others of his large, musical family (and also to denote his abilities as both
composer and organist), François was a Parisian, born and dead. He is
best known for his works for the harpsichord (over 200 such), but he also
wrote prolifically for the organ, instrumental combinations, and the voice.
A large number of his works for harpsichord are based on dances of his
time. These works were frequently program pieces (to judge from their
titles), with programs no longer intelligible to modern audiences since the
references are archaic and many of the more obscure are lost. His works
are a kind of compromise between the polyphonic and homophonic and are
tonally centered. His harpsichord works are arranged in 4 "Books" totalling
27 Suites ("Ordres").

Chamber

C Les Nations (4 Sonatas and Symphonic Suites for 2 Violins and
Continuo) (1726)

$ Cologne Musica Antiqua; DG ARC–410901–1 AH2 (2 discs).

Instrumental

C Book 1 (Ordres 1–5) (1713)

$ Kenneth Gilbert, harpsichord; Harmonia Mundi 351–354 (4 discs).

C Book 2 (Ordres 6–12) (1717)

$ Kenneth Gilbert, harpsichord; Harmonia Mundi 355–358 (4 discs).

C Book 3 (Ordres 13–19) (1722)

$ Kenneth Gilbert, harpsichord; Harmonia Mundi 359–362 (4 discs).

B Book (Ordres 20–27) (1730)

$ Kenneth Gilbert, harpsichord; Harmonia Mundi 363–366 (4 discs).

CRUMB, GEORGE
1929–

Born in Charleston, West Virginia, Crumb is one of the best of the younger American composers (and teachers—at the University of Pennsylvania). He is the recipient of numerous awards for composition and has proven to be an influence on composers younger than he. Crumb's music is idiosyncratic, innovative, and uses the full potential of many of the instruments for which he writes, thought-provoking, and occasionally lyrical.

Instrumental
C Sonata for Solo 'Cello (1955)

$ Robert Sylvester, 'cello; Desto 7169. Includes Hindemith's Sonata for Unaccompanied 'Cello, Op.25 No.3; Wellesz' Sonata for Solo 'Cello, Op.30 and Ysaÿe's Sonata for Unaccompanied 'Cello, Op.28.

Vocal
C Ancient Voices of Children (1970)

* Jan DeGaetani, mezzo–soprano; Michael Dash, boy soprano; Contemporary Chamber Ensemble; Arthur Weisberg, conductor; Nonesuch 71255.

DAHL, INGOLF
1912–1970

Ingolf Dahl, with whom the author studied composition at the University of Southern California, was born in Hamburg, Germany. He is generally considered an American composer, and one of influence in this country and abroad. He is also regarded as a very important teacher of composition. His music is often terse and somewhat dry, but inflected with rhythmic invention and intriguing sonorities. A portion of his Music for Brass Instruments is the theme for the popular syndicated radio program, On First Hearing.

Chamber
C Music for Brass Instruments (Quintet) (1944)

$ American Brass Quintet; Desto 6474–6477 (4 discs). Includes Palestrina's Ricercar sopra il primo tuono; Reicha's Baroque Suite; Four Dances from Lachrimae or Seaven teares Figured in Seaven Passionate Pavans, by Dowland; Five Flemish Dances from Dances: The Third Little Music Book, of Susato; Desperavi and Triumphavi by Michael East; Six 17th Century Dances by Pezel; Anton Simon's Quatuor en forme de sonatine, Op.23 No.1; Ewald's (Brass) Quintet, Op.5, in b flat; In modo religioso, Op.38 of Glazunov; Sonata for Trumpet, Horn and Trombone by Poulenc; Hindemith's Morgenmusik; Bergsma's Suite for Brass Quintet (1945); Five Miniatures of Robert Starer; Elias Tannenbaum's Improvisations and Patterns for Brass Quintet and Tape; Kriki for Brass Quintet of Darijan Bozic and Charles Whittenberg's Triptych for Brass Quintet. This is an excellent survey of the literature peculiar to the brass quintet ensemble, and beautifully performed.

DEBUSSY, CLAUDE
1862–1918

Debussy (born Achille-Claude) was a composer to whom individuality was virtually sacred. Even though, for example, he was much taken with, and fascinated by, the music of Wagner, he realized full well that he had to resist that older master's influence in order to maintain his own independence. The Prélude à l'Après-midi d'un faune ("Prelude to the Afternoon of a Faun") was first performed in 1894 and, with that performance, the school of Impressionism (in music) was born. This despite James Huneker's report in the New York Sun of July 19,1903, that "...the man (i.e., Debussy) is a wraith from the East; his music was heard long ago in the hill temples of Borneo; was made as a symphony to welcome the head-hunters with their ghastly spoils of war!" As a friend of the poet Mallarmé (on whose poem Debussy's Prélude à l'Après-midi d'un faune was based), Debussy was aware of Mallarmé's precept that "To name an object is to sacrifice three-quarters of that enjoyment of the poem which comes from the guessing bit by bit. To suggest it—that is our dream." It was with that in mind that Debussy sought to create his music—through vague yet colorful allusions: the "impressions" of the artist of perceived reality, colored by his own senses and imagination. In the composition of such music no one was more successful than Debussy. As a matter of fact,

59

there is no other composer who is "truly" an Impressionist. In particular, Debussy's harmonic innovations (although still based in tonality and given to pandiatonicism) are probably what remain that aspect of his work which is most easily apprehended, certainly in his piano works. In his orchestral pieces, it is that same harmonic novelty plus his extraordinary orchestral palette which give his works their distinctive quality. Because of the sensibilities with which his works are imbued, Debussy's music requires the greatest sensitivity (and intelligence) on the part of the performing artist in order to be heard properly—it is music which is easily divested of its quality by less than the best in performance. In 1880 and 1881, Debussy visited Moscow (twice), Switzerland and Italy as a music tutor to the children of Tchaikovsky's wealthy patroness: Madame Nadezhda von Meck. It was on these trips that he became familiar with, and was subsequently influenced by, the music of Mussorgsky and Borodin. Oddly, he was not appreciative of the work of Tchaikovsky. Debussy agonized throughout the First World War on two counts: the cancer (from which he suffered for ten years, and ultimately died), and the assault on his beloved France (the Sonata for 'Cello and Piano <1915>, the first of a projected series of six sonatas for diverse instruments, carries the patriotic inscription: "...par C. Debussy, musicien français"). Debussy is a composer whose place in the musical firmament has never been fixed with assurance, yet it is possible that, in the words of one French critic, "No great music has been written in the 20th century after that of Debussy."

Ballet

C Jeux: poème dansé ("Games: A Dance Poem") (1912)

$ Amsterdam Concertgebouw Orchestra; Bernard Haitink, conductor; Philips 6768284 PSI (3 discs). Includes Debussy's Danse sacrée et danse profane ("Sacred and Profane Dances"), for Harp and Strings (1904), with harpist Vera Badings, rated B; Images pour orchestre (1906-1909) (3), Nos.1-3: Gigues ("Jigs," Orchestration Completed by André Caplet); Iberia ("Spain") and Rondes de printemps ("Dances of Spring"), rated A; Marche écossaise sur un thème populaire ("Scottish March on a Popular Theme": the "Earl of Ross March") (1891), rated C; La Mer ("The Sea") (1903-1905), rated A; Nocturnes (1893) (3), Nos.1-3: Nuages ("Clouds"); Fêtes ("Festivals") and Sirènes ("Sirens"), rated B; Prélude à l'aprés-midi d'un faune ("Prelude to the Afternoon of a Faun") (1892-1894), rated A and Première rapsodie for clarinet and piano (1909-1910), with clarinetist George Pieterson (and with orchestral accompaniment instead of piano).

Chamber

B Danse sacrée et danse profane ("Sacred and Profane Dances"), for Harp and Strings (1904)--see entry for Jeux: poème dansé ("Games: A Dance Poem") (1912), under Ballet, immediately supra.

C Sonata for 'Cello and Piano, in d (1915)

$ Mstislav Rostropovich, 'cello; Benjamin, Lord Britten, piano; London 41068, ⧫ 41068. Includes Schubert's Sonata for Arpeggione and Piano, D.821, in a and Robert Schumann's Fünf Stücke im Volkston ("Five Pieces in the Folk Style") for 'Cello and Piano, Op.102, both rated A.

A String Quartet, Op.10, in g

$ Juilliard Quartet; Columbia M-36050. Includes Ravel's String Quartet, in f (1903), also rated A.

* Talich Quartet; Calliope 1893. Includes Ravel's String Quartet, in f (1903), also rated A.

Instrumental

A Children's Corner Suite (1906-1908) (6), Nos.1-6: Doctor Gradus ad Parnassum; Jimbo's Lullaby; Serenade for the Doll; Snow is Dancing; The Little Shepherd and Golliwog's Cakewalk

$ Walter Gieseking, piano; Angel 35067. Includes Debussy's Suite bergamasque (1890-1905) (4), Nos.1-4: Prélude; Menuet; Clair de lune ("Moonlight") and Passepied, also rated A. Although monophonic, this disc is worth the regular price since a monophonic recording of a solo instrument is not a problem, and Gieseking's performances are exquisite.

B Deux Arabesques ("Two Arabesques") (1888)

* Aldo Ciccolini, piano; Seraphim S-60253. Includes Debussy's Ballade (1890); Danse: Tarantelle styrienne (1890); Pour le piano Suite (1896-1901) (3), Nos.1-3: Prélude; Sarabande and Toccata, rated B; Rêverie (1890), rated A and Suite bergamasque (1890-1905) (4), Nos.1-4: Prélude; Menuet; Clair de lune ("Moonlight") and Passepied, rated A.

C En blanc et noir ("In Black and White") For Two Pianos (1915) (3), Nos.1-3

$ Alfons and Aloys Kontarsky, piano(s); DG 2707072 (2 discs). Includes Debussy's Ballade, For Piano Four Hands (1890); "Cortège et air de danse," For Piano, Four Hands, from Cantata L'Enfant prodigue (1884); Lindaraja, For Two Pianos (1901); Marche écossaise sur un thème populaire ("Scottish March on a Popular Theme": the "Earl of Ross March"), For Piano, Four Hands (1891), rated C; Petite Suite, For Two Pianos (1888) (4), Nos.1-4: En bateau ("In a Boat"); Cortège; Menuet and Ballet, For Piano, Four Hands, rated B; Prélude à l'aprés-midi d'un faune ("Prelude to the Afternoon of a Faun") (1892-1894), For Two Pianos, rated A; Six Épigraphes antiques (1915), For Two Pianos (6), Nos.1-6: Pour invoquer Pan, dieu du vent d'été ("To Invoke Pan, God of the Summer Wind"); Pour un tombeau sans nom ("For a Nameless Tomb"); Pour que la nuit soit propice ("For Which the Night is Propitious"); Pour la danseuse aux crotales ("For the Dancing Lady With Castanets"); Pour l'Egyptienne ("For the Egyptian Lady") and Pour remercier la pluie au matin ("Thanks for the Morning Rain"), rated C; Symphonie en si mineur ("Symphony in b"), For Two Pianos (1880) and Ravel's Entre cloches ("Among Bells") from Les sites auriculaires ("Auricular Sites"), (1895-1896) For Two Pianos; Frontispice (1919), For Two Pianos; Ma-Mère l'Oye ("Mother Goose") Suite (1907), For Two Pianos (5), Nos.1-5: Pavane de la belle au bois dormant ("Pavane of Sleeping Beauty"); Petit Poucet ("Tom Thumb"); Laideronette, impératrice des pagodes ("The Ugly Woman, Empress of the Pagodas"); Les Entretiens de la belle et la bête ("Conversations of Beauty and the Beast") and Le Jardin féerique ("The Enchanted Garden"), rated A and Rapsodie espagnole ("Spanish Rhapsody") (1907), For Piano, Four Hands (3), Nos.1-3: Prélude à la nuit ("Prelude in the Fashion of the Night"); Habañera and Féria ("Fiesta"), rated A.

A Estampes ("Engravings") (1903) (3), Nos.1-3: Pagodes ("Pagodas"); Soirée dans Grenade ("Evening Party in Granada") and Jardins sous la pluie ("Gardens in the Rain")

$ Claudio Arrau, piano; Philips 9500965, ◻ 7300965. Includes Debussy's Images (Book I) (1905), (3), Nos.1-3: Reflets dans l'eau ("Reflections on the Water"); Hommage à Rameau ("Homage to Rameau") and Mouvement, and Images (Book II) (1907), (3), Nos.1-3: Cloches à travers les feuilles ("Bells Through the Leaves"); Et la lune descend sur le temple qui fut ("And the Moon Descends to the Temple Which Had Been") and Poissons d'or ("Goldfish"), both rated A.

A Images pour piano: (Book I) (1905), (3), Nos.1-3: Reflets dans l'eau ("Reflections on the Water"); Hommage à Rameau ("Homage to Rameau") and Mouvement, rated A; Images (Book II) (1907), (3), Nos.1-3: Cloches à travers les feuilles ("Bells Through the Leaves"); Et la lune descend sur le temple qui fut ("And the Moon Descends to the Temple Which Had Been") and Poissons d'or ("Goldfish")--see entry for Estampes ("Engravings") (1903) (3), Nos.1-3: Pagodes ("Pagodas"); Soirée dans Grenade ("Evening Party in Granada") and Jardins sous la pluie ("Gardens in the Rain"), immediately supra.

C Marche écossaise sur un thème populaire ("Scottish March on a Popular Theme": the "Earl of Ross March"), For Piano, Four Hands (1891)--see entry for En blanc et noir ("In Black and White") For Two Pianos (1915) (3), Nos.1-3, supra and for orchestral version, see Jeux: poème dansé ("Games: A Dance Poem") (1912), under Ballet, supra.

B Petite Suite, For Two Pianos (1888) (4), Nos.1-4: En bateau ("In a Boat"); Cortège; Menuet and Ballet, For Piano, Four Hands--see entry for En blanc et noir ("In Black and White") For Two Pianos (1915) (3), Nos.1-3, supra.

B Pour le piano Suite (1896-1901) (3), Nos.1-3: Prélude; Sarabande and Toccata--see entry for Deux Arabesques ("Two Arabesques") (1888), supra.

A Prélude à l'aprés-midi d'un faune ("Prelude to the Afternoon of a Faun") (1892-1894), For Two Pianos--see entry for En blanc et noir ("In Black and White") For Two Pianos (1915) (3), Nos.1-3, supra and for orchestral version--see entry for Jeux: poème dansé ("Games: A Dance Poem") (1912), under Ballet, supra.

A Préludes (1910-1913) (24), (12 Each in Books I and II), Nos.1-24
* Paul Jacobs, piano; Nonesuch 73031 (2 discs), 및 N6-3031.

A Rêverie (1890)—see entry for <u>Deux</u> <u>Arabesques</u> ("Two Arabesques") (1888), <u>supra</u>.

C <u>Six</u> <u>Épigraphes</u> <u>antiques</u> (1915), For Two Pianos (6), Nos.1-6: <u>Pour</u> <u>invoquer</u> <u>Pan,</u> <u>dieu</u> <u>du</u> <u>vent</u> <u>d'été</u> ("To Invoke Pan, God of the Summer Wind"); <u>Pour</u> <u>un</u> <u>tombeau</u> <u>sans</u> <u>nom</u> ("For a Nameless Tomb"); <u>Pour</u> <u>que</u> <u>la</u> <u>nuit</u> <u>soit</u> <u>propice</u> ("For Which the Night is Propitious"); <u>Pour</u> <u>la</u> <u>danseuse</u> <u>aux</u> <u>crotales</u> ("For the Dancing Lady With Castanets"); <u>Pour</u> <u>l'Égyptienne</u> ("For the Egyptian Lady") and <u>Pour</u> <u>remercier</u> <u>la</u> <u>pluie</u> <u>au</u> <u>matin</u> ("Thanks for the Morning Rain")—see entry for <u>En</u> <u>blanc</u> <u>et</u> <u>noir</u> ("In Black and White") For Two Pianos (1915) (3), Nos.1-3, <u>supra</u>.

A <u>Suite</u> <u>bergamasque</u> (1890-1905) (4), Nos.1-4: <u>Prélude</u>; <u>Menuet</u>; <u>Clair</u> <u>de</u> <u>lune</u> ("Moonlight") and <u>Passepied</u>—see entries for <u>Children's</u> <u>Corner</u> Suite (1906-1908) (6), Nos.1-6: <u>Doctor</u> <u>Gradus</u> <u>ad</u> <u>Parnassum</u>; <u>Jimbo's</u> <u>Lullaby</u>; <u>Serenade</u> <u>for</u> <u>the</u> <u>Doll</u>; <u>Snow</u> <u>is</u> <u>Dancing</u>; <u>The</u> <u>Little</u> <u>Shepherd</u> and <u>Golliwog's</u> <u>Cakewalk</u> and <u>Deux</u> <u>Arabesques</u> ("Two Arabesques") (1888), both <u>supra</u>.

For orchestral version of <u>Clair</u> <u>de</u> <u>lune</u>—see entry under Ibert, Orchestral, <u>Escales</u> ("Ports of Call") (1922), <u>infra</u>.

Orchestral

A <u>Images</u> <u>pour</u> <u>orchestre</u> (1906-1909) (3), Nos.1-3: <u>Gigues</u> ("Jigs," Orchestration Completed by André Caplet); <u>Iberia</u> ("Spain") and <u>Rondes</u> <u>de</u> <u>printemps</u> ("Dances of Spring")—see entry for <u>Jeux:</u> <u>poème</u> <u>dansé</u> ("Games: A Dance Poem") (1912), under Ballet, <u>supra</u>.

C <u>Marche</u> <u>écossaise</u> <u>sur</u> <u>un</u> <u>thème</u> <u>populaire</u> ("Scottish March on a Popular Theme": the "Earl of Ross March"), For Piano, Four Hands (1891)—see entry for <u>En</u> <u>blanc</u> <u>et</u> <u>noir</u> ("In Black and White") For Two Pianos (1915) (3), Nos.1-3 under Instrumental, <u>supra</u>; for orchestral version, see entry for <u>Jeux:</u> <u>poème</u> <u>dansé</u> ("Games: A Dance Poem") (1912), under Ballet, <u>supra</u>.

A <u>La</u> <u>Mer</u> ("The Sea") (1903-1905)—see entry for <u>Jeux:</u> <u>poème</u> <u>dansé</u> ("Games: A Dance Poem") (1912), under Ballet, <u>supra</u>.

B Nocturnes (1893) (3), Nos.1-3: Nuages ("Clouds"); Fêtes ("Festivals") and Sirènes ("Sirens")--see entry for Jeux: poème dansé ("Games: A Dance Poem") (1912), under Ballet, supra.

A Prélude à l'aprés-midi d'un faune ("Prelude to the Afternoon of a Faun") (1892-1894)--for orchestral version, see entry for Jeux: poème dansé ("Games: A Dance Poem") (1912), under Ballet, supra; for piano version, see entry for En blanc et noir ("In Black and White") For Two Pianos (1915) (3), Nos.1-3 under Instrumental, supra.

DELIBES, LÉO
1836-1991

Léo Delibes (full name Clément-Philibert-Léo Delibes) was, during his lifetime, a well known composer of several operas and a few ballets. Of the operas, only Lakmé has been able to hold the stage with any regularity; of the ballets, only Coppélia and Sylvia (which is actually the better of the two, but less often performed). Delibes' was a melodic, rather than a dramatic, gift, and Lakmé (famous for its difficult coloratura aria, "The Bell Song") is one of the most exotically set works in the operatic literature.

Ballet

B Coppélia Suite (1876)
* Paris Conservatory Orchestra; Roger Desormière, conductor; Vox 513470. Includes Delibes' Sylvia Suite (1870), also rated B.

B Sylvia Suite (1870)--see entry for Coppélia Suite (1876), immediately supra.

Operatic

C Lakmé (1880)
* Mady Mesplé, soprano; Roger Soyer, baritone; Charles Burles, bass; Chorus and Orchestra of the Opéra-Comique, Paris; Alain Lombard, conductor; Seraphim S-6082 (3 discs).

DELIUS, FREDERICK
1862-1934

Delius (full name Fritz Albert Theodor Delius) is the only Impressionistic composer of English birth known to me. He was of German descent, and spent several years as proprietor of an orange-growing plantation in Florida in order to escape from the mercantile career his parents had planned for him. He said that his principal musical influence was Grieg (having studied unsuccessfully with Reinecke). Delius' last years were spent blind and paralyzed (syphilis being the probable cause) in France. His music is highly personal and exhibits a kind of isolation verging on deep loneliness. It is delicate, for the most part, and many listeners find that it lacks impetus or motion. Yet, several of his pieces are well-colored and evocative of nature, and are also full of gentleness and patience. Were it not for Sir Thomas Beecham acting as his champion, Delius' music would almost certainly be unknown today.

Orchestral

C Brigg Fair: "An English Rhapsody" (1907)

* Royal Philharmonic Orchestra; Sir Thomas Beecham, conductor; Seraphim ♮ 4XG-60185. Includes Delius' On Hearing the First Cuckoo in Spring (1912), rated A; Sleigh Ride (1888), rated C; A Song Before Sunrise (1918) and Summer Night on the River (1912).

A On Hearing the First Cuckoo in Spring (1912)--see entry for Brigg Fair: "An English Rhapsody" (1907), supra.

B Over the Hills and Far Away (1895)--see entry for Florida Suite (1886), supra.

C Sleigh Ride (1888)--see entry for Brigg Fair: "An English Rhapsody" (1907), supra.

DES PRÉZ, JOSQUIN
c.1440-1521

Des Préz is more often simply referred to by his first name, Josquin (and sometimes by its diminutive: Jossé), which is rather handy, since his surname has been spelled in a variety of ways (e.g., Desprez, Dupré, Del Prato, etc.). Little is known with certitude about his early years. It is thought that his musical education was obtained as a

66

choir-boy at the church of St. Quentin. Later he studied with his great Flemish countryman, the composer Joannes Okeghem (not to be confused with the philosopher, William of Occam, he of the razor). Josquin had what J.R. Milne called a "...checkered and erratic career...." Milne also quotes G.R. Kieswetter as saying that "Josquin deserves to be classed as one of the greatest musical geniuses of any period," and this opinion is one still held by many musical scholars, in particular for Josquin's stunningly beautiful use of counterpoint. Josquin's works are of essentially two vocal types: works for the church (masses and motets) and secular songs (chansons); in almost all his genius is to be found.

Vocal

B <u>Missa Gaudeamus</u> ("Mass: Therefore Let Us Praise")
$ Capella Cordina; Alejandro Planchart; Lyrichord 7265.

B <u>Recordans de my segnora</u> (á 4)
* Marsha Horgan, soprano; William Zukof, counter-tenor; Elliot Levine, baritone; The Nonesuch Consort; Joshua Rifkin, director; Nonesuch 71261. Includes 15 other songs by the same composer.

DOHNANYI, ERNST VON
1877-1960

Dohnányi was a Hungarian-born pianist and composer who "Teutonicized" his forename from Ernő and added the nobiliary particle "von" later (to give, one assumes, a "dignity and weight" to the whole). Only two of his works are of any popularity today, and those are the ones listed below. His music is essentially third-rate and characteristic of the Late-Romantic (and Austro-Hungarian) type. Dohnányi's grandson, Christoph von Dohnányi, is now the Music Director and Principal Conductor of the Cleveland Orchestra.

Chamber

C Serenade, Op.10, in C
! Jascha Heifetz, violin; William Primrose, viola; Emanuel Feuermann, 'cello; RCA AGM1-4942. Includes the Concerto for Violin (1944) by Gruenberg: the soloist is Heifetz and the accompaniment is provided by the San Francisco Symphony Orchestra with Pierre Monteux conducting.

Concerted

C Variations on a Nursery Song, Op.25 ("Twinkle, Twinkle, Little Star," or, for the polyglot purist, "Ah, vous dirai-je, maman?")

* Julius Katchen, piano; London Philharmonic Orchestra; Sir Adrian Boult, conductor; London STS-15406, 🎜 5-15406. Includes Rachmaninoff's Rhapsody on a Theme of Paganini, Op.43, rated A.

DONIZETTI, GAETANO
1797-1848

Donizetti (full name Domenico Gaetano Maria Donizetti) was an Italian composer of operas which contain charming melodies and are given, like Bellini's, to the then prevailing bel canto style. Only a handful of his works now hold the stage with any regularity.

Operatic

B L'Elisir d'amore ("The Elixir of Love") (1832)

$ Dame Joan Sutherland, soprano; Monica Sinclair, contralto; Luciano Pavarotti, tenor; Dominic Cossa, bass-baritone; Spiro Malas, bass; Ambrosian Singers; English Chamber Orchestra; Sir Richard Bonynge, conductor; London 13101 (3 discs), 🎜 13101.

C La Fille du régiment ("The Daughter of the Regiment") (1840)

$ Dame Joan Sutherland, soprano; Monica Sinclair, contralto; Spiro Malas, bass; Covent Garden Opera Chorus and Orchestra; Sir Richard Bonynge, conductor; London 1273 (2 discs), 🎜 5-1273.

A Lucia di Lammermoor (1835) (After Sir Walter Scott)

$ Dame Joan Sutherland, soprano; Luciano Pavarotti, tenor; Sherrill Milnes, baritone; Nicolai Ghiaurov, bass; Covent Garden Opera Chorus and Orchestra; Sir Richard Bonynge, conductor; London 13103 (3 discs), 🎜 5-13103.

DUKAS, PAUL
1865-1935

There is little to be said of French composer Dukas, except that he was a dedicated teacher, a thorough craftsman, and is now known for but

one work, and that one made immensely popular by Disney's movie
Fantasia (remember M. Mouse trying vainly to stop the onslaught of
brooms?). Oh yes, and Dukas was a sometime critic for La Revue
hebdomadaire (which last word is worth familiarity, especially if one is a
devotee of the Barchester works of Trollope).

Orchestral

A L'Apprenti sorcier ("The Sorcerer's Apprentice") (1897)

$ New York Philharmonic Orchestra; Leonard Bernstein, conductor;
Columbia MS-7165. Includes Mussorgsky's Night on Bald Mountain
(Orchestrated by Rimsky-Korsakov) (1860-1866); Saint-Saëns' Danse
macabre, Op.40 and Richard Strauss' Til Eulenspiegels lustige Streiche
("Til Eulenspiegel's Merry Pranks"), Op.28, all also rated A.

* L'Orchestre de la Suisse Romande; Ernest Ansermet, conductor;
London ₿ STS-15591. Includes Bizet's Jeux d'enfants (Orchestrated by
Bizet from his Work for Piano, 4 Hands, Same Opus), Op.22, rated B;
Chabrier's Joyeuse Marche (1888), rated B; Debussy's Prélude à
l'aprés-midi d'un faune ("Prelude to the Afternoon of a Faun")
(1892-1894), rated A; Honegger's Pacific 237 ("Mouvement symphonique"
No.1) (1924), rated A and Ravel's Rapsodie espagnole ("Spanish Rhapsody")
(1907) (3), Nos.1-3: Prélude à la nuit ("Prelude in the Fashion of the
Night"); Habañera and Féria ("Fiesta"), rated A.

Also--see entry under Honegger, Orchestral, Pacific 231
("Mouvement symphonique" No.1) (1924), infra.

DVOŘÁK, ANTONIN
1841-1904

Born in Bohemia (now Czechoslovakia) on the Vltava River (made
musically famous by Smetana in his Mà Vlast's "Moldau" section, since
the Czech for the Moldau is Vltava), Dvořák was basically a simple
person. He had been an apprentice to his father, a butcher, and was much
devoted to his country's people, music and real estate. He was a barely
accomplished violinist, but had been well schooled in music theory and
organ, and somewhat in composition. He later became a decent enough
violist to perform in the Czech Provisional Theater Orchestra under such a
one as Smetana. Dvořák's music is characterized by lovely melodies,
modestly colorful orchestration, and a good deal of Bohemian national

idiom (but seldom straying far from the academic aspects of the German school of composition). He was helped to no small extent by Brahms, who induced him to write the Slavonic Dances and also introduced Dvořák to Brahms' influential publisher, Simrock. There is virtually no ensemble grouping (both vocal and instrumental) for which Dvořák did not essay some kind of work, but he did his best with chamber, orchestral and symphonic enterprises (his solo piano pieces are very nice, but...), and his operas, a few of which are excellent but not particularly popular in this country. Dvořák visited the United States from 1892-1895, during which time he wrote the Symphony No.9 ("From the New World")--probably his best known work, and two oddments titled American Suite and The American Flag (the latter a cantata), both best forgotten. It may be of interest to Iowans that Dvořák visited the Czech community in Spillville on his summer vacations. By the way, it is not well known that one of Dvořák's first "tour guides" in New York was the estimable music critic, James G. Huneker of the New York World, whom Dvořák, the story goes, promptly "drank under the table" imbibing slivovitz. One more interesting personal sidelight on Dvořák: his great-grandson is the estimable Czech violinist, Josef Suk. Dvořák is among the last of the Brahmsian symphonists (albeit Dvořák is in the middle of the second rank, just behind Tchaikovsky). Dvořák's music is not contrapuntally fascinating, but it is well-crafted and full of his sincere affection and usually sunny disposition.

Chamber

C Quintet for Piano, 2 Violins, Viola and 'Cello, Op.81, in A
$ Artur Rubinstein, piano; Guarneri Quartet; RCA AGL1-4882.

B Serenade for Strings, Op.22, in E
$ Academy of St. Martin-in-the-Fields; Sir Neville Marriner, conductor; Philips 6514145, ♫ 7337145. Includes Dvořák's Serenade for Winds, 'Cellos and String Basses, Op.44, in d, also rated B.

B Serenade for Winds, 'Cellos and String Basses, Op.44, in d--see entry for Serenade for Strings, Op.22, in E, immediately supra.

B String Quartet No.12 ("American"), Op.96, in F
$ Talich Quartet; Calliope 1617, ♫ 4617. Includes Dvořák's String Quartet No.11, Op.61, in C.

B Trio for Piano, Violin and 'Cello ("Dumky"), Op.90, in e

$ Beaux Arts Trio; Philips 802918.

Concerted

A Concerto for 'Cello, Op.104, in b--see entry under Bruch, Concerted, Kol Nidrei, for Cello and Orchestra, Op.47, supra.

C Concerto for Piano, Op.33, in g

* Rudolf Firkusny, piano; St. Louis Symphony Orchestra; Walter Susskind, conductor; Turnabout 34691, 🅱 CT-2145.

C Concerto for Violin, Op.53, in a

* Josef Suk, violin; Czech Philharmonic Orchestra; Karel Ančerl, conductor, Quintessence 7112, 🅱 7112.

Instrumental

B Slavonic Dances (16), Op.46 (8), Nos.1-8: in C, e, D, F, A, A flat, c and g; and Op.72 (8), Nos.1-8: in B, e, F, D flat, b flat, B flat, a and A flat

* Alfred Brendel, piano; Walter Klien, piano; Turnabout 34060.

Also, for orchestral version--see same entry under Orchestral, infra.

Orchestral

A Carnival Overture, Op.92--see entry for Symphony No.5, Op.76, in F, under Symphonic, infra.

B Scherzo Capriccioso, Op.66

$ Cleveland Orchestra; Christoph von Dohnányi, conductor; DG 414422-1 LH, 🅱 414422-4 LH. Includes Dvořák's Symphony No.8, Op.88, in G, rated A.

A Slavonic Dances (16), Op.48 (8), Nos.1-8: in C, e, D, F, A, A flat, c and g; and Op.72 (8), Nos.1-8: in B, e, F, D flat, b flat, B flat, a and A flat

$ Cleveland Orchestra; George Szell, conductor; Columbia MP-38753.

Also--for two piano version of same opus, see same entry under Instrumental, supra.

Symphonic

C Symphony No.1 ("The Bells of Zlonice"), in c (1865)

* London Symphony Orchestra; István Kertész, conductor; Vox SVBX-5137 (3 discs). Includes Dvořák's Symphony No.2, in B flat (1865), rated C; Symphony No.3, in E flat (1873), rated B and Husitská Overture, Op.67.

C Symphony No.2, Op.4, in B flat--see entry for Symphony No.1 ("The Bells of Zlonice"), in c (1865), immediately supra.

B Symphony No.3, Op.10, in E flat--see entry for Symphony No.1 ("The Bells of Zlonice"), in c (1865), supra.

A Symphony No.5, Op.76, in F

* London Symphony Orchestra; István Kertész, conductor; Vox SVBX-5138 (3 discs). Includes Dvořák's Symphonies Nos.4 and 6, Op.13, in d and Op.60, in D, rated B, and the concert overtures Amid Nature, Op.91; Carnival, Op.92, rated A, and My Home, Op.62.

B Symphony No.6, Op.60, in d--see entry for Symphony No.5, Op.6, in F, immediately supra.

B Symphony No.7, Op.70, in d

* Czech Philharmonic Orchestra; Zdeněk Košler, conductor; Quintessence 7126, ♮ 7126.

A Symphony No.8, Op.88, in G

$ Cleveland Orchestra; George Szell, conductor; Columbia MY-38470, ♮ MY-38470.

Also--see entry for Scherzo Capriccioso, Op.66, under Orchestral, supra.

A Symphony No.9 ("From the New World"), Op.95, in e

$ Berlin Philharmonic Orchestra; Rafael Kubelik, conductor; DG 415915-1 GMF, ♮ 415915-4 GMF.

* Vienna Philharmonic Orchestra; Rafael Kubelik, conductor, London ♮ STS-15007.

ELGAR, SIR EDWARD
1857-1934

On first hearing Elgar's _Enigma_ Variations, George Bernard Shaw (only occasionally given to hyperbole) proclaimed the composer to be the greatest English composer since Purcell and the probable inheritor of the mantle of Beethoven. Even Elgar, I think, would have had difficulty with the latter assessment. His works are serious (occasionally inflated), but can be possessed of a Late-Romantic warmth, breadth and intelligence not often encountered among the works of other English composers of his generation.

Concerted

C Concerto for 'Cello, Op.85, in e

$ Lynn Harrell, 'cello; Cleveland Orchestra; Lorin Maazel, conductor; London 7195, ▤ 7195. Includes Tchaikovsky's _Pezzo Capriccioso_, Op.62 and Variations on a Rococo Theme for 'Cello and Orchestra, Op.33, rated B.

B Concerto for Violin, Op.61, in b

$ Pinchas Zukerman, violin; London Philharmonic Orchestra; Daniel Barenboim, conductor; Columbia M-34517.

Orchestral

A _Enigma_ Variations, Op.36

$ London Symphony Orchestra; Sir Adrian Boult, conductor; Angel S-36799, ▤ 4XS-36799. Includes Williams' English Folk Song Suite (1923) and Fantasia on _Greensleeves_ (1934), both also rated A.

C Introduction and Allegro for String Quartet and String Orchestra, Op.47

$ Allegri Quartet; London Sinfonietta; Sir John Barbirolli, conductor; Angel S-36101. Includes Elgar's Serenade for Strings, Op.20, in e and Vaughan Williams' Fantasia on _Greensleeves_ (1934), rated A.

A _Pomp and Circumstance_ March No.1, Op.39, in D

$ London Philharmonic Orchestra; Sir Adrian Boult, conductor; Angel S-37436, ▤ 4XS-37436. The _Pomp and Circumstance_ No.1 is famous for its use in this country as a processional in high school commencements, and, in England as the song Land of Hope and Glory (Elgar ultimately abominated this work as he felt it had been put to jingoistic and xenophobic purposes.) Includes Elgar's remaining 4 Pomp and Circumstance Marches, Op.39 Nos.2-5: in a, c, G and C and Walton's Crown Imperial March (1937), rated B and Orb and Sceptre March (1953), rated C.

ENESCO, GEORGES
1881-1955

Famous as a violin virtuoso, teacher and composer, Roumanian Enesco (born George Enescu) employed the thematic materials of his homeland in many of his works. At present, only one of those works is heard with any frequency, and that one usually as an encore piece.

Orchestral

A Roumanian Rhapsody No.1, Op.11

$ RCA Victor Symphony Orchestra; Leopold Stokowski, conductor; RCA AGL1-5259, ♮ AGL-5259. Includes the orchestral version of Liszt's Hungarian Rhapsody No.2, in c sharp (1874), rated A; Smetana's Overture to The Bartered Bride (1886), rated A and Vltava ("The Moldau") from Má Vlast ("My Fatherland") (1874-1879), rated A.

FALLA, MANUEL DE
1876-1956

Spanish composer Falla, although influenced by the music of his native land, was too sophisticated, worldly-wise and intelligent to be simply a typical composer of the Spanish Nationalistic school. Two each of his ballets and concerted pieces are international in their Neo-Romantic (and, in the case of the Concerto for Harpsichord, Neo-Classical) appeal, and may be heard and enjoyed often.

Ballet

A El Amor brujo ("Love, the Warlock") (1915)

* Victoria de los Angeles, soprano; Philharmonia Orchestra; Carlo Maria Giulini, conductor; Seraphim ♮ 4XG-60405. Includes Ravel's Pavane pour une Infante défunte ("Pavane for a Dead Princess") (1899) and

Rapsodie espagnole ("Spanish Rhapsody") (1907)(3), Nos.1–3: Prélude à la nuit ("Prelude in the Fashion of the Night"); Habañera and Féria ("Fiesta"), both also rated A.

Also--see entry for El Sombrero de tres picos ("The Three-Cornered Hat") (1919), immediately infra.

B El Sombrero de tres picos ("The Three-Cornered Hat") (1919)

$ Colette Boky, soprano; Montreal Symphony Orchestra; Charles Dutoit, conductor; London LDR-71060, ▤ LDR5-71060. Includes Falla's El Amor brujo ("Love, the Warlock") (1915), rated A.

Concerted

C Concerto for Harpsichord and Chamber Orchestra (1923–1926)

$ John Constable, harpsichord; London Sinfonietta; Simon Rattle, conductor; Argo ZRG-921 PSI. Includes Falla's Psyché and El Retablo de Maese Pedro ("Master Peter's Puppet Show") (1923).

B Noches en los jardines de España ("Nights in the Gardens of Spain") (1909–1915)

$ Artur Rubinstein, piano; Philadelphia Orchestra; Eugene Ormandy, conductor; RCA LSC-3165, ▤ RK-1165. Includes Saint-Saëns' Concerto for Piano No.2, Op.22, in g, rated B.

* Gonzalo Soriano, piano; Paris Conservatory Orchestra; Rafael Frühbeck de Burgos, conductor; Angel AE-34422, ▤ AE-34422. Includes Rodrigo's Concierto de Aranjuez for Guitar and Orchestra (1939), rated A. In the Rodrigo work, the artists are guitarist Alirio Diaz with the Spanish National Orchestra, conducted by Frühbeck.

FAURÉ, GABRIEL
1845–1924

Gabriel-Urbain Fauré became a friend and student of Saint Saëns, who was ten years Fauré's senior. It was Saint-Saëns' influence which helped Fauré become a fine pianist and organist, and exposed him to the works of such disparate composers as Liszt and Bach. Fauré, too, became an excellent teacher, numbering among his students Ravel, Enesco and Nadia Boulanger. As a mature composer, Fauré's works are fastidious (like those of Ravel) and representative of the French virtues of his time:

75

intelligence, discretion and reticence. His greatest originality does not encompass form or instrumental color, but rather an honesty and directness which his use of melody and harmony make telling.

Chamber

B Sonata for Violin and Piano, Op.13, in A

$ Jascha Heifetz, violin; Brooks Smith, piano; RCA LM-2074. This is a monophonic recording at full price. Includes Castelnuovo-Tedesco's The Lark for Violin and Piano (1930) and Vitali's Chaconne for Violin, in g. The accompanist to Heifetz in the Vitali is organist Richard Elsasser.

Orchestral

B Pelléas et Mélisande, Op.80 (Incidental Music for the Play by Maeterlinck)

$ New Philharmonia Orchestra; Andrew Davis, conductor; CBS MY-38471, ⓑ MY-38471. Includes Franck's Symphony in d (1886-1888), rated A.

Vocal

B Pavane, Op.50

$ Ambrosian Singers; Philharmonia Orchestra; Andrew Davis; Columbia M-35153. Includes Fauré's Requiem, Op.48, with Lucia Popp, soprano; Siegmund Nimsgern, bass, also rated B.

B Requiem, Op.48--see entry for Pavane, Op.50, immediately supra.

FRANCK, CÉSAR
1822-1890

César Franck (full name César-Auguste Jean Guillaume Hubert Franck) was born in Liège, the son of a Belgian father and German mother. Franck studied at the Conservatoire de Paris and became a naturalized Frenchman. After his studies, he toured as a piano virtuoso for a short time, then settled down to composition. Franck married in 1848, during the French Revolution, and the wedding party only gained access to the church after climbing a barricade (with the assistance of the revolutionaries stationed there). His death was caused, in part, by injuries sustained from being hit by a bus (he lingered for a few months and was then transported elsewhere). Besides composition, Franck was known as a kind and generous soul and as a very fine teacher (among his students were Chausson, d'Indy, Duparc and Ropartz). Only a few of Franck's many compositions are much performed, but these few give testimony to a brilliant talent, rich with melody and, in the case of the Symphony in d, an architectonic skill almost unsurpassed.

Chamber

A Sonata for Violin and Piano, in A (1886)—see entry under Brahms, Chamber, Trio for Horn, Violin and Piano, Op.40, in E flat, supra.

Concerted

A Variations symphonique (Symphonic Variations for Piano and Orchestra) (1885)

$ Sir Clifford Curzon, piano; London Philharmonic Orchestra; Sir Adrian Boult, conductor; London ♮ STS–15407. Includes Litolff's Scherzo from his Concerto symphonique No.4, Op.102 and Grieg's Concerto for Piano, Op.16, in a, rated A.

Also—see entry under d'Indy, Concerted, Symphonie sur un chant montagnard français for Piano and Orchestra, Op.25, infra.

Orchestral

C Le chasseur maudit (Symphonic Poem) ("The Accursed Huntsman") (1882)

$ L'Orchestre de Paris; Daniel Barenboim, conductor; DG 2543821. Includes Franck's Nocturne for Voice and Piano (Orchestrated by Guy Ropartz) (1884) (with Christa Ludwig, mezzo–soprano) and Psyché (Symphonic Poem) (1886–1888).

Symphonic

A Symphony in d (1886–1888)

$ Chicago Symphony Orchestra; Pierre Monteux, conductor; RCA AGL1–5261, ♮ AGL1–5261.

Also—see entry under Fauré, Orchestral, Pelléas et Mélisande, Op.80 (Incidental Music for the Play by Maeterlinck), supra.

GAY, JOHN
1685–1732

Although Gay was a poet and playwright, not a composer, his name is closely associated with The Beggar's Opera (1728) in that he wrote both its dialog and lyrics. The "composer" was one Dr. Johann–Christoph Pepusch. In reality, Pepusch was only the compiler and arranger of the music for the work, since the actual composers included Handel and Purcell, and Pepusch also made use of several popular English and Scottish tunes of the day. The Beggar's Opera is important in that it is the prototype of the English ballad opera, and also because it not only satirizes 17th and early 18th century Italian opera, but all of 17th and early 18th century English morality as well (particularly thos of the legal profession).

Operatic

B The Beggar's Opera (1728)

$ Dame Kiri Te Kanawa, soprano; Dame Joan Sutherland, soprano; Angela Lansbury, mezzo-soprano; James Morris, bass; London Voices; National Philharmonic Orchestra, London; Sir Richard Bonynge, conductor; London Teldec D 252 D 2 FK (2 discs). Must be special ordered.

GERSHWIN, GEORGE
1898-1937

New York born Gershwin's real name was Jacob Gershvin and he was initially famous for his musical comedies. However, he ultimately created works which are at home in the concert hall and opera house. With the exception of a class in harmony taught by Rubin Goldmark, Gershwin was essentially a self-made composer. He had benefited from piano lessons in his youth and went on to become a virtuoso pianist: to this his recordings attest. A brief digression: the orchestrator of the "original" (i.e., for Paul Whiteman's dance band) version of Rhapsody in Blue--Ferde Grofé, told me shortly before his death, that Gershwin had received the commission for the work from Whiteman but had forgotten about it. A few days before the scheduled premiere, Gershwin called Grofé and they got down to the business of writing it in Gershwin's apartment. According to Grofé, they completed it in its entirety in about three days. The feverish rush to complete the work does not intrude itself on the quality of the work. Much of Gershwin's concert music was, for its day, daring and novel, in that it made extensive use of jazz and "Negro" materials. It is these elements which are now recognized, of course, as contributing greatly to Gershwin's winning rhythms and melodies.

Concerted

B Concerto for Piano, in f (1925)

$ Philippe Entremont, piano; Philadelphia Orchestra; Eugene Ormandy, conductor; Columbia MG-30073 (2 discs). Includes the same composer's An American in Paris (1928), rated A; Porgy and Bess (Symphonic Picture, arranged by Robert Russell Bennett); and Rhapsody in Blue for Piano and Orchestra (1924), rated A.

A Rhapsody in Blue for Piano and Orchestra (1924)

$ Leonard Bernstein, piano; Columbia Symphony Orchestra; Leonard Bernstein, conductor; Columbia MY-37242, 𝕭 MY-37242. Includes Gershwin's An American in Paris (1928), rated A.

$ George Gershwin, piano (piano roll); Columbia Jazz Band; Michael Tilson Thomas, conductor; Columbia M-34205, 𝕭 MT-34205. This performance is the original jazz-band (as opposed to symphony orchestra) version, and is very fast paced. Includes Gershwin's An American in Paris (1928), also rated A.

Also--see entry for Concerto for Piano (1925), in f, supra.

Operatic

B Porgy and Bess (1935)

$ Leona Mitchell, soprano; Willard White, bass; McHenry Boatwright, bass-baritone; Florence Quivar, soprano; Cleveland Children's Chorus; Cleveland Chorus and Orchestra; Lorin Maazel, conductor; London 13116 (3 discs), 𝕭 5-13116.

Orchestral

A An American in Paris (1928)--see entries for Concerto for Piano (1925), in f and Rhapsody in Blue for Piano and Orchestra (1924), both under Concerted, supra.

GILBERT AND SULLIVAN--SEE SULLIVAN, SIR ARTHUR

GIORDANO, UMBERTO
1867-1948

Famous now only for his opera Andrea Chenier, Giordano was one of those composers influenced by Mascagni (he of Cavalleria Rusticana) and tended towards his native Italian verismo school of opera. Chenier is a fine exemplum of Giordano's work: somewhat crude, but melodic and powerful.

79

Operatic

B <u>Andrea</u> <u>Chenier</u> (1896)

$ Renata Scotto, soprano; Placido Domingo, tenor; Sherrill Milnes, baritone; John Alldis Choir; National Philharmonic Orchestra, London; James Levine, conductor; RCA ARL3-2046 (3 discs), ☐ ARK3-2046.

GLAZUNOV, ALEXANDER
1865-1936

Born in St. Petersburg (no, not the one in Florida—Glazunov's later became Leningrad), Alexander Konstantinovich studied with Rimsky-Korsakov and is generally thought of as a composer of the Russian Nationalistic school. His was not a great original compositional talent, and his work is heavily influenced by Brahms (probably the only well-known Russian composer so to be). Glazunov produced few works of lasting interest (on this almost everyone agrees, including the Soviet critics).

Ballet

C <u>The</u> <u>Seasons,</u> Op.67

$ Philharmonia Orchestra; Yevgeny Svetlanov, conductor; Angel S-37509, ☐ 4XS-37509. Includes Glazunov's <u>Valses</u> <u>de</u> <u>concert</u> (2), Nos.1-2: Op.47 and Op.51.

GLINKA, MIKHAIL
1804-1857

Glinka (Mikhail Ivanovich) is acknowledged as the first Russian composer whose music gained acceptance outside his native land (he is occasionally called "the father of Russian music"). The catalog of his works is primarily given over to songs and solo piano works (most of them in a lighter artery). It is, however, for his operas <u>Russlan</u> <u>and</u> <u>Ludmilla</u> and <u>A</u> <u>Life</u> <u>for</u> <u>the</u> <u>Tsar,</u> plus a few orchestral pieces, that Glinka is remembered. The most important effect of Glinka's music on those Russian composers who came after him was his assimilation of folk idioms into his works, not through quoting folk themes, but rather by composing his own melodies as verisimilitudes of true folk ones. He was also a pioneer in the use of the whole-tone scale long before the Impressionists made it fashionable. His works possess energy, color, and reflect the national temperament of his time.

Orchestral

B Jota Aragonesa (Spanish Overture No.1) (1845)

* L'Orchestre de la Suisse Romande; Ernest Ansermet, conductor; London ♮ STS5-15385. Includes Glinka's Overture to Russlan and Ludmilla (1838–1841), rated A and Valse Fantasie, in B flat (1856) and Mussorgsky's Khovanshchina: Introduction and "Dance of the Persian Slaves" (1872–1880), rated C and Night on Bald Mountain (Orchestrated by Rimsky-Korsakov) (1860–1866), rated A.

A Russlan and Ludmilla: Overture (1838–1841)--see entries for Jota Aragonesa (Spanish Overture No.1) (1845), immediately supra and under Borodin, Orchestral, Prince Igor (1890) Overture and "Polovtsian Dances," supra.

GLUCK, CHRISTOPH WILLIBALD
1714–1787

Not until he was in his twenty-third year did Gluck seriously devote his attention to the study of composition, and then with the eminent Sammartini. For his time, Gluck was an operatic "modernist" in that he stressed the subordination of the music to the dramatic requirements. He also dispensed with two of the 18th century Italian opera conceits: recitativo secco ("dry," or unaccompanied, recitative) and replaced it with recitativo accompagnato (fully accompanied recitative), and the da capo aria, providing his singers with arias not dependent on repetition for their vocal or theatrical effect. He wrote approximately 45 operas and numerous other works, and his good taste (however limited his work may be by the relative absence of counterpoint) is evident in his high esteem for the music of Mozart.

Operatic

B Orfeo ed Euridice (1762)

* Hanny Steffek, soprano; Teresa Stich-Randall, soprano; Maureen Forrester, contralto; Akadamiechor; Vienna State Opera Orchestra; Sir Charles Mackerras, conductor; Vanguard HM-86-87 (2 discs).

GOTTSCHALK, LOUIS MOREAU
1829–1869

Gottschalk was the Creole son of an English father (of German descent) who held a Ph.D. (from Harvard) and a French mother, who was the daughter of Count Antoine de Brusle, commander of a cavalry regiment and Governor of Santo Domingo. Louis Moreau studied in Paris with Charles Hallé and was one of the foremost piano virtuosi of his day (he was sufficiently accomplished that Chopin praised his playing). Born in New Orleans, Gottschalk absorbed the rhythms and melodic elements of the Caribbean. These are pleasingly reflected in many of his works, most of which are for solo piano. Gottschalk ultimately is reckoned as the first "true" American composer (i.e., using native American rhythmic and melodic elements) and, certainly, this country's first stellar musical performer. He died in Rio de Janeiro of yellow fever.

Instrumental

C The Banjo ("Fantasie grotesque"), Op.15

* Eugene List, piano; Vanguard S-723–724 (2 discs). Includes Gottschalk's The Dying Poet ("A Meditation"), rated B; Souvenir de Porto Rico ("Marche des gibaros" <"March of the White Peasants">) (1859), rated B; Le Bananier ("Chanson Negre"), Op.5; Ojos criollos, Op.37; The Maiden's Blush ("Grand valse du concert"); The Last Hope ("Meditation religieuse"), Op.16; Suis moi ("Follow Me") (Caprice) (1862); Pasquinade (Caprice), Op.59; Tournament galop; Bamboula ("Danse des Negres"); La Savane ("Ballad Creole"), Op.3; Tarantelle, tutti d'orchestra, Op.67 ("Grand Tarantelle for Piano and Orchestra", reconstructed and orchestrated by Hershey Kay) with Reid Nibley, piano, rated C and Symphony: A Night in the Tropics (1859), rated B. Both of the last listed works feature the Utah Symphony Orchestra; Maurice Abravanel, conductor.

B Souvenir de Porto Rico ("Marche des gibaros" <"March of the White Peasants">) (1859)—see entry for The Banjo ("Fantasie grotesque"), Op.15, immediately supra.

Orchestral

C Tarantelle tutti d'orchestra, Op.67 ("Grand Tarantelle for Piano and Orchestra", reconstructed and orchestrated by Hershey Kay)--see entry for The Banjo ("Fantasie grotesque"), Op.15 under Instrumental, supra.

Symphonic

B Symphony: A Night in the Tropics (1859)--see entry for The Banjo ("Fantasie grotesque"), Op.15 under Instrumental, supra.

GOUNOD, CHARLES
1818-1893

Charles-François Gounod was descended from a family of artists (his father, François-Louis, was a painter who was awarded the Grand Prix de Rome in 1783--only the second awarded to that time). No less the son--Charles won the same prize, for music, in 1839. He had studied with Halévy (Bizet's father-in-law) and closely examined the works of Schumann and Berlioz. Although most of his music is devoted to the church, Gounod is most highly thought of for his opera Faust. Of late, pleasing to tell, some other of this master's works have regained the realm of performance. Pleasing to tell because Gounod's music is full of the dramatic opulence, voluptuousness and sentiment(ality) which are so seldom capable of being carried off well, which he did.

Operatic

A Faust (1852-1859)

$ Dame Joan Sutherland, soprano; Franco Corelli, tenor; Nicolai Ghiaurov, bass; Highgate School Choir; Ambrosian Singers; London Symphony Orchestra; Sir Richard Bonynge, conductor; London 1433 (4 discs); 🎵 5-1433.

C Roméo et Juliette (1864)

$$ Catherine Malfitano, soprano; Alfredo Kraus, tenor; José van Dam, bass; Capitole de Toulouse Choeur et Orchestra; Michel Plasson, conductor; Angel DSX-3960 (3 discs), 🎵 DSX-3960.

GRANADOS, ENRIQUE
1867-1916

Granados (full surname: Granados y Campina) was a talented, but minor, Spanish pianist and composer. His two most enduring works are Goyescas and the 12 Spanish Dances. Both of these works, although written for piano, have often been transcribed for guitar and, occasionally, orchestra. Granados died during World War I when his ship was torpedoed by a German submarine. Two facts make this all the more poignant: Granados and his wife had missed the boat on which they were originally scheduled to depart from the U.S. to Spain (because he was delayed by giving a performance for the President of the U.S.); further, he drowned trying, unsuccessfully, to save his wife.

Instrumental

C Goyescas (1911)
$ Alicia de Larrocha, piano; London 7009, ⊕ 5-7009.

C 12 Spanish Dances, Op.37, Nos.1-12
$ Alicia de Larrocha, piano; London 7209, ⊕ 5-7209.

GRIEG, EDVARD
1843-1907

Grieg (his middle name, Hagerup, was his mother's maiden name) had the unusual benefit, for a composer, of having had a secure and seemingly happy childhood. His father, Alexander, was the British consul at Bergen, and Alexander's grandfather was of Scottish extraction (the original spelling of the family name was Greig) and left Scotland after the battle of Culloden. Grieg's mother had been given fine musical training as child and was a pianist of some repute in Bergen. Grieg's family were easily persuaded by the then fashionable violinist, Ole Bull, to send young Edvard off for training at the Leipzig Conservatory where he later studied with Moscheles. A spate of illness befell him in 1860, an illness (pleurisy) from which he never fully recovered (it did, however, take him a long time to succumb). After a career of concertizing (until about 1864), Grieg became interested in folk things (essentially music, naturally) Norwegian, and set about studying them. From 1867, when he married his cousin Nina Hagerup, until his death, Grieg's life was essentially a busy, and almost idyllic one (except for recurrences of pulmonary illness). He often performed with his wife (who was a fine singer) and he composed. He is

84

now accounted as the greatest composer produced by Norway, and one who did much to ensure that the rest of the world had knowledge of Norway's musical heritage.

Concerted

A Concerto for Piano, Op.16, in a

$ Leon Fleisher, piano; Cleveland Orchestra; George Szell, conductor; Columbia MP-38757, ♮ MP-38757. Includes Schumann's Concerto for Concerto for Piano, Op.54, in a, rated A.

Also—see entry under Franck, Concerted, Variations symphonique (Symphonic Variations for Piano and Orchestra) (1885), supra.

Orchestral

C Holberg Suite, Op.40

* Hungarian Chamber Orchestra; Vilmos Tátrai, conductor; Turnabout 34404. Includes Elgar's Serenade for Strings, Op.20, in e (performed by the Hamburg Symphony Orchestra; Alois Springer, conductor) and Sibelius' Rakastava for Strings and Percussion, Op.14 (also performed by the Hamburg Symphony Orchestra under Springer).

B Norwegian Dances, Op.35 (4), No.2—see entry under Alfvén, Orchestral, Swedish Rhapsody No.1 (1904), supra.

A Peer Gynt Incidental Music, Op.23

$$ Lucia Popp, soprano; Ambrosian Singers; Academy of St. Martin-in-the-Fields; Sir Neville Marriner, conductor; Angel DS-37968, ♮ 4DS-37968.

GROFÉ, FERDE
1892-1972

It is difficult to imagine that a composer famous for the Grand Canyon Suite, who was born in New York and whose music is generally as American as pizza, should have been christened Ferdinand Rudolph von Grofé. Ferde (rhymes with "hurdy" as in "hurdy-gurdy"), as he preferred, was sufficiently well tutored (in part by his uncle, a 'cellist with the Los Angeles Philharmonic) in music that he taught for a while at Juilliard. He spent part of his youth playing piano, first in bawdy houses in mining towns in California (Grofé stated that, unlike other, more pretentious "professors," who also had experience playing piano in bordellos, he knew very well what went on "upstairs"), then, later, for the Paul Whiteman band. He also recorded many classical and popular songs on Ampico player piano rolls, something he found particularly lucrative. He was an arranger for George Gershwin (Grofé did the "original" jazz band orchestration for Rhapsody in Blue and the later, similar one, for Gershwin's Concerto for Piano, in F) and he found time to commemorate virtually every State of the Union with a "Suite." The Grand Canyon remains his most often played work (particularly the section titled "On the Trail"—made famous in Philip Morris commercials).

Orchestral

A Grand Canyon Suite (1931)—see entry under Bernstein, Orchestral, Candide Overture (1956), supra.

HANDEL, GEORGE FRIDERIC
1685-1759

Born in Halle, in Saxony (formerly a province of North Germany) to a middle-middle class family, Handel became a naturalized English citizen in 1727. His father, a frugal man who hoped his son would become a businessman, was initially opposed to young Georg Friederich Händel's (so he was baptized) desire for a musical career. Upon the youngster's coming to the attention of the Duke of Saxe-Weissenfels, father Händel acquiesced to the Duke's suggestion that the obviously talented boy be given a proper musical education. George ultimately became well known at the court in Berlin as a keyboard performer. Yet in 1697, after being appointed assistant organist at the Halle Domkirche, Handel entered the University at Halle to study law. While pursuing both careers, Handel's work as a performer was noticed by Telemann. Later, Telemann was to become a friend and sometime mentor. In 1703 Handel left the University for good and auditioned for the position of organist at Lübeck, where Buxtehude was retiring. Like Bach, Handel found the secondary condition of acceptance for the position unacceptable—marrying Buxtehude's daughter (she was ten years older than either Handel or Bach). He was then living in Hamburg and, in the course of performing at the harpsichord in a performance of German composer (and lexicographer) Johann Mattheson's Cleopatra, the jealous Mattheson attempted to gain that performing position for himself. Handel thereupon found himself involved in a duel with Mattheson outside the theater following the performance. Ostensibly, Handel was spared by virtue of a solid button on his waistcoat. After numerous career changes and travels throughout Europe he enjoyed a productive stay in Italy, where he assimilated the operatic style which he was to employ for the remainder of his life. While there he wrote several successful stage pieces. Although he visited England a few times earlier, Handel returned to that country in 1715, never again to leave. He became a favorite of George I (Handel's former patron as the Elector of Hanover—with whom he had had a falling out for previously overstaying his leave in England). Thence were his musical and financial fortunes made. The Water Music was written in 1717 to accompany a "water party" of the King's, held on barges on the Thames. According to a contemporary newspaper report, the King was sufficiently pleased with the work to have it performed three times in its entirety (keep in mind, one performance takes about an hour—George I must have really dug the thing). One more anecdote, whose image can still bring tears to my eyes, is that regarding the premiere of the Royal Fireworks Music in 1749. Written to celebrate the signing of the peace treaty at Aix-la-Chapelle (ending the imbroglio between England and France), the work was performed at a huge celebration in London's Green Park, replete with papier-maché castle-fronts, etc., and accompanied by the setting-off of fireworks. During the concatenated events, the pyrotechnics set the backdrops ablaze, leaving the audience to depart in some haste. Obviously, no one had the presence of mind to ask for the playing of the Water Music. Despite the huge success and popularity of the Messiah to this day (it was composed in 1742 in a period of 23 days), greater is Handel's oratorio Israel in Egypt, composed in 1739. By the way, the popular story of the Messiah's having been written while the composer was sequestered in a room with little food and, taking as his inspiration, a vision of the Virgin, would be even more delightful were it not spurious. His popularity notwithstanding, Handel's talent was never one of the depth of Bach's, yet his music is straightforward, noble, tuneful and wonderfully enjoyable, sufficiently so that he was highly esteemed by both Haydn and Beethoven. Handel did not stray much from the accepted Italian operatic style of his day. Important, however, is that change which he brought to the oratorio, in particular the "British" oratorio. Basing his early efforts on the work of Carissimi, Handel drew his oratorio characters more sharply and decisively, and was not hesitant in giving a good deal of the action to the chorus. Thus was Handel able to solve the problem of incorporating the chorus into the fabric of the dramatic action. Despite his inability to compete with Bach intellectually, Handel's art was sufficiently great that Haydn, hearing the "Hallelujah Chorus" at Westminster Abbey, joined with the audience in rising to his feet, weeping, and was supposedly heard to exclaim, "He is the master of us all."

Choral (A. Oratorios)

B Israel in Egypt (1739)

$ Patricia Clark, soprano; Heather Harper, soprano; Paul Esswood, counter-tenor; Alexander Young, tenor; Michael Rippon, bass; Christopher Keyte, bass; Leeds Festival Chorus; English Chamber Orchestra; Sir Charles Mackerras, conductor; DG 413919-1 GX-2 (2 discs).

C Jephtha (1752)

$ Elizabeth Gale, soprano; Glenys Linos, soprano; Gabriele Sima, contralto; Paul Esswood, counter-tenor; Werner Hollweg, tenor; Thomas Thomaschke, baritone; Arnold Schönberg Choir; Mozart Sängerknaben; Vienna Concentus Musicus; Nikolaus Harnoncourt, conductor; Teldec 4635499 (4 discs), 3435499.

B Judas Maccabaeus (1747)

$ Felicity Palmer, soprano; Dame Janet Baker, mezzo-soprano; Ryland Davies, tenor; John Shirley-Quirk, baritone; Wandsworth School Boys' Choir; English Chamber Orchestra; Sir Charles Mackerras, conductor; DG 413906-1 GX3 (3 discs).

A Messiah (1742)

$ Elizabeth Harwood, soprano; Dame Janet Baker, mezzo-soprano; Paul Esswood, counter-tenor; Robert Tear, tenor; Raimund Herincx, baritone; Ambrosian Singers; English Chamber Orchestra; Sir Charles Mackerras, conductor; Angel S-3705 (3 discs).

* Felicity Palmer, soprano; Helen Watts, contralto; Ryland Davies, tenor; John Shirley-Quirk, baritone; English Chamber Chorus and Orchestra; Raymond Leppard, conductor; RCA CRL3-1426 (3 discs).

Choral (B. Miscellaneous)

B Ode for St. Cecilia's Day (1739)

$ Jill Gomez, soprano; Robert Tear, tenor; King's College Chapel Choir, Cambridge; English Chamber Orchestra; Philip Ledger, conductor; Vanguard 25010.

Concerted

B Concerti for Oboe (1740), Nos.1-2, both in B—see entry under Cimarosa, Concerted, Concerto for Oboe and Strings (Arranged from Melodies of Cimarosa by Arthur Benjamin), supra.

B Concerti for Organ and Strings (12), Op.4 Nos.1-6: in g, B flat, g, F, F and B flat, Op.7 Nos.7-12: in B flat, A, B flat, d, g and B flat

$ Herbert Tachezi, organ; Vienna Concentus Musicus; Nikolaus Harnoncourt, conductor; Teldec 3635282 (3 discs).

Instrumental

C Suites for Harpsichord (1720-1733) (17), (Nos.1-8)

$ Kenneth Gilbert, harpsichord; Harmonia Mundi 447 (2 discs).

Orchestral

B Concerti Grossi, Op.6 (12), (Nos.1-12)

$ English Concert; Trevor Pinnock, conductor; DG ARC-2742002 (3 discs), ♮ 3383002.

A Royal Fireworks Music (1749)

* Jean-François Paillard Chamber Orchestra; Jean-François Paillard, conductor; RCA VICS-1690. Includes Handel's Water Music (Suite) (1717), also rated A.

Also—see entry under Holst, Orchestral, Suite for Band No.1, Op.28a, in E flat, infra.

A Water Music (1717)

$$ Academy of Ancient Music; Christopher Hogwood, conductor; L'Oiseau Lyre DSLO-543, ♮ 543.

* Amsterdam Concertgebouw Orchestra; Eduard van Beinum, conductor; Philips Festivo ♮ 7310171.

Also—see entry for Royal Fireworks Music (1749), immediately supra.

Operatic

C Giulio Cesare (1724)

$ Beverly Sills, soprano; Maureen Forrester, contralto; Beverly Wolff, contralto; Norman Treigle, bass-baritone; New York City Opera Chorus and Orchestra; Julius Rudel, conductor; RCA LSC-6182 (3 discs).

C Rinaldo (1711)
$ Ileana Cotrubas, soprano; Jeanette Scovotti, soprano; Carolyn Watkinson, contralto; Charles Brett, counter-tenor; Paul Esswood, counter-tenor; Ulrik Cold, bass; Grande Ecurie et la Chambre du Roy; Jean-Claude Malgoire, conductor; Columbia M3-34592 (3 discs).

B Serse (1738)
$ Barbara Hendricks, soprano; Carolyn Watkinson, contralto; Ortrun Wenkel, contralto; Paul Esswood, counter-tenor; Ulrik Cold, bass; Grande Ecurie et la Chambre du Roy; Jean-Claude Malgoire, conductor; Columbia CBS M3-36941 (3 discs).

C Tamerlano (1724)
$ Carole Bogard, soprano; Gwendolyn Killebrew, mezzo-soprano; Joanna Simon, mezzo-soprano; Sophia Steffan, mezzo-soprano; Marius Rintzler, bass; Alexander Young, tenor; Copenhagen Chamber Orchestra; John Moriarty, conductor; Cambridge 2902 (4 discs).

HANSON, HOWARD
1896-1981

Howard Harold Hanson, called "conservatively modern" by John Tasker Howard, was born in Wahoo, Nebraska (almost as good as Cole Porter hailing from Peru <rhymes with "we rue">, Indiana, n'est-ce pas?) and received his principal education at Northwestern University. After a stint, first as professor, then Dean of the Conservatory of Fine Arts at the College of the Pacific, he received the American Prix de Rome. He returned to the U.S. and was invited to conduct the New York Symphony Orchestra in his North and West, the invitation coming from Walter Damrosch. He repaired to Rome shortly thereafter and, while there, in 1924, was offered the Directorship of the Eastman School of Music at Rochester, N.Y. (a post he held until 1964). He was given this position at the tender age of 30 by George (the "Kodak" man) Eastman after the latter heard some of Hanson's works conducted by the composer. Hanson's music is firmly based in the European style of Sibelius and Tchaikovsky. It can occasionally overstay its welcome through repetition and lack of weight, but some of it is quite pleasing and certainly has earned a niche in libraries.

Symphonic

C Symphony No.2 ("Romantic"), Op.30

$ Eastman-Rochester Orchestra; Howard Hanson; Mercury 75007, 9 75007. Includes Hanson's The Lament for Beowulf (1925).

HAYDN, FRANZ JOSEPH
1732-1809

It is virtually a truism that when one is asked to list the "greatest composers," Bach, Mozart, Beethoven and Brahms readily spring to mind. If Haydn's name occurs to one, it is usually as an afterthought, and then, more often than not, with a question mark following: "'tis true 'tis pity; and pity 'tis 'tis true." For of all among the "greatest composers," Haydn's name should come as easily as breath itself: he was, was he not, the "father of the symphony?" And among his "lesser" accomplishments are: having had Beethoven for a student for something over a year; being generally considered the propounder of the form of the modern quartet; being generous enough to pronounce Mozart as "...the greatest composer that I know, either personally or by reputation; he has taste, and beyond that the most consummate knowledge of the art of composition." And this is an already acknowledged master of 53 speaking of the 29 year-old Mozart. Another indication of Haydn's reputation is the argument, begun in 1824, that Haydn, born in Rohrau (Lower Austria) is actually of Slavonic descent. It continues to this day: the Hungarians (although not actually Slavs) claim him as a compatriot (the first complete recorded set of his symphonies was made by Antal Doráti conducting the Hungarica Philharmonia, and Hungarian ensembles of various sorts have recorded an immensity of his works on the Hungarian national label: Hungaroton). It must be obvious that Haydn's greatest accomplishments are to be found in the body of his music, and that is some body: 18 operas, incidental music for 6 plays, 16 masses, 104 symphonies, 16 overtures, over 3 dozen divertimenti, about 37 concerti, 83 string quartets, 31 piano, violin and 'cello trios, songs galore, 11 miscellaneous choral/orchestral works (including Die Jahreszeiten <"The Seasons"> and Die Schöpfung <"The Creation">, two works which, on their own, would probably have ensured his immortality), and on and on. Mirabile dictu, this outpouring from a man of humble origins whose musical education began with the benevolent teaching of Johann Mathias Franck, a distant relative to whom Haydn referred as his cousin. Franck must have been an excellent teacher (but the teacher had pretty good material with which to work) and Haydn spoke well of his methods, even though his regimen offered "...more flogging than food." From this "school" Haydn "matriculated" to being a chorister at St. Stephen's Cathedral in Vienna. There he remained for 9 years, with no instruction in harmony or composition. These lacunae Haydn filled through his own efforts. He left St. Stephen's when his voice broke at maturity, found himself a garret wherein he gave lessons, and earnestly studied the works of C.P.E. Bach. In fine, his career soared upon his appointment, in 1761, to the court of Prince Esterházy. Here Haydn was elevated to the position of Kapellmeister, and in the employ of the Esterházys he remained for 29 years, composing the majority of his operas and all the while studying and refining his own art. By this time Haydn was internationally famous and in 1790 he made his first visit to London, at the request of the renowned impressario, Johann Peter Salomon. Haydn was to visit London twice more (1791 and 1794) and for these visits he composed his 12 "London" or "Salomon" Symphonies --generally regarded as his best in this form. Although Haydn was married when he was 28 (his wife was then 32), it was not a happy marriage; (he said of Maria Aloysia that "she has no virtues and it is entirely indifferent to her whether her husband is a shoemaker or an artist"); yet, with characteristic patience, he maintained their unhappy relationship (which did not even offer him the solace of a child, and children were adored by Haydn) for 20 years until her death in 1800. To unconfuse one issue, Haydn composed the song Gott, erhalte Franz den Kaiser ("God Protect Franz the Emperor") out of envy for the English having such a wonderful anthem in God Save the King, feeling that Austria needed something similar. The poet Hauschka was commissioned to write the words, which Haydn then set (in 1797). The Kaiserquartett ("Emperor Quartet"), in which the same melody is heard as the basis for a set of variations, was composed later (probably 1799). The same melody was given new words in 1848 by a revolutionary--cum

92

-professor: Hoffmann von Fallersleben. His work is known to us as Deutschland über alles ("Germany Before All"--not to be translated as either "Germany Over All" <as it was construed when it became a Nazi hymn> or, as Flanders and Swann would have it, "German Overalls"). The "H" number for Haydn works refer to the Hoboken's thematic index.

Chamber

C Die sieben Worte des Erlösers am Kreuze ("The Seven Last Words") (1785)

$ Tátrai Quartet; Hungaroton 12036.

B String Quartets, Op.17 (6), Nos.25-30: in E, F, E flat, c, G ("Recitative") and D

$ Tátrai Quartet; Hungaroton 11382-11384 (3 discs).

A String Quartets, Op.20 (6), Nos.31-36: in E flat ("Sonnenquartette"), C (contains the "Bagpipe Minuet"), g, D ("The Row in Venice"), f, and A

$ Tátrai Quartet; Hungaroton 11332-11334 (3 discs).

B String Quartets, Op.33 (Known Variously as "Gli scherzi," "Jung ern" or "Russian" Quartets) (6), Nos.37-42: in b, E flat ("The Joke"), C ("The Bird"), B flat, G ("How Do You Do?") and D

$ Tátrai Quartet; Hungaroton 11887-11889 (3 discs).

C String Quartets, (The "Prussian Quartets"), Op.50 (6), Nos.44-49: in B flat, C, E flat, f sharp, F ("The Dream") and D (Known variously as "The Frog," "The House on Fire" and "The Row in Vienna")

$ Tátrai Quartet; Hungaroton 11934-11936 (3 discs).

B String Quartets, ("Tost" Quartets), Op.64 (6), Nos.63-68: in C, b, B flat, G, D ("The Lark" or "The Hornpipe") and E flat

$ Tátrai Quartet; Hungaroton 11838-11840 (3 discs).

C String Quartets, ("Apponyi" Quartets), Op.71 (3), Nos.69-71: in B flat, D and E flat

$ Tátrai Quartet; Hungaroton 12246–12248 (3 discs). Includes Haydn's String Quartets, ("Apponyi" Quartets), Op.74 (3), Nos.72–74: in C, F and g ("The Rider"), rated B.

B String Quartets, ("Apponyi" Quartets), Op.74 (3), Nos.72–74: in C, F and g ("The Rider")--see entry for String Quartets, ("Apponyi" Quartets), Op.71 (3), Nos.69–71: in B flat, D and E flat, immediately supra.

A String Quartets, ("Erdödy" Quartets) Op.76 (6), Nos.75–80: in G ("The Farmyard"), d ("Quinten" Quartet, includes the "Hexen-Minuet," "The Bell" and "The Donkey"), C ("Emperor"), B flat ("Sunrise"), D and E flat
$ Tátrai Quartet; Qualiton 1205–1207 (3 discs).

C String Quartets, Op.77 (2), Nos.1–2: in G ("Lobkowitz") and F ("Wait Till the Clouds Roll By")
$ Tátrai Quartet; Hungaroton 11776.

Choral (A. Masses)

B Mass No.3 (Missa Cellensis, or Cäcilienmesse) ("St. Caecilia Mass") (1766)
$$ Judith Nelson, soprano; Margaret Cable, mezzo-soprano; Martyn Hill, tenor; Christ Church Cathedral Choir, Oxford; Academy of Ancient Music; Simon Preston, conductor; L'Oiseau Lyre DSLO-583-584 (2 discs). Includes Haydn's Mass No.3a (Missa Rorate coeli desuper ("The Heavens Descended From Above") (1766).

A Mass No.7 ("Missa in tempore belli" or "Paukenmesse") ("Mass in the Time of War" or "Drum Mass"), in C (1796)
$ April Cantelo, soprano; Helen Watts, contralto; Robert Tear, tenor; Barry McDaniel, baritone; King's College Chapel Choir, Cambridge; Academy of St. Martin-in-the-Fields; George Guest, conductor; Argo 417163-1 PSI, ♮417163-4 PSI. Includes Michael Haydn's Ave Regina for A Capella Chorus.

A Mass No.9 Missa Solemnis ("Nelson Mass"), in d (1798)
$$ Kathrin Graf, soprano; Verena Piller, contralto; Ernst Haefliger, tenor; Jakob Stämpfli, baritone; Bern Chamber Chorus; Bern Chamber Orchestra; Jörg Ewald Dähler, conductor; Claves D-8108.

A Mass No.10 ("Theresien-Messe"), in B flat (1799)

* Elisabeth Speiser, soprano; Maureen Lehane, contralto; Theo Altmeyer, tenor; Wolfgang Schöne, bass; Tolzer Boys' Choir; Collegium Aureum; Franzjosef Maier, conductor; Quintessence 7166, ꕞ 7166.

Choral (B. Oratorios)

A Die Jahreszeiten ("The Seasons") (1801)

* Helen Donath, soprano; Adalbert Kraus, tenor; Kurt Widmer, bass; Ludwigsburg Festival Orchestra; South German Madrigal Choir, Stuttgart; Wolfgang Gönnenwein, conductor; Vox SVBX-5215 (3 discs), ꕞ CBX-5215.

A Die Schöpfung ("The Creation") (1798)

* Heather Harper, soprano; Robert Tear, tenor; John Shirley-Quirk, baritone; King's College Chapel Choir, Cambridge; Academy of St. Martin-in-the-Fields; Sir David Willcocks, conductor; Arabesque 8039 (2 discs), ꕞ 9039.

Concerted

A Concerto for Harpsichord, in D, H.XVIII No.11

* Igor Kipnis, harpsichord; London Strings; Sir Neville Marriner, conductor; Odyssey Y-32980. Includes Mozart's Concerto for Piano No.9, K.271, in E flat, rated B.

C Concerto No.3 (old No.1) for Horn, in D, H.VIId

* Barry Tuckwell, horn; Academy of St. Martin-in-the-Fields; Sir Neville Marriner, conductor; Angel AM-34720, ꕞ AM-34720. Includes Haydn's Concerto No.4 (old No.2) for Horn, in D, H.VIId, also rated C and Michael Haydn's Concerto for Horn, P.134, in D.

C Concerto No.4 (old No.2) for Horn, in D, H.VIId--see entry for Concerto No.3 (old No.1) for Horn, in D, H.VIId, immediately supra.

A Concerto for Oboe, in C, H.VIIgC1 (Attributed)

$ Ingo Goritzki, oboe; Southwest German Chamber Orchestra; Paul Angerer, conductor; Claves D-606, ꕞ D-606. Includes Mozart's Concerto for Oboe, in C, K.314, rated B.

Also--see entry under Cimarosa, Concerted, Concerto for Oboe and Strings (Arranged from Melodies of Cimarosa by Arthur Benjamin), supra.

95

A Concerto for Trumpet, in E flat, H.VIIe

\$ Wynton Marsalis, trumpet; National Philharmonic Orchestra, London; Raymond Leppard, conductor; Columbia IM-37846, ⊟ IMT-37846. Includes Hummel's Concerto for Trumpet and Orchestra, in E flat, rated B and Leopold Mozart's Concerto for Trumpet and Orchestra, in D (1762).

Instrumental

B Fantasia, in C H.XVII4

* Malcolm Bilson, fortepiano; Nonesuch 78016, ⊟ 78016. Includes C.P.E. Bach's Fantasia, in C, W.59/6 and Mozart's Allegro and Andante K.533, in F and Fantasia K.475, in c, rated B.

B Sonatas for Piano (52), Nos.20, 44 and 46, in c (1771), g (1785–1786) and A flat (1768)

\$ Charles Rosen, piano; Vanguard 10131.

Operatic

B Armida (1784)

\$ Jessye Norman, soprano; Norma Burrowes, soprano; Claes-Haakan Ahnsjö, tenor; Samuel Ramey, bass; Lausanne Chamber Orchestra; Antal Doráti, conductor; Philips 6769021 (3 discs).

C Lo speziale ("Der Apotheker") (1768)

\$ Magda Kalmár, soprano; Veronika Kincses, soprano; Attila Fülöp, tenor; István Rozsos, tenor; Ferenc Liszt Chamber Orchestra; György Lehel, conductor; Hungaroton 11926–11927 (2 discs).

Symphonic

C Symphony No.6 ("Le Matin") ("The Morning"), in D (1761)

* Vienna Festival Orchestra; Wilfried Böttcher, conductor; Turnabout 34150. Includes Haydn's Symphonies Nos.7 ("Le Midi") ("The Afternoon"), in C (1761) and 8 ("Le Soir") ("The Evening"), in G (1761), both also rated C.

C Symphony No.7 ("Le Midi") ("The Afternoon"), in C (1761)—see entry for Symphony No.6 ("Le Matin") ("The Morning"), in D (1761), immediately supra.

C Symphony No.8 ("Le Soir") ("The Evening"), in G (1761)--see entry for Symphony No.6 ("Le Matin") ("The Morning"), in D (1761), supra.

B Symphony No.31 ("Hornsignal"), in D (1765)
    * Stuttgart Bach-Collegium; Helmuth Rilling, conductor; Turnabout 34104. Includes Haydn's Symphony No.59 ("Fire"), in A (1767-1768), also rated B.

B Symphony No.44 ("Trauer"), in e (1772)
    $ Orpheus Chamber Orchestra; DG 415365-1 ☒ 415365-4 GH. Includes Haydn's Symphony No.77, in B flat (1783).

A Symphony No.45 ("Farewell"), in f sharp (1772)
    $ Ferenc Liszt Chamber Orchestra; János Rolla, conductor; Hungaroton 12468. Includes Haydn's Symphony No.49 ("La Passione"), in f (1768), also rated A.

C Symphony No.48 ("Maria Theresia"), in C (1772)
    * Zagreb Radio Symphony Orchestra; Antonio Janigro, conductor; Vanguard HM-61. Includes Haydn's Symphony No.49 ("La Passione") in f (1768), rated A.

A Symphony No.49 ("La Passione"), in f (1768)--see entries for Symphony No.45 ("Farewell"), in f sharp (1772), supra and Symphony No.48 ("Maria Theresia"), in C (1772), immediately supra.

B Symphony No.59 ("Fire"), in A (1766-1768)--see entry for Symphony No.31 ("Hornsignal"), in D (1765), supra.

A Symphonies Nos.82-87 (6: The "Paris" Symphonies), in C ("L'Ours") ("The Bear"), in g ("La Poule") ("The Hen"), in E flat, B flat ("La Reine") ("The Queen"), in D and A (1785-1786)
    * London Little Symphony; Leslie Jones, conductor; Nonesuch 73011 (3 discs).

A Symphony No.88, in G (1787)

* Columbia Symphony Orchestra; Bruno Walter, conductor; Odyssey Y-35932. Includes Haydn's Symphony No.100 ("Military"), in G (1794), also rated A.

A Symphonies Nos.93-104 (12: The "London" or "Salomon" Symphonies), in D, G ("Surprise"), c, D ("Miracle"), C, B flat, E flat, G ("Military"), D ("Clock"), B flat, E flat ("Drum Roll") and D ("London") (1791-1795)

* London Little Symphony; Leslie Jones, conductor; Nonesuch 73109 (6 discs).

Also--for Symphony No.100 ("Military"), in G (1794), see entry for Symphony No.88, in G (1787), immediately supra.

HINDEMITH, PAUL
1895-1963

Hindemith was one of those typical, rebellious individuals who left home at the tender age of 11 in order to seek the musical career to which his parents were opposed. He had already received violin lessons (beginning at age 9) and, while making a living in cafe and dance bands, enrolled at Hoch's Conservatory at Frankfurt, at 14. By the time Hindemith was 20 he was the concertmaster of the Frankfurt Opera Orchestra. Later, he took up the viola (upon which instrument he became expert) and performed in the Amar-Hindemith Quartet. It was composition, however, for which he soon became widely known. His previously referred to rebelliousness made itself obvious in his early works (e.g., his opera Mörder, Hoffnung der Frauen, Op.12 and String Quartet No.4, Op.22, in C). As happens with many as they mature (not just artists), Hindemith ultimately became somewhat conservative and a kind of Neo-Classicist, in what Marion M. Scott calls his "back to Bach" period. Certainly this is easily discerned by his profound concern for contrapuntal techniques and his interest in what he called "Gebrauchsmusik," or "useful music." By this Hindemith meant music which was in closer touch with the interests and needs of audiences. In any event, despite his music being recent, Hindemith remains one of the least controversial composers primarily because his works are of a reactionary cast.

Chamber

98

C Sonata for Flute and Piano (1939)

$ Louise DiTullio, flute; Lincoln Mayorga, piano; GSC 3. Includes Hindemith's Echo for Flute and Piano (1944), Duet for Viola and 'Cello (1934) with Sven Reher, viola and Kurt Reher, 'cello and Sonata for Unaccompanied 'Cello, Op.25 No.3 with Kurt Reher, 'cello, rated C.

C String Quartet No.3, Op.22

$ Los Angeles Quartet; GSC 10. Includes Hindemith's String Quartet No.4, Op.32.

Instrumental

C Ludus Tonalis (1943)

$ Richard Tetley-Kardos, piano; Orion 75189.

C Sonata for Unaccompanied 'Cello, Op.25 No.3—see entry for Sonata for Flute and Piano (1936) under Chamber, supra.

Orchestral

B Mathis der Maler Symphony (1934)

$ Philadelphia Orchestra; Eugene Ormandy, conductor; Columbia MS-6562. Includes Hindemith's Symphonic Metamorphosis on Themes by Weber (1944), rated A.

A Symphonic Metamorphosis on Themes by Weber (1944)—see entry for Mathis der Maler Symphony (1934), immediately supra.

HOLST, GUSTAV
1874-1934

The family background of Gustav Theodore Holst (full real name: Gustavus Theodore von Holst) is rather an interesting one. The Holsts had originally been Swedish but settled in the Baltic portion of Russia in the early 18th century. Gustav's great-grandfather, Matthias von Holst, migrated to England in 1807 with his 8-year-old son, Gustavus. Gustavus married an Englishwoman, and their son, Adolf, wed Clara Lediard, an English pianist. These were the parents of Gustav, who discontinued the use of the "von" at the outbreak of World War I (presumably to help ensure his not being taken for German). Despite all of this, Holst is definitely an English composer in every sense. After organ lessons from his father and piano instruction from his mother, Holst won a scholarship to the Royal College of Music (take heart, oh you impatient youth, he did it on the 8th or 9th attempt), where he studied composition with Stanford. He also studied trombone with such success that he was able to earn his way as a trombonist with the Carl Ross Opera Company. Holst later turned to teaching (ultimately at the Royal College of Music—probably to his great satisfaction) and thence to full-time composing. Many of Holst's musical inspirations were derived from literature (e.g., Keats, the Rig Veda, Hardy, etc.) and are programmatic in that sense. His music is not greatly innovative but makes full use of the potential of the orchestra (or voice), and is colorful, introspective, poetic, and (as in the "Mars" section of The Planets) can be quite powerful. Holst is a minor composer (not to the English, of course), but one who is easily apprehended and appreciated.

Ballet

B Music from the Opera The Perfect Fool, Op.39

* London Philharmonic Orchestra; Sir Adrian Boult, conductor; Decca Jubilee JB 49. Must be special ordered. Includes Holst's The Hymn of Jesus, Op.37 (performed by the BBC Chorus and Symphony Orchestra under Boult), rated C and Egdon Heath, Op.47, rated B.

Orchestral

B Egdon Heath, Op.47—see entry for Music from the Opera The Perfect Fool, Op.39 under Ballet, supra.

A The Planets, Op.32

$ Philharmonia Orchestra; Sir Adrian Boult, conductor; Angel S-36420, ₿ 4XS-26420.

B Suite No.1 for Band, Op.28a, in E flat

$$ Cleveland Winds; Frederick Fennell, conductor; Telarc DG 10038. Includes J.S. Bach's S.561 Fantasia for Organ, in G, Holst's Suite No.2 for Band, Op.28b, in F, also rated B, and Handel's Royal Fireworks Music (1749), rated A.

B Suite No.1 for Band, Op.28b, in F—see entry for Suite No.1 for Band, Op.28a, in E flat, immediately supra.

HONEGGER, ARTHUR

1892-1955

Born in La Havre of Swiss parents, Arthur Oscar Honegger studied at the Conservatoire de Paris (with Widor and d'Indy). He first came to public attention with the Paris performance of his masque Le Dit des jeux du monde, in 1918. He followed this with other stage works, ultimately turning to choral and symphonic pieces. In 1920, the critic Henri Collet named a group of young French composers "The Six," as a kind of answer to the Russian group known as "The Five." The six named were: Auric, Durey, Honegger, Milhaud, Poulenc and Germaine Tailleferre. Only Honegger, Milhaud and Poulenc have retained any lasting fame. Honegger's style incorporated elaborate counterpoint, rich harmonies (with what some call "harsh" polytonalities), and melodies which, on occasion, use atonal features. His works are definitely of minor quality, but some have found popularity in the concert hall and on recordings.

Operatic

C Le Roi David ("King David") (1921)

$ Martial Singher, baritone; Netania Davrath, soprano; Utah Symphony Orchestra; Maurice Abravanel, conductor; Vanguard 2117-2118 (2 discs).

Orchestral

A Pacific 231 ("Mouvement symphonique" No.1) (1924)—see entries under Dukas, Orchestral, L'Apprenti sorcier (1897) ("The Sorcerer's Apprentice"), supra and under Ibert, Orchestral, Divertissement (1930), infra.

Symphonic

C Symphony No.3 ("Liturgique") (1945-1946)

$ Orchestre de la Suisse Romande; Ernest Ansermet, conductor; London 414435-1 LE, ♮ 414435-4 LE. Includes Honegger's Symphony No.4 ("Deliciae basiliensis") (1946).

HOVHANESS, ALAN
1911-

American-born Alan Hovhaness' music is reflective more of the East than West and, in part, this is due to his Armenian heritage. Through the repetition of themes Hovhaness is often able to achieve an almost "hypnotic" effect. More often than not his work is programmatic, exotic and mystical. Probably the work for which he is best known, at this writing, is the one commissioned by André Kostelanetz, titled And God Created Great Whales, which interpolates recordings of actual "whale songs" into an orchestral text. As usual, the music is gentle, contemplative, and novel.

Orchestral

C And God Created Great Whales (1970)

$ Orchestra; André Kostelanetz, conductor; Columbia M–34537. Includes Hovhaness' Fantasy on Japanese Woodprints, Op.211 and Rubaiyat of Omar Khayyam (1977).

Symphonic

B Symphony No.2 ("Mysterious Mountain"), Op.132

* Chicago Symphony Orchestra; Fritz Reiner, conductor; RCA AGL–1–4215, ♮ AGL–1–4215. Includes Stravinsky's Le Baiser de la fée ("The Fairy's Kiss" Suite: "Divertimento") (1928), rated B.

HUBAY, JENÖ
1858–1937

Hubay was a well-known Hungarian violin virtuoso and very minor composer. One work, and one work only, still keeps his name before the pubic, and that is listed below.

Concerted

B Hejre Kati ("Hey There, Katie"), for Violin and Orchestra, Op.99

* Aaron Rosand, violin; Orchestra of Radio Luxembourg; Louis de Froment, conductor; Candide 31064. Includes Ernst's Concerto for Violin, Op.23, in d and Ysaÿe's Chant d'hiver ("Song of Winter"), for Violin and Chamber Orchestra.

HUMMEL, JOHANN NEPOMUK
1778–1837

Although Hummel was considered possessed of sufficient talent by Mozart that the great one took the young Hummel into his home and provided him with instruction for 2 years, Hummel is hardly heard any more, except for a couple of concerti. During his lifetime, Hummel was thought to be an outstanding conductor, composer and pianist. Most of his music is rather slight, but is stylish and typical of his classical German training and period.

Concerted

C Concerto for Bassoon and Orchestra, in F

* George Zukerman, bassoon; Württemberg Chamber Orchestra; Jörg Faerber, conductor; Turnabout 34348. Includes Hummel's Concerto for Piano, Op.73, in G and Rondo for Piano ("La Galante"), Op.120. These latter 2 pieces feature Martin Galling, piano.

B Concerto for Trumpet and Orchestra, in E flat--see entry under Haydn, Concerted, Concerto for Trumpet, in E flat, H.VIIe, supra.

HUMPERDINCK, ENGELBERT
1854-1921

Humperdinck was not the most imaginative German composer of all time, but through Hansel und Gretel has certainly found a kind of niche. The work is based on the musical techniques of Wagner (without his genius) and, in truth, does not deserve its popularity (a folktale about 2 innocent children, with a Wagnerian musical texture and orchestration?); yet people do seem to have taken it to their hearts. By the way, why would any popular singer want to be known by this composer's name? Why not "Jan Dismas Zelenka" or "Walther von der Vogelweide?"

Operatic

B Hansel und Gretel (1893)

$ Ileana Cotrubas, soprano; Elisabeth Söderström, soprano; Christa Ludwig, mezzo-soprano; Dame Kiri Te Kanawa, soprano; Frederica von Stade, mezzo-soprano; Siegmund Nimsgern, bass; Cologne Opera Children's Chorus; Cologne Gürzenich Orchestra; Sir John Pritchard, conductor; Columbia M2-35898 (2 discs).

IBERT, JACQUES
1890-1962

Having studied at the Conservatoire de Paris with Fauré, French composer Jacques-François Antoine Ibert won the Prix de Rome in 1919 (after serving with the French military in World War I). Ibert's music is eclectic and relies mostly on the tools of Impressionism and Neo-Classicism, sometimes being so reminiscent of Ravel as to be a bit confusing. It is possessed of a definitely brittle Parisian wit (e.g., Divertissement) and warmth.

Orchestral

B Divertissement (1930)

* City of Birmingham, England, Symphony Orchestra; Louis Frémaux, conductor; Arabesque 8035, ♮ 9035. Includes Honegger's Pacific 231 ("Mouvement symphonique" No.1) (1924), rated A and, Poulenc's Les Biches Suite (1924) and Satie's Trois Gymnopédies ("Three 'Barefooted' Dances"), (Nos.1 and 3) (1888), rated A.

A Escales ("Ports of Call") (1922)

$ Philadelphia Orchestra; Eugene Ormandy, conductor; Columbia MS-6474. Includes Chabrier's España Rhapsody (1883), rated A; Debussy's Clair de lune from Suite bergamasque (1890-1905) (4), Nos.1-4: Prélude; Menuet; Clair de lune ("Moonlight") and Passepied, rated A; Ravel's Boléro (1927), Pavane pour une Infante défunte ("Pavane for a Dead Princess") (1899), and La Valse ("The Waltz") (1919-1920), all also rated A.

D'INDY, VINCENT
1851-1931

Paul-Marie-Théodore-Vincent d'Indy was born to an upper middle class family and was raised by his paternal grandmother--a woman of great strength and moral rectitude (the which no one surpasses the upper middle-class French). She ensured that the young Vincent was provided with an exemplary (to her lights) upbringing: one filled with discipline, virtue, and, happily for the precocious youngster, a thorough musical education. Early on he made the acquaintance of such luminaries as Bizet, Massenet, Saint-Saëns, etc. He began his studies with Franck (at the Conservatoire de Paris) in 1872, and from then on Franck became one of the most important influences in his musical thinking. On visiting Germany for the first time, in 1873, he met Liszt, Brahms and Wagner. d'Indy fell under the spell of Wagner's music and became one of his principal champions. d'Indy's debut as a composer was in 1874, and his work was not well received. It was not until 1883 that d'Indy received acceptance by the critics, this for his opera La Chant de la cloche. d'Indy's music is still generally thought to be less French than German: primarily for his highly intellectual approach to his art. Those opposed to his cerebral music were wont to prefer the more sensuous work of Debussy. In 1894 d'Indy cofounded the Schola Cantorum (with Charles Bordes and Alexandre Guilamant) which music school became one of the preeminent ones in the world. As taught at the Schola, the principal gods of music were Bach, Beethoven, Wagner and Franck. d'Indy wrote several operas, incidental music for 3 plays, a number of choral, vocal, instrumental, orchestral and concerted works, but remains best known for his "Symphony on a French Mountain Air."

Concerted

B Symphonie sur un chant montagnard français ("Symphony on a French Mountain Air") for Piano and Orchestra, Op.25

* Robert Casadesus, piano; Philadelphia Orchestra; Eugene Ormandy, conductor; Odyssey Y-31274. Includes Franck's Variations symphonique (Symphonic Variations for Piano and Orchestra) (1885), rated A.

IPPOLITOV—IVANOV, MIKHAIL
1859–1935

Born as Mikhail Mikhailovich Ivanov, the composer added the Ippolitov to ensure that he would not be confused with a music critic named Michael Ivanov. As a child, he studied the violin and, in 1876, he entered the St. Petersburg Conservatory, where he studied composition with Rimsky-Korsakov. He is noted for his studies of the music of the various races living in the Caucasus, particularly his book titled On the National Songs of Georgia (i.e., Stalin's, not the one famous for Ty Cobb). Ippolitov-Ivanov's music is charmingly melodious and usually filled with color and vitality.

Orchestral

B Caucasian Sketches Suite, Op.10

* Utah Symphony Orchestra; Maurice Abravanel, conductor; Vanguard C-10060. Includes Rimsky-Korsakov's Symphony No.2 ("Antar"), Op.9, rated C.

IVES, CHARLES
1874-1954

Often thought of as either an incredibly capable musical amateur (by Castelnuovo-Tedesco, among others) or a fascinating dilettante with musical aspirations, Charles Edward Ives is certainly peculiarly American and probably among the most important of this country's composers. Ives' first musical training came from his father, George Ives, a Civil War military band leader. Charles graduated from Yale, having studied music there with Horatio Parker. Prior to Yale, Ives had studied organ with Dudley Buck and served as organist at churches in New Jersey and New York. Ives' professional career was not really as a composer, but rather as a business man and executive in the insurance field. He formed, with Julian Myrick, the firm of Ives and Myrick in 1916, which became quite successful. Ives retired from business completely in 1930, at which time he essentially stopped writing music. Most of his important works were written between 1906 and 1916. His music is characterized by a variety of idiosyncrasies including polytonality, polyrhythms, and the use of nostalgic American hymns, songs and folk songs in such a manner as to be evocative but not saccharine. His masterpieces are the Concord Sonata, for piano and Three Places in New England, for orchestra. Ives' first 2 Symphonies are in the late 19th century Romantic style: lyrical, melodic, and formal. His genius was long unrecognized (not until about the 1930s were his works even performed), but now his originality and influence are readily acknowledged.

Chamber

C String Quartet No.1 ("A Revival Service") (1896)

$ Juilliard Quartet; Columbia MP-39752, 🅱 MP-39752. Includes Ives' String Quartet No.2 (1913), also rated C.

C String Quartet No.2 (1913)—see entry for String Quartet No.1 ("A Revival Service") (1896), immediately supra.

106

C Sonatas for Violin and Piano 4), (No.1: 1908; No.2: 1910; No.3: 1914 and No.4 <"Children's Day at the Camp Meeting">: 1915)

* Paul Zukofsky, violin; Gilbert Kalish, piano; Nonesuch 73025 (2 discs).

B The Unanswered Question for Chamber Orchestra (1908)

$ New York Philharmonic Orchestra; Leonard Bernstein, conductor; Columbia MP-38777, 🄱 MP-38777. Includes Ives' Central Park in the Dark (1898-1907) with Seiji Ozawa and Maurice Peress as assistant conductors; Decoration Day from the Symphony: Holidays (1904-1913), rated C and Symphony No.3 (1901-1904), rated B.

Instrumental

A Sonata for Piano No.2 ("Concord, Mass., 1840-1860") (1905-1915)

* Gilbert Kalish, piano; Nonesuch 71337.

Orchestral

A Three Places in New England (1903-1914)—see entry under Copland, Orchestral, Fanfare for the Common Man (1944), supra.

Symphonic

C Decoration Day from Symphony: Holidays (1904-1913)—see entry for The Unanswered Question for Chamber Orchestra (1908) under Chamber, supra.

B Symphony No.3 (1901-1904)—see entry for The Unanswered Question for Chamber Orchestra (1904-1913) under Chamber, supra.

A Symphony No.4 (1910-1916)

$ American Symphony Orchestra; Schola Cantorum of New York; Leopold Stokowski, conductor (assisted by David Katz and José Serebrier); Columbia MS-6775.

JANÁČEK, LEOŠ
1854-1928

Janáček is one of those composers whose worth has been known to musicians for some time but is a relative novelty to the general public. He was given a fine basic musical education, first at the Augustine monastery at Brno, in his native Czechoslovakia, as a chorister, then at the Brno Teachers Training School and, finally, at the Prague Organ School (College of Music). Later, he attended the Leipzig and Vienna Conservatories. He returned to Brno in 1880 and was successful in founding the Brno Organ School (College of Music). He became an intimate of Dvořák's, who admired Janáček's work but was somewhat "alarmed" at the harmonies Janáček employed. Janáček's life was one marked by a succession of peculiar circumstances. As a person he was eccentric and stubborn, but lovable, and his music reflects his fascination with things psychological. Janáček was unhappily married (in 1884), and had two children—both of whom preceded him in death. He did not begin to show his compositional genius until he was past the age of 40. His style was greatly influenced by several factors. He studied Moravian folk songs and attempted to incorporate into his own music their "speech" patterns in such a way as to determine the "arch" of his themes. Also, he based his harmonies on the work of Helmholtz, the German physicist and acoustician. Melodies did not pour forth from Janáček, rather he employed essentially the same group of melodies from work to work. Yet he was able to alter their character to suit varying contexts by changing their emphases, rhythms and textures. Although Janáček's masterpiece, the opera Jenufa, was written during the years 1894-1903 (and is really titled Jejï pastorkyňa, "Her Foster-Daughter"), it was not publicly performed (except once, rather perfunctorily, at Brno in 1904) until 1916 in Prague. Once Jenufa gained the stage, Janáček's international reputation became assured. Along with Berg's Wozzeck, Jenufa is one of the operatic masterpieces of the 20th century. Janáček's other great works are (Kátya Kabanová), the Slavonic <or Glagolitic> Mass, and From the House of the Dead. All of these last mentioned date after 1916, when the 62-year-old Janáček met, and fell in love with, Mrs. Kamila Stössl. Although Mrs. Stössl was considerably younger than Janáček, and their relationship being a platonic one, that relationship served as a rejuvenation for the composer's powers, accounting, to some extent, for the remarkable outburst of creativity which took place during the last 11 years of his life. It would be a mistake to leave the impression that Janáček's only important works are operas. His 2 String Quartets, Sinfonietta, instrumental and chamber works are also of great value and are finally gaining the recognition that is their due.

Chamber

C Concertino for Piano and Chamber Orchestra (1925)

$ Rudolf Firkusny, piano; Bavarian Radio Symphony Orchestra; Rafael Kubelik, conductor; DG 2721251 (2 discs). Includes Janáček's Capriccio for Piano, Left Hand (1926), rated C; In the Mist, Four Pieces for Piano (1912), rated B; Sonata for Piano, "October 1, 1905" (also known as "From the Street"), rated B; On an Overgrown Path (1902-1908) and Theme and Variations (1880).

B String Quartet No.1 ("Kreutzer") (1923)

* Janáček Quartet; Quintessence 7193, ▣ 7193. Includes Janáček's String Quartet No.2 ("Intimate Pages") (1927-1928), rated A.

A String Quartet No.2 ("Intimate Pages") (1927-1928)--see entry for String Quartet No.1 ("Kreutzer") (1923), immediately supra.

Choral

A Slavonic Mass (also known as Glagolitic Mass) (1926)

$ Teresa Kubiak, soprano; Anne Collins, mezzo-soprano; Robert Tear, tenor; Wolfgang Sch5one, bass; John Birch, Organ; Brighton Festival Chorus; Royal Philharmonic Orchestra; Rudolf Kempe, conductor; London 411726-1 LJ, ▣ 411726-4 LJ.

Instrumental

C Capriccio for Piano, Left Hand (1926)--see entry for Concertino for Piano and Chamber Orchestra (1925) under Chamber, supra.

B In the Mist, Four Pieces for Piano (1912)--see entry for Concertino for Piano and Chamber Orchestra (1925) under Chamber, supra.

B Sonata for Piano, "October 1, 1905" (also known as "From the Street")--see entry for Concertino for Piano and Chamber Orchestra (1925) under Chamber, supra.

Operatic

B The Cunning Little Vixen (1921-1923)

$ Lucia Popp, soprano; Éva Randová, mezzo-soprano; Rudolf Jedlicka, bass; Vienna State Opera Chorus; Vienna Philharmonic Orchestra; Sir Charles Mackerras, conductor; London LDR-72010 (2 discs), ▣ LDR-72010.

C From the House of the Dead (1928)

$ Jiri Zahradniček, tenor; Ivo Zidek, tenor; Václav Zitek, baritone; Vienna State Opera Chorus; Vienna Philharmonic Orchestra; Sir Charles Mackerras, conductor; London LDR-10036 (2 discs), ⊟ LDR-10036.

A Jenufa (1894-1903)

$ Lucia Popp, soprano; Elisabeth Söderström, soprano; Éva Randová, mezzo-soprano; Marie Mrázová, contralto; Peter Dvorsky, tenor; Wieslaw Ochman, tenor; Rudolf Jedlicka, bass; Vienna State Opera Chorus; Vienna Philharmonic Orchestra; Sir Charles Mackerras, conductor; London LDR-73009 (3 discs), ⊟ LDR-73009.

C Kátya Kabanová (1919-1921)

$ Nadezda Kniplová, soprano; Elisabeth Söderström, soprano; Peter Dvorsky, tenor; Vienna State Opera Chorus; Vienna Philharmonic Orchestra; Sir Charles Mackerras, conductor; London 12109 (2 discs), ⊟ 5-12109.

B The Makropoulos Affair (1923-1925)

$ Elisabeth Söderström, soprano; Peter Dvorsky, tenor; Benno Blachut, tenor; Vienna State Opera Chorus; Vienna Philharmonic Orchestra; Sir Charles Mackerras, conductor; London 12116 (2 discs), ⊟ 5-12216.

Orchestral

B Sinfonietta (1926)

* Czech Philharmonic Orchestra; Karel Ančerl, conductor; Quintessence 7184, ⊟ 7184.   Includes Janáček's Taras Bulba (Slavonic Rhapsody after Gogol) (1918), rated C.

C Taras Bulba (Slavonic Rhapsody after Gogol) (1918)--see entry for Sinfonietta (1926), immediately supra.

JOPLIN, SCOTT
1868-1917

Born in Texarkana, Joplin was a Black composer who wrote over 50 piano rags--the works upon which his primary fame rests.   Such titles as

The Maple Leaf Rag, The Entertainer, Chrysanthemum, The Stop Time Rag, etc., are familiar to most aficionados of popular American music. Joplin was taught to play the piano at home and later undertook serious studies, including courses at George Smith College in Sedalia, Missouri. Despite his recent recognition as a composer of virtually perfect miniatures (some go so far as to compare him to Mozart or Chopin), his largest undertaking went unnoticed until the 1970s--his opera Treemonisha. Although Treemonisha is a flawed, and rather naive work, it is one of rare talent, honesty and simplicity (in the best sense). Joplin died penniless and insane, the victim of syphilis.

Operatic

B Treemonisha (1911)

$ Carmen Balthrop, soprano; Betty Lou Allen, mezzo-soprano; Willard White, bass; Houston Grand Opera Chorus and Orchestra; Gunther Schuller, conductor; DG 2707083 (2 discs).

KABALEVSKY, DMITRI
1904-1987

Kabalevsky is a relatively minor contemporary Russian composer who received his musical education at the Scriabin Music School and the Moscow Conservatory. He seems not to have benefited greatly from his compositional studies with Miaskovsky, and was appointed, in 1939, a professor at the Moscow Conservatory. Most of his work is typical of the "accepted" academic school required by the Soviets (usually referred to as "Soviet Realism"--the old love affair between boy and tractor kind of stuff). He has been fond of using Russian folk songs in his works, and some few of his musical enterprises have become popular outside the Soviet sphere, mainly because of their vitality and rather slapstick humor.

Orchestral

B Comedians (Suite for Small Orchestra), Op.26

* Vienna State Opera Orchestra; Vladimir Golschmann, conductor; Vanguard S-207, ◪ S-207. Includes Khachaturian's Gayne Ballet Suites 1 and 2 (1942), rated A.

KHACHATURIAN, ARAM
1903-1978

111

Despite having been born in Tiflis (formerly Tbilisi), the capital of Soviet Georgia, Khachaturian was essentially an Armenian composer whose music exhibits his Armenian roots. Indifferent to music at first, he became interested in that art when he was about 19. At 26, he enrolled at the Moscow Conservatory and studied under Miaskovsky. Others who do not determine the courses of their lives until relatively late should take heart from Khachaturian's example: he did not receive his diploma from the Conservatory until he was 31. Khachaturian is principally known for his ballet music, music which not only makes use of the folklore of Armenia, but also draws upon the national characteristics of Georgia, the Ukraine, Turkey, etc. As might be expected, Khachaturian's work is filled with color, brio, lovely melodies and a fine earthiness.

Ballet

A Gayne Ballet (excerpts) (1942)

$ London Symphony Orchestra; Aram Khachaturian, conductor; Angel S-37411, 图 S-37411. Includes Khachaturian's Spartacus Ballet Suite (1953). Gayne contains the very popular "Sabre Dance."

$ National Philharmonic Orchestra; Loris Tjeknavorian, conductor; RCA CRL2-2263 (2 discs).

Also--see entry under Kabalevsky, Orchestral, Comedians (Suite for Small Orchestra), Op.26, supra.

Concerted

C Concerto for Piano (1936)

$ Philippe Entremont, piano; New Philharmonia Orchestra; Seiji Ozawa, conductor; Columbia M-31075. Includes Liszt's Hungarian Fantasia for Piano and Orchestra (1852), rated B.

B Concerto for Violin (1940)

* David Oistrakh, violin; Moscow Radio Symphony Orchestra; Aram Khachaturian, conductor; Odyssey/Melodiya Y-34608.

KODÁLY, ZOLTÁN
1882-1967

Along with Béla Bartók, his friend and colleague, Kodály is one of the two most important Hungarian composers of this century. Kodály's

112

parents were avid amateur musicians who were not loath to provide young Zoltán with a musical education. He attended the University of Budapest and the Budapest Academy of Music. Early on, Kodály became interested both in composition and Hungarian musical folklore and musicology. Wishing to determine what the real Hungarian musical ethos was, he found that most of the existing Hungarian folk music collections were inaccurate and of little use to him. In 1905 he set out on an expedition to collect, for himself, what he could of northwestern Hungarian folk music. He published his findings, and the following year began his important association with Bartók. Also in 1906, Kodály took his Ph.D. at the Péter Pázmány University of Sciences in Budapest. The following year found Kodály with an appointment as a teacher of theory at the Academy of Music in Budapest. Between continuing to collect Hungarian folk music and teaching, Kodály found time to compose extensively. His first international recognition as a composer seems to have come in 1926 with the performance of Psalmus Hungaricus (at Zurich), which was approximately concomitant with the beginning of his interest in composing large scale choral works. Kodály's most popular (and famous) work, the opera Háry János, also received a performance in 1926 (in Budapest) which seems to have put the seal on his reputation as an estimable composer. In his music, Kodály appropriated some of the stylistic and technical elements of the French Impressionists. He imposed upon this a polyphonic discipline reminiscent of Palestrina, yet all the while employing an Hungarian underpinning in his rhythms, melodic turns, and tonalities. His 85 years allowed him to produce a large catalog of works which, in the main, are of excellent quality.

Chamber

B Sonata for 'Cello and Piano, Op.4

$ Miklós Perényi, 'cello; Jenő Jandó, piano; Hungaroton 11864. Includes Kodály's Sonata for Unaccompanied 'Cello, Op.8, rated B.

C String Quartet No.1, Op.2

$ Kodály Quartet; Hungaroton 12362. Includes Kodály's String Quartet No.2, Op.10, rated B.

B String Quartet No.2, Op.10--see entry for String Quartet No.1, Op.2, immediately supra.

Choral

B <u>Psalmus Hungaricus</u> for Tenor, Chorus and Orchestra, Op.13

$ József Simándy, tenor; Budapest Chorus; Hungarian State Orchestra; Antal Doráti, conductor; Hungaroton 11392, ♭ 11392. Includes Kodály's Variations on an Hungarian Folk Song (<u>Peacock</u> Variations) (1939), rated C.

Instrumental

B Sonata for Unaccompanied 'Cello, Op.8 see entry for Sonata for 'Cello and Piano, Op.4 under Instrumental, <u>supra</u>.

Operatic

B <u>Háry János</u>, Op.15

$ Klára Takács, mezzo-soprano; Sándor Sólyom Nagy, baritone; József Gregor, bass; Hungarian State Opera; János Ferencsik, conductor; Hungaroton 12187-121899 (3 discs), ♭ 12187-12189.

Orchestral

B <u>Dances of Galanta</u> (1933)

$ Hungarian Radio Orchestra; György Lehel, conductor; Hungaroton 12252, ♭ 12252. Includes Kodály's <u>Dances of Marosszék</u> (1930) and Variations on an Hungarian Folk Song (<u>Peacock</u> Variations) (1939), rated C.

A <u>Háry János</u> Suite (1926)

$$ London Philharmonic Orchestra; Klaus Tennstedt, conductor; Angel DS-38095, ♭ 4DS-38095. Includes Prokofiev's <u>Lieutenant Kijé</u> Suite, Op.60, also rated A.

C Variations on an Hungarian Folk Song (<u>Peacock</u> Variations) (1939)--see entries for <u>Dances of Galanta</u> (1933), <u>supra</u> and <u>Psalmus Hungaricus</u> for Tenor, Chorus and Orchestra, Op.13 under Choral, <u>supra</u>.

LALO, ÉDOUARD
1823-1892

Victor-Antoine-Édouard Lalo was a French composer of Spanish descent, which heritage marks his best known work: the <u>Symphonie espagnole</u>. After studying composition and the violin and attending the Conservatoire de Paris, Lalo played viola in the Armingaud-Jacquard

Quartet.   He began composing in earnest in 1865, and met with some success.   Lalo's works are in a Romantic cast: nicely orchestrated, melodic, neatly rhythmic and well constructed.

Concerted

B Concerto for 'Cello and Orchestra, in d (1876)

$ Yo Yo Ma, 'cello; L'Orchestre National de France; Lorin Maazel, conductor; Columbia IM-35848, ♮ HMT-35848.   Includes Saint Saëns' Concerto for 'Cello No.1, Op.33, in a, also rated B.

B Symphonie espagnole for Violin and Orchestra, Op.21

* Sir Yehudi Menuhin, violin; Philharmonia Orchestra; Sir Eugene Goossens, conductor; Seraphim ♮ 4XG-60370.   Includes Saint-Saëns' Havanaise for Violin and Orchestra, Op.83 and Introduction and Rondo Capriccioso for Violin and Orchestra, Op.28, both also rated B.

* Aaron Rosand, violin; Southwest German Radio Symphony Orchestra; Tibor Szöke, conductor; Vox 511590.   Includes Saint-Saëns' Concerto for Violin No.3, Op.61, in b, rated B.

LEONCAVALLO, RUGGERO
1857-1919

Leoncavallo was an Italian composer who remains extremely well known but for one work, his opera Pagliacci. After taking a degree at the Conservatorio di Napoli, he left to begin work on an opera based on the tragic life of the English poet Thomas Chatterton. Probably for the best, the opera's production was called off by the impressario, leaving Leoncavallo to earn his way as a piano player in cafes in a variety of countries, from Germany to Turkey. As with many younger composers of his era, Leoncavallo came under the influence of the music of Wagner, whose scores he studied assiduously.   Betimes, Mascagni's opera, Cavalleria Rusticana, was published in 1888 and received tumultuously at its first performances in 1890. Leoncavallo, taking his cue from Mascagni, wrote Pagliacci in the verismo style (it is based on an actual incident in Calabria). It was first performed in 1892 with Toscanini conducting. It was an instant success, but Leoncavallo, despite a few other later works which were somewhat esteemed, never was able to duplicate the reception given Pagliacci.

Operatic

A <u>Pagliacci</u> (1892)

$ Mirella Freni, soprano; Luciano Pavarotti, tenor; Ingvar Wixell, baritone; London Voices; Finchley Children's Music Group; National Philharmonic Orchestra, London; Giuseppe Patané, conductor; London D-13125 (3 discs). Includes Mascagni's <u>Cavalleria Rusticana</u> (1889), also rated A.

LISZT, FRANZ
1811-1886

Franz (real first name Ferencz) Liszt's life is one of the most curious and exciting in the annals of music. He was born in Hungary, the son of a steward in the service of Prince Esterházy (the patron family of Haydn), who was also a musical amateur sufficiently good to be able to teach the young Franz the rudiments of piano playing. Oddly, despite Franz' later interest in Hungarian folk music, his principal language was German, and he never learned the Hungarian language very well. He made his public debut at the age of 9 and, based on his exceptional performance, was the recipient of funds donated by a group of Hungarian aristocrats. This donation enabled him to underwrite his musical studies for 6 years. To that end, he went to Vienna and undertook lessons with Carl Czerny, who had studied with Beethoven. In fact, Liszt gave a concert on April 13, 1823 to which Beethoven was to be in the audience, unfortunately for all concerned, Beethoven did not attend. Liszt thence journeyed to Paris to seek entrance to the Conservatoire de Paris, but Cherubini (who was then the director of that institution) refused to admit him ostensibly because the Conservatoire was only open to French citizens (in actuality, Cherubini was not disposed to admitting child prodigies)--he made no exception in the case of Liszt, despite the latter's large reputation. Instead of a formal musical education, Liszt studied composition with Reicha and, at age 13, wrote an operetta in one act titled <u>Don Sanche</u>. He toured Switzerland, France and England and then, in 1827, on the death of his father, settled in Paris, where he became friends with Victor Hugo, George Sand, Chopin and Berlioz, among others of that ilk. In 1833 he met the Countess d'Agoult (known better by her nom de plume, Daniel Stern), with whom he had a 6 year affair and 3 children, which affair ended in 1839. One of the issue of this liaison was a daughter named Cosima, who became the wife of conductor and Wagner champion Hans von Bülow. Cosima is famous in her own right for later having an affair with, and then becoming the wife of, Wagner. Between the years 1839 to 1847, Liszt was lionized everywhere he travelled, and was considered the premier pianist of his time. This does not mean that Liszt was not savaged, either in the press or privately. The entry for November 19, 1870 in George Templeton Strong's diary reads, in part: "The Liszt Concerto is filthy and vile. It suggests Chinese orchestral performances as described by enterprising and self-sacrificing travelers. This may be a specimen of the School of the Future for aught I know. If it is, the future will throw the works of Haydn, Mozart and Beethoven into the rubbish bin." And in the press one finds (January 7, 1843 of the Dramatic and Musical Review, London): "Liszt is a mere commonplace person, with his hair on end--a snob out of Bedlam. He writes the ugliest music extant." Liszt was always a generous artist and was the benefactor, in one way or another, of several of his colleagues, including Beethoven (whose monument at Bonn would not have been erected with rather smart alacrity without Liszt's efforts and cash), Chopin (whose works he often performed in public) and Wagner, to whom he was more than a father-in-law (he was also a mentor and sounding-board, pun intentional). Liszt formed another romantic attachment in 1848, this time with the Russian Princess Carolyne von Sayn-Wittgenstein, and they took up residence at their house in Weimar. It was this paramour who led Liszt towards orthodox Catholicism, and in 1865 Pope Pius IX conferred the title of Abbé upon him. His full life was crowned with many honors from several nations, and it was not unusual for one to encounter people born in the last half of the 19th century who claimed to be illegitimate offspring of Liszt's: such was his famed prowess with the ladies (and his reputation as a composer-pianist). Liszt's piano works are legendary for their difficulty and ingenuity--requiring physical endurance and great dexterity. Most of his music has a philosophical (essentially religious or mystical) quality which is virtually unique to him. In the realm of orchestral music, his principal contribution was the "invention" of the one-movement symphonic poem, a device based on the transformation of themes, without actually being in the theme-and-variations "form." Although previous composers had employed similar concepts, it was Liszt who brought it to full fruition.

This concept, along with Berlioz' _idée fixe_, became the basis for Wagner's system of the _Leitmotiv_. In addition to his piano and orchestral works, Liszt was a master of choral writing, and some of his efforts in this vein are among the best in the literature. In fine, he is ranked as the greatest of Hungarian composers (except for Bartók), and among the most important composers of the 19th century.

Choral

B _Christus_ (Oratorio) (1855–1859)

$ Éva Andor, soprano; Zsuzsa Németh, contralto; József Réti, tenor; Sándor Nagy, baritone; József Gregor, bass; Sándor Margittay, organ; Budapest Chorus; Zoltán Kodály Girls' Chorus; Hungarian State Orchestra; Miklós Forrai, conductor; Hungaroton 11506–11508 (3 discs).

C Mass: _Hungarian Coronation_ (1867)

$ Veronika Kinces, soprano; Klára Takács, contralto; Dénes Gulyás, tenor; László Polgár, bass; Hungarian Radio Chorus; Budapest Symphony Orchestra; György Lehel, conductor; Hungaroton 12148, ⊟ 12148.

C _Missa solemnis_ (1855–1858)

$ Veronika Kinces, soprano; Klára Takács, contralto; György Korondy, tenor; József Gregor, bass; Sándor Margittay, organ; Hungarian Radio Chorus; Budapest Symphony Orchestra; János Ferencsik, conductor; Hungaroton 11861, ⊟ 11861.

Concerted

A Concerto for Piano No.1, in E flat (1830–1856)

* Ivan Davis, piano; Royal Philharmonic Orchestra; Edward Downes, conductor; London ⊟ STS5–15562. Includes Liszt's Concerto for Piano No.2, in A (1839–1861), rated B.

$ Claudio Arrau, piano; London Symphony Orchestra; Sir Colin Davis, conductor; Philips 412926–1 PM, ⊟ 412926–4 PM. Includes Liszt's Concerto for Piano in A (1839–1861), rated B.

Also--see entry under Chopin, Concerted, Concerto for Piano No.1, Op.11, in e, _supra_.

B Concerto for Piano No.2, in A (1839–1861)--see entries for Concerto for Piano No.1, in E flat (1830–1856), immediately _supra_.

B Hungarian Fantasia for Piano and Orchestra (1852)--see entry under Khachaturian, Concerted, Concerto for Piano (1936), supra.

C Totentanz for Piano and Orchestra (Paraphrase on Dies irae) (1838-1859)

* Alfred Brendel, piano; Vienna Symphony Orchestra; Michael Gielen, conductor; Turnabout 34265. Includes Liszt's Wanderer Fantasie for Piano and Orchestra (after Schubert) (1851), rated B.

$ Byron Janis, piano; Chicago Symphony Orchestra; Fritz Reiner, conductor; RCA ARP1-4668, ⏚ ARP1-4668. Includes Schumann's Concerto for Piano, Op.54, in a, rated A.

B (Wanderer Fantasie for Piano and Orchestra (after Schubert) (1851)--see entry for Totentanz for Piano and Orchestra (Paraphrase on Dies irae) (1838-1859), immediately supra.

Instrumental

B Années de pèlerinage (Premiere année: Suisse; Deuxieme année: Italie; Venezia e Napoli: Supplement aux Années de pèlerinage, Deuxieme volume; Troiseme année) (26), (Nos.1-26)

$ Lazar Berman, piano; DG 2740175 (3 discs). Must be special ordered.

A Hungarian Rhapsodies (19)

* Alfred Brendel, piano; Vanguard C-10035. Includes Nos.2, in c sharp (1847); 3, in B flat (1853); 8, in f sharp (1853); 13, in a (1853); 15 (Rákóczy March), in a (1871) and 17, in d (1882). It is the No.2 which is the most famous.

For orchestral version of No.2, in c sharp (1847)--see entries for Mazeppa, Symphonic Poem No.6 (1851), under Orchestral, infra and under Enesco, Orchestral, Roumanian Rhapsody No.1, Op.11, supra.

A Sonata for Piano, in b (1853)

$ Tamás Vásáry, piano; DG 415918-1 GMF. Includes Liszt's Polonaise No.2, in E (1851) and Réminiscences de Don Juan (After Mozart) (1841).

A Transcendental Études (12), (Nos.1-12) (1851)

$ Claudio Arrau, piano; Philips 6747412 (2 discs), ♮ 7505081. Includes Liszt's Études de concert (3), (1848) Nos.1-3: in A flat, f and D flat.

Orchestral

B A Faust Symphony (1854-1857)

* Ferdinand Koch, tenor; Southwest German Chorus; Southwest German Radio Symphony Orchestra; Jascha Horenstein, conductor; Turnabout 34491.

A Hungarian Rhapsody No.2, in c sharp (1847) orchestral version (1874)—see entries under Enesco, Orchestral, Roumanian Rhapsody No.,1, Op.11, supra, Mazeppa, Symphonic Poem No. 6 (1851), immediately infra and Mephisto Waltz No.2 (1880-1881), infra.

C Mazeppa, Symphonic Poem No. 6 (1851)

* Boston Pops Orchestra; Arthur Fiedler, conductor; RCA Victrola ♮ ALK1-4475. Includes Liszt's Hungarian Rhapsody Nos.2, in c harp (1874), rated B and 6, in D flat (1874), Les Préludes, Symphonic Poem No.3 (1848), rated A and Rákóczy March (1865), rated B.

A Mephisto Waltz No.2 (1880-1881)

$ Philadelphia Orchestra; Eugene Ormandy, conductor; Columbia MY-37772, ♮ MY-37772. Includes Liszt's Hungarian Rhapsody No.2, in c sharp (1847) orchestral version and Les Préludes, Symphonic Poem No.3 (1848), both also rated A.

A Les Préludes, Symphonic Poem No.3 (1848)—see entries for Mephisto Waltz No.2 (1880-1881), immediately supra and Mazeppa, Symphonic Poem No.6 (1851), supra.

B Rákóczy March (1865)—see entry for Mazeppa, Symphonic Poem No.6 (1851), supra.

MACDOWELL, EDWARD
1860-1908

Edward Alexander MacDowell was an American composer whose importance in the music of this country is not insignificant. He was born in New York and began his music studies (piano, initially) quite early, and then left to continue his education at the Conservatoire de Paris, in 1876. In Paris he devoted his time to piano performance and composition, studying the latter with Joachim Raff. The greatest early influence on MacDowell's compositional style was that of Raff. MacDowell left Paris to take up a position on the faculty of the Conservatory at Darmstadt, as principal piano pedagogue. After a year at Darmstadt he moved to Frankfurt and worked as a private piano teacher. In 1882, at the invitation of Raff, he went to Weimar and met (and played his Concerto for Piano No.1 for) Liszt. The old Liszt invited MacDowell to perform his (i.e., MacDowell's) <u>Modern Suite</u> for Piano at the Allgemeiner Deutscher Musikverein at Weimar in 1882. MacDowell married Marian Nevins in 1884. She was an erstwhile pupil of his and, both during and after his life, was the "keeper of MacDowell's flame." MacDowell, for most of the remainder of his life (which was not all that long), gave himself over to less concertizing and more composition and teaching. In 1905 he became ill with what was described as "deterioration of the brain" (result of syphilis) and ultimately became insane, in which state he died. After his death, Mrs. MacDowell transferred their Peterborough, New Hampshire summer home to the MacDowell Memorial Association. This property became a well-known "artist's retreat" at which litterateurs and composers could spend their summers, working at their crafts, with the need to pay virtually nothing for room and board. Most of MacDowell's works are for solo piano; there are a few orchestral ones and 2 concerti for piano. His music is marked by late 19th century Romanticism and he was given to assigning programmatic titles (often referring to flora, and other natural <and sometimes supernatural> phenomena) to many of his pieces. MacDowell's creations are still fresh-sounding and poetic. Probably most important, MacDowell was the first modern American composer to infuse his music with native idioms (e.g., rhythm, melodies, etc.) and became, therefore, a kind of "role model" to the succeeding generation of American composers. His works are now, unfortunately, undervalued and underperformed.

Concerted

B Concerto for Piano No.2, in d, Op.23

* Eugene List, piano; Westphalian Symphony Orchestra, Recklinghausen; Siegfried Landau, conductor; Turnabout 34535. Includes MacDowell's Suite No.2 ("Indian") for Orchestra, Op.48, rated C.

Instrumental

B Woodland Sketches for Piano, Op.51

* Charles Fierro, piano; Nonesuch 71411, 🎵 71411. Includes MacDowell's Two Fantastic Pieces, Op.17, and piano pieces of Ethelbert Nevin (he of Mighty Lak' a Rose infamy). No.1 of the Woodland Sketches is the once popular "To a Wild Rose."

Orchestral

C Suite No.2 ("Indian") for Orchestra, Op.48--see entry for Concerto for Piano No.2, in d, Op.23 under Concerted, supra.

MAHLER, GUSTAV
1860-1911

Mahler was born in Kališt, Bohemia (now Austria) to comfortably middle-class Jewish parents and was the second in a family of 12. Upon completing grammar school in 1875, he attended the Conservatory in Vienna until 1878. Concurrently, from 1877 to 1879, he also attended the University of Vienna, taking courses in history, history of music and philosophy. His musical education was a firm one, his instructors at the Conservatory having been excellent. In 1880 Mahler wended his way (I've always wanted to use that) to Hall, in Austria, to become the Kapellmeister there. Also in 1880 he completed his first work of consequence: Das klagende Lied. In succeeding years he held a variety of conducting positions, moving from Ljubljana to Vienna and, in 1886 to Leipzig (replacing the great Anton Seidl) as assistant to Arthur Nikisch (one of the greatest conductors of the century), where he conducted many of Wagner's operas. Seidl, by the way, was the conductor of the old New York Philharmonic Orchestra at the time of his death (in 1898, of ptomaine poisoning). In 1888 Mahler was appointed Director (the first time he had held such a title) of the Royal Opera in Budapest. In this post he exhibited exceptional managerial and organizational talents. It was also in this year that he composed his Symphony No.1. During the years 1891 to 1897 he filled the position of Kapellmeister of the Hamburg Opera, a comedown from his previous jobs, but one which allowed him more time for composition. On the strong recommendation of Brahms, Mahler was appointed <u>Kapellmeister</u> of the Court Opera in Vienna in 1897 (the year of Brahms' death). Mahler spent ten years with the Court Opera since, not long after returning to Vienna, his position was elevated to include that of Artistic Director (somewhat analagous to the position now enjoyed by James Levine at the Metropolitan Opera). Mahler was always concerned about his own mortality and many of his works indicate this inner struggle with morbidity. Given this turn of mind, it is not surprising that he made a concerted effort, beginning in 1907 (5 years after his marriage to the incredible Alma Schindler, later the spouse of Franz Werfel and Walter Gropius, and mistress to uncounted minions), to amass an amount of money sufficient to support himself and his family in order to spend his time in unfettered composing. During 1907 and 1908 Mahler was the conductor of the New York Philharmonic Orchestra. He returned to this country once more, in 1910, but his health was precarious and he returned to Europe, where he conducted a few more times and then died of pneumonia in Vienna the following year. Mahler was influenced by both Bruckner and Wagner and also, oddly, by an ethos (Nicolas Slonimsky calls it "melos"--I think it deeper than that) peculiarly rustic, and specifically, Austrian. Mahler was less an innovator than a Romantic eclectic, culminating the melos (and here the word seems more appropriate) of the last half of the 19th century. Bruno Walter, a student of Mahler's, said of him that his work was of a "...radical subjectivity...which filled my heart with a sort of intensely personal satisfaction...." And Mahler himself said, "Only when I experience do I compose--only when I compose do I experience" (from a letter to Arthur Seidl, the German musicologist and critic, dated February 17, 1897). Yet, as recently as June 4, 1952, R.D. Darrell, writing in <u>Down Beat,</u> could say of the Mahler Symphony No.8: "If you are perverse enough to endure over an hour of masochistic aural flagellation, here's your chance! This grandiose 'Symphony of a Thousand', with all its elephantine forces, fatuous mysticism and screaming hysteria, adds up to a sublimely ridiculous minus-zero." <u>Chacun à son</u> ....

Symphonic

A Symphony No.1 ("Titan"), in D (1888)

* London Philharmonic Orchestra; Klaus Tennstedt, conductor; Angel AM-34744, 🄫 AM-34744.

$ Columbia Symphony Orchestra; Bruno Walter, conductor; Columbia MY-37235, ◾ MY-37235.

A Symphony No.2 ("Resurrection"), in c (1894)

* Emilia Cundari, soprano; Maureen Forrester, contralto; Westminster Choir; New York Philharmonic Orchestra; Bruno Walter, conductor; Odyssey Y2-30848 (2 discs), ◾ YT-30848.

$$ Edith Mathis, soprano; Doris Soffel, contralto; London Philharmonic Chorus and Orchestra; Klaus Tennstedt, conductor; Angel DS-3916 (2 discs), ◾ DS-3916.

B Symphony No.3, in d (1895)

$ Marilyn Horne, mezzo-soprano; Glen Ellyn Children's Chorus; Chicago Symphony Orchestra and Chorus; James Levine, conductor; ARL2-1757 (2 discs), ◾ CRK2-1757.

A Symphony No.4, in G (1900)

$$ Lucia Popp, soprano; London Philharmonic Orchestra; Klaus Tennstedt; conductor; Angel DS-37954, ◾ DS-37954.

B Symphony No.5, in c sharp (1902)

$ Bavarian Radio Symphony Orchestra; Rafael Kubelik, conductor; DG 2543535, ◾ 3343535.

! New York Philharmonic Orchestra; Bruno Walter, conductor; Odyssey 32260016E (2 discs). Includes Mahler's <u>Kindertotenlieder</u> ("Songs on the Deaths of Children") (1902) with Kathleen Ferrier, contralto, rated A.

C Symphony No.6, in a (1904)

$$ London Philharmonic Orchestra; Klaus Tennstedt, conductor; Angel DS-3945 (2 discs).

C Symphony No.7, in e (1905)

$$ London Philharmonic Orchestra; Klaus Tennstedt, conductor; Angel DS-3908 (2 discs), ◾ 4X2S-3908.

$ Utah Symphony Orchestra; Maurice Abravanel, conductor; Vanguard 71141-71142 (2 discs).

B Symphony No.8 ("Symphony of a Thousand"), in E flat (1907)

$ Arleen Augér, soprano; Heather Harper, soprano; Lucia Popp, soprano; Yvonne Minton, mezzo-soprano; Helen Watts, contralto; René Kollo, tenor; John Shirley-Quirk, baritone; Martti Talvela, bass; Vienna Choir Boys; Vienna State Opera Chorus; Vienna Singverein der Gesellschaft der Musikfreunde; Chicago Symphony Orchestra; Sir George Solti, conductor; London 1295 (2 discs), ⬚ 5-1295

C Symphony No.9, in D (1909)

* Columbia Symphony Orchestra; Bruno Walter, conductor; Odyssey Y2-30308 (2 discs).

$ Amsterdam Concertgebouw Orchestra; Bernard Haitink, conductor; Philips 6700021 (2 discs).

C Symphony No.10 (Unfinished), in F sharp (1910)

$ Philadelphia Orchestra; James Levine, conductor; RCA ARC2-4553 (2 discs), ⬚ ARK2-4553. This version was revised and completed by Deryck Cooke.

Vocal

A Kindertotenlieder ("Songs on the Deaths of Children") (1902)--see entry for Symphony No.5, in c sharp (1902) under Symphonic, supra and Lieder eines fahrenden Gesellen ("Songs of a Wayfaring Youth") (1883), infra.

B Des Knaben Wunderhorn ("The Youth's Magic Horn") (1888)

* Maureen Forrester, contralto; Heinz Rehfuss, bass-baritone; Vienna Festival Orchestra; Felix Prohaska, conductor; Vanguard S-285.

A Das Lied von der Erde ("The Song of the Earth") (1908)

$ Dame Janet Baker, mezzo-soprano; James King, tenor; Amsterdam Concertgebouw Orchestra; Bernard Haitink, conductor; Philips 412927-1 PM, ⬚ 412927-4 PM.

$ Mildred Miller, mezzo-soprano; Ernst Haefliger, tenor; New York Philharmonic Orchestra; Bruno Walter, conductor; Columbia MP-39027, ⬚ MP-39027.

B <u>Lieder</u> <u>eines</u> <u>fahrenden</u> <u>Gesellen</u> ("Songs of a Wayfaring Youth") (1883)

! Dietrich Fischer-Dieskau, baritone; Philharmonia Orchestra; Wilhelm Furtwängler, conductor; Seraphim 60272. Includes Mahler's <u>Kindertotenlieder</u> ("Songs on the Deaths of Children") (1902) with Fischer-Dieskau, but here accompanied by the Berlin Philharmonic Orchestra; Rudolf Kempe, conductor, rated A.

B <u>Rückert</u> Lieder (5 Songs on Poems of Rückert) (1902)

$ Dame Janet Baker, mezzo-soprano; New Philharmonia Orchestra; Sir John Barbirolli, conductor; Angel S-36796. Includes Elgar's <u>Sea Pictures,</u> Op.37 (Song Cycle).

MARCELLO, ALESSANDRO
1669-1747

Marcello was a Venetian musician, mathematician and philosopher (and published his compositions under the pseudonym Eterico Stinfalico). His younger brother, Benedetto, became a better known composer and was even, for many years, credited with writing Alessandro's best known work, the Concerto for Oboe.

Concerted

B Concerto for Oboe and Strings, in d (1716)

$ Heinz Holliger, oboe; Geneva Baroque Orchestra; Jean-Marie Auberson, conductor; Pearl 561. Includes C.P.E. Bach's Concerto for Oboe, W.165, in E flat; J.S. Bach's S.1060, Concerto for Violin, Oboe and Strings, in d (with Lorand Fenyves, violin), rated A and Bellini's Concerto for Oboe and Strings, in E flat (1824).

MASCAGNI, PIETRO
1863-1945

Italian opera composer Mascagni's father was a baker who wanted his son to become an attorney. However, contrary to popular lore, Mascagni's father did not interfere with his son's plans to become a musician. The composer studied for a time with Ponchielli at the Milan Conservatory, but finding the study of counterpoint and the fugue not to his taste, Mascagni left and wandered through Italy as a conductor with a variety of traveling opera companies. He finally settled near Foggia, married, and supported himself by giving piano lessons. In 1889, his manuscript of the opera Cavalleria Rusticana (which, as has often been said, is neither chivalric nor rustic) won first prize in a competition sponsored by the publisher Sonzongo. The work was given its premiere in 1890 and was an instant success. Cavalleria is generally recognized as the first opera in the style known as verismo. After Cavalleria, Mascagni's fame fell into decline, none of his succeeding efforts approached his masterpiece in acclaim. During the ascent of the Fascists in Italy, Mascagni allied himself with their cause and this added no further lustre to his name. In sum, he is essentially known as a "one opera composer."

Operatic

A Cavalleria Rusticana (1889)—see entry under Leoncavallo, Operatic, Pagliacci (1892), supra.

MASSENET, JULES
1842-1912

Jules-Émile Frédéric Massenet was sufficiently endowed with talent that he was admitted to the Conservatoire de Paris at the age either 11 or 12, having studied piano with his mother. Massenet's professor of composition was Ambroise Thomas. In 1863 Massenet won the Prix de Rome with a cantata titled David Rizzio (the subject being the famous "friend" and private foreign secretary of Mary, Queen of Scots). Having had some minor works published and produced, Massenet did not become fully recognized as a major talent until after the Franco-Prussian War. It was in 1872 that the production of his opera, Don César de Bazan, brought him to the forefront of the younger French composers and, on the death of Bizet (in 1875), he assumed the position of premier French opera composer. In 1878 Massenet became a member of the faculty of the Conservatoire, a position he retained until his death. His catalog contains 26 operas, 3 ballets, incidental music for 14 plays and 7 orchestral suites. Lawrence W. Haward says of Massenet: "...he was a sufficiently astute musician not merely to reflect the taste of his day (which he gratified by his regular and effortless supply of what Vincent d'Indy called a 'discreet

127

and semi-religious eroticism'), but even to some extent to mould it. By grafting the idiom of Gounod on to something like the method of Wagner with a sensibility to the requirements of singers and an understanding of effective though conventional characterization that belonged essentially to the theatre, he succeeded in appealing to 'the average sensual man' without alienating those who expected opera to be something more than a series of pleasant tunes." It has also been said that "to have heard Manon is to have heard all of Massenet." This writer disagrees with the latter sentiment and finds in Massenet, as have many of his admirers, a keen French sensibility: genteel, rhapsodic and observant. Absent the pith of greater composers, Massenet's music still bears up remarkably well on hearing after hearing.

Ballet

B Le Cid Suite

$ City of Birmingham, England, Symphony Orchestra; Louis Frémaux, conductor; Klavier 522. Includes Massenet's Scènes pittoresques (1874) and "Dernier sommeil de la vierge" from La Vierge Oratorio (1880).

Operatic

C Le Cid (1885)

$ Grace Bumbry, mezzo-soprano; Placido Domingo, tenor; Paul Plishka, bass; Byrne Camp Chorale; New York Opera Orchestra; Eve Queler, conductor; Columbia M3-34211 (3 discs).

A Manon (1884)

$$ Ileana Cotrubas, soprano; Alfredo Kraus, tenor; Charles Burles, bass; José van Dam, bass; Capitole de Toulouse Choeur et Orchestre; Michel Plasson, conductor; Angel DSX-3946 (3 discs), ▤ DSX-3946.

C Werther (After Goethe) (1892)

$ Christiane Barbaux, soprano; Tatiana Troyanos, mezzo-soprano; Alfredo Krauss, tenor; Matteo Manuguerra, baritone; Children's Choir; London Philharmonic Orchestra; Michel Plasson, conductor; Angel SZX-3894 (3 discs), ▤ 4Z3X-3894.

MENDELSSOHN, FELIX
1809-1847

Despite his short life (or as some twits might say, his "untimely death"), the name "Felix" is most appropriate to Mendelssohn (whose full name was Jacob Ludwig Felix Mendelssohn Bartholdy). He was the grandson of the renowned Jewish philosopher, Moses Mendelssohn (the model for the title character in Lessing's Nathan der Weise), and son of Abraham Mendelssohn and Lea Salomon. Felix' forebears were decidedly Jewish but, on moving to Berlin from Hamburg, Abraham converted to Protestantism (specifically, Lutheranism) and added "Bartholdy" to the family name to distinguish it from those Mendelssohns who remained in their original faith. The "Bartholdy," incidentally, came from the Salomon family, one member of which was Jacob Salomon-Bartholdy (an uncle of Felix', and Prussian Consul-General in Rome). The Mendelssohn Bartholdy family was a well-to-do (they were in banking) and prominent one, and all of the three children of Abraham and Lea were talented. It was Felix' brother Paul who employed the hyphenated form of "Mendelssohn-Bartholdy," and, therefore, Felix' name is not his nom juste when the hyphen is used in it. As is not unusual, Felix received his first musical training, in the form of piano lessons, from his mother. He went on with private tutors in music, languages and painting. His teacher of composition, Carl Zelter, recognized the true musical genius of Mendelssohn. Felix gave his first public performance (in a chamber concert) in 1818. In 1819 he entered the Berlin Singakademie. In 1821 Felix was introduced to Goethe at Weimar, by Zelter. By 1824 Felix had established himself, at least in Zelter's eyes, as a mature composer and, in 1825, Felix accompanied his father to Paris, where the "mature composer" of 16 met Cherubini in order to determine what musical prospects might lie ahead for Felix. Father and son returned to Berlin where, during the same year, Felix wrote the overture to A Midsummer Night's Dream of Shakespeare. It, and the Octet (Op.20) of the previous year, give ample proof of Mendelssohn's awesome talent at an almost ridiculous age. Further, try as he might, he never again exceeded the quality of those early pieces. In addition to his own compositions, Mendelssohn was instrumental in the revival of interest in Bach's vocal music, the young composer having already resurrected and given a public performance of the St. Matthew Passion in 1828. Mendelssohn was well-travelled, making many journeys to most of Europe and the British Isles. In 1837 he married

Cécile-Charlotte-Sophie Jeanrenaud, the German-born daughter of a minister of the French Reformed Church. Their marriage was a happy one and produced 5 children. According to a contemporary description, Cécile was "...not a striking person in any way, neither extraordinarily clever, brilliantly witty, nor exceptionally accomplished." It is agreed, however, that she was pleasant, and developed into an efficient Hausfrau. Mendelssohn was unusually close to his sister Fanny, herself an accomplished composer (several of her works were long misattributed to her brother). Fanny's death, in May, 1847, was probably the greatest blow which Felix had to endure. His own health was undermined and he followed Fanny in death 6 months later. Mendelssohn's music, although essentially Romantic in content, is decidedly Classical in form, and through his exquisite taste and intelligence, his best work is almost on par with that of the greatest composers. During the Nazi rule of Germany (and in keeping with Wagner's pronouncements regarding the pejorative "Jewish" influence on music) Mendelssohn's name and music were expunged from all books published in Germany at that time, and the playing of his music was verboten.

Chamber

A Octet for Strings, Op.20, in E flat

$ Melos Ensemble; Arabesque 8017, ⊟ 9017. Includes Spohr's Double Quartet for Strings, Op.65, in d.

B String Quartets (7), Nos.1-7: Op.12, in E flat; Op.13, in a; Op.44, Nos.1-3, in D, e and E flat; Op.80, in f and Op.81, in E (Unfinished)

$ Melos String Quartet; DG 2740267 (4 discs). Includes Mendelssohn's String Quartet, Op.0, in E flat (1837).

A Trios for Piano, Violin and 'Cello (2), Nos.1-2: Op.49, in d and Op.66, in c

$ Isaac Stern, violin; Leonard Rose, 'cello; Eugene Istomin, piano; Columbia M-35835, ⊟ M-35835.

Choral

C Elijah, Op.70 (Oratorio)

$ Gwyneth Jones, soprano; Dame Janet Baker, mezzo-soprano; Nicolai Gedda, tenor; Dietrich Fischer-Dieskau, baritone; New Philharmonia Orchestra; Rafael Frühbeck de Burgos, conductor; Angel S-3738 (3 discs).

Concerted

B Concerti for Piano (2), Nos.1–2: Op.25, in g and Op.40, in d

$ John Ogdon, piano; London Symphony Orchestra; Aldo Ceccato, conductor; Klavier 531. Includes Mendelssohn's Rondo brilliant for Piano and Orchestra, Op.29, in E flat.

A Concerto for Violin, Op.64, in e

$ Jascha Heifetz, violin; Boston Symphony Orchestra; Charles Munch, conductor; RCA LSC–3304, ♭ RK–1284. Includes Tchaikovsky's Concerto for Violin, Op.35, in D, also rated A.

Instrumental

B Lieder ohne Worte ("Songs Without Words") (48), Nos.1–48: Op.19, Nos.1–6; Op.30, Nos.7–12; Op.38, Nos.13–18; Op.53, Nos.19–24; Op.62, Nos.25–30; Op.67, Nos.31–36; Op.85, Nos.37–42 and Op.102, Nos.43–48

$ Daniel Barenboim, piano; DG 2709052 (3 discs).

Orchestral

A Hebrides (or "Fingal's Cave") Overture, Op.26

$ Vienna Philharmonic Orchestra; Christoph von Dohnányi, conductor; London LDR–10003, ♭ LDR–10003. Includes Mendelssohn's Meeresstille und glückliche Fahrt ("Calm Sea and Prosperous Voyage") Overture, Op.27, rated B and Symphony No.4, Op.90, in A ("Italian"), rated A.

B Meeresstille und glückliche Fahrt ("Calm Sea and Prosperous Voyage") Overture, Op.27—see entry for Hebrides (or "Fingal's Cave") Overture, Op.26, immediately supra.

A Midsummer Night's Dream, Op.21 and 61 (Incidental Music After Shakespeare)

* Heather Harper, soprano; Dame Janet Baker, mezzo–soprano; Philharmonia Chorus and Orchestra; Otto Klemperer, conductor; Angel AE–34445; ♭ AE–34445.

Symphonic

C Symphony No.1, Op.11, in c

$ London Philharmonic Orchestra; Bernard Haitink, conductor; Philips ♭ 7300803. Includes the same composer's Symphony No.4 ("Italian"), Op.90, in A, rated B.

Also—see entry for Symphony No.2 (<u>Lobgesang</u>) ("Hymn of Praise"), Op.52, in B flat.

C Symphony No.2 (<u>Lobgesang</u>) ("Hymn of Praise"), Op.52, in B flat

* Helen Donath, soprano; Rotraud Hansmann, soprano; Waldemar Kmentt, tenor; New Philharmonia Chorus and Orchestra; Wolfgang Sawallisch, conductor; Philips Festivo 6770054 (2 discs). Includes Mendelssohn's Symphony No.1, Op.11, in c, rated C.

A Symphony No.3 ("Scottish"), Op.56, in a

$ Chicago Symphony Orchestra; Sir George Solti, conductor; London 414665-1 LH, ⊟ 414665-4 LH. Includes Mendelssohn's Symphony No.4 ("Italian"), Op.90, in A, also rated A.

A Symphony No.4 ("Italian"), Op.90, in A—see entries for <u>Meeresstille</u> <u>und</u> <u>glückliche</u> <u>Fahrt</u> ("Calm Sea and Prosperous Voyage") Overture, Op.27 under Orchestral, <u>supra</u>, Symphony No.3 ("Scottish"), Op.56, in a, immediately <u>supra</u> and Symphony No.5 ("Resurrection"), Op.107, in d, immediately <u>infra.</u>

B Symphony No.5 ("Resurrection"), Op.107, in d

$ Berlin Philharmonic Orchestra; Herbert von Karajan, conductor; DG 2530416. Includes Mendelssohn's Symphony No.4 ("Italian"), Op.90, in A, rated A.

MENOTTI, GIAN CARLO
1911–

Although Menotti is thought of as the foremost American composer of opera in the 20th century, he was born in (and retains the citizenship of) Italy. He studied at the Conservatory in Milan (a city only occasionally known for opera) and continued his studies at the Curtis Institute, composing his first opera, <u>Amelia</u> <u>Goes</u> <u>to</u> <u>the</u> <u>Ball,</u> when he was 23. It was produced by the Metropolitan in New York 3 years later. Since <u>Amelia,</u> Menotti has had a number of successes, even to the extent of having a film made of one of his best, <u>The</u> <u>Medium.</u> Menotti's operas, though decidedly modern, owe their heritage to the <u>verismo</u> school of

Mascagni. His works are "tuneful," exceptionally dramatic in their choice of plots and music, and, wonder of wonders, seem to be enjoyed by wide audiences (especially Amahl and the Night Visitors, which was commissioned expressly for television production by NBC, and which has become a Christmas fixture since 1951). Menotti founded the Spoleto (Italy) Festival of Two Worlds (celebrating music both old and new), and also its American counterpart in Charleston, South Carolina, in 1977. As of this writing, Menotti's new opera, Goya (commissioned by Placido Domingo, who has been portraying the title role) was given its premiere performance in Washington, D.C. to something akin to acclaim.

Ballet

C Sebastian (1944)

$ London Symphony Orchestra; José Serebrier, conductor; Desto 6432.

Operatic

A Amahl and the Night Visitors (1951)

$ Robert King, boy soprano; John McCollum, tenor; Robert Patterson, baritone; NBC Television Production Orchestra; Herbert Grossman, conductor; RCA LSC-2762.

B The Medium (1946)

$ Judith Blegen, soprano; Regina Resnik, soprano; Washington Opera Society; Jorge Mester, conductor; Columbia MS-7387.

MESSIAEN, OLIVIER
1908–

Olivier-Eugène Prosper Charles Messiaen is a French composer and organist who has influenced numerous of his students, among them: Boulez, Xenakis and Stockhausen. On his birth, Messiaen's mother wrote a volume of verse titled L'Ame en bourgeon ("The Burgeoning Spirit"). Nicolas Slonimsky attributes the composer's mysticism to the influence of his mother and her book. In 1916, when he was 8, Messiaen taught himself to play the piano, and to compose. At the age of 11 he entered the Conservatoire de Paris and studied with Dukas and the organist-composer, Marcel Dupré. At the Conservatoire, Messiaen won several prizes in a variety of musical fields. He was appointed organist at the Église de

Trinité in Paris in 1931, which post he held until he was imprisoned by the Germans during World War II. He was repatriated in 1942, and resumed his job at Trinité, and in the same year, was appointed to the faculty of the Conservatoire. Messiaen's music is, in his words, "...at the service of the dogmas of Catholic theology." In his work, Messiaen employs a variety of devices and sounds, methods, rhythms and ideas, from imitating the songs of birds and the timbres of Javanese and Balinese ensembles, to Gregorian chant. His ensembles may contain odd percussion instruments and electronic devices (e.g., Ondes Martenot) in addition to traditional ones. He is unafraid of dissonance, idiosyncratic harmonies and the bizarre in general.

Chamber

B Le Merle noir ("The Blackbird") for Flute and Piano (1950)

* Paige Brook, flute; Robert Levin, piano; Candide 31050, 🅱 CT-4822. Includes Messiaen's Quatuor pour la fin du temps ("Quartet for the End of Time") for Clarinet, Violin, 'Cello and Piano (1941) with Joseph Rabbai, clarinet; Isidore Cohen, violin; Timothy Eddy, 'cello and Robert Levin, piano, rated A.

A Quatuor pour la fin du temps ("Quartet for the End of Time") for Clarinet, Violin, 'Cello and Piano (1941)--see entry for Le Merle noir ("The Blackbird") for Flute and Piano (1950), immediately supra.

Instrumental

C Vingt regards sur l'Enfant Jesus ("Twenty Views of the Infant Jesus") (1944)

* Jocy de Oliveria, piano; Vox SVBX-5486 (3 discs).

Symphonic

B Turangaîla Symphonie for Piano, Ondes Martenot and Orchestra (1946)

$ Yvonne Loriod, piano; Jeanne Loriod, Ondes Martenot; Luxembourg Radio Orchestra; Louis de Froment, conductor; Forlane UM-6504-6505 (2 discs), 🅱 UMK-6504-6505.

MEYERBEER, GIACOMO
1791-1864

Born Jakob Liebmann Beer, the composer added the "Meyer" on receiving a large legacy from a rich uncle (whose last name was Meyer). Although of German birth, Meyerbeer is considered by many to be the architect of French "grand opera." In the usual fashion for composers, Meyerbeer began by studying the piano. The then old Clementi, who had given up teaching, took on Meyerbeer because of the boy's promise as a performer. At age 7, Meyerbeer gave his first public concert, in which he played Mozart's Concerto for Piano No.20, in d, no mean achievement for an adult, let alone, etc. His family arranged for Meyerbeer to study composition with Carl Zelter (also Mendelssohn's teacher) and, in 1810, with the eccentric and celebrated Abbé Vogler, at his "Tonschule" at Darmstadt. Among Meyerbeer's fellow students was Carl Maria von Weber, with whom he remained friends for the remainder of Weber's life. Meyerbeer left in 1812 and repaired to Vienna to seek his fortune. There he heard Hummel perform at the piano and was simultaneously impressed and depressed (the latter at his own apparent relative incompetence). While in Vienna, he wrote a good deal of piano music (which he did not publish) and also performed. He was heard by Moscheles who seems to have been much impressed by Meyerbeer's prowess as a pianist. The Italian composer Salieri, having heard an early comic opera of Meyerbeer's (Alimelek), suggested that he attempt writing in the Italian opera style, found his suggestion taken at its root--Meyerbeer moved to Venice in 1815. There, with Rossini's operas the vogue, Meyerbeer assimilated a good deal of the prevailing style, foregoing his own plodding and Germanic one. In Venice Meyerbeer found easy success. For the reason of seeing one of his works produced there, Meyerbeer ultimately took up residence in Paris, the city in which he found his greatest audience and in which he spent most of the remainder of his life. Meyerbeer's best works are unique in their admixture of Italian style melodies, Germanic harmony and Gallic wit and piquance. They are singable, rhythmic, offer pageantry and endure despite Wagner's abjuration of them.

Operatic

C Le Prophète (1849)

$ Renata Scotto, soprano; Marilyn Horne, mezzo-soprano; Jerome Hines, bass-baritone; Ambrosian Opera Chorus; Royal Philharmonic Orchestra; Henry Lewis, conductor; Columbia M4-34340 (4 discs).

MILHAUD, DARIUS
1892-1974

Milhaud was born in Aix-en-Provence to a wealthy and long established Franco-Jewish family. He exhibited an interest and talnt for music at age 3, but because of his high-strung and delicate nature, he did not receive regular music lessons until he was 11, at which time he studied the violin. Milhaud began his education at the Conservatoire de Paris in 1909. World War I interrupted his studies and he was not able to compete for the Prix de Rome (the winning of which has often proven to be a passport to fame). Instead, in 1917, at the urging of his classmate and friend, Paul Claudel, who had been appointed French Minister to Brazil, Milhaud journeyed to that country as secretary to Claudel. The general ambience of Brazil, and, naturally, the musical one specifically, made a deep impression on Milhaud, as evidenced by his Saudades do Brasil of 1920-1921--this, even though he was in the country for less than 2 years. Returning to Paris, Milhaud became a member of a group of artists including Satie, Honegger, Poulenc and Cocteau, and was numbered as one of the "ensemble" of composers labelled "Les Six." After his marriage to his cousin Madeleine, Milhaud travelled extensively, and in his travels assimilated many of the national musical characteristics of the countries he visited. In addition to the South American rhythms and melodic turns, he made use of jazz, polytonality (found in Indian and North African music) and the syncopations peculiar to different speech patterns. He experimented with a host of techniques, including polyrhythms, electronic instruments, Classical Greek declamation, etc. It is not surprising, therefore, to find a good deal of innovative color and activity in Milhaud's music. He left little of any great profundity, but his music has the ability to please through its humor, vitality and total lack of sentimentality.

Ballet

C Le Boeuf sur le toit ("The Nothing-Doing Bar") (1919)

$$ L'Orchestre du Théâtre des Champs-Elysées; Darius Milhaud, conductor; Charlin SLC-17. Includes Milhaud's La Création du Monde ("The Creation of the World") (1923), rated B.

B La Création du Monde ("The Creation of the World") (1923)--see entry for Le boeuf sur le toit ("The Nothing-Doing Bar") (1919), immediately supra.

Instrumental

C Saudades do Brasil (1920-1921)

* William Bolcom, piano; Nonesuch 71316.

MONTEVERDI, CLAUDIO
1567-1643

Very few facts are known about the early life of the great Italian composer Monteverdi. He was born in Cremona and his father, Baldassare, was a physician who turned his son's musical education over to Marc' Antonio Ingegneri (who was musicae prefectus of the Cremona cathedral at the time). Under Ingegneri, Monteverdi studied viol and organ performance and, as a chorister, young Claudio also learned vocal polyphony. It would appear that he was appointed to the household of Vincenzo (I) Gonzaga, Duke of Mantua, in 1590. With the Duke, he travelled to Hungary and Flanders. Monteverdi married one Claudia Cattaneo, a singer in the Duke's court, about 1595. She died in 1607, leaving Monteverdi with 2 very small sons. Also in 1607, Monteverdi completed L'Orfeo, probably the earliest opera still staged with any frequency. This work won its composer immediate acclaim and was followed by an outpouring of madrigals and other operas (some now lost). On the death of Vincenzo, Monteverdi was dismissed from the court and elected maestro di cappella at St. Mark's Cathedral in Venice, in 1613. In Venice he remained until his death. Monteverdi continued to be creative into the last year of his long life and, much like Verdi, gave the world masterpieces in his old age--his last work being the wonderful L' incoronazione di Poppea. It is difficult to overestimate the importance of Monteverdi with regards the development of music. After excelling in the art of the old polyphonic madrigal, in 1614 he turned away from that aspect of music and perfected the relatively new one of thorough-bass. It is Monteverdi who is usually considered the father of modern operatic composition. He was an iconoclast who, like Beethoven, enlarged the orchestra, made use of newly invented violin performance devices, and brought a new sense of the dramatic to opera--all this while crafting some of the most beautiful music ever to derive from a pen held by a human hand.

Operatic

A L'incoronazione di Poppea ("The Coronation of Poppea") (1642)

$ Cathy Berberian, soprano; Helen Donath, soprano; Elisabeth Söderström, soprano; Paul Esswood, counter-tenor; Vienna Concentus Musicus; Nikolaus Harnoncourt, conductor; Teldec 5635247 (5 discs).

B L'Orfeo (1607)

$ Cathy Berberian, soprano; Rotraud Hansmann, soprano; Eiko Katonosaka, soprano; Lajos Kozma, tenor; Nigel Rogers, tenor; Max van Egmond, bass; Jacques Villisech, bass; Capella Antiqua München; Vienna Concentus Musicus; Nikolaus Harnoncourt, conductor; Teldec 3635020 (3 discs).

B Il Ritorno d'Ulisse in patria ("Ulysses' Return to His Homeland") (1641)

$ Margaret Baker-Genovesi, soprano; Rotraud Hansmann, soprano; Paul Esswood, counter-tenor; Ladislaus Anderko, tenor; Sven-Olof Eliasson, tenor; Kurt Equiluz, tenor; Max van Egmond, bass; Vienna Concentus Musicus; Nikolaus Harnoncourt, conductor; Teldec 4635024 (4 discs).

Vocal

B Vespero della Beata Virgine ("Vespers of the Blessed Virgin") (1610)

$ Rotraud Hansmann, soprano; Irmgard Jacobeit, soprano; Nigel Rogers, tenor; Bert van t'Hoff, tenor; Max van Egmond, baritone, Jacques Villisech, bass; Monteverdi Chorus, Hamburg; Capella Antiqua, Munich; Vienna Concentus Musicus; Nikolaus Harnoncourt, conductor; Teldec 2635045 (2 discs).

MOURET, JEAN—JOSEPH
1682-1738

Mouret was a French composer who served in the court of the Duchess of Maine in Paris and composed ballets and operas, the majority of which are forgotten. The Fanfare listed below is familiar as the theme of

138

"Masterpiece Theater" and, despite its relative brilliance, has become somewhat of a bore through too great a familiarity.

Orchestral

A Fanfares for Violins, Oboe, Bassoons, Trumpets and Percussion (1729)

* Jean-François Paillard Chamber Orchestra; Jean-François Paillard, conductor; Musical Heritage Society 1624F. Includes Lully's Suite of Symphonies; Suite française in g, by an anonymous student of Lully and Lully's Suite of Symphonies from "D'Amadis."

MOZART, WOLFGANG AMADEUS
1756-1791

Christened Johannes Chrysostomus Wolfgangus Theophilius Mozart, and born in Salzburg, on January 27, 1756, Mozart is, in the opinion of the majority of music historians and musicologists, the greatest composer of the western world. His father, Leopold, was a well-established and esteemed musician in the court of Hieronymus von Colloredo, Archbishop of Salzburg. Leopold's book, Versuch einer gründlichen Violinschule ("Attempt to Elucidate the Basis for a Violin Method") was long in print in many languages and was one of the best known and accepted texts of violin pedagogy. Musical talent showed itself early in Leopold's son. Wolfgang (who, with the help of his father, rang changes on his name, most particularly the "Theophilius" <"Beloved of God">, which was tried as "Gottlieb" <"Beloved of God"> and finally settled on Amadeus ("Beloved of God">) was an eager 3-year-old audience during the music lessons given his elder sister Maria Anna. As children, she was known as "Nannerl" and he as "Wolferl." The always observant Leopold immediately began his son's musical education, first on the harpsichord, later on the violin. Mozart's incredible aptitude showed itself in his 4th year, by which time, besides playing pieces of increasing difficulty written for him by his father, he began composing pieces of his own, which Leopold wrote down for him. By the time he was 5, Wolferl could distinguish, and remember, differences in pitch as slight as an eighth of a tone. It could not be said of him, as Fermat said of one de Mere: "Il a très bon esprit, mais il n'est pas géométre: c'est comme vous savez, un grand défaut," since Mozart was also interested by, and capable in, mathematics. The enterprising Leopold took his children (Nannerl was also a prodigy) on their first performance excursion to Munich in 1762 (Nannerl was 11, Wolferl, 5) to play for the Bavarian Elector. Later the same year the entire family journeyed to Vienna and the children performed for the Emperor Franz and Empress Maria Theresa (and, incidentally, the visiting 7-year-old Marie Antoinette). The Emperor pronounced Wolfgang a kleiner Hexenmeister ("little sorcerer") and Wolfgang (who had asked that the court composer, Wagenseil, act as his page-turner since, as Wolfgang stated, "I am playing a concerto of yours so you must turn over for me") ended up in Maria Theresa's lap and, with the ingenuousness of childhood, bestowed a kiss on her. A number of tours were made by the children and Leopold, to Paris, London, Antwerp, etc., and everywhere Wolfgang triumphed. Not the least of the child's talents was the ability to extemporize faultlessly on any theme set before him. To some superstitious audiences Wolfgang was thought to be possessed of divine powers, to others, diabolical ones. During the tours and during the respites, Wolfgang composed. His first symphony dates from 1764, his first opera from 1767. In 1770, in a private audience with Pope Clement XIV, the papal Order of the Golden Spur was conferred upon Wolfgang, after which he was "Signor Cavaliere Amadeo"--a title he wore lightly. After a series of tests at the Accademia Filarmonica in Bologna, he was admitted to that rarefied circle with the title of compositore (he was only 14), the following year he became maestro di cappella. Perforce his travels, Mozart became a true polyglot which faculty, combined with his natural playfulness and wit, made for charming conversation and correspondence (he signs a letter to his sister, written in Rome on April 25, 1770, as: "Wolfgango in germania e amadeo Mozartt <sic> in italia"). December 26, 1770 saw the first performance of Mitridate, rè di Ponto in Milan. It was an immediate success. Mozart's teen-age years were extraordinarily fruitful and he went from success to success. Yet, although his powers had matured beyond his older contemporaries, by the time he was 22, he found it virtually impossible to obtain an appointment of any consequence. While on a visit to Paris with his mother, Anna, in 1778, Anna fell ill and died. Indicative of Mozart's sensitivity, he first wrote Leopold that Anna was merely ill, and was able, over a time, to soften the shock of her death for his father. During his return to Salzburg, Wolfgang stopped in Munich to spend time with friends, the von Webers. He had fallen in love with one of the daughters, Aloysia, but she, having gotten him to write arias for her use (she was to become a famous singer), ultimately showed no further interest in him. On returning to Salzburg he was given the position of Konzertmeister and organist to the court and cathedral, this through the good offices of Leopold. Because of the Archbishop's jealousy, Mozart's petitions to travel (with an eye to bettering his station) were refused. Finally, while enjoying the reception given his opera Idomeneo, whose premiere in Munich (1781) he was overseeing, the Archbishop summarily summoned Mozart to join him in Vienna. Here he was forced to live and dine with the Archbishop's menials. Neither was Wolfgang allowed to give solo performances anywhere but in the Archbishop's residence, nor to give any concerts. In answer to the entreaties of the nobility, Archbishop Colloredo allowed Mozart to attend, and take part in, the concert of the Tonkünstler-Societät. This was his last concert while in the employ of the vain and detested (not only by Mozart, but also the nobility generally) Archbishop. Wolfgang had tendered his resignation and, as an answer, quite literally got the boot from the Archbishop's high-steward. Mozart returned to Vienna and ostensibly fell in love with Aloysia von Weber's younger sister, Constanze. Most likely Constanze was a substitute for Aloysia (and a rather poor one at that: she was an inept housekeeper, scatterbrained, rather intemperate, and given to hypochondria). I say ostensibly since he continued to correspond with and, on occasion, see Aloysia. In Vienna Mozart eked out a living primarily through composing and teaching. For recreation he played billiards (at which he was supposedly expert) and, according to Constanze, dancing. Towards the end of his brief life Mozart, who had been brought up to be a pious Catholic, turned to freemasonry (which is thoroughly reflected in his penultimate opera, Die Zauberflöte). During his last few days of life, Mozart, although moribund, continued to work on his Requiem, with which he was occupied until his last hours--seeming to realize that the work was for himself. The work was dictated to his friend and student, Süssmayer, not to Salieri, as the movie Amadeus would have it. The official cause of death was typhus (more likely, it was renal failure); but overwork, lack of money (Constanze's health, also precarious at that time, occasioned large medical bills), and frustration were all probably culpable. With regards Constanze's "precarious health:" she died in 1842, aged 79, outliving her husband by 51 years (and Beethoven by 15); "precarious" indeed. Mozart was first buried in a regular, "proper" grave, but the "cash flow" problems he had had in life continued after his death. Because the costs of his funeral were not paid in time, his remains were removed to an unmarked pauper's grave. Only recently, however, has there been news that his grave may have been rediscovered. The notion of Mozart's having been poisoned by his rival Salieri was given some credibility since Mozart, during his last days, indicated that he felt so ill that he believed he was being poisoned. Salieri didn't help himself by commenting, after Mozart's death, that "It is indeed a pity to lose so great a genius, but his death is a good thing for us. If he had lived longer, not a soul would have given us a bit of bread for our compositions." Salieri vehemently denied the accusations and his friend, Kapellmeister Schwanenberg, when told of the conjecture, replied, "Fools, what has he done to deserve so great an honor?" However, Pushkin's poem, Mozart and Salieri (later set as an opera by Rimsky-Korsakov), did little to improve Salieri's standing in the eye of history. And to those who believe Mozart to have been the consummate boor and social maladroit depicted in both the play and movie titled Amadeus, that is about as likely as the assumption that Chekov's plays are actually light farces. Rather than expound on Mozart's music, I defer to the graceful words of Paul Henry Lang, "...everything that seems childlike and simple in Mozart's music is in reality an infinitely intense and complicated cosmos....We must not forget that Mozart was the child of an era customarily called the 'golden age' ... <and> the child of the golden age need not experiment, he need not demolish the form material he is offered in order to build a new edifice out of the ruins. He simply takes the gifts of his epoch, intact, and, as a self-evident matter, utilizes them at will....Mozart grasped the form material of his epoch ... with the liberty of the artist of the golden age. He shuffled them like a pack of cards and the result was a strikingly original and individual world." The catalog of Mozart's works (the one usually used and originally compiled by Köchel, hence the "K" numbers) contains over 620 entries—all by a man who never saw his 36th birthday.

Chamber

B Divertimento No.15 for 2 Horns and Strings, in B flat, K.287
* Collegium Aureum; Quintessence 7195, ⑧ 7195.

C Ein musikalischer Spass ("A Musical Joke"), K.522

$ Gerd Seifert, horn; Helmut Klier, horn; Amadeus Quartet; DG 2531253, ▤ 3301253. Includes Mozart's Serenade ("Eine kleine Nachtmusik") for Strings, in G, K.525, rated A.

B Quartets for Flute and Strings (4), Nos.1-4: in D, K.285; in G, K.285a; in C, K.285b and K.298, in C
    $ Jean-Pierre Rampal, flute; Isaac Stern, violin; Alexander Schneider, violin; Leonard Rose, 'cello; Columbia MP-39758, ▤ MP-39758.

A Quartet for Oboe and Strings, in F, K.370
    $ Ray Still, oboe; Itzhak Perlman, violin; Pinchas Zukerman, viola; Lynn Harrell, 'cello; Angel S-37756, ▤ S-37756. Includes Johann Christian Bach's Quartet for Oboe and Strings, in B flat; Carl Stamitz's Quartet for Oboe and Strings, Op.8 No.4, in E flat and Vanhal's Quartet for Oboe and Strings, Op.7 No.1, in F.
    Also--see entries for Quintet for Horn and Strings, in E flat, K.407 and Quintet for Clarinet and Strings, in A, K.581, both _infra_.

B Quartet for Piano and Strings, in E flat, K.493
    $ Artur Rubinstein, piano; Guarneri Quartet; RCA ARL1-2676, ▤ ARK1-2676. Includes Mozart's Quartet for Piano and Strings, in g, K.478, also rated B.

B Quartet for Piano and Strings, in g, K.478--see entry for Quartet for Piano and Strings, in E flat, K.493, immediately _supra_.

A Quintet for Clarinet and Strings, in A, K.581
    $ Gervase De Peyer, clarinet; Amadeus Quartet; DG 2530720. Includes Mozart's Quartet for Oboe and Strings, in F, K.370, also rated A. The oboe soloist in the K.370 is Lothar Koch.

C Quintet for Horn and Strings, in E flat, K.407
    $ Hermann Baumann, horn; Esterházy Quartet; Teldec 642173, ▤ 442173. Includes Mozart's Quartet for Oboe and Strings, in F, K.370 with Michel Piquet, oboe, rated A.

B Serenade No.6 ("Serenata Notturna"), in D, K.239

$$ Academy of Ancient Music; Christopher Hogwood, conductor; L'Oiseau Lyre 411720-1, ☒ 411720-4. Includes the same composer's Notturno for 4 Orchestras, K.269a and Serenade ("Eine kleine Nachtmusik") for Strings, in G, K.525, rated A.

B Serenade No.9 ("Posthorn"), in D, K.320
* Collegium Aureum; Quintessence 7118, ☒ 7118.

A Serenade No.10 for 13 Winds, in B flat, K.361
$ Marlboro Festival Ensemble; Marcel Moyse, conductor; Marlboro 11.
$ Collegium Aureum; Pro Arte PAD-137, ☒ PAD-137.

A Serenade ("Eine kleine Nachtmusik") for Strings, in G, K.525
* Collegium Aureum; Quintessence 7087, ☒ 7087. Includes Mozart's Divertimento No.7 for Bassoon, 2 Horns and Strings, in D, K.205.
* Columbia Symphony Orchestra; Bruno Walter, conductor; Columbia MY-37774, ☒ MY-37774. Includes Mozart's Masonic Funeral Music, K.477 and Overtures to Der Schauspieldirektor ("The Impressario"), K.486; Così fan tutte ("Thus Are All Women"), K.588; Le nozze di Figaro ("The Marriage of Figaro"), K.492 and Die Zauberflöte ("The Magic Flute"), K.620, all Overtures also rated A.
Also--see entries for Ein musikalischer Spass ("A Musical Joke"), K.522 and Serenade No.6 ("Serenata Notturna"), in D, K.239, both supra.

A String Quartets No.14-19 ("Haydn") (6), Nos.14-19: K.387, in G, K.387; in d, K.421; in E, K.428; in B flat ("The Hunt"), K.458; in A, K.464 and in C ("The Dissonant"), K.465
$ Juilliard Quartet; Columbia M3-37856 (3 discs), ☒ M3-37856.

B String Quartet No.20, in D, K.499
$ Guarneri Quartet; RCA ARL1-4687, ☒ ARL1-4687. Includes the same composer's String Quartet No.21, in D, K.575, rated A.

A String Quartet No.21, in D, K.575--see entry for String Quartet No.20, in D, K.499, immediately supra.

A String Quartet No.22, in B flat, K.589

$ Berg Quartet; Teldec 642042, ♮ 442042. Includes Mozart's String Quartet No.23, in F, K.590, rated C.

C String Quartet No.23, in F, K.590—see entry for String Quartet No.22, in B flat, K.589, immediately supra.

C String Quintet, in C, K.515

* William Primrose, viola; Griller Quartet; Vanguard HM-29. Includes Mozart's String Quintet, in g, K.516, rated B.

B String Quintet, in g, K.516—see entry for String Quintet, in C, K.515, immediately supra.

B Trios for Piano, Violin and Cello (7), Nos.1-7: in B flat, K.254; in d, K.442; in G, K.496; in B flat, K.502; in E, K.542; in C, K.548 and in G, K.564

* Beaux Arts Trio; Philips Festivo ♮ 7650017 (3 discs).

Choral

B Ave, verum corpus, K.618—see entries for Missa brevis, in C, K.259, infra and Exsultate jubilate (Motet for Soprano and Orchestra), K.165 under Vocal, infra.

B Mass ("Coronation), in C, K.317

$ Edda Moser, soprano; Julia Hamari, contralto; Nicolai Gedda, tenor; Dietrich Fischer-Dieskau, baritone; Bavarian Radio Symphony Orchestra; Eugen Jochum, conductor; Angel S-37283. Includes Mozart's Vesperae solemnes de confessore, in C, K.339, rated C.

B Mass ("The Great"), in c, K.427

* Ileana Cotrubas, soprano; Dame Kiri Te Kanawa, soprano; Werner Krenn, tenor; Hans Sotin, bass; John Alldis Choir; New Philharmonia Orchestra; Raymond Leppard, conductor; Angel AM-34710, ♮ AM-34710.

C Missa brevis, in C, K.259

$ Vienna Cathedral Chorus and Orchestra; Ferdinand Grossman, conductor; Philips Festivo 6570079. Includes Mozart's Ave, verum corpus, K.618, rated B and Missa brevis ("Spatzenmesse"), in C, K.220.

A Requiem, K.626
$ Helen Donath, soprano; Christa Ludwig, mezzo-soprano; Robert Tear, tenor; John Shirley-Quirk, baritone; Robert Lloyd, bass; Philharmonia Chorus and Orchestra; Carlo Maria Giulini, conductor; Angel SZ-37600.

C Vesperae solemnes de confessore, in C, K.339--see entries for Mass ("Coronation"), in C, K.317, supra and Exsultate jubilate (Motet for Soprano and Orchestra), K.165 under Vocal, infra.

Concerted
C Andante for Flute and Orchestra, in C, K.315
$ Julius Baker, flute; I Solisti di Zagreb; Antonio Janigro, conductor; Vanguard 71153. Includes Mozart's Concerti for Flute (2), Nos.1-2: in G, K.313 and in D, K.314, rated B.

B Concerto for Bassoon, in B flat, K.191
$ Milan Turkovic, bassoon; Salzburg Mozarteum Camerata Academica; Leopold Hager, conductor; Teldec 642361. Includes the same composer's Concerto for Oboe, in C, K.314 (with Jürg Schaftlein, oboe), rated B.

A Concerto for Clarinet, in A, K.622
* Jack Brymer, clarinet; Academy of St. Martin-in-the-Fields; Sir Neville Marriner, conductor; Philips ▉ 7300301. Includes Mozart's Concerto for Flute and Harp, in C, K.299 (with Claude Monteux, flute and Ossian Ellis, harp), rated B.
$ Robert Marcellus, clarinet; Cleveland Orchestra; George Szell, conductor; Columbia CBS MY-37810, ▉ MY-37810. Includes Mozart's Sinfonia Concertante for Violin, Viola and Orchestra, in E flat, K.364 with Rafael Druian, violin and Abraham Skernick, viola, also rated A.

B Concerti for Flute (2), Nos.1-2: in G, K.313 and in D, K.314--see entry for Andante for Flute and Orchestra, in C, K.315, supra.

146

B Concerto for Flute and Harp, in C, K.299

$ Jean-Pierre Rampal, flute; Marielle Nordmann, harp; English Chamber Orchestra; Jean-Pierre Rampal, conductor; Columbia CBS M-35875, ⬥ MT-35875. Includes Mozart's Concerto for Oboe, in C, K.314 with Pierre Pierlot, oboe, rated B and Rondo for Flute and Orchestra, in D, K.Anh.184, also rated B.

Also--see entries for Concerto for Clarinet, in A, K.622, supra and Fantasia for Organ, in f, K.608, infra.

A Concerti for Horn (4), Nos.1-4: in D, K.412; in E flat, K.417; in E flat, K.447 and in E flat, K.495

$ Hermann Baumann, natural horn; Vienna Concentus Musicus; Nikolaus Harnoncourt, conductor; Teldec 641272, ⬥ 641272.

* Barry Tuckwell, horn; London Symphony Orchestra; Peter Maag, conductor; London 41015, ⬥ 41015.

B Concerto for Oboe, in C, K.314--see entries for Concerto for Bassoon, in B flat, K.191, supra and under Haydn, Concerted, Concerto for Oboe, in C, H.VIIgC1 (Attributed), supra.

B Concerto for Piano No.9, in E flat, K.271

* Alfred Brendel, piano; I Solisti de Zagreb; Antonio Janigro, conductor; Vanguard HM-30. Includes Mozart's Concerto for Piano No.14, in E flat, K.449, rated C.

Also--see entry under Haydn, Concerted, Concerto for Harpsichord, in D, H.XVIII No.11, supra.

C Concerto for Piano No.12, in A, K.414

$ Vladimir Ashkenazy, piano; Philharmonia Orchestra; Vladimir Ashkenazy, conductor; London LDR-71056, ⬥ LDR-71056. Includes Mozart's Concerto for Piano No.13, in C, K.378B.

C Concerto for Piano No.14, in E flat, K.449--see entry for Concerto No.9, in E flat, K.271, supra.

B Concerto for Piano No.17, in G, K.453

$ Vladimir Ashkenazy, piano; Philharmonia Orchestra; Vladimir Ashkenazy, conductor; London 7104, 🎵 5-7104. Includes Mozart's Concerto for Piano No.21 (Known as the "Elvira Madigan" Concerto), in C, K.467, rated A.

A Concerto for Piano No.19, in F, K.459

$ Maurizio Pollini, piano; Vienna Philharmonic Orchestra; Karl Böhm, conductor; DG 2530716. Includes Mozart's Concerto for Piano No.23, in A, K.488, also rated A.

A Concerto for Piano No.20, in d, K.466

$ Friedrich Gulda, piano; Vienna Philharmonic Orchestra; Claudio Abbado, conductor; DG 415842-1 GGA, 🎵 415842-4 GGA. Includes Mozart's Concerto for Piano No.21 (Known as the "Elvira Madigan" Concerto), in C, K.467, also rated A.

A Concerto for Piano No.21 (Known as the "Elvira Madigan" Concerto), in C, K.467

$ Alfred Brendel, piano; Academy of St. Martin-in-the-Fields; Sir Neville Marriner, conductor; Philips 6514148, 🎵 7337148. Includes Mozart's Concerto for Piano No.15, in B flat, K.450.

$ Friedrich Gulda, piano; Vienna Philharmonic Orchestra; Claudio Abbado, conductor; DG 2543508, 🎵 3343508. Includes Mozart's Concerto No.27 for Piano and Orchestra, in B flat, K.595, also rated B.

Also--see entries for Concerto for Piano No.17, in G, K.453, supra; Concerto for Piano No.20, in d, K.466, immediately supra and Concerto for Piano No.24, in c, K.491, infra.

C Concerto for Piano No.22, in E flat, K.482

$ Alfred Brendel, piano; Academy of St. Martin-in-the-Fields; Sir Neville Marriner, conductor; Philips 9500145, 🎵 7300521. Includes the same composer's Rondos for Piano and Orchestra, in D, K.382, rated B and in A, K.386.

A Concerto for Piano No.23, in A, K.488--see entries for Concerto for Piano No.19, in F, K.459, supra and Concerto for Piano No.26 ("Coronation"),in D, K.537, infra.

B Concerto for Piano No.24, in c, K.491

$ Robert Casadesus, piano; Cleveland Orchestra; George Szell, conductor; Columbia MY-38523, ❚ MY-38523. Includes Mozart's Concerto for Piano No.21, in C, K.467, rated A.

B Concerto for Piano No.25, in C, K.503

$ Vladimir Ashkenazy, piano; Philharmonia Orchestra; Vladimir Ashkenazy, conductor; London 411810-1 LH, ❚ 411810-4 LH. Includes Mozart's Concerto for Piano No.26, ("Coronation"), in D, K.537, rated B.

* Alfred Brendel, piano; Vienna Pro Musica Orchestra; Paul Angerer, conductor; Turnabout 34129. Includes Mozart's Concerto for Piano No.27, in B flat, K.595, also rated B.

B Concerto for Piano No.26 ("Coronation"),in D, K.537

$ Friedrich Gulda, piano; Amsterdam Concertgebouw Orchestra; Nikolaus Harnoncourt, conductor; Teldec 42970. Includes Mozart's Concerto for Piano No.23, in A, K.488.

Also—see entry for Concerto for Piano No.25, in C, K.503, immediately supra.

B Concerto for Piano No.27, in B flat, K.595—see entries for Concerto for Piano No.21 (Known as the "Elvira Madigan" Concerto), in C, K.467 and Concerto for Piano No.25, in C, K.503, both supra.

B Concerto for 2 Pianos, in E flat, K.365

$ Alfred Brendel, piano; Imogen Cooper, piano; Academy of St. Martin-in-the-Fields; Sir Neville Marriner, conductor; Philips 416364-1 PH, ❚ 416364-4 PH. Includes Mozart's Concerto for 3 Pianos, in F, K.242 (with Fou Ts'ong, piano), rated C.

C Concerto for 3 Pianos, in F, K.242—see entry for Concerto for 2 Pianos, in E flat, K.365, immediately supra.

C Concerto for Violin No.3, in G, K.216

* David Oistrakh, violin; Berlin Philharmonic Orchestra; David Oistrakh, conductor; Angel AM-34709, 🎵 AM-34709.   Includes Mozart's Concerto for Violin No.4, in D, K.218, rated A.

A Concerto for Violin No.4, in D, K.218

\$ Jascha Heifetz, violin; New Symphony Orchestra, London; Sir Malcolm Sargent, conductor; RCA AGL1-5250, 🎵 AGL1-5250.   Includes the same composer's Concerto for Violin No.5 ("Turkish"), in A, K.219, rated A.   In the K.219, the accompanying ensemble is unnamed, and the conductor is Heifetz.

Also--see entries under Bruch, Concerted, Concerto for Violin, Op.26, in g, supra and Concerto for Violin No.3, in G, K.216, immediately supra.

A Concerto for Violin No.5 ("Turkish"), in A, K.219

* David Oistrakh, violin; Berlin Philharmonic Orchestra; David Oistrakh, conductor; Angel AM-34737, 🎵 AM-34737.   Includes Mozart's Sinfonia Concertante for Violin, Viola and Orchestra, in E flat, K.364, also rated A.   The soloists in the K.364 are Igor Oistrakh, violin and David Oistrakh, viola.

Also--see entry for Concerto for Violin No.4, in D, K.218, immediately supra.

B Rondo for Flute and Orchestra, in D, K.Anh.184--see entry for Concerto for Flute and Harp, in C, K.299, supra.

B Rondo for Piano and Orchestra, in D, K.382--see entry for Concerto for Piano No.22, in E flat, K.482, supra.

B Sinfonia Concertante for Oboe, Clarinet, Bassoon, Horn and Strings, in E flat, K.Anh.9 (297b)

* Orpheus Chamber Orchestra; Nonesuch 79009, 🎵 79009.   Includes Mozart's Idomeneo, rè di Creta ("Idomeneo, King of Crete"), K.366 (Ballet Music), rated A.

A Sinfonia Concertante for Violin, Viola and Orchestra, in E flat, K.364

* Josef Suk, violin; Milan Skampa, viola; Czech Philharmonic Orchestra; Kurt Redel, conductor; Quintessence 7106, ♭ 7106.

Also--see entries for Concerto for Clarinet, in A, K.622 and Concerto for Violin No.5 ("Turkish"), in A, K.219, both supra.

Instrumental

C Fantasia, in c, K.396

* Alfred Brendel, piano; Vanguard C-10043. Includes the same composer's Rondo, in a, K.511, rated B; Sonata No.8, in a, K.310 and Variations (on a Minuet by DuPort), K.573.

A Fantasia for Organ, in f, K.608

* Helmut Rilling, organ; Turnabout 34087. Includes Mozart's Adagio, in C, K.617a and Concerto for Flute and Harp, in C, K.299, rated B.

B Rondo, in a, K.511--see entry for Fantasia, in c, K.396, supra.

B Sonata No.11, in A, K.331

$ Alfred Brendel, piano; Philips 9500025, ♭ 7300474. Includes Mozart's Adagio, K.540, in b and Sonata No.13, K.333, in B flat, rated C.

C Sonata No.13, in B flat, K.333--see entry for Sonata No.11, in A, K.331, immediately supra.

C Sonata No.15, in C, K.545

$ Alicia De Larrocha, piano; London 7085, ♭ 7085. Includes Mozart's Sonatas Nos.12, in F, K.332 and 17, in D, K.576, also rated C.

C Sonata No.17, in D, K.576--see entry for Sonata No.15, in C, K.545, immediately supra.

Operatic

B La clemenza di Tito ("The Clemency of Titus"), K.621

$ Lucia Popp, soprano; Dame Janet Baker, mezzo-soprano; Yvonne Minton, mezzo-soprano; Frederica Von Stade, mezzo-soprano; Stuart Burrows, tenor; Robert Lloyd, bass; Vienna State Opera Chorus and Orchestra; Sir Colin Davis, conductor; Philips 6703079 (3 discs), ♭7699038.

A <u>Così fan tutte</u> ("Thus Are All Women"), K.588

$ Elisabeth Schwarzkopf, soprano; Hanny Steffek, soprano; Christa Ludwig, mezzo-soprano; Alfredo Kraus, tenor; Giuseppe Taddei, baritone; Walter Berry, baritone; Philharmonia Chorus and Orchestra; Karl Böhm, conductor; Angel S-3631 (4 discs).

A <u>Don Giovanni,</u> K.527

$ Elisabeth Schwarzkopf, soprano; Dame Joan Sutherland, soprano; Luigi Alva, tenor; Giuseppe Taddei, baritone; Eberhard Wächter, baritone; Gottlob Frick, bass; Philharmonia Chorus and Orchestra; Carlo Maria Giulini, conductor; Angel S-3605 (3 discs), ▣ 4X3X-3605.

A <u>Die</u> <u>Entführung</u> <u>aus</u> <u>dem</u> <u>Serail</u> ("The Abduction from the Seraglio"), K.384

$ Arleen Augér, soprano; Reri Grist, soprano; Peter Schreier, tenor; Kurt Moll, bass; Dresden State Chorus and Orchestra; Karl Böhm, conductor; DG 2709051 (3 discs), ▣ 2709051. Includes Mozart's <u>Der Schauspieldirektor</u> ("The Impressario"), K.486, rated C.

B <u>Idomeneo, rè di Creta</u> ("Idomeneo, King of Crete"), K.366

* Edda Moser, soprano; Anneliese Rothenberger, soprano; Eberhard Büchner, tenor; Nicolai Gedda, tenor; Theo Adam, bass; Dresden State Opera Chorus and Orchestra; Hans Schmidt-Isserstedt, conductor; Arabesque 8054 (4 discs), ▣ 9054.

A <u>Le nozze di Figaro</u> ("The Marriage of Figaro"), K.492

$ Gundula Janowitz, soprano; Edith Mathis, soprano; Tatiana Troyanos, mezzo-soprano; Dietrich Fischer-Dieskau, baritone; Hermann Prey, baritone; German Opera Chorus and Orchestra; Karl Böhm, conductor; DG 2711007 (4 discs), ▣ 3371005.

C <u>Der Schauspieldirektor</u> ("The Impressario"), K.486--see entry for <u>Die</u> <u>Entführung</u> <u>aus</u> <u>dem</u> <u>Serail</u> ("The Abduction from the Seraglio"), K.384, <u>supra</u>.

A <u>Die Zauberflöte</u> ("The Magic Flute"), K.620

$ Gundula Janowitz, soprano; Christa Ludwig, mezzo-soprano; Nicolai Gedda, tenor; Walter Berry, baritone; Gottlob Frick, bass; Philharmonia Chorus and Orchestra; Otto Klemperer, conductor; Angel S-3651 (3 discs).

Orchestral

A Overtures: Così fan tutte ("Thus Are All Women"), K.588; Don Giovanni, K.527; Die Zauberflöte ("The Magic Flute"), K.620; Die Entführung aus dem Serail ("The Abduction from the Seraglio"), K.384; Idomeneo, rè di Creta ("Idomeneo, King of Crete"), K.366; La clemenza di Tito ("The Clemency of Titus"), K.621; Le Nozze di Figaro ("The Marriage of Figaro"), K.492; Der Schauspieldirektor ("The Impressario"), K.486 and Lucio Silla, K.135.

$$ Academy of St. Martin-in-the-Fields; Sir Neville Marriner, conductor; Angel DS-37879, 🎵 DS-37879.

Also--for Overtures to: Der Schauspieldirektor ("The Impressario"), K.486; Così fan tutte ("Thus Are All Women"), K.588; Le Nozze di Figaro ("The Marriage of Figaro"), K.492 and Die Zauberflöte ("The Magic Flute"), K.620, see entry for Serenade ("Eine kleine Nachtmusik") for Strings, K.525, in G under Chamber supra.

Also--for Overture to Idomeneo, rè di Creta ("Idomeneo, King of Crete"), K.366, see entry for Sinfonia Concertante for Oboe, Clarinet, Bassoon, Horn and Strings, in E flat, K.Anh.9 (297b) under Concerted, supra.

Symphonic

B Symphony No.25, in g, K.183

$$ Academy of Ancient Music; Christopher Hogwood, conductor; L'Oiseau Lyre 414472-1 OH, 🎵 414472-4 OH. Includes Mozart's Symphonies Nos.26-27, in E flat, K.184 and in G, K.199, both rated C.

$ Academy of St. Martin-in-the-Fields; Sir Neville Marriner, conductor; London 411717-1 LT; 🎵 411717-4 LT. Includes Mozart's Symphony No. 29, in A, K.201, rated A.

C Symphony No.26, in E flat, K.184--see entry for Symphony No.25, in g, K.183, immediately supra.

C Symphony No.27, in G, K.199--see entry for Symphony No.25, in g, K.183, supra.

B Symphony No.28, in C, K.200

$ Dresden State Orchestra; Sir Colin Davis, conductor; Philips 6514206, ♮ 7337206. Includes Mozart's Symphony No.41 ("Jupiter"), in C, K.551, rated A.

A Symphony No.29, in A, K.201--see entry for Symphony No.25, in g, K.183, supra.

B Symphony No.31 ("Paris"), in D, K.297

$ Amsterdam Concertgebouw Orchestra; Nikolaus Harnoncourt, conductor; Teldec 642817, ♮ 642817. Includes the same composer's Symphony No.33, in B flat, K.319, also rated B.

B Symphony No.32, in G, K.318

$ Berlin Philharmonic Orchestra; Herbert von Karajan, conductor; DG 2531136, ♮ 3301136. Includes Mozart's Symphonies Nos.35 ("Haffner"), in D, K.385 and 36 ("Linz"), in C, K.425, both rated A.

B Symphony No.33, in B flat, K.319--see entry for Symphony No.31 ("Paris"), in D, K.297, supra.

B Symphony No.34, in C, K.388

$ Amsterdam Concertgebouw Orchestra; Nikolaus Harnoncourt, conductor; Teldec 642703, ♮ 442703. Includes Mozart's Symphony No.35 ("Haffner"), in D, K.285, rated A.

A Symphony No.35 ("Haffner"), in D, K.385

$$ Academy of Ancient Music; Christopher Hogwood, conductor; L'Oiseau Lyre DSLO-602, ♮ DSLO-602. Includes Mozart's Symphony No.36 ("Linz"), in C, K.425, also rated A.

Also--see entries for Symphony No.32, in G, K.318, supra and Symphony No.36 ("Linz"), in C, K.425, immediately supra.

A Symphony No.36 ("Linz"), in C, K.425

* Hungarica Philharmonia; Peter Maag, conductor; Vox ♮ CT-2295. Includes Mozart's Symphony No.38 ("Prague"), in D, K.503, also rated A.

$ Columbia Symphony Orchestra; Bruno Walter, conductor; Columbia MY-38473, ♫ MY-38473. Includes Mozart's Symphony No.38 ("Prague"), in D, K.504, also rated A.

Also--see entry for Symphony No.32, in G, K.318, supra.

A Symphony No.38 ("Prague"), in D, K.504

$$ Academy of Ancient Music; Christopher Hogwood, conductor; L'Oiseau Lyre 410233-1 OH, ♫ 410233-4 OH. Includes Mozart's Symphony No.39, in E flat, K.543, also rated A.

Also--see entries for Symphony No.32, in G, K.318, supra and Symphony No.36 ("Linz"), in C, K.425, immediately supra.

A Symphony No.39, in E flat, K.543--see entry for Symphony No.38 ("Prague"), in D, K.504, immediately supra.

A Symphony No.40, in g, K.550

* Philharmonia Orchestra; Otto Klemperer, conductor; Angel AE-34405, ♫ AE-34405. Includes Mozart's Symphony No.41 ("Jupiter"), in C, K.551, also rated A.

$ Vienna Philharmonic Orchestra; Karl Böhm, conductor; DG 2530780, ♫ 3300780. Includes Mozart's Symphony No.41 ("Jupiter"), in C, K.551, also rated A.

A Symphony No.41 ("Jupiter"), in C, K.551--see entries for Symphony No.28, in C, K.200 supra and Symphony No.40,in g, K.550, immediately supra.

Vocal

A Exsultate jubilate (Motet for Soprano and Orchestra)), K.165

$ Dame Kiri Te Kanawa, soprano; London Symphony Orchestra; Sir Colin Davis, conductor; Philips 6500271. Includes Mozart's Ave, verum corpus, K.618, rated B, Kyrie, in d, K.368a and Vesperae solemnes de confessore, in C, K.339, rated C.

MUSSORGSKY, MODEST
1839-1881

Mussorgsky (full name: Modest Petrovich) is ordinarily considered to be among the very greatest of Russian composers yet his total output was small when compared to others such as Mozart, Beethoven or even Tchaikovsky (who was sufficiently unawed by Mussorgsky as to write that Mussorgsky's music was so slapdash as to be a "sad spectacle"). Mussorgsky was born to a middle-class landowner and was taught the elements of piano playing by his mother. The family intended that Modest should follow a military career and he dutifully entered the Cadet School of the Guards in St. Petersburg. While at the School he took classes in history and philosophy and was in the School Choir. He also composed some easily forgotten frivolities, which Mussorgsky père obligingly had published. Mussorgsky also attempted to set Victor Hugo's Han d'Islande as an opera: the work was never produced. After leaving the Cadet School, Mussorgsky enjoyed himself as a young officer and piano-playing-cum-composing dilettante. Having met Borodin, Dargomizhsky, Cui and Balakirev, and having suffered what was probably a nervous breakdown, Mussorgsky resigned his military commission in 1858 and studied in earnest with Balakirev. In 1863 the Mussorgsky family estate was lost and Modest took a "collegiate secretarial" civil service position with the Chief Engineering Department of the Ministry of Communications (in fact, the job was a clerical one). Typical of Mussorgsky's psychological difficulties, in 1866 he was promoted to the rank of titular councilor, and was dismissed from that position 4 months later. Being a spiritual progenitor of "flower children," Mussorgsky joined a commune and lived with 5 other aspiring aesthetes. In 1867, having repaired to his brother's house in Minkino, Mussorgsky finally began to create works of quality, some of which were published and, happily for their composer, recognized. In 1868 he began work on his chef-d'oeuvre: Boris Godounov, using Pushkin's play for the bulk of his libretto. The vocal score was completed in July 1869; he finished the entire score in December of the same year. The work was in 7 scenes and, in 1871, the work was rejected for performance by the executive opera committee of the Maryinsky Theater. It was about this time that Mussorgsky, in his frustration and despair, turned to serious bibulosity. Ultimately, it was his alcoholism that was the cause of his relatively early death (actually, it would appear that his drinking brought on a form of epilepsy, and it was the coupling of the two which abbreviated his life). He completed the second version in 1872 and it, too, was rejected. In 1873, Mussorgsky was reemployed by the government, and in 1874 he completed the "revised" second version of Boris, which was finally performed that year. For most of the remainder of his life, Mussorgsky drifted through a variety of governmental positions, none well-paying, and all the while he composed. He succumbed after suffering several days of numerous "fits" due to his "alcoholic epilepsy." Mussorgsky's work has a spiritual kinship with the literary jewels of Dostoevsky: both were fascinated with the human psyche, both plumbed the depths of the despair which could descend upon that evanescent entity, and both were concerned less with finesse and craftsmanship than with communication on an elemental level. Mussorgsky deeply despaired his lack of formal training, yet he was sufficiently self-possessed that that lack could not vanquish his need to create. There is a wonderful portrait of Mussorgsky by Repin: in it, Repin captures both the alcoholic and genius which were the composer.

Instrumental

A Pictures at an Exhibition for Piano (1874)

! Vladimir Horowitz, piano; RCA LSC-3278E. Includes the Ravel orchestration of the same work, performed by the NBC Symphony Orchestra, conducted by Arturo Toscanini.

Also--see orchestral versions of same entry under Orchestral, infra.

Operatic

A Boris Godounov (1874)

$ Galina Vishnevskaya, soprano; Aleksei Maslennikov, tenor; Ludovic Spiess, tenor; Nicolai Ghiaurov, bass; Martti Talvela, bass; Wiener Sängerknabenchor; Chorus of the Vienna State Opera; Bulgarian Radio (Sofia) Chorus; Vienna Philharmonic Orchestra; Herbert von Karajan, conductor; London 1439 (4 discs).

Orchestral

C Khovanshchina: Introduction and "Dance of the Persian Slaves" (1872-1880)--see entry under Glinka, Orchestral, Jota Aragonesa (Spanish Overture No.1) (1845), supra.

A Night on Bald Mountain (Orchestrated by Rimsky-Korsakov) (1860-1866)--see entries under Borodin, Orchestral, Prince Igor Overture and "Polovtsian Dances" (1890); Dukas, Orchestral, L'Apprenti sorcier

157

("The Sorcerer's Apprentice") (1897) and Glinka, Orchestral, Jota Aragonesa (Spanish Overture No.1) (1845), all supra, and Pictures at an Exhibition (Orchestrated by Ravel) (1874), immediately infra.

A Pictures at an Exhibition (Orchestrated by Ravel) (1874)

$$ Cleveland Orchestra; Lorin Maazel, conductor; Telarc DG-10042. Includes Mussorgsky's Night on Bald Mountain (Orchestrated by Rimsky-Korsakov) (1860-1866), also rated A.

Also--see solo piano (and additional orchestral versions) of same entry under Instrumental, supra and under Britten, Orchestral, Young Person's Guide to the Orchestra, Op.34, supra.

NIELSEN, CARL
1865-1931

Carl August Nielsen is generally accorded the position of premier composer of his native Denmark. Coming from a poor family, several family friends assisted in his being able to attend the Royal Conservatory in Copenhagen. There he became a student of the illustrious Niels Gade, considered the founder of the modern school of Scandinavian composition. Nielsen left the Conservatory after only 2 years and became a second violinist in the orchestra of the Theater Royal. In 1890 Nielsen obtained a state subsidy which enabled him to travel to Germany, France and Italy. In Paris he met the Danish sculptress, Anne Marie Broderson, who later became Mrs. Nielsen. Nielsen began work on his Symphony No.1 in 1892 and, during the same period, he came under the influence of such "moderns" as Brahms, Grieg and Liszt. Throughout most of the remainder of his career, Nielsen both conducted and composed (a wise combination, since he was able to program several of his own works). Nielsen is usually thought of as a symphonist and it is in that genre that he produced his finest works. Although his music is often felt to be "difficult," it is not all that inaccessible, and can prove very rewarding in its novel approach to tonality. Despite Nielsen's gift not being a lyrical one (say, like Grieg's), his music is possessed of melody and rather interesting use of folk idioms and harmonies.

Symphonic
C Symphony No.2 ("The Four Temperaments"), Op.16

* Tivoli Concert Symphony; Carl Garaguly, conductor; Turnabout
37049.

C Symphony No.3 ("Sinfonia espansiva"), Op.27
$ Royal Danish Orchestra; Leonard Bernstein, conductor; Columbia
MP–39071, 🄱 MP–39071.

B Symphony No.4 ("The Inextinguishable"), Op.29
$ Berlin Philharmonic Orchestra; Herbert von Karajan, conductor;
DG 2532029, 🄱 3302029.

C Symphony No.6 ("Sinfonia semplice") (1924–1925)
* Music for Westchester Symphony Orchestra; Siegfried Landau,
conductor; Turnabout 34182. Includes Sibelius' Humoresques for Violin (6),
Nos.1–6: Op.87b and Op.89, performed by Aaron Rosand, violin and the
Southwest German Radio Symphony Orchestra conducted by Tibor Szöke.

OFFENBACH, JACQUES
1819–1880

Offenbach's real name was Jakob Eberst and like many "French"
opera and operetta composers, was of German birth. His father was a
cantor of the synagogue at Cologne and, given the paternal interest in
music, young Jacques (as he styled himself, once established in France)
was sent to study at that Mecca of musicians, the Conservatoire de Paris,
this in 1833. He left after a year, having concentrated on 'cello
performance without distinction (and with a disinclination towards serious
study). In his youth he wrote several minor pieces for the 'cello. For a
time he was a 'cellist in the Opéra-Comique in Paris while, at the same
time, working assiduously to bring his name before the public by giving
concerts. He wrote a succession of moderately successful operettas and
also was the manager of a rather small theater on the Champs-Élysées.
In 1855 he produced his first noteworthy work: Le Papillon, which was a
ballet-pantomime. In 1861 he gave up management and became what is in
modern parlance a "producer." As an operetta composer, Offenbach wrote
something over 100 of the things. His music is essentially frivolous, but
does contain an effervescent and light melodic quality which is quite

engaging. It was Offenbach who suggested to Johann Strauss, Jr., that in order to increase his income, Strauss ought to turn to operetta. For this alone, the world owes him a debt of thanks, since Die Fledermaus was a product of that suggestion. I cannot resist recounting a sign I once saw on the door of a record shop in Beverly Hills, it read: "Closed for lunch. Bach in an hour, Offenbach sooner."

Ballet

A Gaîté Parisienne (Arranged by Manuel Rosenthal) (1938)

$ New York Philharmonic Orchestra; Leonard Bernstein, conductor; Columbia ▣ MT-31013. Includes Bizet's L'Arlésienne Suite No.1 (1872) (Incidental Music for a Play by Alphonse Daudet), also rated A.

$ Pittsburgh Symphony Orchestra; André Previn, conductor; Philips 6514367, ▣ 7337367.

Operatic

B Les Contes d'Hoffmann ("The Tales of Hoffmann") (Completed by Ernest Guiraud) (1881)

$ Dame Joan Sutherland, soprano; Huguette Tourangeau, mezzo-soprano; Hugues Cuénod, tenor; Placido Domingo, tenor; Gabriel Bacquier, baritone; Pro Arte Chorus, Lausanne; L'Orchestre de la Suisse Romande; Sir Richard Bonynge, conductor; London 13106 (3 discs), ▣ 5-13106.

C La Grande-Duchesse de Gérolstein (1867)

$ Régine Crespin, soprano; Mady Mesplé, soprano; Alain Vanzo, tenor; Robert Massard, baritone; Charles Burles, bass; Capitole de Toulouse Orchestre; Michel Plasson, conductor; Columbia M2-34576 (2 discs).

ORFF, CARL
1895-1982

Carl Orff, born in Munich, combined the 3 careers of composer, educator and musicologist. He studied at the Munich Academy of Music and, after a time spent in coaching and conducting, became a faculty member of the Munich Hochschule für Musik. In 1925 he cofounded, with Dorothee Günther, the Günther Schule. The basis for education at this rather novel school was laid by Jacques-Dalcroze in his system of "eurythmics." Orff was particularly interested in teaching children to play percussion instruments as a means of bringing them to musical self-expression. His own compositions are marked by a variety of vital rhythms, simple melodies, the use of monodic forms (countered by some dissonances), and the employment of antique verse. I am reminded of the somewhat dubious story of the conductor who was rehearsing the premiere of the Orff opera, Die Kluge, and had some difficulty understanding a particular passage. Said conductor could not understand why his orchestral and vocal colleagues laughed long and well when he said, in a discouraged fashion, "In order to do this properly, we'll have to get Orff."

Choral

B Carmina Burana (Scenic Cantata) (1935-1936)

* Lucia Popp, soprano; Gerhard Unger, tenor; John Noble, baritone; Raymond Wolansky, bass; New Philharmonia Chorus and Orchestra; Rafael Frühbeck de Burgos, conductor; Angel AE-34484, ☐ AE-34484.

PACHELBEL, JOHANN
1653-1706

Better known during his life as an organist than as a composer, Pachelbel was born in Nuremberg and had a fine musical education. Suffice it for us that his Kanon is one of the works most often requested on classical music stations today.

Orchestral

A Kanon—see entry under Albinoni, Orchestral, Adagio, in g, supra.

PAGANINI, NICCOLO
1782-1840

Paganini is one of the most fascinating and charismatic figures in the annals of western music. He was born in Genoa to a family of modest means. His father was a mandolin player who was able to teach young Niccolo the rudiments of violin playing (the strings of the two instruments are tuned exactly alike, and the left hand positions are similar). Paganini fils soon exhausted his father's meager abilities and progressed to studying with one Servetto, a local orchestral violinist. From Servetto, he "graduated" to Giacomo Costa, maestro di cappella of the San Lorenzo Cathedral. Paganini made his debut at the age of 9, performing a set of variations of his own composition on a patriotic French air, La Carmagnole. At Costa's urging Niccolo's father allowed the child to perform a solo in church each Sunday. Paganini later counted these experiences as important because of the rigors involved. Finally, as had happened with his father, Paganini progressed beyond Costa's ability to teach him and he was brought to study with Alessandro Rolla, then a renowned violinist, conductor and teacher. Ostensibly, on arriving in Parma to present themselves, the Paganinis, pére et fils, found Rolla ill and abed. While awaiting Rolla's decision to see them, Niccolo took up a fiddle which lay handily on a table in the waiting room, and began to play. According to the story, Rolla forgot his illness, asked that the "professor" be brought to him, and declared that, "'Tis a child." He then stated that he could teach Niccolo nothing and suggested that Paganini's father take the boy to study with Ferdinando Paer. Paer was then in Germany so Niccolo studied instead with Paer's master, Ghiretti. This Niccolo did for 6 months, and so concluded his formal musical education-- he was about 13. He began his concertizing while still not quite 14, and also began to compose seriously. Through the kindness of a French merchant he was loaned a Guarnerius instrument which, upon hearing Paganini perform, the owner refused to reclaim. Later, on a challenge from a painter named Pasini, he won a Stradivarius by performing a difficult concerto on first sight. Additionally, during this time Paganini was involved in countless amorous adventures, gambling and performing. From 1801 to 1804 Paganini, living with a "lady of rank" in Tuscany, discontinued performing. While in Tuscany he took up the guitar and became a virtuoso on that instrument also. When he did return to the concert stage his playing was possessed of such great technical facility, and so exquisitely refined (remembering that much of what he played was written by himself expressly to display his powers), that rumors abounded that only one in league with Satan could perform in such a manner. Foolishly, Paganini did not challenge these rumors but, rather, encouraged them. Ultimately he was forced to renounce them publicly in the press. Paganini died in Nice, age 57. Because of those old Satanic rumors, he was not administered the last rites and he was not interred in holy ground until 5 years after his death. As a performer, virtually no violinist was able to match him until

162

Jascha Heifetz, who could exhibit the same kind of technical phenomena: double and triple stops, left hand pizzicatti, clean, "whistling" harmonics--in single and double stops, etc. Paganini's compositions (all exclusively for, or featuring, the violin) remain mainstays of that instrument's literature and are much enjoyed despite their obvious lack of compositional mastery. They contain lovely melodies, show off the instrument as almost no other works can, and the public adores them.

Concerted

A Concerto for Violin No.1, Op.6, in D

* Ruggiero Ricci, violin; London Symphony Orchestra; Anthony Collins, conductor; Turnabout 34527E. Includes Paganini's Concerto for Violin No.2, Op.7, in d, rated B.

* Michael Rabin, violin; Philharmonia Orchestra; Sir Eugene Goossens, conductor; Seraphim ⊟ 4XG-60222. Includes Wienawski's Concerto for Violin No.2, Op.22, in d, rated B.

B Concerto for Violin No.2, Op.7, in b--see entry for Concerto for Violin No.1, Op.6, in D, immediately supra.

Instrumental

A Caprices (24), Nos.1-24, Op.1

\$ Itzhak Perlman, violin; Angel S-36860, ⊟ S-36860.

* Ruggiero Ricci, violin; Turnabout 34528.

PALESTRINA, GIOVANNI
c.1525-1594

Giovanni Pierluigi da Palestrina derived his surname from the Italian city of his birth (his true family name being Pierluigi). As is not uncommon with anyone (let alone composers) born well over 400 years ago, not too much is known regarding his formative period. He was probably a chorister in the cathedral of Sant' Agapit, in Palestrina. On the appointment of the Bishop of Palestrina to the post of Archbishop of the basilica of Santa Maria Maggiore in Rome in 1534, young Giovanni appears to have been taken along and became a student at the choir school there. From 1544 to 1551 Palestrina was the organist and maestro di canto at the cathedral of Palestrina. During that period he seems to have married Lucrezia Gori and became the father of two sons. When the composer was about 26, the former Bishop of Palestrina, Cardinal del Monte, was elevated to the papal throne, becoming Pope Julius III. Palestrina was sent for and he became the master of the Capella Juliana, that is, the choir responsible for the ceremonial music at St. Peter's Basilica. A year later Julius III died and was replaced by Pope Marcellus, whom Palestrina immortalized in his Missa Papae Marcelli. Pope Marcellus died about three years after his election. He was followed by Paul IV who dismissed from papal service all married choristers, including Palestrina. Following an illness about that time, Palestrina held a few musical posts in different churches, ultimately becoming interested in music somewhat more secular (and less given to religious rigor). This did not last long and, in 1570 he returned to St. Peter's. There was an attempt on the part of Santa Maria Maggiore (Rome) to lure him away, but the authorities at St. Peter's increased his salary and, in 1578, gave him the title of Master of Music at the Vatican Basilica. Due to the seemingly unending wars Italy underwent during that period, several epidemics swept Italy from about 1572 to 1580. To one, or more, of these Palestrina lost his two sons, two brothers and his wife. After his own illness in 1578, and the death of his wife in 1580, Palestrina decided to join the priesthood. Pope Gregory was sufficiently pleased with this decision that he conferred upon him a vacancy at the Cathedral of Ferrentina. Suddenly, however, in 1581, Palestrina, having made the acquaintance of a wealthy widow, Virginia Dormuli, married her secretly and, obviously, was forced to abandon the priesthood to which he had not quite ascended. The widow Dormuli's first husband had been a successful furrier and Palestrina carried on the business--the marriage is thought to have been one of the "financial" type, and both parties seemed happy with the arrangement. During the ten years he managed the fur business he wrote some of his best works. Afterwards, although Palestrina was never nominally the chief of the papal singers, he was considered to be the official composer to the choir. On his death, Palestrina's funeral brought out great numbers of people, and he was entombed in the Capella Nuova at the old St. Peter's. His coffin bears the inscription: Princeps Musicae. Palestrina is regarded as the greatest composer officially to have served the Catholic Church. He produced 93 masses, over 600 motets and a host of other types of vocal works. His music is marked by polish (brought about by careful revision), rhythmic subtlety, a combination of alternating homophony and polyphony (particularly in his later works), the use of plainsong melodies, and an inventiveness in the use of voices that is virtually orchestral.

Choral

B Missa brevis (1570)

$ St. John's College Choir, Cambridge; George Guest, conductor; Argo ZRG-690 PSI. Includes Palestrina's Missa Assumpta est Maria.

A Missa Papae Marcelli (1567)

$ Westminster Abbey Choir; Simon Preston, conductor; DG ARC-415517-1 AH, ♮ 415517-4 AH. Includes Palestrina's Missa Tu est Petrus; Allegri's Misere; Felice Anerio's Venite ad me omnes; Giovanelli's Jubilate and Giovanni Maria Nanino's Haec dies.

PENDERECKI, KRZYSZTOF
1933-

Penderecki (pronounced as "Pen-der-ét-ski," accent on the third syllable) is among the two (along with Witold Lutoslawski) foremost living ultra-modern Polish composers. His use of a variety of techniques for producing extraordinary sounds from ordinary orchestral instruments, and his attempts at creating his own notational system are but a couple of examples of his "newness." He first came to prominence in this country with his keening and effective work called Threnody for the Victims of Hiroshima for Strings. His later Passion According to St. Luke was hailed a masterpiece even though it makes incredible demands on both the performers and the audience.

Choral

C Passion According to St. Luke (1962-1965)

$ Steania Woytowicz, soprano; Andrezjej Hiolski, baritone; Bernard Ladysz, bass; Boys' Choir of Cracow; Cracow Philharmonic Chorus and Orchestra; Henryk Czyz, conductor; EMI 157-99 660-61 (2 discs). Must be special ordered.

PERGOLESI, GIOVANNI BATTISTA
1710-1736

Italian composer Pergolesi was an accomplished violinist and composer, most notably of music for the church and of operas. He is best remembered today for his La serva padrona ("The Maid as Mistress") and for the fact that Stravinsky incorporated several Pergolesi themes in his ballet Pulcinella.

Choral

C Stabat Mater (1736)

$ Margaret Marshal, soprano; Lucia Valentini-Terrani, mezzo-soprano; London Symphony Orchestra; Claudio Abbado, conductor; DG 415103-1 GH, ▣ 415103-4 GH.

PISTON, WALTER
1894-1976

Walter Hamor Piston descended from an Italian family (the surname was originally Pistone) and was born in Rockland, Maine. After graduating from Harvard he studied with Nadia Boulanger at the École Normale de Musique in Paris. On his return to the U.S., in 1926, he was appointed to the music faculty of Harvard, from which he retired (as professor emeritus) in 1960. His earlier works display a Neo-Classical bent, but as he grew older (mid-1960s) he toyed with the dodecaphonic system. Although he wrote better works, he is principally known for his ballet, the Incredible Flutist (giving the lie to purists who insist on "flautist").

Ballet

B Incredible Flutist (1938)

$ Louisville Orchestra; Jorge Mester, conductor; Louisville 755. Includes Dudley Buck's Festival Overture on The Star-Spangled Banner (1887).

PONCHIELLI, AMILCARE
1834-1886

Ponchielli's name has come down to us primarily for a piece ("Dance of the Hours") from his operatic masterwork: La Gioconda. Many will remember the "Dance of the Hours" as the marvelously ridiculous ballet for hippopotami, elephants, et al., in Disney's Fantasia. Ponchielli was born in Cremona and attended the Milan Conservatorio from 1843 to

1854. His first success came with the opera I promessi sposi, in 1856. La Gioconda was written in 1876 and the libretto was by Boito (also librettist to Verdi, besides being an accomplished composer in his own right). Gioconda is now that upon which Ponchielli's fame rests. About the most interesting personal thing regarding Ponchielli, aside from his having been an instructor to Puccini and Mascagni, is that his given name is the modern Italian for the name of Hannibal's father.

Operatic

B La Gioconda (1876)

$ Montserrat Caballé, soprano; Agnes Baltsa, mezzo-soprano; Luciano Pavarotti, tenor; Sherrill Milnes, baritone; Nicolai Ghiaurov, bass; London Opera Chorus, National Philharmonic Orchestra, London; Bruno Bartoletti, conductor; London LDR-73005 (3 discs), ▤ LDR5-73005.

POULENC, FRANÇIS
1899-1963

Although Poulenc's parents forced a classical education upon him, the French composer still managed to study piano and composition via tutors. His compositional models were Ravel and Satie, and the young Poulenc was one of the group bearing the appellation "Les Six." His music is brilliantly conceived, full of typical French sarcasm, wit and humor, and often given to "Ravellian" melodic lines.

Chamber

B Aubade for Piano and 18 Instruments (1929)

$ François-René Duchable, piano; Rotterdam Philharmonic Orchestra; James Conlon, conductor; Erato NUM-75203, ▤ MCE-75203. Includes Poulenc's Concerto for Piano and Orchestra, in c sharp (1949) and Concerto for Two Pianos and Orchestra, in d, (1932), rated B. The second pianist in the Concerto for Two Pianos is Jean-Philippe Collard.

Choral

B Gloria, in G (1961)

$$ Sylvia McNair, soprano; Michael Murray, organ; Atlanta Symphony Chorus and Orchestra; Robert Shaw, conductor; Telarc DG-10077. Includes Poulenc's Concerto for Organ, Strings and Tympani, in g (1941).

Concerted

B Concerto for Piano and Orchestra, in c sharp (1949)--see entry for <u>Aubade</u> for Piano and 18 Instruments (1929), under Chamber, <u>supra</u>.

PROKOFIEV, SERGEI
1891-1953

Prokofiev's mother was an accomplished amateur pianist and his musical education began with her. He began composing, albeit crudely, at the age of 9 (an opera titled <u>The Giant</u>), and completed 3 more operas by the time he began his teen-age years. At 13 he entered the St. Petersburg Conservatory where he studied with Rimsky-Korsakov and Tcherepnin, having already studied privately with Glière. At his graduation he received the Anton Rubinstein Prize for piano performance and composition (the prize consisted of a grand piano; the work with which he won it was his Concerto for Piano, No.1)--he was 23. His first important works for orchestra were his <u>Scythian</u> Suite and his Symphony No.1, called the "Classical." In the latter work he emulated, but did not parody, the form of the 18th century, while the content of the work was decidedly modern. During the years 1918 to 1927 Prokofiev traveled widely, mostly to such centers of culture and sophistication as London, Paris, Tokyo, Chicago, etc. From January 1927 on, he returned to Russia as a permanent resident, but he occasionally visited western cities to perform. Prokofiev had a running battle with Soviet authorities regarding the "Sovietness" of his compositions since, according to the authorities, his work was "decadent" and did not sufficiently reflect Soviet values (i.e., his work was too modern and not adequately hackneyed to be easily understood either by the Soviet arbiters of music or the public). Some of his works (e.g., <u>Peter and the Wolf, Songs of Our Days,</u> etc.) were written as intentional sops to quiet his critics. Despite having to produce such trivia he also created several works of lasting worth like <u>Romeo and Juliet, Lieutenant Kijé</u> and the Symphony No.5. Whatever his political problems, Prokofiev's genius was able to surmount the impedimenta which the Soviet academicians, political hacks and party-line press critics had strewn before him. His death remained unreported for several days in the West since it occurred on precisely the same day as that of his old antagonist--Stalin. Along with Bartók and Stravinsky, Prokofiev is probably among the greatest composers truly belonging to the 20th century, that is, those who spent the majority of their working lives after 1900. Prokofiev was not so much imbued with the virtual necessity to innovate in music as were the other two.

Ballet

B <u>Cinderella</u>, Op.87

$$ London Symphony Orchestra; André Previn, conductor; Angel DS-3944 (2 discs), ⊟ DS-3944.

B <u>Romeo</u> <u>and</u> <u>Juliet</u>, Op.64

$ London Symphony Orchestra; André Previn, conductor; Angel S-3802 (3 discs), ⊟ 4X3S-3802.

A <u>Romeo</u> <u>and</u> <u>Juliet</u> Suites (2), Nos.1-2: Op.64a and Op.64b

$ National Symphony Orchestra; Mstislav Rostropovich, conductor; DG 2532087, ⊟ 330287.

Chamber

B Overture on Hebrew Themes, Op.34

$ Gabrielli Quartet; Vladimir Ashkenazy, piano; Keith Puddy, clarinet; London 7062, ⊟ 5-7062. Includes Prokofiev's Piano Concerti No.1, in D flat, Op.10, rated B and No.2, in g, Op.16 (performed by pianist Ashkenazy with the London Symphony Orchestra conducted by André Previn), rated C.

B Sonata for Flute and Piano, Op.94

$ Louise DiTullio, flute; Virginia DiTullio, piano; Crystal 311. Includes Sancan's Sonatine pour flute et piano.

C String Quartet No.1, Op.50

* Sequoia Quartet; Nonesuch 79048, ⊟ 79048-4. Includes Prokofiev's String Quartet No.2, Op.92, rated B.

B String Quartet No.2, Op.92--see entry for String Quartet No.1, Op.50, immediately <u>supra</u>.

Choral

A <u>Alexander</u> <u>Nevsky</u> (Cantata from the Film of the Same Name), Op.78

* Lili Chookasian; Westminster Choir; New York Philharmonic Orchestra; Thomas Schippers, conductor; Odyssey ▇ YT-31014.

$ Elena Obraztsova, mezzo-soprano; London Symphony Chorus and Orchestra; Claudio Abbado, conductor; DG 253 1202 IMS. Must be special ordered.

Concerted

B Concerto for Piano No.1, in D flat, Op.10--see entry for Overture on Hebrew Themes, Op.34 under Chamber, <u>supra</u>.

C Concerto for Piano No.2, Op.16, in g--see entry for Overture on Hebrew Themes, Op.34 under Chamber, <u>supra</u>.

A Concerto for Piano No.3, Op.26, in C
$ Martha Argerich, piano; Berlin Philharmonic Orchestra; Claudio Abbado, conductor; DG 139349. Includes Ravel's Concerto for Piano, in G (1930-1931), also rated A.

C Concerto for Violin No.1, Op.19, in D
$ Isaac Stern, violin; Philadelphia Orchestra; Eugene Ormandy, conductor; Columbia MY-38525, ▇ MY-38525. Includes the same composer's Concerto for Violin No.2, Op.63, in g, rated B.

B Concerto for Violin No.2, Op.63, in g--see entry for Concerto for Violin No.1, Op.19, in D, immediately <u>supra</u>.

Instrumental

B Sonata for Piano No.7, Op.83, in B flat
$ Maurizio Pollini, piano; DG 2530225.   Includes Stravinsky's <u>Petrouchka</u>: 3 Scenes for Piano (1921), rated C.

C <u>Visions fugitives</u> (20), Op.22
$ Sviatoslav Richter, piano; DG 2543812.   Includes Nos.3, 6, 9; Prokofiev's Concerto for Piano No.5, Op.55, in G and Prokofiev's Sonata for Piano No.8, in B flat, Op.84. Must be special ordered.

Orchestral

A <u>Lieutenant Kijé</u> Suite, Op.60--see entry under Kodály, Orchestral, <u>Háry János</u> Suite (1926), <u>supra</u>.

C Love for Three Oranges Suite, Op.33

* Moscow Radio Symphony Orchestra; Gennady Rozhdestvensky, conductor; Quintessence 7196, ♮ 7196. Includes Prokofiev's Portraits (Suite from The Gambler), Op.49 and Seven, They Are Seven (Cantata), Op.30. The "March" from Love for Three Oranges was the theme for the old radio program, "The FBI in Peace and War" (if there is any irony in that, I leave it for you to discern).

A Peter and the Wolf, Op.67

* Sir Ralph Richardson, narrator; London Symphony Orchestra; Sir Malcolm Sargent, conductor; London STS-15114, ♮ 5-15114. Includes Prokofiev's Symphony No.1 ("Classical"), in D, Op.25, also rated A.

Symphonic

A Symphony No.1 ("Classical"), Op.25, in D—see entries for Peter and the Wolf, Op.67 under Orchestral, supra and Symphony No.7, Op.131, in C sharp, infra.

A Symphony No.5, Op.100, in B flat

* Boston Symphony Orchestra; Erich Leinsdorf, conductor; RCA ♮ ALK1-4485.

$ Israel Philharmonic Orchestra; Leonard Bernstein, conductor; Columbia IM-35877, ♮ HMT-35877.

C Symphony No.7, Op.131, in C sharp

* Moscow Radio Symphony Orchestra; Gennady Rozhdestvensky, conductor; Quintessence 7138, ♮ 7138. Includes Prokofiev's Symphony No.1 ("Classical"), Op.25, in D, rated A.

PUCCINI, GIACOMO
1858-1924

One yclept (my wife, in proofing this, comments "you've got to be kidding," I reply—"?") Giacomo Antonio Domenico Michele Secondo Maria Puccini probably could not have helped becoming one of Italy's greatest musicians: his ancestors, back to Giacomo (c.1712-1781), Antonio (1747-1832) and through to his grandfather, Domenico (1771-1815) and father, Michele (1813-1864) were all eminent composers. The Puccini with which we deal, like his forebears, made his name by writing operas (some of his ancestors dabbled in other forms, and so did their most illustrious son). Born in Lucca, he quickly exhausted that city's musical pedagogy and, with a pension given him by the Queen of Italy, he entered the Milan Conservatorio. His composition instructor was the eminent Ponchielli, on whose suggestion he undertook his first operatic composition, Le villi. Although Puccini's instructors were not impressed, one of his fellow students, Boito, was. With the help of some other students, Boito managed to get Le villi performed at the Teatro dal Verme in Milan, in 1884. It received another performance the following year, in an enlarged version, at La Scala: not too shabby for the 27-year-old struggling composer. Still, Puccini's first real success was with the production of Manon Lescaut, in 1893. With the production of La Bohème in Turin in 1896, Puccini became known as the chief of the younger Italian composers. After Bohème came Madama Butterfly and Tosca--each a raving success. Then came a period of attempts at novelty and, unfortunately, failure. La fanciulla del West ("The Girl of the Golden West"), La Rondine and Il Trittico ("The Triptych"): not one of these has ever made it into the "regular" Puccini repertoire, where performances every year are de rigueur. Puccini's last opera, Turandot was almost complete at the time of his death (due to throat cancer), and was completed by Franco Alfano. Puccini was a person of special simplicity, both in his tastes (except for women: his wife often put a sleeping potion in his soup when an attractive female was dining with them) and his self-esteem. He once commented: "Just think of it, if I hadn't hit on music I should never have been able to do anything in the world." He refused, insofar as possible, to make any public speeches, and enjoyed travel and also the serenity of the countryside. His music is echt Romantic, even indulging in occasional sentimentality but, more often than not, balanced by a charming sense of humor and reality. It seems odd now that the well-known American critic, William Foster Apthorp, could write (in the April 12, 1901 Boston Evening Transcript): "At the first hearing much, perhaps most, of Puccini's Tosca sounds exceedingly, even ingeniously, ugly. Every now and then one comes across the most ear-flaying succession of chords; then the instrumentation, although nearly always characteristic, is often distinctly rawboned and hideous; the composer shows a well-nigh diabolical ingenuity in massing together harsh, ill-sounding timbres. As for harmony, Puccini, like some of his countrymen--Arrigo Boito, for example--shows that his ear is far less sensitive to the unpleasant effect of cross-relations and illogical succession of chords than to that of harsh and complex dissonances." What would Apthorp have written regarding, say, Stravinsky?

Operatic

A La Bohème (1896)

* Victoria De los Angeles, soprano; Jussi Björling, tenor; Robert Merrill, baritone; RCA Victor Chorus and Orchestra; Sir Thomas Beecham, conductor; Seraphim S-6099 (2 discs), ▤ 4X2G-6099.

$ Mirella Freni, soprano; Luciano Pavarotti, tenor; Nicolai Ghiaurov, bass; Berlin Opera Chorus; Berlin Philharmonic Orchestra; Herbert von Karajan, conductor; London 1299 (2 discs), ▤ 5-1299.

A Madama Butterfly (1904)

$ Victoria De los Angeles, soprano; Jussi Björling, tenor; Rome Opera Chorus and Orchestra; Gabriele Santini, conductor; Angel S-3604 (3 discs), ▤ S-3604.

B Manon Lescaut (1893)

$ Montserrat Caballé, soprano; Placido Domingo, tenor; Vicente Sardinero, bass; Ambrosian Opera Chorus; Philharmonia Orchestra; Bruno Bartoletti, conductor; Angel S-3782 (2 discs), ▤ 4X2X-3782.

A Tosca (1900)

$ Birgit Nilsson, soprano; Franco Corelli, tenor; Dietrich Fischer-Dieskau, baritone; Chorus and Orchestra of the Academy of Santa Cecilia, Rome; Lorin Maazel, conductor; London 42001 (2 discs), ▤ 42001.

$ Katia Ricciarelli, soprano; Jos' Carreras, tenor; Ruggero Raimondi, bass; Deutsche Oper Chor; Berlin Philharmonic Orchestra; Herbert von Karajan, conductor; DG 2707121 (2 discs).

B Il Trittico ("The Triptych") (Includes Gianni Schicchi; Suor Angelica and Il Tabarro) (1918)

$ Ileana Cotrubas, soprano; Renata Scotto, soprano; Marilyn Horne, mezzo-soprano; Placido Domingo, tenor; Tito Gobbi, baritone; Ingvar Wixell, baritone; Ambrosian Opera Chorus; New Philharmonia Orchestra; Lorin Maazel, conductor; Columbia M3-35912 (3 discs).

A <u>Turandot</u> (1926)

$ Montserrat Caballé, soprano; Dame Joan Sutherland, soprano; Luciano Pavarotti, tenor; Nicolai Ghiaurov, bass; John Alldis Choir; London Philharmonic Orchestra; Zubin Mehta, conductor; London 13108 (3 discs), ⑧ 5-13108.

PURCELL, HENRY
c.1658-1695

Purcell (preferred <in this case, more accurately, "received"> pronunciation asks that the accent be on the first syllable) is considered one of the greatest, if not the greatest, of English composers. He was born in London to a family with a distinguished musical history, his father being Thomas Purcell, Gentleman of the Chapel Royal and, jointly, Master of the King's Band of Music. Henry became a chorister of the Chapel Royal in 1669 and remained there until 1673, when his voice "changed." Ostensibly, Henry was composing as early as 1670. After the "breakage" of his voice he became Assistant Keeper of the King's Instruments, and, in 1679, was appointed Organist of Westminster Abbey. By 1683 he had become Keeper of the King's Wind Instruments (where are such titles today?) with a salary of 60 pounds sterling (which he occasionally had difficulty collecting). Naturally, he was composing all through this period, and performing, at the organ, for the coronations which took place (James II, and then, William and Mary). His birthday ode for Queen Mary (1692) has a title which is rather reminiscent of <u>Porgy</u> <u>and</u> <u>Bess</u> (it certainly is in the right vernacular): <u>Love's</u> <u>Goddess</u> <u>Sure</u> <u>Was</u> <u>Blind</u> (probably to be followed by the song, "A Woman is a Sometime Thing"). Purcell was married in about 1681, and fathered 6 children, 3 of whom predeceased him. Much honor was heaped upon him on his death (such a cliché ought to close with: "and much earth, too"), and he was interred in Westminster Abbey beneath the organ. A tablet on a pillar near the grave was erected by Annabella, Lady Howard, which tablet reads: "Here lyes HENRY PURCELL Esqr. Who left this Life And is gone to that Blessed Place Where only his Harmony can be exceeded." He was 37, and Percy Scholes rightfully laments that "His early death must ever be regarded as a national calamity." He might just as well as substituted "world" for "national."

Operatic

A Dido and Aeneas (1689)

$ Emma Kirkby, soprano; Judith Nelson, soprano; David Thomas, bass, Taverner Choir; Taverner Players; Andrew Parrott, conductor; Chandos 1034.

B The Fairy Queen (1692)

$ Deller Consort; Harmonia Mundi 231 (3 discs).

Orchestral

B Abdelazar, or the Moor's Revenge Suite (1695)

$$ Academy of Ancient Music; Christopher Hogwood, conductor; L'Oiseau Lyre DSLO-504. Includes Purcell's Distressed Innocence, or The Princess of Persia Suite (1690; The Gordian Knot Untied Suites Nos.1 and 2 (1691), rated B and The Married Beau, or The Curious Impertinent Suite (1694). Abdelazar contains the famous "Round-O" (i.e., "rondo") used as the thematic basis by Benjamin, Lord Britten, in his Young Person's Guide to the Orchestra.

B The Gordian Knot Untied Suites Nos.1 and 2 (1691)--see entry for Abdelazar, or the Moor's Revenge (1695), immediately supra.

Vocal

B Come Ye Sons of Art ("Ode for the Birthday of Queen Mary") (1694)

$ Felicity Lott, soprano; Charles Brett, counter-tenor; John Williams, counter-tenor; Thomas Allen, bass; Equale Brass Ensemble; Monteverdi Chorus and Orchestra, London; John Eliot Gardiner, conductor; Erato STU-70911. Includes Purcell's Funeral Music for Queen Mary (1695).

C Love's Goddess Sure Was Blind ("Ode on the Birthday of Queen Mary II") (1692)

$$ Christina Clarke, soprano; Honor Sheppard, soprano; Alfred Deller, counter-tenor; Mark Deller, counter-tenor; John Buttrey, tenor; Neil Jenkins, tenor; Maurice Bevan, baritone; Jane Ryan, viola da gamba; Robert Elliott, harpsichord; Deller Consort, London; Stour Music Chamber

Orchestra; Alfred Deller, conductor; Harmonia Mundi 222. Includes <u>Ode</u> <u>on</u> <u>St.</u> <u>Cecilia's</u> <u>Day</u> ("Welcome to all the Pleasures") (1683), rated A.

A <u>Ode</u> <u>on</u> <u>St.</u> <u>Cecilia's</u> <u>Day</u> ("Welcome to all the Pleasures") (1683)--see entry for <u>Love's</u> <u>Goddess</u> <u>Sure</u> <u>Was</u> <u>Blind</u> ("Ode on the Birthday of Queen Mary II") (1692), immediately <u>supra</u>.

RACHMANINOFF, SERGEI
1873-1943

Sergei Vassilievich Rachmaninoff was born to an aristocratic family of old Russia. He entered the Conservatory at St. Petersburg at age 9, majoring in piano performance. At 12 he matriculated to the Moscow Conservatory and continued studying the piano, but also took classes with Taneyev and Arensky in composition and theory. In 1892, at 19, he took the gold medal for composition and wrote the work which, for many years was "the" Rachmaninoff piece: the Prelude in c sharp. In 1893 he joined the faculty of the Maryinsky Institute for Girls in Moscow, and his Symphony No.1 (written in 1895) was premiered in London in 1909. It was badly received and Rachmaninoff destroyed the manuscript (the players' parts were saved and the work has been found to be somewhat better than the composer thought). The Symphony No.2 (1907) fared considerably better on its public appearance. It was his Concerto for Piano No.2, however, which brought him enduring acclaim. It was first performed in 1901 in Moscow, and was much emulated by other Russian composers. Rachmaninoff left his homeland in 1917 and ultimately took up residence in the U.S., becoming a citizen of this country shortly before his death. In appearance, Rachmaninoff was very tall and spare, and his physiognomy always seemed beset by unspeakable inner tragedy. His music is too cosmopolitan to be considered exemplary of Russian influence except, perhaps, for his masterful use of orchestral coloration. This relatively quiet, solitary soul was one of the greatest pianists of his time, and also a great composer for his instrument: it has often been said that Rachmaninoff's works verge on the unplayable because of their abundant technical demands (such handfuls of notes to the bar!). It is, however, his Romantically lyrical quality which yet endears him to audiences in much the same fashion that Tchaikovsky's music does. The Piano Concerto No.2

has the slow movement which was set as a popular song ("Full Moon and Empty Arms" <sensitive listeners have been known to suffer reverse peristalsis on hearing it so>), and the Rhapsody on a Theme of Paganini has the breath-catchingly lovely inversion of the theme in the 18th variation.

Concerted

C Concerto for Piano No.1, Op.1, in f sharp

* Earl Wild, piano; Royal Philharmonic Orchestra; Jascha Horenstein, conductor; Quintessence 7052, ◘ 7052. Includes Rachmaninoff's Isle of the Dead (Symphonic Poem), Op.29, also rated C.

A Concerto for Piano No.2, Op.18, in c

$ Vladimir Ashkenazy, piano; Moscow Philharmonic Orchestra; Kiril Kondrashin, conductor; London 41001, ◘ 41001. Includes Rachmaninoff's Études-Tableaux, Op.39, rated B.

$ Cecile Licad, piano; Chicago Symphony Orchestra; Claudio Abbado, conductor; CBS IM-38672, ◘ IMT-38672. Includes Rachmaninoff's Rhapsody on a Theme of Paganini, Op.43, also rated A.

A Concerto for Piano No.3, Op.30, in d

$ Vladimir Ashkenazy, piano; London Symphony Orchestra; Anatole Fistoulari, conductor; London 41023, ◘ 41023.

A Rhapsody on a Theme of Paganini, Op.43--see entries for Concerto for Piano No.2, Op.18, in c, supra and under Dohnányi, Concerted, Variations on a Nursery Song, Op.25 ("Twinkle, Twinkle, Little Star"), supra.

Instrumental

B Études-Tableaux, Op.39--see entry for Concerto for Piano No.2, Op.18, in c under Concerted, supra.

A Prelude, Op.32 No.2, in c sharp--see entry for Preludes for Piano, Op.23 (10), Nos.1-10 and Op.32 (13) Nos.1-13, immediately infra.

B Preludes for Piano, Op.23 (10), Nos.1-10 and Op.32 (13) Nos.1-13

$ Vladimir Ashkenazy, piano; London 2241 (2 discs), ◘ 5-2241. Includes the Prelude, Op.32 No.2, in c sharp (the famous one), rated A.

Orchestral

C Isle of the Dead (Symphonic Poem), Op.29--see entry for Concerto for Piano No.1, Op.1, in f sharp under Concerted, supra.

B Symphonic Dances, Op.45

* Moscow Philharmonic Orchestra; Kiril Kondrashin, conductor; Quintessence 7136, ⊞ 7136. Includes Rachmaninoff's Russian Songs for Chorus and Orchestra, Op.41 (3), Nos.1-3, performed by the Bolshoi Theater Chorus and Orchestra, conducted by Yevgeny Svetlanov.

Symphonic

C Symphony No.1, Op.13, in d

* St. Louis Symphony Orchestra; Leonard Slatkin, conductor; Candide 31099, ⊞ Vox CT-2183.

A Symphony No.2, Op.27, in e

\$ Amsterdam Concertgebouw Orchestra; Vladimir Ashkenazy, conductor; London LDR-71063, ⊞ LDR5-71063.

* Philadelphia Orchestra; Eugene Ormandy, conductor; RCA ⊞ ALK1-4978.

B Symphony No.3, Op.44, in a

* Moscow Radio Symphony Orchestra; Yevgeny Svetlanov, conductor; Allegro 88108, ⊞ 88108.

Vocal

B Vocalise, Op.34 No.14--see entry under Canteloube, Vocal, Chants d'Auvergne ("Songs of the Auvergne"), supra.

RAVEL, MAURICE
1875-1937

Joseph-Maurice Ravel was born near the Swiss border, in Basses-Pyrénées, his father being a Swiss and his mother of Basque background. His parents met in Spain in 1873 and were married in 1874. The offspring of this rather odd couple was to become the quintessential French composer of his time. The family moved to Paris in 1875, and Maurice began piano lessons (no, not from his mother) at age 7 and began to study harmony at 11. At age 14 he entered the Conservatoire de Paris where he studied composition with Fauré. Ravel became interested in the music of Liszt, Chabrier, Satie and the contemporary Russian composers (e.g., Rimsky-Korsakov, Tchaikovsky, etc.). In 1898 he began work on an opera, Shéhérazade. Although he did not publish Shéhérazade as an opera, some of it found its way into his song cycle of the same name. Due to what may have been political intrigue, Ravel never won the Grand Prix de Rome. Still, some of his early works were performed, but to essentially unsympathetic ears (Ravel had become known as something of a musical revolutionary). During World War I he served in the air force of France in some auxiliary fashion. His health was fragile and, in 1916, he was removed from the scene of action to a hospital. Little of consequence transpired in Ravel's life after his failure to gain the Grand Prix, except for the works he produced and his performing tours, on which he played virtually no works but his own. In his private life he was a dandy (for a tour of the U.S. lasting about 2 months, he brought 50 pastel colored silk shirts, etc.), reticent and a bachelor. In 1920 he was offered the Legion of Honor which he refused. He never taught formally, although Manuel Rosenthal did study with him privately, as did a handful of others. His music was first thought to be but a reflection of that of Debussy but, on careful examination and consideration, it is not really Impressionistic. Technically, he is essentially a Neo–Classicist, but one given to fabulous colorations, timbres, sensitivities and exquisite craftsmanship. Ravel prided himself that there was not one extraneous note to be found in any of his works; and though some of his pieces are contained of true emotion, there is never anything resembling vulgarity, or sentimentality. If anything, they are aloof and restrained, marked by a sympathetic quality which is never intrusive. They are as perfect pearls, or the microscopic crystalline formations from which some scientists derive untold pleasure.

Ballet

A Daphnis et Chloé (1909–1912)

$ Montreal Symphony Chorus and Orchestra; Charles Dutoit, conductor; London LDR-71028, ☰ LDR5-71028.

A Ma Mère l'Oye Suite ("Mother Goose" Suite) (1907) (5) (Nos.1–5: Pavane de la belle au bois dormant <"Pavane of Sleeping Beauty">; Petit Poucet <"Tom Thumb">; Laideronette, impératrice des pagodes <"The Ugly Woman, Empress of the Pagodas">; Les Entretiens de la belle et la

179

bête <"The Conversations of Beauty and the Beast"> and Le Jardin féerique <"The Enchanted Garden">)

$ Orchestre de Paris; Jean Martinon, conductor; Angel S-37149, ▣ S-37149. Includes Ravel's Valses nobles et sentimentales (1911) and Tzigane ("Gypsies") for Violin and Orchestra, (1924) (with Itzhak Perlman, violin), both also rated A.

Also--see entry under Chamber, Introduction and Allegro for Harp, Flute, Clarinet and String Quartet (1906), infra.

Also--for piano, four hands version of same entry see entry under Debussy, Instrumental, En blanc et noir ("In Black and White") for Two Pianos (3) (Nos.1-3) (1915), supra.

A La Valse ("The Waltz") (1919-1920)

$ Orchestre de Paris; Jean Martinon, conductor; Angel S-37147, ▣ S-37147. Includes Ravel's Boléro (1927); Rapsodie espagnole ("Spanish Rhapsody") (1907), Nos.1-3: Prélude à la nuit ("Prelude in the Fashion of the Night"); Habañera and Féria ("Fiesta"), both rated A, and Shéhérazade: Ouverture de féerie (1898).

Also--see entries under Dukas, Orchestral, L'Apprenti sorcier ("The Sorcerer's Apprentice") (1897) and Ibert, Orchestral, Escales ("Ports of Call") (1922), both supra.

Chamber

A Introduction and Allegro for Harp, Flute, Clarinet and String Quartet (1906)

* Chicago Symphony Orchestra; Jean Martinon, conductor; RCA AGL1-5061, ▣ AGL1-5061. Includes Ravel's Alborada del gracioso ("Morning Song of the Jester") (1905), Ma Mère l'Oye Suite ("Mother Goose" Suite) (1907) (5) (Nos.1-5: Pavane de la belle au bois dormant <"Pavane of Sleeping Beauty">; Petit Poucet <"Tom Thumb">; Laideronette, impératrice des pagodes <"The Ugly Woman, Empress of the Pagodas">; Les Entretiens de la belle et la bête <"The Conversations of Beauty and the Beast"> and Le Jardin féerique <"The Enchanted Garden">) and Rapsodie espagnole ("Spanish Rhapsody") (1907), Nos.1-3: Prélude à la nuit ("Prelude in the Fashion of the Night"); Habañera and Féria ("Fiesta"), all rated A.

A String Quartet, in F (1902-1903)--see entry under Debussy, Chamber, String Quartet, Op.10, in g, supra.

B Trio for Violin, 'Cello and Piano (1914)

$ Beaux Arts Trio; Philips 411141-1 PH, 411141-4 PH. Includes Chausson's Trio for Violin, 'Cello and Piano, in g, Op.3.

* Caecilian Trio; Turnabout 37007, CT-7007. Includes Ravel's Sonata for Violin and Piano (1923-1927).

Concerted

A Concerto for Piano, in G (1930-1931)

$ Jean-Phillipe Collard, piano; L'Orchestre National de France; Lorin Maazel, conductor; Angel SZ-37730. Includes Ravel's Concerto for Piano, for the Left Hand, in D (1930-1931), also rated A.

Also--see entry under Prokofiev, Concerted, Concerto for Piano No.3, Op.26, in C, supra.

A Concerto for Piano, for the Left Hand, in D (1930-1931)--see entry for Concerto for Piano, in G (1930-1931), immediately supra.

A Tzigane ("Gypsies") for Violin and Orchestra, (1924)--see entry for Ma Mère l'Oye Suite ("Mother Goose" Suite) (1907) (5) (Nos.1-5: Pavane de la belle au bois dormant <"Pavane of Sleeping Beauty">; Petit Poucet <"Tom Thumb">; Laideronette, impératrice des pagodes <"The Ugly Woman, Empress of the Pagodas">; Les Entretiens de la belle et la bête <"The Conversations of Beauty and the Beast"> and Le Jardin féerique <"The Enchanted Garden">) under Ballet, supra.

Instrumental

A Gaspard de la nuit ("Gaspard of the Night"--after Bertrand) (3) (Nos.1-3: Ondine; Le Gibet <"The Gibbet"> and Scarbo) (1908)

$ Deszö Ránki, piano; Hungaroton 12317. Includes Ravel's Menuet antique (1895), Sonatine (1903-1905) and Valses nobles et sentimentales (1911), rated A.

$ Werner Haas, piano; Erato EPR-15552, MCE-15552. Includes Ravel's Miroirs ("Mirrors") (5) (Nos.1-5: Noctuelles <"Night Butterflies">; Oiseaux tristes <"Sad Birds">; Une Barque sur l'océan <"A Boat on the Ocean">; Alborada del gracioso <"Morning Song of the Jester"> and La

Vallée des cloches <"Valley of the Bells"> (1905), rated A and Jeux d'eau ("Games of the Water"), rated B.

B Jeux d'eau ("Games of the Waters")--see entry for Gaspard de la nuit ("Gaspard of the Night"--after Bertrand) (3) (Nos.1-3: Ondine; Le Gibet <"The Gibbet"> and Scarbo) (1908), immediately supra.

A Miroirs ("Mirrors") (5) (Nos.1-5: Noctuelles <"Night Butterflies">; Oiseaux tristes <"Sad Birds">; Une Barque sur l'océan <"A Boat on the Ocean">; Alborada del gracioso <"Morning Song of the Jester"> and La Vallée des cloches <"Valley of the Bells"> (1905)--see entry for Gaspard de la nuit ("Gaspard of the Night"--after Bertrand) (3) (Nos.1-3: Ondine; Le Gibet <"The Gibbet"> and Scarbo) (1908), supra.

Also--for orchestral version of Une Barque sur l'océan ("A Boat on the Ocean"), see entry for Alborada del gracioso ("Morning Song of the Jester") (1905), under Orchestral, infra.

A Rapsodie espagnole ("Spanish Rhapsody") (1907), For Piano, Four Hands (3), Nos.1-3: Prélude à la nuit ("Prelude in the Fashion of the Night"); Habañera and Féria ("Fiesta")--see entry under Debussy, Instrumental, En blanc et noir ("In Black and White") For Two Pianos (1915) (3), Nos.1-3, supra.

Also--for orchestral version, see same entry under Orchestral, infra.

Operatic

B L'Enfant et les sortilèges ("The Child and the Sorceries") (1920-1925)

$$ Arleen Augér, soprano; Jane Berbie, soprano; Lynda Richardson, soprano; Susan Davenny Wyner, soprano; Jocelyne Taillon, mezzo-soprano; Linda Finnie, contralto; Philip Langridge, tenor; Philippe Huttenlocher, baritone; Jules Bastin, bass; Ambrosian Opera Chorus; London Symphony Orchestra; André Previn, conductor; Angel DS-37869, ▨ 4DS-37869.

Orchestral

A Alborada del gracioso ("Morning Song of the Jester") (1905)

$ Orchestre de Paris; Jean Martinon, conductor; Angel S-37150, ▨ S-37150. Includes the same composer's Une Barque sur l'océan ("A Boat on the Ocean") from Miroirs ("Mirrors") (5) (Nos.1-5: Noctuelles <"Night

Butterflies">; Oiseaux tristes <"Sad Birds">; Une Barque sur l'océan <"A
Boat on the Ocean">; Alborada del gracioso <"Morning Song of the
Jester"> and La Vallée des cloches <"Valley of the Bells">) (1905), rated
A, Menuet antique (1895), Pavane pour une Infante défunte ("Pavane for
a Dead Princess") (1899), rated A and La Tombeau de Couperin ("Homage
to Couperin") (4) (Nos.1-4: Prélude; Forlane; Menuet and Rigaudon)
(1914-1917), also rated A.

    Also--see entry under Chamber, Introduction and Allegro for Harp,
Flute, Clarinet and String Quartet (1906), supra.

    A Boléro (1927)--see entries for La Valse ("The Waltz")
(1919-1920) under Ballet, supra and Alborada del gracioso ("Morning Song
of the Jester") (1905), immediately supra and under Dukas, Orchestral,
L'Apprenti sorcier ("The Sorcerer's Apprentice") (1897) and Ibert,
Orchestral, Escales ("Ports of Call") (1922), both supra.

    A Pavane pour une Infante défunte ("Pavane for a Dead Princess")
(1899)--see entry for Alborada del gracioso ("Morning Song of the Jester")
(1905), supra and under Falla, Ballet, El Amor brujo ("Love, the Warlock")
(1915) and Ibert, Orchestral, Escales ("Ports of Call") (1922), both supra.

    A Rapsodie espagnole ("Spanish Rhapsody") (1907), Nos.1-3:
Prélude à la nuit ("Prelude in the Fashion of the Night"); Habañera
and Féria ("Fiesta")--see entries under Ballet, La Valse ("The Waltz")
(1919-1920); Chamber, Introduction and Allegro for Harp, Flute, Clarinet
and String Quartet (1906); Falla, Ballet, El Amor brujo ("Love, the
Warlock") (1915) and Dukas, Orchestral, L'Apprenti sorcier ("The
Sorcerer's Apprentice") (1897), all supra.

    Also--for two piano version, see entry under Debussy, Instrumental,
En blanc et noir ("In Black and White") For Two Pianos (3) (Nos.1-3)
(1915), supra.

    A La Tombeau de Couperin ("Homage to Couperin") (4) (Nos.1-4:
Prélude; Forlane; Menuet and Rigaudon) (1914-1917)--see entry for
Alborada del gracioso ("Morning Song of the Jester") (1905), supra.

A <u>Valses nobles et sentimentales</u> (1911)--see entries under Ballet, Ma Mère l'Oye Suite ("Mother Goose" Suite) (1907) (5) (Nos.1-5: <u>Pavane de la belle au bois dormant</u> <"Pavane of Sleeping Beauty">; <u>Petit Poucet</u> <"Tom Thumb">; <u>Laideronette, impératrice des pagodes</u> <"The Ugly Woman, Empress of the Pagodas">; <u>Les Entretiens de la belle et la bête</u> <"The Conversations of Beauty and the Beast"> and <u>Le Jardin féerique</u> <"The Enchanted Garden">) under Ballet, <u>supra</u> and, for piano version of same entry, see entry for <u>Gaspard de la nuit</u> ("Gaspard of the Night" --after Bertrand) (3) (Nos.1-3: <u>Ondine; Le Gibet</u> <"The Gibbet"> and <u>Scarbo</u>) (1908) under Instrumental, <u>supra</u>.

Vocal

B <u>Chansons madécasses</u> for Voice, Flute, 'Cello and Piano (3) (Nos.1-3: <u>Nahandève; Aoua!</u> and <u>Il est doux</u>) (1925-1926)

$ Frederica von Stade, soprano; Boston Symphony Orchestra; Seiji Ozawa, conductor; Columbia ♭ HMT-36665. Includes Ravel's <u>Deux Mélodies hébraïques</u> (2) (Nos.1-2: <u>Kaddisch</u> and <u>L'Énigme éternelle</u>) (1914) and <u>Shéhérazade</u> (Song Cycle) (3) (Nos.1-3: <u>Asie; La Flûte enchantée</u> and <u>L'Indifférent</u>) (1903), both also rated B.

B <u>Deux Mélodies hébraïques</u> (2) (Nos.1-2: <u>Kaddisch</u> and L'Énigme éternelle) (1914)--see entry for <u>Chansons madécasses</u> for Voice, Flute, 'Cello and Piano (3) (Nos.1-3: <u>Nahandève; Aoua!</u> and <u>Il est doux</u>) (1925-1926) immediately <u>supra</u>.

B <u>Shéhérazade</u> (Song Cycle) (3) (Nos.1-3: <u>Asie; La Flûte enchantée</u> and <u>L'Indifférent</u>) (1903)--see entry for <u>Chansons madécasses</u> for Voice, Flute, 'Cello and Piano (3) (Nos.1-3: <u>Nahandève; Aoua!</u> and <u>Il est doux</u>) (1925-1926), <u>supra</u>.

RESPIGHI, OTTORINO
1879-1936

Born in Bologna, Respighi studied violin and viola at the Liceo Musicale in the city of his birth. He also studied composition at the Bologna Conservatory. Receiving his diploma from the Liceo in 1899, he travelled to Russia to take the first violist's chair with the St. Petersburg Opera Orchestra. While there he became a composition and orchestration

184

student of Rimsky-Korsakov. This latter aspect of his education became a decided influence on the emphasis on orchestration in his works. During the period 1903 to 1908 Respighi busied himself with performing as a solo violinist and with the Mugellini Quartet, based in his home town. In addition he took a diploma in composition, and studied under Max Bruch in Berlin. The first work of Respighi to receive public performance was a concerto for piano, in 1902. He became known, however, after the production of his opera Semiràma, in 1910. For a time, he was a faculty member, then director of the prestigious Conservatorio di Santa Cecilia in Rome. He resigned from this institution in 1925 to pursue the careers of conductor and composer. In 1919 he married a pupil of his, Elsa Oliverie-Sangiacomo, who was a singer and 15 years his junior (she survived him by about 40 years). Despite having written at least 8 operas, Respighi's reputation is now entirely based upon his symphonic poems, which are descriptive of Rome. The musical style of Respighi is typically lyrical, evocative (e.g., the use of a recording of a nightingale in the score of "The Pines of Rome"), sensual and one which depends mightily on the effects of brilliant orchestration (having studied with Rimsky-Korsakov, and considering the influence of Richard Strauss, q.e.d.). He is a better composer than often thought, but not as good as his principal mentors.

Ballet

B Ancient Airs and Dances for the Lute (3 sets) (Sets 1-3) (1917, 1924 and 1932)

$ Los Angeles Chamber Orchestra; Sir Neville Marriner, conductor; Angel S-37301, 4XS-37301.

A La Boutique fantasque ("The Fantastic Toyshop") (After Rossini) (1919)--see entry under Britten, Orchestral, Matinées musicales (After Rossini), Op.24, supra.

Orchestral

B Feste Romane ("Roman Festivals") (1929)

$ Philadelphia Orchestra; Eugene Ormandy, conductor; Columbia MG-32308 (2 discs). Includes Respighi's Fontane di Roma ("Fountains of Rome") (1917) and I Pini di Roma ("The Pines of Rome") (1924), both rated A; Gli Uccelli ("The Birds") (On Themes of Pasquini, Rameau, et al.) (1927), rated B and Vetrate di chiesa ("Church Windows") (1927), rated C.

185

A Fontane di Roma ("Fountains of Rome") (1917)--see entry for Feste Romane ("Roman Festivals") (1929), immediately supra.

A I Pini di Roma ("The Pines of Rome") (1924)--see entry for Feste Romane ("Roman Festivals") (1929), supra.

B Gli Uccelli ("The Birds") (On Themes of Pasquini, Rameau, et al.) (1927)--see entry for Feste Romane ("Roman Festivals") (1929), supra.

C Vetrate di chiesa ("Church Windows") (1927)--see entry for Feste Romane ("Roman Festivals") (1929), supra.

RIMSKY—KORSAKOV, NIKOLAI
1844-1908

Nikolai Andreyevich Rimsky-Korsakov is among the preeminent Russian (not Soviet) composers and was born in Tikhvin (Novgorod District) to an aristocratic and landed family. At 6 he began studying the piano and he exhibited definite musical talent, but this was thought unsuitable for the child of such a family and, in 1856, he was sent to the Naval College in St. Petersburg, whence he graduated in 1862. He had met Balakirev in 1861 and, along with Cui, Mussorgsky and Borodin, had begun to study music intensively. Rimsky was sent on a cruise which lasted 3 years, but during which he completed his Symphony No.1 (keeping in correspondence with Balakirev) which received its first public performance (Balakirev conducting) in December, 1865. The audience at the Free School of Music in St. Petersburg received the work warmly and were rather surprised when a young man in naval uniform was presented as the composer. Rimsky was able to remain in St. Petersburg and resumed his interrupted musical studies. He produced several works between 1865 and 1873, at which time he resigned his naval commission (but keeping a civil service position, until 1884, as Inspector of Naval Bands). In 1871 he received an appointment to the faculty of the St. Petersburg Conservatory, a post he kept until 1905, often declining the directorship of the Moscow Conservatory in order to remain in his beloved St. Petersburg. He was forced to resign from the St. Petersburg Conservatory in 1905 because he had supported, through publication of a letter in the press, the autonomy of the Conservatory, and had lent his support to the students in the abortive revolution of that year. He was reinstated (after the resignations, in sympathy, of Glazunov, Liadov, et al.). Rimsky-Korsakov was a happy family man (he had married a pianist, Nadezhda Nikolayevna Purgold) whose son, Andrei, became an eminent historian of Russian music. As an educator, Rimsky was outstanding. Among his students were Ippolitov-Ivanov, Glazunov, Liadov, Arensky and Stravinsky. Rimsky-Korsakov was one of the greatest orchestrators of all time, in company with Berlioz and Liszt (Rimsky's text on orchestration was definitive until but a few decades ago). He was daring in his use of harmony and progressions, the latter of which, particularly, sound quite "modern." He was fully adept in the use of classical forms, but more often than not, tended to eschew form in favor of lush melodies and their loose (and simple) development. Although he was grouped with "The Five," he easily transcended the capabilities of the others (except, of course, for Mussorgsky): he is more on par with his admiring colleague, Tchaikovsky.

Orchestral

A Capriccio espagnol, Op.34

$ Montreal Symphony Orchestra; Charles Dutoit, conductor; London 410253-1, ▤ 410253-4. Includes Rimsky-Korsakov's Scheherezade, Op.35, also rated A.

B Le Coq d'or ("The Golden Cockerel") Suite (1907)

* Boston Pops Orchestra; Arthur Fiedler, conductor; RCA ▤ ALK1-4460. Includes Rossini's William Tell Overture (1829) and Tchaikovsky's Marche slave, Op.31, both rated A.

B Russian Easter Overture, Op.36

$ Rotterdam Philharmonic Orchestra; David Zinman, conductor; Philips 9500971. Includes Rimsky-Korsakov's Symphony No.2 ("Antar"), Op.9, also rated B.

C Sadko: A Musical Picture, Op.5

* Royal Philharmonic Orchestra; Leopold Stokowski, RCA AGL1-5213, ▤ AGL1-5213.

A (Scheherezade, Op.35

$$ London Symphony Orchestra; Loris Tjeknavorian, conductor; Chalfont SDG-304.

* Royal Philharmonic Orchestra; Sir Thomas Beecham, conductor; Angel AE-34417, ♮ AE-34417.

Also--see entry for Capriccio espagnol, Op.34, supra.

C Tsar Saltan: Suite, Op.57

* State Academic Symphony Orchestra; Yevgeny Svetlanov, conductor; Quintessence 7189, ♮ 7189. Includes Rimsky-Korsakov's Legend of the Invisible City of Kitezh (1903-1905) Excerpts.

Symphonic

B Symphony No.2 ("Antar"), Op.9--see entries for Russian Easter Overture, Op.36 under Orchestral, supra and under Ippolitov-Ivanov, Orchestral, Caucasian Sketches Suite, Op.10, supra.

RODRIGO, JOAQUIN
1902-

Born in Sagunt, in the province of Valencia, Spanish composer Rodrigo lost his sight at the age of 3. After studies with musicians in Valencia he worked with Dukas in Paris at the École Normale de Musique from 1927 to 1932. He returned to Spain in 1933 and was awarded a scholarship, which enabled him to return to Paris and continue his education. He became a permanent resident of Spain in 1939. He is a composer of works which, because of their Romantic lyricism and conventional harmonies, etc., sound older than they are. His music is filled with Spanish color and folk elements.

Concerted

A Concierto de Aranjuez for Guitar and Orchestra (1939)

$ John Williams, guitar; Philharmonia Orchestra; Louis Frémaux, conductor; Columbia IM-37848, ♮ IMT-37848. Includes Rodrigo's Fantasia para un gentilhombre for Guitar and Orchestra (1954), rated B.

Also--see entries under Castelnuovo-Tedesco, Concerted, Concerto for Guitar, Op.99, in D and Falla, Concerted, Noches en los jardines de España ("Nights in the Gardens of Spain") (1909-1915), both supra.

B Fantasia para un gentilhombre for Guitar and Orchestra
(1954)--see entry for Concierto de Aranjuez for Guitar and Orchestra
(1939), immediately supra.

ROSSINI, GIOACCHINO
1792-1868

Baptized Gioacchino Antonio, Rossini is, along with Verdi and
Puccini, in the very forefront of Italian opera composers. He was born in
Pesaro, where his father was both town trumpeter and inspector of
slaughter-houses. In 1796 paterfamilias Rossini was incarcerated for siding
with the French in the political upheavals of that year. With papa in
prison, mama took to the stage as an opera buffa prima donna with not a
little success. Upon his release from jail, papa became an orchestral
performer in his wife's travelling company. They left little Gioacchino in
Bologna, cared for by a pork butcher (a pork butcher in Bologna?). It was
in this city that the budding composer received his initial musical
education: 3 years of harpsichord lessons and, from Angel Tesei, singing
and harmony lessons. By the time he was 10, he was a modestly
accomplished singer, and just in the nick of time, too, since his mother's
voice had deteriorated and he took to singing in church services for
remuneration. At 13 he was singing in the theater and, no slouch, playing
horn alongside his father. By a stroke of good fortune, the commanding
engineer in Bologna, Cavaliere Giusti, took a liking to Rossini and opened
the world of literature to him by reading and explaining the works of the
Italian poets to the youngster. In 1807 Rossini was admitted to the Liceo
Comunale at Bologna, where he studied counterpoint with Padre Mattei
and 'cello with Cavedagni. Gioacchino had already been composing (e.g.,
songs, short pieces for horn duo, other chamber works, etc.). After a year
at the Liceo, Rossini won a prize with a cantata. As a student Rossini
was much taken with the works of Mozart and thereby earned (from his
schoolmates) the nickname, "The Little German." Leaving the Liceo soon
after, Rossini wrote his first comic opera, La Cambiale di matrimonio
("The Matrimonial Market") which was produced in Venice in 1810. In
1813, after accepting a commission from the Grand Theatre in Venice,
Rossini was pursued by the manager of the San Moise Theatre (also in
Venice) to fulfill an agreement to write an opera and the impressario

189

forced a rather dreadful, but ostensibly serious, libretto upon Rossini. Had Rossini followed the plan of the libretto it would probably have been a disaster. Instead, he turned the work (Il Signor Bruschino) into a comic one, filled with bizarre effects (e.g., in the overture, the second violins mark each bar of one long passage by tapping their bows on their music stands; the bass and soprano each sing at the high and low extremes of their registers, respectively; a funeral march is performed at one of the most humorous junctures in the work, etc.). Despite the complaints of the audience (thinking they were to see an opera seria) and the producer, Rossini could not be influenced to make any changes--he had enjoyed his joke too much to give way. His next work was a box office smash and a succès d'estime: Tancredi. Its production in February 1813 created what Percy Scholes calls a "madness" for the work and, naturally, for its composer. Thenceforth was Rossini fully established as the opera buffa composer nonpareil (sans égal even). So facile was he as a composer that he was able to write the whole of Il Barbiere di Siviglia in 13 days (using a previously composed overture, one from a work which had not done well--he was given to "reworking" and reusing portions of earlier compositions of his own in order to meet his febrile compositional pace). In an undated letter to an unknown composer, Rossini offered his famous and inimitable advice on how to compose a overture: "Wait until the evening before the opening night. Nothing primes inspiration more than necessity, whether it be the presence of a copyist waiting for your work or the prodding of an impressario tearing his hair. In my time, all the impressarios in Italy were bald at thirty. I composed the overture to Otello in a little room in the Barbaja palace wherein the baldest and fiercest of directors had forcibly locked me with a lone plate of spaghetti and the threat that I would not be allowed to leave the room until I had written the last note. I wrote the overture to La Gazza ladra the day of its opening in the theater itself, where I was imprisoned by the director and under the surveillance of four stagehands who were instructed to throw my original text through the window, page by page, to the copyists waiting below to transcribe it. In default of pages, they were ordered to throw me out the window bodily. ...I composed the overture to Conte Ory while fishing .... The overture for William Tell was composed under more or less similar circumstances. And as for Mosé, I did not write one." In 1822 he married the soprano Isabella Colbran (she had been the mistress of the impressario, Barbaja--a friend of Rossini's). Because she had a rather nice annuity and she was also 7 years older than he, Rossini was accused of marrying her for money (especially since her vocal powers were declining), but he had courted her for some time and may well have loved her. In 1843 he underwent surgical treatment for a urinary problem (either a kidney stone or gonorrhea--take your pick). Rossini and Isabella separated in 1837 and, since she died in 1845, he married Olympe Pelissier in 1847. In 1848 Rossini quit Bologna for Florence when, in 1855, he repaired to Paris, where he spent the rest of his life. During the years 1815 to 1823, Rossini wrote some 20 operas--an absolutely incredible feat, especially considering that almost all were raving successes. After writing William Tell in 1829, Rossini retired from composing opera--this due to a variety of circumstances, including French national politics. He said, though, that in his youth the melodies had chased him, but later, since he had to chase the melodies, composition was no longer fun. He did, however, write his lovely Stabat Mater and several songs and about 180 short pieces (which he generically titled Péchés de ma viellesse <"Sins of My Old Age">). In his retirement Rossini was well known as a host to lavish soirees, to which came the literary, musical and artistic giants, youngsters, etc., to partake of lively repartee, philosophical and artistic conversations and, naturally, the exquisite cuisine of the wealthy and generous host (Rossini was a gourmet who could be seduced about as easily either by a succulent dish or an attractive "dish" of another sort). His music is ever popular--his operas are performed with astounding regularity, and the overtures are still to be heard everywhere. The reasons for this popularity are easy to explain: Rossini's music is lively, witty, filled with easily whistled melodies, colorfully orchestrated, is never condescending and does not demand great intellectual powers to be appreciated.

Operatic

A Il Barbiere di Siviglia ("The Barber of Seville") (1816)

$ Marilyn Horne, mezzo-soprano; Leo Nucci, baritone; Enzo Dara, bass; Samuel Ramey, bass; Chorus and Orchestra of the Academy of Santa Cecilia, Rome; Riccardo Chailly, conductor; Columbia I3-M-37862 (3 discs), ▣ I3-M-37862.

B La Cenerentola ("Cinderella") (1817)

191

$ Teresa Berganza, soprano; Luigi Alva, tenor; Renato Capecchi, baritone; Ugo Trama, bass; Chorus and Orchestra of the London Symphony; Claudio Abbado, conductor; DG 2709039 (3 discs).

B <u>William Tell</u> (1829)

$ Mirella Freni, soprano; Graziella Sciutti, soprano; Sherrill Milnes, baritone; Nicolai Ghiaurov, bass; Ambrosian Singers; National Philharmonic Orchestra, London; Riccardo Chailly, conductor; London 1446 (5 discs), ▣ 5-1446.

Orchestral

A Overtures: <u>Cenerentola</u> ("Cinderella") (1817); <u>La Gazza ladra</u> ("The Thieving Magpie") (1817); <u>Semiramide</u> (1823); <u>Tancredi</u> (1813) and <u>William Tell</u> (1829)

* Philharmonia Orchestra; Carlo Maria Giulini, conductor; Seraphim ▣ 4XG-60058.

Also—for <u>William Tell</u> Overture (1829) see entry under Rimsky-Korsakov, Orchestral, <u>Le Coq d'or</u> ("The Golden Cockerel") Suite (1907), <u>supra.</u>

A Overtures: <u>Il Barbiere di Siviglia</u> ("The Barber of Seville") (1816); <u>La Gazza ladra</u> ("The Thieving Magpie") (1817); <u>La Scala di seta</u> ("The Silken Ladder") (1812); <u>Semiramide</u> (1823) and <u>William Tell</u> Overture (1829)

$ London Symphony Orchestra; Pierino Gamba, conductor; London 41027, ▣ 41027.

A Overtures: <u>L'Italiana in Algeri</u> ("The Italian Woman in Algiers") (1813); <u>Il Barbiere di Siviglia</u> ("The Barber of Seville") (1816); <u>Il Signor Bruschino</u> (1813) and <u>La Scala di seta</u> ("The Silken Ladder") (1812)

* Philharmonia Orchestra; Carlo Maria Giulini, conductor; Seraphim ▣ 4XG-60138. Includes Verdi's Overtures to <u>La Forza del destino</u> ("The Force of Destiny") (1862); <u>La Traviata</u> (1853), both rated A, and the Preludes to Acts I and III of <u>I Vespri siciliani</u> (1856).

SAINT—SAËNS, CAMILLE
1835-1921

Charles-Camille Saint-Saëns (rhymes with "Man-Lawns"), despite his rather regal-sounding name, was the son of a peasant father and middle-class mother. His mother was widowed while Camille was quite young, and he was given piano lessons, beginning almost in infancy, by his mother and her great-aunt. He gave a public performance when he was 4 and by age 7 was a pupil of the celebrated pianist, Camille-Marie Stamaty (himself a pupil of Mendelssohn). Saint-Saëns made his formal debut at 11, in which he performed an entire Mozart concerto and a movement from one of Beethoven's. In 1848 he was a student at the Conservatoire de Paris, studying organ with François Benoist (taking a second prize after his first year) and composition with Halévy. He was appointed organist of the Église de Saint-Merry in 1853 and, in 1857, gained the important post of organist at the Madeleine. Additionally, in 1855, his Symphony No.1 had been performed by the Société Sainte-Cécile. All the while he was composing and gaining a reputation as an organist and pianist of virtuosity and taste. He started writing operas in 1864 and, by the end of his life, had written 13. Despite this not insignificant number of operas (of which only Samson et Dalila, written in 1877, is still regularly performed), it was in instrumental and orchestral music that he achieved lasting fame. His work combines the flair for the exotic to be found most often in such Russian composers as Rimsky-Korsakov, plus a nice refinement and Classical (and French) regard for reticence and form. Despite the Wagnerian influences roiling about him, Saint-Saëns kept his musical barque on his own, untroubled and self-possessed, course.

Chamber

B Sonata No.1 for Violin and Piano, in d, Op.75

$ Jascha Heifetz, violin; Brooks Smith, piano; RCA LSC-2978. Includes Sibelius' Nocturne No.3, Op.3 (arranged by Michael Press); Wieniawski's Capriccio-Valse, Op.7, rated C; Rachmaninoff's Daisies, Op.38 No.3 (transcribed by Heifetz) and Falla's Nana: (Bereceuse) and Jota.

Concerted

A Carnival of the Animals ("Grand Zoological Fantasy") for Two Pianos and Orchestra (1886)

* Aldo Ciccolini, piano; Alexis Weissenberg, piano; Paris Conservatory Orchestra; Georges Prêtre, conductor; Angel AE-34452, 目 AE-34452. Includes Saint-Saëns' Concerto for Piano No.2, Op.22, in g,

rated B. The performers in the Concerto are Ciccolini accompanied by the L'Orchestre de Paris conducted by Serge Baudo.

B Concerto for 'Cello No.1, Op.33, in a

* Jacqueline Du Pré, 'cello; New Philharmonia Orchestra; Daniel Barenboim, conductor; Angel AE-34490, ▤ AE-34490. Includes Robert Schumann's Concerto for 'Cello, Op.129, in a, rated A.

Also—see entry under Lalo, Concerted, Concerto for 'Cello and Orchestra, in d (1876), supra.

B Concerto for Piano No.2, Op.22, in g

$ Pascal Rogé, piano; Royal Philharmonic Orchestra; Charles Dutoit, conductor; London 7253, ▤ 7253. Includes Saint-Saëns' Concerto for Piano No.4, Op.33, in c, also rated B.

Also—see entry for Carnival of the Animals ("Grand Zoological Fantasy") for Two Pianos and Orchestra (1886), supra.

B Concerto for Piano No.4, Op.44, in c—see entry for Concerto for Piano No.2, Op.22, in g, immediately supra.

B Concerto for Violin No.3, Op.61, in b

$ Itzhak Perlman, violin; Orchestre de Paris; Daniel Barenboim, conductor; DG 4105261 GH, ▤ 410526-4 GH. Includes Wienawski's Concerto for Violin No.2, Op.22, in d, rated B.

Also—see entry under Lalo, Concerted, Symphonie espagnole for Violin and Orchestra, Op.21, supra.

A Havanaise for Violin and Orchestra, Op.83

$ Jascha Heifetz, violin; RCA Symphony Orchestra; William Steinberg, conductor; RCA LSC-3232(e). Includes Saint-Saëns' Introduction and Rondo Capriccioso for Violin and Orchestra, Op.28, rated A; Brahms' Hungarian Dance No.7, in A (1868) with Heifetz and the Los Angeles Philharmonic Orchestra conducted by Alfred Wallenstein, rated A; Chausson's Poème for Violin and Orchestra, Op.25: here Heifetz is accompanied by the same orchestra, but with Izler Solomon conducting, rated B; Sarasate's Zigeunerweisen ("Gypsy Airs") for Violin and Orchestra, Op.20 No.1, rated B and Waxman's Carmen Fantasy (Based on

Themes from Bizet's Carmen) (1947), in this the RCA Symphony Orchestra is conducted by Donald Voorhees.

Also--see entry under Ravel, Concerted, Tzigane ("Gypsies") for Violin and Orchestra (1924), supra.

A Introduction and Rondo Capriccioso for Violin and Orchestra, Op. 28--see entries under Chausson, Concerted, Poème for Violin and Orchestra, Op.25, supra; Ravel, Concerted, Tzigane ("Gypsies") for Violin and Orchestra (1924) and Havanaise for Violin and Orchestra, Op.83, immediately supra.

Orchestral

A "Bacchanale" from Samson and Dalila, Op.47

$ Orchestre de Paris; Daniel Barenboim, conductor; DG 415847-1 GGA, ▤ 415847-4 GGA. Includes Saint-Saëns' Danse macabre, Op.40 and Symphony No.3 ("Organ"), Op.78, in c, both also rated A. In the Symphony, Barenboim conducts the Chicago Symphony Orchestra, and the organist is Gaston Litaize.

A Danse macabre, Op.40--see entries for "Bacchanale" from Samson and Dalila, Op.47, immediately supra and under Dukas, Orchestral, L'Apprenti sorcier ("The Sorcerer's Apprentice") (1897), supra.

Symphonic

A Symphony No.3 ("Organ"), Op.78, in c

$$ Michael Murray, organ; Philadelphia Orchestra; Eugene Ormandy, conductor; Telarc 10051.

* Pierre Segon, organ; L'Orchestre de la Suisse Romande; Ernest Ansermet, conductor; London ▤ STS5-15154.

Also--see entry under Orchestral, "Bacchanale" from Samson and Dalila, Op.47, supra.

SALIERI, ANTONIO
1750-1825

Student of Austrian composer Florian Leopold Gassman and of the German-Bohemian composer, Christoph Willibald Gluck, Salieri was an Italian composer of operas, in particular. He was talented but also given to court (and other) intriguing in order to achieve his ends, which ends

195

included a variety of musical posts: <u>Kapellmeister</u> at the court in Vienna, and conductor of the Vienna Tonkünstler-Sozietät. The likelihood of Salieri's having poisoned Mozart is about the same as that of Sir Francis Bacon's having written the poems of Yeats.

Concerted

B Concerto for Flute and Oboe, in C--see entry under Cimarosa, Concerted, Concerto for Oboe and Strings (Arranged from Melodies of Cimarosa by Arthur Benjamin), <u>supra</u>.

SARASATE, PABLO DE
1844-1908

Pablo Martin Melitón Sarasate y Navascues was a native of Pamplona who studied at the Conservatoire de Paris and won first prizes in solfège and violin. He went on to become one of the greatest violinists of his era. He lived sufficiently long to be able to have his playing (admittedly beyond its peak) recorded by the phonograph, then in its infancy. His fame was international: it rested on an infallible technique and an impeccable sense of style.

Concerted

B <u>Zigeunerweisen</u> ("Gypsy Airs") for Violin and Orchestra, Op.20 No.1--see entries under Chausson, Concerted, <u>Poème</u> for Violin and Orchestra, Op.25, <u>supra</u> and Saint-Saëns, Concerted, <u>Havanaise</u> for Violin and Orchestra, Op.83, <u>supra</u>.

Instrumental

C <u>Navarra</u> for 2 Violins, Op.33

* Aaron Rosand, violin; Vox 512760. Includes Sarasate's Spanish Dances, Op.21, 22, 23 and 26, rated B.

B Spanish Dances, Op.21, 22, 23 and 26--see entry for <u>Navarra</u> for 2 Violins, Op.33, immediately <u>supra</u>.

SATIE, ERIK
1866-1925

Born to a French father and a London-born mother of Scottish parentage, composer Erik-Alfred-Leslie Satie was one of a number of

French eccentrics who exerted enormous influence on both their contemporaries and on the composers who came after. Satie's parents moved from Honfleur (the composer's birthplace) to Paris while Erik was a relatively small child. He was left in the care of his grandparents. An uncle, Adrien, was close to little Erik and was probably of some influence on the development of the child's personality, Adrien being quite an eccentric himself. At the age of 12 Erik moved to Paris to join his parents. He attended the Conservatoire de Paris from 1879 to 1886. The faculty of the Conservatoire did not approve of Satie's compositions; the academicians nothwithstanding, Satie began to publish his piano pieces in 1887. At about the same time he became fascinated with the Rosicrucian religious sect and with the study of plainsong. Concurrently, he was an habitué of the Montmartre cafes favored by the "Bohemian" artists. He became a pianist in cafes in Montmartre and, in 1890, was befriended by Debussy (their friendship ended in estrangement not long before Debussy's death). After a 7-year spell in the industrial suburb of Arcueil (which was now his regular residence), Satie began studying counterpoint with d'Indy and Roussel at the Schola Cantorum (this in 1905, when Satie was 40). He received a diploma (honored with a très bon) which allowed him, then, to present something in the way of credentials to those of his critics who considered him a humbug. For most of the rest of his life Satie was accepted both as a musician and as a creature of strange behavior (and confirmed bachelorhood, although stories abound about his having had his way with ladies in the cafes in which he worked: such occurrences usually after the cafe closed and he had finished another of his frequent chores—sweeping up the "joint"). Regarding Satie's music, it is difficult to explain much of his beliefs or any "school" to which he might have belonged, since he professed adherence to none (except, perhaps, the Rosicrucians, and no one is certain about that). Rather, his music tends towards mysticism, odd harmonies, melodies which could be well organized (and yet beautiful, or boring, or provocative) and Classical elements (and here is where his most profound influence on the likes of Ravel is to be found). He was a friend to Cocteau, Picasso and Diaghilev, among others, and despite the movements they represented (e.g., cubism, dadaism, etc.), he remained aloof from them. A word to the wise: with Satie, pay no attention to those of his titles which may seem très outré since such titles were usually only a sardonic attention–getting device, or, possibly, a means of self–defense.

Ballet

C <u>Parade</u> (1917)

* Utah Symphony Orchestra; Maurice Abravanel, conductor; Vanguard C–10037–10038 (2 discs). Includes Satie's <u>Mercure</u> (1924); <u>Relâche</u> (Ballet) (1924); <u>Trois Gymnopédies</u> ("Three 'Barefooted' Dances") (Nos.1 and 3 Orchestrated by Debussy), rated A and <u>Trois Morceaux en forme de poire</u> ("Three Pieces in the Shape of a Pear") (1903); <u>La Belle Exentrique</u> (1920); <u>Cinq Grimaces pour le Songe d'une nuit d'été</u> (Five Affectations for "A Dream of a Summer Night") (1914); <u>En habit de cheval</u> ("In the Attire of a Horse") (1911); <u>Deux Préludes et une Gnossienne</u> ("Two Preludes and a Little Gnostic") (1890 and 1892); <u>Le Fils des Étoiles</u> ("The Son of the Stars") (1891) and <u>Jack in the Box</u> (1899).

Instrumental

A <u>Trois Gymnopédies</u> ("Three 'Barefooted' Dances") (1888)

$ Aldo Ciccolini, piano; Angel S–36482. Includes Satie's <u>Croquis et agaceries d'un gros bonhomme en bois</u> ("Sketches and Exasperations of a Big Wooden Blockhead") (1913); <u>Heures séculaires et instantanées</u> ("Time–honored and Instantaneous Hours") (1914); <u>Trois Avant dernières pensées</u> ("Three Penultimate Thoughts") (1915); <u>Trois Gnossiennes</u> ("Three Little Gnostics") (1888); <u>Trois Morceaux en forme de poire</u> ("Three Pieces in the Shape of a Pear") (1903); <u>Trois Nocturnes</u> (1919) and <u>Trois Valses distinguées du précieux dégoûté</u> ("Three Waltzes of an Affected, Disgusted Man") (1914).

Also––for orchestral version of Nos.1 and 3, see entries under Orchestral, <u>infra</u> and under Ibert, Orchestral, <u>Divertissement</u> (1930), <u>supra</u>.

Orchestral

A <u>Trois Gymnopédies</u> ("Three 'Barefooted' Dances") (Nos.1 and 3 Orchestrated by Debussy)––see entries for <u>Parade</u> (1917) under Ballet, <u>supra</u> and under Ibert, Orchestral, <u>Divertissement</u> (1930), <u>supra</u>.

SCARLATTI, DOMENICO
1685–1757

Giuseppe Domenico Scarlatti was the son of the exceedingly famous composer, Alessandro Scarlatti (of whom no less than Edward J. Dent calls "...the founder of the Neapolitan school of the 18th century."). Indeed, the entire male line of the Scarlatti family of that period appears to have been comprised of illustrious composers: Domenico, obviously didn't have a choice (one of the few examples in music where a composer didn't have to wrangle with his father because said father wanted his son to become a doctor, lawyer, accountant, mayor, lobbyist, or member of some other "respectable" profession). Having studied with his father, Domenico became organist of the royal chapel in Naples at the age of 16. At 18 he achieved notoriety as an opera composer and in 1705 he was sent to study with Gasparini in Venice. In 1709 he was in Rome at the same time as Handel. The two of them engaged in a friendly keyboard performance-cum -contest. It was adjudged that Handel won on the organ but was bested by Scarlatti on the harpsichord. From that time forward, the pair remained the best of friends, each having a healthy respect for the talents of the other. Also in 1709, Scarlatti came into the employ of Maria Casimira, Queen of Poland, and wrote several operas for her private theater. After the Queen left Rome, in 1714, Scarlatti took the position of maestro di cappella to the Portuguese ambassador to Rome. Following several other changes of employment, Scarlatti finally found himself appointed to the royal chapel in Lisbon as maestro. When one of his patronesses, the Infanta Maria Barbara, married the Prince of the Asturias, Scarlatti moved with his employer to the court in Madrid, there to spend the rest of his life (he had previously made 2 trips back to Italy: in 1724, to visit his father, and in 1729, to marry Maria Caterina Gentile). Scarlatti's first wife died in 1739, and he remarried, this time to a Spanish woman, Anastasia Ximenes(?), at some later (and not known for a certitude) date. Scarlatti fathered 9 children, 5 with Maria and 4 with Anastasia. Scarlatti's music (and he is best known for his works for solo harpsichord), once he removed himself to Spain, was written in an odd amalgam of the homophonic style with an earthy appreciation for the Spanish culture (some aver they can hear castanets, guitars, flamenco elements, etc., in Scarlatti's harpsichord works). Scarlatti's pieces for solo harpsichord (generically named by him Esercizi <numbering 555>, but known individually as sonatas) having been cataloged by both Alessandro Longo and, more recently, Ralph Kirkpatrick, they therefore bear both "L" and

"K" numbers. An oddment of history: Scarlatti, Bach and Handel all have the same birth year.

Instrumental

A Sonatas for Harpsichord

* Luciano Sgrizzi, harpsichord; Nonesuch 71094. Includes the following 16 sonatas: K.15, 162, 517, 191, 532, 212, 355, 227, 146, 515, 290, 445, 184, 307 and 475.

SCHOENBERG, ARNOLD
1874-1951

Born in Vienna, Arnold Schoenberg (surname originally Schönberg) began with little formal musical training other than violin and counterpoint studies, the former in the Vienna Realschule, the latter privately with Alexander von Zemlinsky. Virtually single-handedly, Schoenberg founded the "Second Viennese" (i.e., "Post-Romantic," after the Schubert-through-Mahler era) school: that is, one in which the 12-tone system ("dodecaphony") is preeminent, and the normal tonic system was essentially abandoned. As an admirer of Mahler's music, Schoenberg's early works were based pretty much on that master's style. His first real success came in 1902 with the Sextet for Strings titled Verklärte Nacht ("Transfigured Night") (written in 1889)--still his most popular work. Schoenberg's influence, from the 1920s until the mid-1960s, was immense. He numbered among his students (and worshippers) Alban Berg, Webern, Krenek and Dallappiccola. Among those who did not study with him but who emit his radiance are the likes of Messiaen, Boulez, Stockhausen and Xenakis. From 1935 to 1936, Schoenberg was on the faculty of the University of Southern California, and from 1936 almost to his death, at the University of California at Los Angeles. He became an American citizen in 1941. Although Schoenberg's importance as a force for change in the musical direction of this century cannot be denied, a taste for his music, per se, is about as difficult for most people to develop as one for catfish-eyeball stew.

Chamber

C Chamber Symphony No.1, Op.9, in E

* Los Angeles Chamber Orchestra; Gerard Schwarz, conductor; Nonesuch 79001. Includes Schoenberg's Five Pieces for Orchestra, Op.16, also rated C.

Choral

B Gurre-Lieder (1900–1901)

$ Jessye Norman, soprano; Tatiana Troyanos, mezzo-soprano; James McCracken, tenor; Werner Klemperer, narrator; Tanglewood Festival Chorus; Boston Symphony Orchestra; Seiji Ozawa, conductor; Philips 6769038 (2 discs), ▣ 7699124.

Orchestral

C Begleitungsmusik zu einer Lichtspielscene, Op.34--see entry for Variations for Orchestra, Op.31, infra.

C Five Pieces for Orchestra, Op.16--see entries for Chamber Symphony No.1, Op.9, in E under Chamber, supra and Variations for Orchestra, Op.31, immediately infra.

C Variations for Orchestra, Op.31

$ BBC Symphony Orchestra; Pierre Boulez, conductor; Columbia M-35882. Includes Schoenberg's Begleitungsmusik zu einer Lichtspielscene, Op.34, Five Pieces for Orchestra, Op.16, rated C and Survivor from Warsaw, Op.46.

A Verklärte Nacht ("Transfigured Night") (Orchestrated by Schoenberg from his String Sextet, Same Opus Number), Op.4

$ Ensemble InterContemporain; Pierre Boulez, conductor; Columbia IM-39566, IMT-39566. Includes Schoenberg's Suite for Chamber Ensemble, Op.29.

Vocal

B Pierrot lunaire (Song Cycle), Op.21

* Jan De Gaetani, soprano; Contemporary Chamber Ensemble; Arthur Weisberg, conductor; Nonesuch 71251.

SCHUBERT, FRANZ
1797–1828

Franz Peter Schubert is undoubtedly the greatest composer born in Vienna. His father was a schoolmaster; his mother had been a domestic servant. The family was moderately comfortable and, had all the children survived beyond their infancies, Franz would have had 11 or so siblings. Only he and 3 others of their parents' children did survive. Of these, Franz and his brother Ferdinand became well known (Ferdinand for works on musical pedagogy). Franz was taught to play the violin by his father, an amateur 'cellist. He learned to play the piano from lessons given him by his eldest brother, Ignaz. It was not long (in 1805, when Franz was 8) before the boy informed his instructors, with childish honesty and not impudence, that they had nothing more to teach him. Franz also indicated that he would have to make his own way. When he was 9 or 10, Franz' father entrusted his musical education to Michael Holzer, organist of their parish church in Liechtenthal. Franz was taught singing, harmony and organ performance by Holzer. According to Holzer's own admission, Schubert was soon beyond what Holzer had to offer: "If I wished to instruct him in anything fresh, he already knew it. Consequently I have given him no actual tuition <i.e., tutoring> but merely talked to him, and watched him with silent astonishment." In 1808 Schubert was taken on as a choirboy at the court chapel; this engendered admission to the Imperial and Royal Seminary. Among his instructors there was Salieri, and in this institution, too, Schubert was considered out of the ordinary. In short order he was given the seat as concertmaster of the school orchestra. By this time the Schubert family's financial situation was terrible, and young Franz had to admit to one of his instructors that he had not the money to purchase the manuscript paper requisite to his needs. The instructor, who had taken Schubert under his conducting arm, provided him with all the paper he could use. In the absence of the regular orchestra director (Wenzel Ruzicka), Schubert often conducted. This was a marvelous opportunity for one so young and gifted to become familiar, not only with the contemporary orchestral repertoire (e.g., Haydn, Mozart, Beethoven, etc.) but also with conducting technique. Ultimately, Schubert's education began to be supervised by Salieri himself, this to extend even after Franz left the Seminary (belying Salieri's meanness). In 1810 Schubert had written his first (that is, with any certainty) composition: a sonata for 2 pianos. His first song dates from 1811. In 1813 Schubert wrote his first symphony and was dismissed from the Seminary because his voice had changed. Schubert's mother had died in 1812, and his father remarried in 1813. Anna Kleyenböck, Franz' new stepmother was a generous and kind soul, and she provided him with "loans" from her housekeeping allowance. Bowing to his father's desires, Franz entered a training-school for elementary school teachers in 1813. By the fall of the next year he was teaching at his father's school. He continued studying with Salieri until 1816. Many musicologists feel that it was the inadequacy of his formal musical education which was to blame for the occasional flaws one finds in his mature music. The principal flaw, and the one most easily discerned, is that which shows up as an inability to organize his longer works coherently. He was somewhat impetuous and this is ascribed to his volatile and poetic nature. Yet it does not seem likely that Salieri would not have provided him with all of the rudiments that a well-equipped composer of the early 19th century would have been deemed to need. Quite possibly, the flaws to be found found in Schubert's works may simply have been caused by the haste with which he worked. Looking at the incredible output that began in 1814 and ended with his death, only 14 years later, it is no wonder that there are some lapses: 13 operas, incidental music for 3 plays, over 25 works for the church, 10 works for chorus and orchestra, over 40 works for chorus and piano, about 30 works for unaccompanied chorus, 15 orchestral works, 3 pieces for violin and orchestra, 26 assorted chamber works, about 40 piano works, about 580 songs (there are 634 in all) and an assortment of about another 30 miscellaneous pieces. Going back to Schubert's life: in 1816, after drudging along teaching, he attempted to get a job as music master in a school devoted to training elementary school teachers. In this he failed and he left off teaching in order to live with 2 friends and try full-time composing. In 1817, he was back to teaching but, in 1818, he was offered the position of music-master to the children of Count Johann Esterházy in Zelész, Hungary. He happily accepted, and never returned to classroom teaching. He returned with the Esterházy family to Vienna in late 1818 and, in early 1819, his one-act operetta Die Zwillingsbrüder was produced. This, with the productions of others of his works, began to bring him to the attention of the Viennese musical public. During the period until early 1821, Schubert lived with a few different friends then, finally, moved into his own lodgings. For the remainder of his life he moved haphazardly, having no real home, living in poverty in a succession of poor rooms (sometimes alone, sometimes with friends). In 1822 Schubert contracted syphilis and his already weakened health began to break almost immediately. During his last years, Schubert was increasingly productive, and the products are of exceptional quality. He died in November of 1828, of complications brought on by an attack of typhus. A good deal of Schubert's music is very well known to the public, and it is much loved for its easy approachability, its beautiful melodies and for the sensitivity of its emotional content. No one, either before or after him, wrote better songs, and few wrote string quartets to equal his. One anecdote in a lighter vein: there lived in Dresden a double-bass player and composer by the name of Franz Anton Schubert. When the "real" Schubert submitted the manuscript of his great song, Der Erlkönig, the publisher (Breitkopf and Härtel, in Leipzig), declining to publish it, returned it to the only Franz Schubert of whom they knew: naturally, the wrong one. This virtual non-entity indignantly wrote back to the publisher, "I have further to inform you that some ten days ago I received a valued letter from you in which you enclosed the manuscript of Goethe's Der Erlkönig alleged to be set by me. With the greatest astonishment I state that this cantata (sic) was never composed by me. I shall retain the same in my possession to learn, if possible, who sent you that sort of trash in such an impolite manner and also to discover the fellow who has thus misused my name." Schubert's works were indexed by Otto Deutsch, ergo the "D" numbers.

Chamber

C Introduction and Variations for Flute and Piano, D.802

$ Jean-Pierre Rampal, flute; Robert Veyron-Lacroix, piano; RCA AGL1-4141, ▣ AGL1-4141. Includes Reinecke's Sonata for Flute and Piano ("Undine"), Op.167 and Robert Schumann's Romances for Oboe and Piano, Op.94 (3), Nos.1-3 (in these performances, the oboe part is transcribed for flute), also rated C.

A Octet for Strings and Winds, D.803

* Boston Symphony Chamber Players; Nonesuch 79046, ▣ 79046-4.

B Phantasie for Violin and Piano, in C, D.934

$ Zino Francescatti, violin; Eugenio Bagnoli, piano; Columbia CMS-6829. Includes Schubert's Sonatinas for Violin and Piano (3), Nos.1-3: D.384 and D.408, also rated B.

A Piano Quintet ("The Trout"), in d, D.667

$$ Sviatoslav Richter, piano; Georg Hörtnagel, bass viol; Borodin Quartet; Angel DS-37846.

A Sonata for Arpeggione and Piano, in a, D.821--see entry for Sonata for 'Cello and Piano, in d (1915) under Debussy, Chamber, _supra._

A String Quartet No.12 ("Quartettsatz"), in c, D.703

$ Portland Quartet; Arabesque 6536. Includes Schubert's Quartet No.14 ("Death and the Maiden"), D.810, in d, also rated A.

A String Quartet No.14 ("Death and the Maiden"), D.810, in d

$ Melos Quartet; DG 419064-1 GGA, ▣ 419064-4 GGA.

Also--see entry for String Quartet No.12 ("Quartettsatz"), in c, D.703, immediately _supra._

B String Quartet No.15, in g, D.887

$ Guarneri Quartet; RCA ARL1-3003.

A Trios for Piano, Violin and 'Cello (2), Nos.1-2: D.898 in B flat and D.929, in E flat

$ Artur Rubinstein, piano; Henryk Szeryng, violin; Pierre Fournier, 'cello; RCA ARL2-0731 (2 discs).

Choral

C _Lazarus_ (Easter Cantata), D.689

$ Sheila Armstrong, soprano; Anthony Rolfe Johnson, tenor; ORTF Chorus and Orchestra; Theodore Guschlbauer, conductor; Erato STU-71442 (2 discs).

B Mass No.2, in G, D.167

$ Vienna Boys' Choir; Vienna Symphony Orchestra; Uwe Christian Harrer, conductor; Philips 6514262, ▣ 7337262. Includes Schubert's _Deutsche_ Messe, D.872.

C Mass No.4, in C, D.452

* Vienna State Opera Chorus and Orchestra; George Barati, conductor; Lyrichord 7101.

Instrumental

C Allegretto, in d, D.915

$ Claudio Arrau, piano; Philips 9500755. Includes Schubert's Sonata No.19, in c, D.958, rated B.

A Fantasia ("Wanderer"), in C, D.760

$ Maurizio Pollini, piano; DG 2530473. Includes Schubert's Sonata No.16, in a, D.845, rated B.

B Impromptus (8), Nos.1-8: D.899 and D.935

* Alfred Brendel, piano; Turnabout 34481, 𝕭 CT-2130.

A <u>Moments</u> <u>musicaux</u> (6), Nos.1-6: D.946

* Emil Gilels, piano; Allegro 88100, 𝕭 88100. Includes Robert Schumann's <u>Nachtstücke</u> (4) Nos.1-4, Op.23, rated B.

C Piano Pieces (3), Nos.1-3: D.946

* Gilbert Kalish, piano; Nonesuch 71386. Includes Schubert's Sonata ("Unfinished"), in C, D.840, also rated C.

B Sonata No.14, in a, D.784

$ Paul Badura-Skoda, piano; RCA AGL1-2707. Includes Schubert's Sonata No.20, in A, D.959, also rated B.

C Sonata ("Unfinished"), in C, D.840--see entry for Piano Pieces (3), Nos.1-3: D.946, <u>supra</u>.

B Sonata No.16, in a, D.845--see entry for Fantasia ("Wanderer"), in C, D.760, <u>supra</u>.

B Sonata No.19, in c, D.958--see entry for Allegretto, D.915, in d, <u>supra</u>.

B Sonata No.20, in A, D.959--see entry for Sonata No.14, in a, D.784, <u>supra</u>.

A Sonata No.21, in B flat, D.960

$ Claudio Arrau, piano; Philips 9500928, ◙ 7300928.

Orchestral

A Rosamunde: Incidental Music, D.797

* Oksana Sowiak, contralto; Hungarica Philharmonia; Peter Maag; conductor; Turnabout 34330, ◙ CT-4330.

Symphonic

A Symphony No.3, in D, D.200

* Hungarica Philharmonia; Peter Maag, conductor; Turnabout 34361. Includes Schubert's Symphony No.4 ("Tragic"), in c, D.417, also rated A.

A Symphony No.4 ("Tragic"), in c, D.417—see entry for Symphony No.3, in D, D.200, immediately supra.

A Symphony No.5, in B flat, D.485

* Hungarica Philharmonia; Peter Maag, conductor; Turnabout 34474. Includes Schubert's Symphony No.6 ("Little"), in C, D.589, rated B.

* Philharmonia Orchestra; Otto Klemperer, conductor; Angel AE-34444, ◙ AE-34444. Includes Schubert's Symphony No.8 ("Unfinished"), in b, D.759, also rated A.

B Symphony No.6 ("Little"), in C, D.589—see entry for Symphony No.5, in B flat, D.485, immediately supra.

A Symphony No.8 ("Unfinished"), in b, D.759—see entry for Symphony No.5, in B flat, D.485, supra.

A Symphony No.9 (The "Great"), in C, D.944

* Berlin Philharmonic Orchestra; Herbert von Karajan, conductor; AM-34731, ◙ Am-34731.

Vocal

B Der Hirt auf dem Felsen ("The Shepherd on the Rock") for Soprano, Clarinet and Piano, D.965

$ Elly Ameling, soprano; Guy Depuis, clarinet; Irwin Gage, piano; Peters PLE-123. Must be special ordered. Includes Schubert's songs Auf dem Strom ("On the Stream"), D.943; Gott im Frühling ("God in Spring"),

D.448; <u>Herbst</u> ("Autumn"), D.945; <u>Kanzonen,</u> D.688; <u>Die</u> <u>Sommernacht</u> ("The Summer Night"), D.289 and <u>Winterabend</u> ("Winter Evening"), D.938.

A <u>Die</u> <u>schöne</u> <u>Müllerin</u> ("The Lovely Miller's Daughter") (Song Cycle), D.795

$ Ernst Haefliger, tenor; Jörg Ewald Dähler, piano; Claves 8301, ▤ 8301.

A <u>Schwanengesang</u> ("Swan Song") (Song Cycle), D.957

$ Ernst Haefliger, tenor; Jörg Ewald Dähler, piano; Claves D-8506.

A <u>Die</u> <u>Winterreise</u> ("The Journey in Winter") (Song Cycle), D.911

$ Dietrich Fischer-Dieskau, baritone, Daniel Barenboim, piano; DG 2707118 (2 discs), ▤ 3301237.

A Various Lieder

$ Dietrich Fischer-Dieskau, baritone; Gerald Moore, piano; Angel S-36341. Includes <u>Am</u> <u>Tage</u> <u>Aller</u> <u>Seelen</u> ("On All-Souls Day"), D.343; <u>Auf</u> <u>dem</u> <u>Wasser</u> <u>zu</u> <u>singen</u> ("To Be Sung on the Water"), D.774; <u>Du</u> <u>bist</u> <u>die</u> <u>Ruh'</u> ("You Are the Peace"), D.776; <u>Der</u> <u>Erlkönig</u> ("The Erl-King"), D.328; <u>Die</u> <u>Forelle</u> ("The Trout"), D.550; <u>Heidenröslein</u> ("The Little Heath-Rose"), D.257; <u>Der</u> <u>Jüngling</u> <u>an</u> <u>der</u> <u>Quelle</u> ("Youth at Its Source"), D.300; <u>Lachen</u> <u>und</u> <u>weinen</u> ("Laughing and Weeping"), D.777; <u>Lied</u> <u>im</u> <u>Grünen</u> ("Song in the Green Time"), D.917; <u>Sei</u> <u>mir</u> <u>gegrüsst!</u> ("Be Greeted By Me"), D.741; <u>Seligkeit</u> ("Blessedness"), D.433; <u>Ständchen</u> ("Serenade"), D.410; <u>Ständchen</u> ("Serenade"), D.889; <u>Der</u> <u>Tod</u> <u>und</u> <u>das</u> <u>Mädchen</u> ("Death and the Maiden"), D.531 and <u>Der</u> <u>Wanderer</u> ("The Wanderer"), D.649.

SCHUMANN, ROBERT
1810-1856

Robert Alexander Schumann was the 5th and youngest child to a father who was a Saxon bookseller, publisher and author and a mother who was the daughter of a surgeon. The family was solidly fixed in the middle-class financial stratum and quite comfortable. Robert began his education at the age of 6 with private tutoring; he did not display any precocity at that time. He also began receiving piano lessons then, his teacher being the organist of St. Mary's Church, in Schumann's home town of Zwickau (Saxony). He started composing when he was 7 and by the time he was 11 he was writing works for chorus and orchestra. The happy circumstance of being the son of a man who not only owned a bookshop, but also an extensive private library, allowed Robert to read voraciously (if not always judiciously--he seemed to devour everything he could reach) and to develop, ultimately, into an extremely literate young man. At 10 he entered the Zwickau Lyceum and remained there until he was 18. On receiving his diploma he became a law student at the University of Leipzig, then matriculated to the University of Heidelberg, but gave up formal education when he was 20. His father had died in 1826, and it had been his wish that Robert become a member of the bar. When Robert indicated to his mother, in 1830, that he wished to pursue a career in music, she allowed him to follow this line and permitted him to return to Leipzig to study with Professor Friedrich Wieck. Wieck had heard Schumann perform on the piano, and he wrote Robert's mother that he believed that, given proper training, Robert could become one of the foremost pianists. Wieck had no doubts of Robert's ability save one: he felt Schumann lacked the necessary focus and discipline to apply himself steadily (particularly in what Wieck called "dry, cold theory") for 3 years. Schumann was taken as a student by Wieck then, but on a 6-month trial basis. Schumann went to live with Wieck in October, 1830. Wieck was then more interested in furthering the career of his daughter, the prodigy Clara, than in being available to Schumann. In 1831 Schumann wrote to Hummel requesting that that master take him on as a pupil. In his letter Schumann described his dissatisfaction with Wieck--both regarding his teaching (or, rather, the lack of it) and his theories of music. Nothing came of this, especially since, in 1832, while taking thorough-bass and piano lessons with the composer-teacher, Heinrich Dorn, Schumann tried to strengthen the ordinarily weak ring fingers by using a mechanical device and succeeded in disabling the ring finger of his right hand, thereby ending his potential career as a virtuoso. All the while Robert composed, and principally these were works for the piano (including the "Abegg" Variations, Papillons, etc.). Clara Wieck gave the first public performances of many of Schumann's early piano works. In 1833 Schumann moved to his own apartment in Leipzig. He had known tragedy early: in

1826 his only sister, Emilie, who was both physically and mentally handicapped, drowned herself. In 1833 his sister-in-law died, and Schumann either attempted, or thought seriously about, suicide by jumping from the window of his 4th floor rooms. Thereafter he always had a morbid fear of heights and would live only on the first floor of a building. While he was composing and publishing his works, he was also engaged in literary endeavors, particularly music criticism and in publishing his music journal, the Neue Leipziger Zeitschrift für Musik, in which journal he publicly recognized Chopin as a new musical genius. In 1834 the Wiecks accepted a 17-year-old girl as a border and music student. The girl went under the name of Ernestine von Fricken, and Schumann, believing her to be the daughter of a "wealthy" Baron von Fricken, promptly fell in love with her. It turned out that Ernestine was probably the Baron's illegitimate daughter; in any event, when he got wind of the proposed marriage of Ernestine and Robert, the good Baron spirited her back to their home in Asch and formally adopted her. On November 25, 1835 Robert and Clara Wieck indulged in their first osculation and it became obvious to them that they were truly in love (Ernestine was formally relieved of her engagement to Robert on January 1, 1836). Clara was 6 months short of her 16th birthday at this time. Fairly soon after this Professor Wieck became aware of his daughter's inclinations and wrote to Schumann forbidding him to see Clara. Clara, the obedient daughter, did not see Robert for some time; in fact, by the beginning of 1837, Schumann appears to have become resigned to losing her. Soon, however, there was a reconciliation and Robert formally asked her father's permission for them to be married in October of 1837. Wieck's response was to remove Clara from Leipzig for 7 months on a concert tour. Schumann was once again contemplating suicide. On Clara's return, in May 1838 they saw each other often, but whenever they were separated, Schumann suffered deep depression. Finally, in 1839, after Clara weakened in her insistence that, prior to marriage, Robert had to be sufficiently well-off financially that she could be assured of comfort, and after Robert instituted a suit against her father for her "release" (and Professor Wieck countersued, claiming, among other things, that Robert was a drunk), Clara agreed to become betrothed. They were married in September, 1840. In the same year Robert received a Ph.D. from the University of Jena (a degree he sought and obtained without coursework, dissertation or examination).

Clara was a well-known and admired pianist at the time she married Schumann, and for some time he had to put up with being recognized as "Clara Wieck's husband." During the majority of his years of marriage Schumann produced many of his best works. During a trip to Russia, in 1844, he had suffered recurring bouts of severe melancholy, and slights, real or imagined, aggravated this problem: he developed insomnia, wept, and for periods was unable to work. Among the slights was his being passed over for the position of Director of the Leipzig Gewandhaus concerts after Mendelssohn's resignation (the inferior Gade got the job). The Schumanns had 8 children, and Schumann's mental stability was weakened even further after the death of his youngest child, Emil, in 1847. Despite being at the height of his creative powers, his mind began to crumble. In 1853 he was forced to resign his post as the Musical Director of Düsseldorf. His mental affliction (brought on by syphilis) now took the form of aural hallucinations: hearing beautiful music constantly. The beautiful music was replaced later by frightful sounds. Throughout the last part of his life, Schumann had been a friend to the ever-faithful and younger Brahms. It was Brahms, now, who attempted to help Clara carry on her own and her family's lives, while Robert was hospitalized with his final illness. In 1854 Schumann tried to drown himself in the Rhine. He finally died, not able to speak (and seeming to recognize but barely his beloved Clara), in the company of Clara and Brahms, about 2 months after his 46th birthday. Schumann's music is marked by a peculiar genius: he was a true Romantic and his works offer delicate melodies, subtle emotional content and truly rhapsodical fancies. His best efforts are those for piano, and his songs. In his orchestral works he becomes mired in the worst aspects of German art: his orchestrations are plodding, colorless and dull; likewise the melodic content (which tends to be inflated) is without intelligent or vital development. As with most Romantic composers, his greatest works tend to have been inspired by literary works. In sum, Schumann, along with Beethoven, Chopin and Liszt, remains one of the greatest of keyboard composers.

Chamber

A Fünf Stücke im Volkston ("Five Pieces in the Folk Style") for 'Cello and Piano, Op.102--see entry under Debussy, Chamber, Sonata for 'Cello and Piano, in d (1915), supra.

B Quartet for Piano and Strings, Op.47, in E flat

$ Glenn Gould, piano; Juilliard Quartet; Columbia D3S–806 (3 discs). Includes Schumann's String Quartets, Op.41 (3), Nos.1-3: in a, F and A, rated B and Quintet for Piano and Strings, Op.44, in E flat, featuring pianist Leonard Bernstein, rated A.

A Quintet for Piano and Strings, Op.44, in E flat--see entry for Quartet for Piano and Strings, Op.47, in E flat, immediately supra.

C Romances for Oboe and Piano, Op.94 (3), Nos.1-3--see entry under Schubert, Chamber, Introduction and Variations for Flute and Piano, D.802, supra.

B String Quartet No.1, Op.41, in a--see entry for Quartet for Piano and Strings, Op.47, in E flat, supra.

B String Quartet No.2, Op.41, in F--see entry for Quartet for Piano and Strings, Op.47, in E flat, supra.

B String Quartet No.3, Op.43, in A--see entry for Quartet for Piano and Strings, Op.47, in E flat, supra.

A Trio for Violin, 'Cello and Piano No.1, Op.63, in d

$ Beaux Arts Trio; Philips 670051 (2 discs). Includes the same composer's Trios for Violin, 'Cello and Piano Nos.2-3, Op.80 and 110, in F and g, rated A and Clara Schumann's Trio for Violin, 'Cello and Piano, Op.17, in g.

A Trio for Violin, 'Cello and Piano No.2, Op.80, in F--see entry for Trio for Violin, 'Cello and Piano No.1, Op.63, in d, immediately supra.

A Trio for Violin, 'Cello and Piano No.3, Op.110, g--see entry for Trio for Violin, 'Cello and Piano No.1, Op.63, in d, supra.

Concerted

A Concerto for 'Cello, Op.129, in a--see entry under Saint-Saëns, Concerted, Concerto No.1, for Cello, Op.33, in a, supra.

A Concerto for Piano, Op.54, in a--see entries under Liszt, Concerted, <u>Totentanz</u> for Piano and Orchestra (Paraphrase on <u>Dies irae</u>) (1838-1839) and Grieg, Concerted, Concerto for Piano, Op.16, in a, both <u>supra</u>.

Instrumental

B Arabeske for Piano, Op.18, in C

$ Artur Rubinstein, piano; RCA LSC-3108, ☒ RK-1153. Includes Schumann's <u>Kreisleriana</u>, Op.16, rated A.

A <u>Carnaval</u>, Op.9

$ Artur Rubinstein, piano; RCA AGL1-4879. Includes Schumann's Fantasiestücke, Op.12, rated B.

B <u>Davidsbündlertänze</u>, Op.6

$ Murray Perahia, piano; Columbia M-32299. Includes the same composer's Fantasiestücke, Op.12, rated A.

A Fantasia for Piano, Op.17, in C

$ Maurizio Pollini, piano; DG 2530379. Includes Schumann's Sonata No.1, Op.11, in f sharp, rated B.

B Fantasiestücke, Op.12--see entry for <u>Davidsbündlertänze</u>, Op.6, <u>supra</u>.

A <u>Kinderscenen</u>, Op.15

$ Claudio Arrau, piano; Philips 6500395. Includes Schumann's Blumenstück, Op.19, in D flat; <u>Papillons</u>, Op.2, rated B and Romances (3), Nos.1-3: Op.28, rated B.

A <u>Kreisleriana</u>, Op.16--see entry for Arabeske for Piano, Op.18, in C, <u>supra</u>.

B <u>Nachtstücke</u> (4) Nos.1-4, Op.23--see entry under Schubert, Instrumental, <u>Moments Musicaux</u> (6), Nos.1-6, D.946, <u>supra</u>.

B <u>Papillons</u>, Op.2--see entry for <u>Kinderscenen</u>, Op.15, <u>supra</u>.

213

B Romances (3), Nos.1-3: Op.28--see entry for <u>Kinderscenen</u>, Op.15, <u>supra</u>.

B Sonata No.1, Op.11, in f sharp--see entry for Fantasia for Piano, Op.17, in C, <u>supra</u>.

B Sonata No.3, Op.14, in f

$ Vladimir Horowitz, piano; RCA ARL1-1766, ♮ ARL1-1766. Includes Scriabin's Sonata No.5, Op.53, in F sharp, rated A.

Orchestral

B <u>Manfred</u> Overture, Op.115

$ Vienna Philharmonic Orchestra; Giuseppe Sinopoli, conductor; DG 410863-1 GH, ♮ 410863-4 GH. Includes Schumann's Symphony No.2, Op.61, in C, rated c.

Symphonic

A Symphony No.1 ("Spring"), Op.38, in B flat

$ Cleveland Orchestra; George Szell, conductor; Columbia MY-38468, ♮ MY-38468. Includes Schumann's Symphony No.4, Op.120, in d, also rated A.

C Symphony No.2, Op.61, in C

$ Hungarian State Orchestra; Giuseppe Patané, conductor; Hungaroton 12278.

Also--see entry for <u>Manfred</u> Overture, Op.115 under Orchestral, <u>supra</u>.

B Symphony No.3 ("Rhenish"), Op.97, in E flat

$ Vienna Philharmonic Orchestra; Sir George Solti, conductor; London ♮ STS5-15575. Includes Schumann's Symphony No.4, Op.120, in d, rated A.

A Symphony No.4, Op.120, in d--see entries for Symphony No.1 ("Spring"), Op.38, in B flat <u>supra</u>and Symphony No.3 ("Rhenish"), Op.97, in E flat, immediately <u>supra</u>.

Vocal

A <u>Dichterliebe</u> ("Love of a Poet") (Song Cycle), Op.48

$$ Olaf Bär, baritone; Geoffrey Parsons, piano; Angel DFO-38120, B DFO-38120. Includes Schumann's Liederkreis ("Song Cycle"), Op.39, rated B.

A Frauenliebe und -leben ("Women's Loves and Lives") (Song Cycle), Op.42
$ Evelyn Lear, soprano; Roger Vignoles, piano; Chandos 1009. Includes Schumann's Liederkreis ("Song Cycle"), Op.39, rated B.

B Liederkreis ("Song Cycle"), Op.39--see entries for Dichterliebe ("Love of a Poet") (Song Cycle), Op.48, supra and Frauenliebe und -leben ("Women's Loves and Lives") (Song Cycle), Op.42, immediately supra.

SCHÜTZ, HEINRICH
1585-1672

Born 100 years before Johann Sebastian Bach, the extraordinary German composer Heinrich Schütz (his surname is occasionally found in the Latin form, "Sagittarius") had a thorough musical education which included study in his own country and in Venice. The majority of his works were written for the church and are extremely fine examples of combining the best in the early German music with the newer, Italianate, school which incorporated greater warmth and emotion. Schütz was an artist typical of the Renaissance.

Choral

B St. Luke's Passion
* Karl Markus, tenor; Franz Müller-Heuser, baritone; Cologne Pro Musica Vocal Ensemble and Orchestra; Johannes Hömberg, conductor; Vox SVBX-5102 (3 discs). Includes Schütz' St. John's Passion and St. Matthew's Passion.

SCRIABIN, ALEXANDER
1872-1915

Russian composer Scriabin (sometimes spelled Skriabin) is surely one of the most singular artists ever to have graced music. His principal training was received at the Moscow Conservatory, where he studied composition with Taneyev and piano with Safonov. He graduated in 1892 with a gold medal in piano, but did not receive a diploma because he could not pass the final examinations in Arensky's course on the fugue. Although he was a gifted pianist, most of Scriabin's energy was devoted to composition. His personal disposition led him to mysticism. In 1897 he married Vera Isakovich, a pianist. They separated in 1905, and he began an affair with Tatiana Schloezer which was to last the rest of his life (they had 3 children). He died of toxemia, the result of a lip abscess. Scriabin was much ahead of his time in both his compositions and the manner in which he wished them performed. He had devised a theory relating specific colors of the spectrum to certain sounds, and a color organ was designed (principally for the performance of "Prometheus") which would project colored lights attuned to assigned sounds. If this seems like the son et lumière displays of the late 1960s and early 1970s, it is because they are directly related. His music is rich in original harmonic textures (he had developed a "synthetic" or "mystical" chord of 6 notes), he approximates atonality, and his piano pieces are of legendary technical difficulty.

Symphonic

B Symphony No.3 ("Divine Poem"), Op.43

$ USSR State Radio Orchestra; Vladimir Fedoseyev, conductor; Vox C-9030, ▇ C-9030.

A Symphony No.4 ("Poem of Ecstasy"), Op.54

$ Boston Symphony Orchestra; Claudio Abbado, conductor; DG 2530137. Includes Tchaikovsky's Romeo and Juliet (1880), also rated A.

SHOSTAKOVICH, DMITRI
1906-1975

One of the most eminent Soviet composers, Shostakovich was born in St. Petersburg not long before it became Leningrad. His family was in good economic straights: his father was a professional in the civil service and his mother a professional pianist. Shostakovich was a student at the Leningrad Conservatory from 1915 to 1925 and his principal composition instructor was Glazunov. His first work of real importance was his opera Lady Macbeth of Mtsensk in 1934, and was based on the work by Leskov.

216

In this early minor masterpiece (which was excoriated by Soviet officialdom as noise unbefitting Soviet music), Shostakovich had already begun employing those devices which would become identified with his later music: occasional use of the form itself (in this case, opera) for the purpose of parodying earlier use of that form, a cool detachment and sense of irony, the use of the waltz as a means of caricature and the use of well-known melodies by other composers (sometimes for obvious reasons, sometimes for obscure or unknown ones). As did Prokofiev, Shostakovich had his ups and downs with the Soviet cultural and political establishments. The zenith of his official recognition came with his Symphony No.7 ("Leningrad"), first performed in 1942, which commemorated the siege of Leningrad and was played incessantly throughout the rest of the war, not only by the Soviets, but by all the Allies. His Symphony No.13 ("Babi Yar"), after Yevtushenko's poem concerning the German massacre of the Jews in Babi Yar, brought Shostakovich into disfavor again since there was no mention in the text of others (e.g., Ukrainians, Poles, etc.) who had similarly suffered there. He had been ill for several years with cardiac problems, and the rather short leash he was allowed by the Soviet system probably did not lengthen his life, which ended with a heart attack.

Ballet

B <u>Age</u> <u>of</u> <u>Gold</u> Suite, Op.22

* Chicago Symphony Orchestra; Leopold Stokowski, conductor; RCA AGL1-5063, ▣ AGL1-5063. Includes Shostakovich's Symphony No.6, Op.54.

$ London Philharmonic Orchestra; Bernard Haitink, conductor; London LDR-10015 (2 discs), ▣ LDR-10015. Includes Shostakovich's Symphony No.7 ("Leningrad"), Op.60, rated B.

Chamber

B Sonata for Viola and Piano, Op.147

$ Fyodor Druzhnin, viola; Mikhail Muntyan, piano; Columbia/Melodiya M-35109. Includes Shostakovich's Sonata for Violin and Piano, Op.134, featuring Gidon Kremer, violin and André Gavrilov, piano, also rated B.

B Sonata for Violin and Piano, Op.134--see entry for Sonata for Viola and Piano, Op.147, immediately <u>supra</u>.

217

B String Quartet No.3, Op.110, in F

$$ Fitzwilliam Quartet; L'Oiseau Lyre DSLO-28. Includes the same composer's String Quartet No.11, Op.122, in f.

C Trio for Violin, 'Cello and Piano No.2, Op.67, in e

$ Oslo Trio; Simax PS-1014. Includes Shostakovich's Trio for Violin, 'Cello and Piano No.1, Op.8, in c.

Concerted

C Concerto for 'Cello, Op.107, in E flat

$ Mstislav Rostropovich, 'cello; Philadelphia Orchestra; Eugene Ormandy, conductor; Columbia MP-38750, ☐ MP-38750. Includes Shostakovich's Symphony No.1, Op.10, in F, rated B.

B Concerto No.1 for Piano and Trumpet, Op.35

$ André Previn, piano; William Vacchiano, trumpet; New York Philharmonic Orchestra; Leonard Bernstein, conductor; Columbia MP-38892, ☐ MP-38892. Includes Shostakovich's Concerto for Piano, Op.102, in F.

Symphonic

B Symphony No.1, Op.10, in F--see entry for Concerto for 'Cello, Op.107, in E flat under Concerted, supra.

A Symphony No.5, Op.47

$$ Cleveland Orchestra; Lorin Maazel, conductor; Telarc DG 10067.

* USSR Symphony Orchestra; Maxim Shostakovich, conductor; Quintessence 7202, ☐ 7202.

$ New York Philharmonic Orchestra; Leonard Bernstein, conductor; Columbia CBS MY-37218, ☐ MY-37218.

B Symphony No.7 ("Leningrad"), Op.60--see entry for Age of Gold Suite, Op.22 under Ballet, supra.

C Symphony No.10, Op.93, in e

$ Berlin Philharmonic Orchestra; Herbert von Karajan, conductor; DG 2532030, ☐ 3302030.

B Symphony No.14, Op.135

$ Galina Vishnevskaya, soprano; Mark Reshetin, bass; Moscow Philharmonic Orchestra; Mstislav Rostropovich, conductor; Columbia/Melodiya M-34507.

B Symphony No.15, Op.141, in A
$ London Philharmonic Orchestra; Bernard Haitink, conductor; London 7130.

SIBELIUS, JEAN
1865-1957

The greatest of all Finnish composers was christened Johan Julius Christian Sibelius; his father was a physician and his mother had come from a family known for its clerics. He was provided a classical education including piano and violin lessons beginning at age 9. He studied law at the University of Helsingfors but left there before finishing his first semester to study at the Helsingfors Conservatory. The first public performances given any of his works were in 1889. He received a government grant to study abroad and went first to Berlin and thence to Vienna to work on composition with Goldmark. In 1897 the Finnish government provided him with a lifetime grant, by means of which he could devote himself fully to composition and occasional conducting. He repaired to a country home in Järvenpää in 1904 and there spent almost all the rest of his life. He early turned to Finnish national themes for inspiration (e.g., the Kalevala--the Finnish national epic, historical figures like King Christian II, etc.); and his countrymen were, and have remained, imbued with extraordinary, but justifiable, pride concerning Sibelius: virtually their national treasure. His early music drew upon the German Romanticism of the late 19th century. This he abandoned and found his own voice, as it were, through a highly personal system. Sibelius' later works are organic in their form, but are virtually the inverse of the traditional method of presenting a theme and then developing it. In Sibelius' works, very often the development ultimately leads to the theme from which it sprang. He did not use Finnish folk melodies in his works; rather, he emulated his native tongue's speech patterns and also folk music rhythms. Most of his works are as majestic, powerful and as awesome as the lakes and mountains he found about him. In his finest efforts there is

219

a strength of character and purpose that seems to combine the best of Tchaikovsky and Brahms. He also could employ a light, and often tender, touch, as in the Symphony No.3. His Finlandia was forbidden to be performed, whistled, etc., during the Nazi occupation of Finland; the work was considered so nationalistic as to incite sabotage (or, also, it may well have been used by Finnish patriots as a kind of signal). The work is now synonymous with Finnish courage, patriotism, and determination.

Chamber

C Rakastava for Strings and Percussion, Op.14

* Hallé Orchestra; Sir John Barbirolli, conductor; Turnabout 34883, ▤ 34883. Includes Sibelius' Pelléas et Mélisande Suite, Op.46, rated B; Scénes historiques (6), Nos.1-2: Op.25 and Swan of Tuonela from 4 Legends from the Kalevala (Lemminkáinen and the Maidens; Lemminkáinen in Tuonela; Swan of Tuonela and Lemminkáinen's Return), Op.22, rated A.

B String Quartet ("Voces intimae"), Op.56, in d

* Copenhagen Quartet; Turnabout 37010, ▤ CT-7010. Includes Grieg's String Quartet, Op.27, in g.

Concerted

A Concerto for Violin, Op.47, in d

\$ Zino Francescatti, violin; New York Philharmonic Orchestra; Leonard Bernstein, conductor; Columbia MP-38770, ▤ MP-38770. Includes Walton's Concerto for Violin and Orchestra (1939), rated B.

* David Oistrakh, violin; Philadelphia Orchestra; Eugene Ormandy, conductor; Odyssey YT-30489. Includes Sibelius' Swan of Tuonela from 4 Legends from the Kalevala (Lemminkáinen and the Maidens; Lemminkáinen in Tuonela; Swan of Tuonela and Lemminkáinen's Return), Op.22, also rated A.

Instrumental

C Lyric Pieces for Piano (4), Nos.1-4, Op.74

\$ Erik Tawastsjerna, piano; Bis 196. Includes Sibelius' 2 Rondinos, Op.68; Sonatinas (3), Nos.1-3, Op.67 and 13 Pieces for Piano, Op.76.

Also--see entry under Alfvén, Orchestral, Swedish Rhapsody No.1 (1904), supra.

Orchestral

A Finlandia, Op.26

* Hallé Orchestra; Sir John Barbirolli, conductor; Angel AM-34712, ☐ AM-34712. Includes the same composer's <u>Karelia</u> Suite, Op.11, rated B; <u>Lemminkáinen's</u> <u>Return</u> from 4 Legends from the <u>Kalevala</u> (<u>Lemminkáinen</u> <u>and</u> <u>the</u> <u>Maidens</u>; <u>Lemminkáinen</u> <u>in</u> <u>Tuonela</u>; <u>Swan</u> <u>of</u> <u>Tuonela</u> and <u>Lemminkáinen's</u> <u>Return</u>), Op.22, also rated A; <u>Pohjola's</u> <u>Daughter</u>, Op.49, rated B and <u>Valse</u> <u>triste</u> from <u>Kuolema</u>, Op.44, rated A.

Also--see entries for Symphony No.1, Op.39, in e, <u>infra</u> and under Alfvén, Orchestral, Swedish Rhapsody No.1 (1904), <u>supra</u>.

A 4 Legends from the <u>Kalevala</u> (<u>Lemminkáinen</u> <u>and</u> <u>the</u> <u>Maidens</u>; <u>Lemminkáinen</u> <u>in</u> <u>Tuonela</u>; <u>Swan</u> <u>of</u> <u>Tuonela</u> and <u>Lemminkáinen's</u> <u>Return</u>), Op.22

$ Scottish National Orchestra; Sir Alexander Gibson, conductor; Chandos CBR-1026.

B <u>Karelia</u> Suite, Op.11--see entries for <u>Finlandia</u>, Op.26, <u>supra</u> and under Alfvén, Orchestral, Swedish Rhapsody No.1 (1904), <u>supra</u>.

A <u>Lemminkáinen's</u> <u>Return</u> from 4 Legends from the <u>Kalevala</u> (<u>Lemminkáinen</u> <u>and</u> <u>the</u> <u>Maidens</u>; <u>Lemminkáinen</u> <u>in</u> <u>Tuonela</u>; <u>Swan</u> <u>of</u> <u>Tuonela</u> and <u>Lemminkáinen's</u> <u>Return</u>), Op.22--see entries for <u>Finlandia</u>, Op.26, <u>supra</u> and 4 Legends from the <u>Kalevala</u> (<u>Lemminkáinen</u> <u>and</u> <u>the</u> <u>Maidens</u>; <u>Lemminkáinen</u> <u>in</u> <u>Tuonela</u>; <u>Swan</u> <u>of</u> <u>Tuonela</u> and <u>Lemminkáinen's</u> <u>Return</u>), Op.22, <u>supra</u>.

B <u>Pohjola's</u> <u>Daughter</u>, Op.49--see entry for <u>Finlandia</u>, Op.26, <u>supra</u>.

A <u>Swan</u> <u>of</u> <u>Tuonela</u> from 4 Legends from the <u>Kalevala</u> (<u>Lemminkáinen</u> <u>and</u> <u>the</u> <u>Maidens</u>; <u>Lemminkáinen</u> <u>in</u> <u>Tuonela</u>; <u>Swan</u> <u>of</u> <u>Tuonela</u> and <u>Lemminkáinen's</u> <u>Return</u>), Op.22--see entries for <u>Rakastava</u> for Strings and Percussion, Op.14 under Chamber, <u>supra</u>; Concerto for Violin, Op.47, in d under Concerted, <u>supra</u>; 4 Legends from the <u>Kalevala</u> (<u>Lemminkáinen</u> <u>and</u> <u>the</u> <u>Maidens</u>; <u>Lemminkáinen</u> <u>in</u> <u>Tuonela</u>; <u>Swan</u> <u>of</u> <u>Tuonela</u> and <u>Lemminkáinen's</u> <u>Return</u>), Op.22, <u>supra</u> and Symphony No.1, Op.39, in e under Symphonic, <u>infra</u>.

C <u>Tapiola</u>, Op.112

$ Philadelphia Orchestra; Eugene Ormandy, conductor; RCA ARL1-3978, ◘ ARL1-3978. Includes Sibelius' Symphony No.4, Op.63, in a, rated B.

Also--see entry for Symphony No.1, Op.39, in e under Symphonic, <u>infra</u>.

A <u>Valse</u> <u>triste</u> from <u>Kuolema</u>, Op.44--see entry for <u>Finlandia</u>, Op.26, <u>supra</u>.

Symphonic

A Symphony No.1, Op.39, in e

$ Boston Symphony Orchestra; Sir Colin Davis, conductor; Philips 6709011 (5 discs), ◘ 7699143. Includes Sibelius' Symphony No.2, Op.43, in D, rated A; Symphony No.3, Op.52, in C, rated B; Symphony No.4, Op.63, in a, rated B; Symphony No.5, Op.82, in E flat, rated A; Symphony No.6, Op.104, in d, rated C; Symphony No.7, Op.105, in C, rated A; <u>Finlandia</u>, Op.26, rated A; <u>Swan</u> <u>of</u> <u>Tuonela</u> from 4 Legends from the <u>Kalevala</u> (<u>Lemminkáinen</u> <u>and</u> <u>the</u> <u>Maidens</u>; <u>Lemminkáinen</u> <u>in</u> <u>Tuonela</u>; <u>Swan</u> <u>of</u> <u>Tuonela</u> and <u>Lemminkáinen's</u> <u>Return</u>), Op.22, rated A and <u>Tapiola</u>, Op.112, rated C.

A Symphony No.2, Op.43, in D

* Philadelphia Orchestra; Eugene Ormandy, conductor; Odyssey ◘ YT-30046.

Also--see entry for Symphony No.1, Op.39, in e, immediately <u>supra</u>.

B Symphony No.3, Op.52, in C--see entry for Symphony No.1, Op.39, in e, <u>supra</u>.

B Symphony No.4, Op.63, in a--see entry for Symphony No.1, Op.39, in e, <u>supra</u>.

A Symphony No.5, Op.82, in E flat--see entry for Symphony No.1, Op.39, in e, <u>supra</u>.

C Symphony No.6, Op.104, in d--see entry for Symphony No.1, Op.39, in e, <u>supra</u>.

222

A Symphony No.7, Op.105, in C—see entry for Symphony No.1, Op.39, in e, <u>supra</u>.

SMETANA, BEDRICH
1824-1884

Smetana (whose last name translates to "sour cream") began his musical career as a pianist. He had been something of a prodigy and made his public debut at the age of 6. As a child he had often played piano duets with Kateřina Kolařf, and they were married in 1849. With the encouragement and assistance of Liszt, Smetana opened a music school in Prague (Smetana was a native Bohemian) and was successful as a performer and teacher, but his compositions were not well received until 1866, when <u>The Bartered Bride</u> was given its premiere and was met with enthusiasm. Thence he went from success to success, but the effects of tertiary syphilis became apparent in 1882 (i.e., virtual total deafness and aural hallucinations which included hearing a constant and perfect "A") and he was sent to a mental institution, in which institution he died, hopelessly insane. Smetana is considered the father of the Bohemian (now Czech) Nationalistic school of composition. His music is melodic, filled with good humor and earthiness, but seems a bit old-fashioned (it did even in his own time).

Operatic
B <u>The Bartered Bride</u> (1863-1866)

$ Gabriela Beňačková-Cápová, soprano; Peter Dvorsky, tenor; Richard Novák, tenor; Czech Philharmonic Chorus and Orchestra; Zdeněk Košler, conductor; Supraphon 3511-3513 (3 discs).

Orchestral
A <u>The Bartered Bride</u> Overture—see entry under Enesco, Orchestral, Roumanian Dance No.1, Op.11, <u>supra</u>.

B <u>Má Vlast</u> ("My Fatherland") (1874-1879)

$ Boston Symphony Orchestra; Rafael Kubelik, conductor; DG 2707054 (2 discs).

! Czech Philharmonic Orchestra; Václav Talich, conductor; Quintessence 7168. No.2 of this 6 part cycle of symphonic poems is the famous Vltava ("The Moldau"), which itself is rated A.

A Vltava ("The Moldau") from Má Vlast ("My Fatherland") (1874–1879)—see entries under Enesco, Orchestral, Roumanian Rhapsody No.1, Op.11, supra and Má Vlast ("My Fatherland") (1874–1879), immediately supra.

SPOHR, LUDWIG
1784–1859

Born in Braunschweig, Germany, Spohr received his musical education essentially from private tutors. He undertook his first performing (as a violinist) tour at the age of 14. He was known to practice 10 hours a day at the age of 18 (he is said to have not had a weak constitution, that seems like a bit of understatement). His composing began in about 1806 and he wrote operas, concerti (particularly for the violin), choral works, etc. His compositions are not terribly distinguished, with but a few exceptions.

Chamber

B Nonet, Op.31, in F

$ Nash Ensemble; CRD 1054, ◙ 4054. Includes Spohr's Octet, Op.32, in E.

STRAUSS, JOHANN, JR.
1825–1899

The story of the feuding Viennese Strausses: Johann Sr. and Johann Jr., has too often been told to take up space here. Suffice it that Johann the Younger became a violinist, orchestra conductor (his own ensemble) and composer of almost 500 waltzes, polkas, galops, etc., and was crowned the "Waltz King." It should be noted that the form of many of Strauss' waltzes is virtually that of a small, early, 4 movement symphony. His principal stage works are Die Fledermaus ("The Bat") and Der Zigeunerbaron ("The Gypsy Baron"). He was married thrice, and neither went insane nor died of syphilis.

224

Operatic

A <u>Die Fledermaus</u> ("The Bat") (1874)

$ Hilde Gueden, soprano; Regina Resnik, soprano; Eberhard Wächter, baritone; Vienna State Opera Chorus; Vienna Philharmonic Orchestra; Herbert von Karajan, conductor; London 1319 (3 discs), ♫ 1319.

Orchestral

A <u>Emperor</u> Waltz, Op.437

* Vienna State Opera Orchestra; Jascha Horenstein, conductor; Quintessence 7051. Includes <u>On the Beautiful Blue Danube</u> Waltz, Op.314; <u>Tales from the Vienna Woods</u> Waltz, Op.325; <u>Viennese Blood</u> Waltz, Op.354 and <u>Wine, Women and Song</u> Waltz, Op.333, all rated A.

A <u>On the Beautiful Blue Danube</u> Waltz, Op.314--see entry for <u>Emperor</u> Waltz, Op.437 <u>Emperor</u> Waltz, Op.437, immediately <u>supra</u>.

A <u>Tales from the Vienna Woods</u> Waltz, Op.325--see entry for <u>Emperor</u> Waltz, Op.437, <u>supra</u>.

A <u>Viennese Blood</u> Waltz, Op.354--see entry for <u>Emperor</u> Waltz, Op.437, <u>supra</u>.

A <u>Wine, Women and Song</u> Waltz, Op.333--see entry for <u>Emperor</u> Waltz, Op.437, <u>supra</u>.

STRAUSS, RICHARD
1864-1949

This Munich-born Strauss' father was a famous French horn player (in the Munich Opera Orchestra) who began Richard's musical education at the age of 4. Richard's mother was of the well-known brewing firm family, Pschorr (the "ps" is pronounced as in "Georg Bernhard Pshaw"). Richard's first composition was a polka written when he was 6. After completing the requirements for graduation from the Gymnasium he attended the University of Munich from 1882 to 1883. He had already had his first large work, the Symphony in d, performed publicly in 1881. With other of Strauss' works also performed by 1883, the great conductor, Hans von Bülow (friend of Wagner's, whose wife <daughter of Liszt> had left von Bülow to take up with Wagner) took Strauss as his assistant conductor for the Bülow Orchestra in Meiningen. Bülow left Meiningen in 1885 and Strauss succeeded him as the director of the orchestra, but only for one year. In 1886 Strauss was appointed to the conducting staff of the Court Opera at Munich. Here he remained for 3 years and was able, perforce light conducting duties, to compose several works. He married the soprano, Pauline de Ahna, in 1894. Around the turn of the century Strauss was one of the busiest, and most sought-after, conductors in the world. Betimes, his works, which were considered "ultra-modern," even going beyond Wagnerian modernism, created controversies everywhere. No one work did so more than his opera <u>Salome</u> (after Oscar Wilde), which was considered lascivious, degrading and bloodthirsty. Since he remained in Germany during World War II (despite his son Franz having married into a Jewish family), he was tried as a Nazi at a special court in Munich after the war, and was exonerated. Strauss' music is lavish in its high-flown emotional content, filled with Wagnerian and Mahlerian lushness and portentousness and is considered by many the height of decadence (especially when compared to the dry, spare work of one such as Prokofiev). By the way, given his father's profession, it is assumed that Strauss' tendency to use (some would say overuse) the French horn must have been genetic.

Concerted

B Concerto for Horn No.1, Op.11, in E flat

$ Dennis Brain, horn; Philharmonia Orchestra; Wolfgang Sawallisch, conductor; Angel 35496. Includes Strauss' Concerto for Horn No.2, in E flat (1942), rated A. This is a a full-priced monophonic recording.

A Concerto for Horn No.2, in E flat (1942)—see entry for Concerto for Horn No.1, Op.11, in E flat, <u>supra.</u>

C Concerto for Oboe, in D (1945)

$ Heinz Holliger, oboe; Cincinnati Symphony Orchestra; Michael Gielen, conductor; Vox C-9064, ▤ C-9064. Includes Lutoslawski's Concerto for Oboe, Harp and Chamber Orchestra (1980) (with harpist Ursula Holliger).

B <u>Don Quixote</u> for 'Cello and Orchestra, Op.35

* Antonio Janigro, 'cello; Chicago Symphony Orchestra; Fritz Reiner, conductor; RCA Victrola ▣ ALK1-4976.

Operatic

B Ariadne auf Naxos, Op.60

$ Edita Gruberová, soprano; Leontyne Price, soprano; Tatiana Troyanos, mezzo-soprano; René Kollo, tenor; Walter Berry, baritone; Erich Kunz, baritone; baritone; London Philharmonic Orchestra; Sir George Solti, conductor; London 13131 (3 discs), ▣ 13131.

B Elektra, Op.58

$ Marie Collier, soprano; Birgit Nilsson, soprano; Regina Resnik, soprano; Gerhard Stolze, tenor; Tom Krause, baritone; Vienna Opera Chorus; Vienna Philharmonic Orchestra; Sir George Solti, conductor; London 1269 (2 discs), ▣ 5-1269.

A Der Rosenkavalier, Op.59

$ Elisabeth Schwarzkopf, soprano; Christa Ludwig, mezzo-soprano; Otto Edelmann, bass-baritone; Philharmonia Orchestra; Herbert von Karajan, conductor; Angel SDX-3970 (4 discs), ▣ SDX-3970.

Orchestral

A Also sprach Zarathustra ("Thus Spake Zarathustra"), Op.30

$ Chicago Symphony Orchestra; Fritz Reiner, conductor; RCA ARP1-4583, ▣ ARP1-4583. The opening of Also sprach has achieved a degree of popularity since its use as a theme in the movie 2001.

A "Dance of the Seven Veils" from Salomé, Op.54--see entry for Don Juan, Op.20, infra.

B Ein Heldenleben ("A Hero's Life"), Op.40

$ Chicago Symphony Orchestra; Fritz Reiner, conductor; RCA ATL1-4100, ▣ ATL1-4100.

A Don Juan, Op.20

* Philharmonia Orchestra; Otto Klemperer, conductor; Angel AE-34472, ▣ AE-34472. Includes Strauss' "Dance of the Seven Veils" from Salomé, Op.54, rated A, Til Eulenspiegels lustige Streiche ("Til

227

Eulenspiegel's Merry Pranks"), Op.28, rated A and Tod und Verklärung ("Death and Transfiguration"), Op.24, rated B.

A Til Eulenspiegels lustige Streiche ("Til Eulenspiegel's Merry Pranks"), Op.28--see entries for Also sprach Zarathustra ("Thus Spake Zarathustra"), Op.30 and Don Juan, Op.20, both supra, and under Dukas, Orchestral, Danse macabre, Op.40, supra.

B Tod und Verklärung ("Death and Transfiguration"), Op.24--see entries for Don Juan, Op.20, supra and under Elgar, Orchestral, Enigma Variations, Op.36, supra.

Vocal

A 4 Last Songs (1946)

$ Elisabeth Schwarzkopf, soprano; Berlin Radio Orchestra; George Szell, conductor; Angel S-36347. Includes Strauss' songs: Die heiligen drei Könige, Op.56 No.6; Freundlich Vision, Op.48 No.1; Muttertändelei, Op.43 No.2; Waldseligkeit, Op.49 No.1 and Zueignung, Op.10 No.1.

STRAVINSKY, IGOR
1882-1971

Even though this century still has more than a decade until its expiration, there are many who believe that Igor Feodorovich Stravinsky is the greatest composer to grace this hundred years. Born near St. Petersburg, and the son of one of the greatest Russian bassos of the last century, Stravinsky was sent to the University at St. Petersburg to study law, and there he remained until he was 23, taking his degree in law but never putting it to use. When Stravinsky was 19 he met Rimsky-Korsakov, who encouraged him to study composition. Stravinsky took private lessons from Rimsky from 1907 until Rimsky's death, the following year. Stravinsky later acknowledged the huge debt he owed to his mentor's instruction. In 1910 Stravinsky became known to the musical world, this through his ballet, The Firebird. It was commissioned and performed by the Russian Ballet company of Diaghilev in Paris, and caused a sensation. Despite the success achieved in 1911, by his Petrouchka, also with Diaghilev's organization, there was nothing to compare with the riot created in 1913, when Diaghilev produced Le Sacre du printemps. The

Parisians in attendance were nearly equally divided into pros and cons, and, given such carryings on as ripping up seats, screaming, whistling, etc. (indecorous, even in Paris), the work could not but succeed (if only as a succès fou, both in the literal and connoted senses). Stravinsky went from this Russian style of "barbarism" in his music to other approaches, including Neo-Classical, etc. He was also a distinguished conductor and an estimable pianist. He became a citizen of the U.S. in 1945. His music, at least that which is most often performed, is original in its abandonment of traditional harmonies, rhythms and set melodies. His orchestral colorations are novel in the extreme, his harmonies very often employ dissonances and his rhythms change with great frequency. His true value probably has yet to be determined, but he has certainly proven to be the most influential composer of this century, if not the greatest.

Ballet

C Appollon Musagète (1928)

* St. John's Smith Square Orchestra; John Lubbock, conductor; Nonesuch 71401, ❚ 71401. Includes the same composer's Orpheus Ballet (1947).

B Le Baiser de la Fée ("The Fairy's Kiss" Suite: Divertimento) (1928)—see entry under Hovhaness, Symphonic, Symphony No.2 ("Mysterious Mountain"), Op.132, supra.

A Firebird (1910)

$ New York Philharmonic Orchestra; Pierre Boulez, conductor; Columbia M-33508.

* L'Orchestre de la Suisse Romande; Ernest Ansermet, conductor; London ❚ STS5-15139.

A Petrouchka (1911)

$ Chicago Symphony Orchestra; James Levine, conductor; RCA ARL1-2615, ❚ ARL1-2615. This is the revised, 1947, version.

$ New York Philharmonic Orchestra; Pierre Boulez, conductor; Columbia M-31076, ❚ M-31076. This is the 1911 version.

A Le Sacre du printemps ("The Rite of Spring") (1913)

$ Columbia Symphony Orchestra; Igor Stravinsky, conductor; Columbia MP-38765, ▤ MP-38765.

* Paris Conservatory Orchestra; Pierre Monteux, conductor; London ▤ STS5-15318.

Chamber

C L'Histoire du soldat ("A Soldier's Tale") (1918)

$ Sir John Gielgud, narrator; Tom Courtenay, speaker; Ron Moody, speaker; Boston Symphony Chamber Players; DG 2530609, ▤ 3335456.

C Octet for Wind Instruments (1923)

$ Columbia Chamber Ensemble; Igor Stravinsky, conductor; Columbia M-30579. Includes Stravinsky's Concertino for 12 Instruments (1952); Ebony Concerto for Clarinet (1945) with George Pieterson, clarinet, rated C; Pastorale (1908) (with Israel Baker, violin) and Ragtime for 11 Instruments (1918).

Concerted

B Concerto for Violin, in D (1931)

$ Isaac Stern, violin; Columbia Symphony Orchestra; Igor Stravinsky, conductor; Columbia MS-6331. Includes Stravinsky's Symphony in 3 Movements (1945), also rated B.

C Ebony Concerto for Clarinet (1945)--see entry for Octet for Wind Instruments (1923) under Chamber, supra.

Operatic

C The Rake's Progress (1951)

$ Judith Raskin, soprano; Alexander Young, tenor; John Reardon, baritone; Sadler's Wells Chorus; Royal Philharmonic Orchestra; Igor Stravinsky, conductor M3S-710 (3 discs).

Orchestral

B Circus Polka (1942)

$ Columbia Chamber Orchestra; Igor Stravinsky, conductor; Columbia M-31729. Includes Stravinsky's Dumbarton Oaks Concerto for 16 Wind Instruments, in E flat (1938), rated B; 4 Études for Orchestra (1930) and 8 Instrumental Miniatures for 15 Players (1962).

B Dumbarton Oaks Concerto for 16 Wind Instruments, in E flat (1938)--see entry for Circus Polka, immediately supra.

Symphonic

A Symphony in C (1940)

$ Canadian Broadcasting Symphony Orchestra; Igor Stravinsky, conductor; Columbia MS-6548. Includes Stravinsky's Symphony of Psalms (1930), with the Toronto Festival Chorus, also rated A.

B Symphony in 3 Movements (1945)--see entry for Concerto for Violin, in D (1931) under Concerted, supra.

A Symphony of Psalms (1930)--see entry for Symphony in C (1940), supra.

SULLIVAN, SIR ARTHUR
1842-1900

The names of Sir Arthur Seymour Sullivan and Sir William Schwenck Gilbert (1836-1911) are inextricably linked by virtue of the wondrous successes of their "operas" (actually English comic operas, or extravaganzas of satire and wit). Sullivan was, before working with (and even, to some extent, during and after) Gilbert, a musician of impeccable training (Royal Academy of Music) and instincts (much in the way of operas, cantatas and other works which proved dreadfully boring, especially when at his most serious). He was much honored, both in England and abroad (e.g., Chevalier of the Legion of Honor, etc.) and, one supposes, took himself rather superceriously. Gilbert died, always keeping to form, by trying to save a young lady he thought to be drowning (it was a prank on her part): this when he was 75, no less.

Operatic

B Gondoliers (1889)

$ D'Oyly Carte Opera Company; London 40211 (2 discs), ▤ 40211.

A H.M.S. Pinafore (1878)

$ D'Oyly Carte Opera Company; London 1209 (2 discs), ▤ 5-1209.

B Iolanthe (1882)

$ D'Oyly Carte Opera Company; London 414145-1 LJ2 (2 discs), ▤ 414145-4 LJ2.

A <u>Mikado</u> (1885)

$ D'Oyly Carte Opera Company; London 12103 (2 discs), ⊟ 5-12103.

A <u>Pirates</u> <u>of</u> <u>Penzance</u> (1879)

$ D'Oyly Carte Opera Company; London 42003 (2 discs), ⊟ 42003.

TCHAIKOVSKY, PIOTR ILYICH
1840-1893

Tchaikovsky was born to a sensible family, one which was above average economically (his father was the government inspector of mines for the area of Piotr's birthplace--Votinsk, in the District of Viatka, in the Urals). The family was so sensible that none, except the child, were musical and they did not notice any particular musical ability in Piotr, probably because they were not looking for any. Piotr was sensitive and rather excitable, but he was considered a "winning child" and his education at home came from his French governess and a music teacher (the latter from about the time he was 7). In 1850 the family moved to St. Petersburg and Piotr was sent to classes to prepare him for the School of Jurisprudence. In 1859 he went to work as a "first-class clerk" for the Ministry of Justice. He also attended classes at the School of Jurisprudence where he joined the choral class, all the while continuing piano lessons. None of his instructors, however, considered him to be a genius-in-the-making. It was not until he was about 20 that Tchaikovsky began to have misgivings about the choice of his career. In 1861 he attended classes at the relatively new Russian Musical Society and, although he felt himself to be a musician, he continued to work indifferently for the Ministry of Justice. After 2 years the Society's classes developed into the St. Petersburg Conservatory, with Anton Rubinstein as its founder-director. Faced with the dilemma of how to continue the pursuit of his happiness: music, Tchaikovsky quit his place of employment and thereby faced an impoverished existence as he continued his musical studies. His mother had died in 1855 of cholera, and Tchaikovsky had been closely (nay, obsessively) attached to her. In addition, his father's fortunes had waned and the best he could provide his son was money for the barest of existences. Rubinstein sent him some music students for private tutoring, but during this period Tchaikovsky's earnings never exceeded about $25 a month.   After completing his education at the Conservatory in 1865, Tchaikovsky was offered a position as professor of harmony at the Conservatory in Moscow (the offer came from the head of the Conservatory, Anton Rubinstein's brother, Nicolai), which he accepted. For several years Tchaikovsky and Rubinstein shared rooms together, an advantage to Tchaikovsky since Rubinstein was influential and was able to secure performances of many of Tchaikovsky's works. Despite some success in Moscow, Tchaikovsky would have preferred appreciation in St. Petersburg, yet he also wanted the solitude of the country (he spent most of his summers with his married sister, Alexandra Davidoff and her family: her husband was the manager of a wealthy family estate outside of Kiev, and Tchaikovsky long found in her a confidante, and much enjoyed her children). Early in 1868 Tchaikovsky became friends with some of "The Five" (specifically, Balakirev, Borodin, Mussorgsky and Rimsky-Korsakov) and their nationalistic influence was most strongly evident in his Symphony No.2 ("Little Russian"). Also in 1868, Tchaikovsky was "courted" by the Belgian singer Désirée Artôt (she was 33, he 28) but they parted in 1869 (when she married Mariano Padilla, a Spanish baritone of some regard). For the next several years Tchaikovsky was busily working on various projects, some operatic, some orchestral, etc. In 1876 he was suffering from nervous exhaustion and he repaired to Vichy to "take the waters." The same year he worked as correspondent for a Russian journal covering the first Bayreuth festival. His return to St. Petersburg proved to be a disappointment since one of his operas (Tcherevichky) was badly received despite a good deal of preparation. In 1876, also, he began the strange, and famous, friendship with Madame Nadezhda Filaretovna von Meck, a wealthy widow with 11 children, who became his patroness (providing him with 6,000 rubles a year), yet they never really met (they corresponded for 13 years) even when he stayed at the von Meck estate. Madame von Meck ultimately terminated their "relationship" in 1890, probably because her health at that time was on the wane. In 1877 Tchaikovsky committed what his brother, Modest, wrote was a "rash act." Tchaikovsky was known to be a homosexual (as was Modest, also a confidant of his) and desperately wished to quell the rumors concerning his sexual preference. He allowed himself to be bullied into a marriage with one of his students, Antonina Milyukova. Antonina was an attractive 28–year–old blonde who threatened suicide if Tchaikovsky did not marry her. She was not terribly intelligent (she knew of his homosexuality but was convinced she could "cure" him of it), psychoneurotic, and also a nymphomaniac. Tchaikovsky saw this as a way to quash the gossip regarding his sexuality and they were, therefore, wed. In 5 days Tchaikovsky was beside himself, writing to Modest of his loathing for Antonina. He attempted suicide by trying to drown himself (or contract pneumonia) in the Moskva River: he only got wet. Needless to add, Antonina and he separated rather quickly (she died in a hospital for the insane, 40 years later, in 1917). Through all of this, Madame von Meck remained loyal to her protege. During the years remaining to him, Tchaikovsky, despite suffering from neurasthenia and morbidity in varying degrees, and these occasionally offset by periods of mania (when a work was well received, as with his opera Pique Dame <"The Queen of Spades"> in 1890), travelled extensively to conduct his works, thus driving himself to further exhaustion. Towards the middle of 1893, Tchaikovsky, finishing the Symphony No.6 ("Pathétique") and readying it for performance, wrote to the Grand Duke Konstantin Konstantinovich that he (i.e., Tchaikovsky) had put his entire soul into that work. He was pleased with his effort yet he was fearful of how it might be received. His fears were justified: the reception at its October 1893 premiere was cool. There is recent conjecture that the story of his death due to self–induced cholera is nothing more than an elaborate ruse to disguise the actual cause of his death: suicide which was ordered by the reigning monarch because Tchaikovsky had had an embarrassing liaison with one of the younger members of the Imperial family. Nicholas Slonimsky (in the 6th edition of Baker's Biographical Dictionary of Musicians, New York, Schirmer, 1978) posits that Tchaikovsky was given the choice of a term in Siberia or taking a poison which mimicked the symptoms (and the terminal result) of cholera. His work remains, and it is among the finest produced by any composer, with the exception of that handful of the very greatest. Tchaikovsky was well aware of the shortcomings of the weakest of his music, but that which was best (as in the Symphonies Nos.4 and 6, and the opera Eugen Onegin) he also knew, and to that best he entrusted his immortality. He is among the last of the great Romantic composers and his music is typical of that group: radiant orchestration, gorgeous melodies which easily flowed from him, the influence of literature upon his subjects, and that peculiar introspection, melancholy and nervousness which comes from too close an examination of, or concern for, one's own psychic navel. An interesting aspect of Tchaikovsky's last efforts, particularly the orchestral suite from The Voyevoda, Op.78 and the Concert Overture: The Storm, Op.76, is an inclination towards (or, perhaps, a searching for) what ultimately became the elements of the Impressionistic school. The harmonies, fleeting hints of melodies, etc., seem to presage the later work of Debussy. In any event, his work is there to be enjoyed, despite the carping of snobs and aesthetic poseurs.

Ballet

A The Nutcracker, Op.71
$ London Symphony Orchestra; André Previn, conductor; Angel S-3788 (2 discs), ▤ 4X2S-3788.
* L'Orchestre de la Suisse Romande; Ernest Ansermet, conductor; London STS-15433-15434 (2 discs), ▤ STS-15433-15434.

A The Nutcracker Suite, Op.71a
* L'Orchestre de la Suisse Romande; Ernest Ansermet, conductor; London STS-15569, ▤ STS-15569. Includes Tchaikovsky's Suite No.2, Op.53, in C.

A Sleeping Beauty, Op.66
$ London Symphony Orchestra; André Previn, conductor; Angel SX-3812 (3 discs), ▤ 4X3S-3812.

A Sleeping Beauty, Op.66 (Excerpts)
$ Philadelphia Orchestra; Eugene Ormandy, conductor; Columbia MS-6279.

A Swan Lake, Op.20
$ London Symphony Orchestra; André Previn, conductor; Angel SX-3834 (3 discs), ▤ 4X3S-3834.

A Swan Lake, Op.20 (Excerpts)
$ Philadelphia Orchestra; Eugene Ormandy, conductor; RCA ARL1-0030, ▤ ARK1-0030.

Chamber

235

B String Quartet No.1, Op.11, in D

$ Guarneri Quartet; RCA ARL1-5419, ⌷ ARL1-5419. Includes Verdi's String Quartet, in e (1873).

C Trio for Piano, Violin and 'Cello, Op.50, in a

$ Itzhak Perlman, violin; Lynn Harrell, 'cello; Vladimir Ashkenazy, piano; Angel SZ-37678.

Concerted

A Concerto for Piano No.1, Op.23, in b flat

* Sir Clifford Curzon, piano; Vienna Philharmonic Orchestra; Sir George Solti, conductor; London STS-15471, ⌷ 5-15471.

$ Sviatoslav Richter, piano; Vienna Symphony Orchestra; Herbert von Karajan, conductor; DG 138822.

A Concerto for Violin, Op.35, in D

* David Oistrakh, violin; Philadelphia Orchestra; Eugene Ormandy, conductor; Odyssey Y-30312, ⌷ YT-30312.

Also--see entry under Mendelssohn, Concerted, Concerto for Violin, Op.64, in e, <u>supra</u>.

A Variations on a Rococo Theme for 'Cello and Orchestra, Op.33--see entry under Elgar, Concerted, Concerto for 'Cello, Op.85, in e, <u>supra</u>.

Operatic

A <u>Eugen Onegin</u>, Op.24

$ Teresa Kubiak, soprano; Stuart Burrows, tenor; Bernd Weikl, baritone; Nicolai Ghiaurov, bass; John Alldis Choir; Royal Opera House Chorus and Orchestra, Covent Garden; Sir George Solti; London 13112 (3 discs).

Orchestral

A <u>Capriccio italien</u>, Op.45

$ Minneapolis Symphony Orchestra; Antal Doráti, conductor; Mercury ⌷ 75001. Includes Tchaikovsky's Overture <u>1812</u>, Op.49, rated A.

B <u>Francesca da Rimini</u>, Op.32

$ Israel Philharmonic Orchestra; Leonard Bernstein, conductor; DG 4109901-1 GS, ▣ 410990-4 GS. Includes Tchaikovsky's <u>Romeo</u> <u>and</u> <u>Juliet</u> (1870), rated A.

C <u>Hamlet</u> Fantasy Overture, Op.67
   * Vienna Philharmonic Orchestra; Lorin Maazel, conductor; London STS-15472, ▣ STS-15427. Includes Tchaikovsky's <u>Romeo</u> <u>and</u> <u>Juliet</u> (1870), rated A.
   $ New York Philharmonic Orchestra; Leonard Bernstein, conductor; Columbia M-34128, ▣ MT-34128. Includes the same composer's Serenade for Strings, Op.48, in C, rated A. This latter contains one of the most popular Tchaikovsky waltzes.

A <u>Marche</u> <u>slave</u>, Op.31--see entry under Rimsky-Korsakov, Orchestral, <u>Le</u> <u>Coq</u> <u>d'or</u> ("The Golden Cockerel") Suite (1907), <u>supra</u>.

A Overture <u>1812</u>, Op.49--see entry for <u>Capriccio</u> <u>italien</u>, Op.45, <u>supra</u>.

A <u>Romeo</u> <u>and</u> <u>Juliet</u> (1870)--see entries for <u>Francesca</u> <u>da</u> <u>Rimini</u>, Op.32,; <u>Hamlet</u> Fantasy Overture, Op.67, both <u>supra</u> and under Scriabin, Symphonic, Symphony No.4 ("Poem of Ecstasy"), <u>supra</u>.

A Serenade for Strings, Op.48, in C--see entry for <u>Hamlet</u> Fantasy Overture, Op.67, <u>supra</u>.

Symphonic
B Symphony No.1 ("Winter Daydreams"), Op.13, in g
   * USSR Symphony Orchestra; Yevgeny Svetlanov, conductor; Quintessence 7091, ▣ 7091.

A Symphony No.2 ("Little Russian"), Op.17, in c
   * USSR Symphony Orchestra; Yevgeny Svetlanov, conductor; Quintessence 7090, ▣ 7090.

B Symphony No.3 ("Polish"), Op.29, in D
   * USSR Symphony Orchestra; Yevgeny Svetlanov, conductor; Quintessence 7164, ▣ 7164.

A Symphony No.4, Op.36, in f

$ Boston Symphony Orchestra; Pierre Monteux, conductor; RCA AGL1-5254, ♮ AGL1-5254.

$ Leningrad Philharmonic Orchestra; Yevgeny Mravinsky, conductor; DG 415928-1 GMF, ♮ 415928-4 GMF.

A Symphony No.5, Op.64, in e

$ Leningrad Philharmonic Orchestra; Yevgeny Mravinsky, conductor; DG 2535236.

* New Philharmonia Orchestra; Leopold Stokowski, conductor; London ♮ STS5-15559.

A Symphony No.6 ("Pathétique"), Op.74, in b

* Chicago Symphony Orchestra; Fritz Reiner, conductor; RCA AGL1-5258, AGL1-5258.

$ Leningrad Philharmonic Orchestra; Yevgeny Mravinsky, conductor; DG 2535237, ♮ 3335237.

* Philharmonia Orchestra; Otto Klemperer, conductor; Seraphim ♮ 4XG-60416.

TELEMANN, GEORG PHILIPP
1681-1767

Telemann was an almost entirely self-taught composer whose "basic training" came through the diligent study of the scores of great masters. That he was successful can be seen in two ways: Bach held him in no little regard, and his music is still performed today. Telemann is among the most prolific composers ever to have lived: somewhere about 40 operas, about 3,000 cantatas and motets (enough church services to go 12 years, daily, without repeating any), more than 600 overtures (many of these rudimentary symphonies), etc. He was a very highly skilled contrapuntalist (Handel stated that Telemann could write an 8 part motet as quickly and easily as most people write an epistle). Telemann's music is a fusion of the German contrapuntal style with Italian operatic melodies and warmth.

Concerted

B Suite for Flute and Strings, in a

238

$ James Galway, flute; I Solisti di Zagreb; RCA AGL1-5443, ▣ AGL1-5443. Includes Telemann's Concerto for Flute and Orchestra.

THOMAS, AMBROISE
1811-1896

The son of a musician, Charles-Louis-Ambroise Thomas learned musical scales while memorizing the alphabet. He was a student at the Conservatoire de Paris from 1828 to 1832, winning numerous medals and the Grand Prix de Rome. Thomas became one of the best, and best known, composers in the Romantic style of French opera. He was the director of the Conservatoire from 1871 until his death (one of the longer tenures of that post). He is now remembered only for his opera Mignon (based on Goethe's Wilhelm Meister).

Operatic

B Mignon (After Goethe's Wilhelm Meister) (1866)

$ Ruth Welting, soprano; Marilyn Horne, mezzo-soprano; Frederica Von Stade, mezzo-soprano; Alain Vanzo, tenor; Nicola Zaccaria, bass; Ambrosian Opera Chorus; Philharmonia Orchestra; Antonio de Almeida, conductor; Columbia M4-34590 (4 discs).

THOMSON, VIRGIL
1896-

Thomson is a musician who has been at home in a number of habitats: music critic (New York Herald Tribune, from 1940 to 1954), composer of operas, composer of film music (The River, Louisiana Story, etc.) and composer of absolute music. His education was received at Harvard and in private study with Nadia Boulanger, among others. His music is dry, eclectic, modern, occasionally wistful, but not boring. As a side note, the title of the opera The Mother of Us All refers to Susan B. Anthony; its libretto was written by Gertrude Stein (likewise Four Saints in 3 Acts. His Francophilia was sufficient to earn him membership in the French Legion of Honor.

Chamber

C Autumn (Concertino for Harp, Strings and Percussion) (1954)

239

$ Los Angeles Chamber Orchestra; Sir Neville Marriner, conductor; Angel S-37300. Includes Thomson's music for the film The Plow That Broke the Plains (1939), rated B.

Operatic

C Four Saints in 3 Acts (1934)

* Florence Quivar, soprano; Clamma Dale, soprano; Betty Lou Allen, mezzo-soprano; Benjamin Matthews, bass-baritone; Chorus and Orchestra of Our Time; Joel Thome, conductor; Nonesuch 79035 (2 discs).

B The Mother of Us All (1947)

$ Batyah Godfrey, soprano; Mignon Dunn, mezzo-soprano; Helen Vanni, mezzo-soprano; James Atherton, tenor; Philip Booth, baritone; Santa Fe Opera Chorus and Orchestra; Raymond Leppard, conductor; New World 288-289 (2 discs).

Orchestral

B The Plow That Broke the Plains (1939)--see entry for Autumn (Concertino for Harp, Strings and Percussion) (1954) under Chamber, supra.

VARÈSE, EDGARD
1883-1965

For a man who wrote only about a dozen works (not counting a few songs and a handful of efforts never completed), Varèse has exerted a phenomenal influence, especially since few of his own works are much performed, primarily because they require exotic instruments or objects or electronic devices. Varèse was born in Paris and came of French and Italian parents. He attended the Schola Cantorum in Paris, studying with d'Indy and Roussel in composition, counterpoint and fugue, and organ with Widor. He moved to the U.S. in 1916 and remained until his death. There is no way to characterize his music other than to say that it is hyper-modern, idiosyncratic, often noisy, and frequently moving. The two discs listed below will supply you with more than enough Varèse, unless you or your patrons get hooked, and if you do, be warned that there aren't many more works of Varèse's to buy.

Instrumental

A Density 21.5 (1936)

* Hans Reissberger, flute; Die Reihe Ensemble, Vienna; Friedrich Cerha, conductor; Candide 31028. Includes Varèse's Hyperprism (1923); Intégrales (1925); Ionisation (1931); Octandre (1924) and Offrandes (1921).

Orchestral

B Amériques (1918–1922)

* Utah Symphony Orchestra; Maurice Abravanel, conductor; Vanguard S–274. Includes Varèse's Nocturnal (1961).

VAUGHAN WILLIAMS, RALPH
1872–1958

The name of Ralph Vaughan Williams seems to create some difficulties for those who are not English, so I shall try to sort out a couple of problems at the outset: Williams is his surname, Vaughan his middle, and his first name is properly pronounced "Rafe." With that settled: Williams was sent to Trinity College, Cambridge after 2 years of study at the Royal College of Music. After taking his degree at Cambridge he returned to the Royal College of Music to further his studies, particularly in composition. He had also become an accomplished organist. After a trip to the Bayreuth festival in 1896 (and not wanting for money, his father was sufficiently endowed pecuniarily as to preclude that kind of misfortune) Williams took his doctorate in music from Cambridge in 1901. Having already studied with Bruch in Berlin, he travelled to Paris in 1909 to work with Ravel. This is somewhat odd since Williams was already something of an established composer. About the turn of the century he had become interested in English folk songs, and thereafter some element or other of that interest may be found in his works. His long life was essentially uneventful. He was much taken with the music of Sibelius and his work bears the same type of individuality and nationalism (without the latter being overweeningly obvious) as that of the object of his esteem. His music tends towards thick harmonic structure and, often, a rather slow, deliberate, sometimes otherworldly pace.

Concerted

B The Lark Ascending (Romance for Violin and Orchestra) (1914)

\$ Iona Brown, violin; Academy of St. Martin-in-the-Fields; Sir Neville Marriner, conductor; Argo ZRG–696, ⬛ 15696. Includes Williams'

Fantasia on a Theme of Thomas Tallis (1910), rated B and Fantasia on Greensleeves (1934), rated A.

Orchestral

A Fantasia on Greensleeves (1934)--see entries under Elgar, Orchestral, Enigma Variations, Op.36 and Introduction and Allegro for String Quartet and String Orchestra, Op.47, supra and The Lark Ascending (Romance for Violin and Orchestra) (1914) under Concerted, supra.

A English Folk Song Suite (1923)--see entry under Elgar, Orchestral, Enigma Variations, Op.36, supra.

B Fantasia on a Theme of Thomas Tallis (1910)--see entry The Lark Ascending (Romance for Violin and Orchestra) (1914) under Concerted, supra.

Symphonic

B Symphony No.1 ("A Sea Symphony") (1910)

$ London Symphony Orchestra; André Previn, conductor; RCA AGL1-4212, ♮ AGL1-4212.

A Symphony No.2 ("London") (1914, 1920)

* London Philharmonic Orchestra; Sir Adrian Boult, conductor; Angel AE-34438, ♮ AE-34438.

B Symphony No.3 ("Pastoral") (1922)

$ London Symphony Orchestra; Andr' Previn, conductor; RCA LSC-3281. Includes Williams' Concerto for Bass Tuba and Orchestra (1954).

A Symphony No.4, in f (1934)

* London Philharmonic Orchestra; Sir Adrian Boult, conductor; Angel AE-34478, ♮ AE-34478. Includes Williams' Symphony No.5, in D (1943).

B Symphony No.7 ("Sinfonia Antartica") (1953)

$ Norma Burrowes, soprano; London Philharmonic Orchestra; Sir Adrian Boult, conductor; Angel S-36763.

VERDI, GIUSEPPE
1813-1901

Verdi's life has lately been of sufficient interest that it merited a series of programs on the public television network. Yet, by and large, his life was not really all that fascinating. He was born as Fortunio Giuseppe Francesco Verdi to a humble tavern keeper in Le Roncole, near Busseto, in the Duchy of Parma. He was taught by local musicians, including the organist of his home town. Despite being financed by a local patron (Antonio Barezzi) to attend the Conservatory at Milan, Verdi was denied admission there for several reasons (all legitimate, including his poor piano playing and his lack of background in composition). With the financial help of Barezzi, Verdi undertook private study in Milan with Vincenzo Lavigna. After a year of such study he returned home, probably to take up the position of the town's music-master since the previous occupant of that position (Ferdinando Provesi, one of Verdi's early teachers) had died. Due to local politics, Verdi failed to get the job permanently, and he returned to Milan and his studies with Lavigna. In 1836 Verdi married Barezzi's daughter and was given the post as music-master, which post he had previously sought. He remained in Busseto for 3 years. During the time between his appointment (1835) and his removal of his new family to Milan (1840), Verdi's two infant children and his wife died. Further, his first opera bombed at La Scala. In 1842 his opera, Nabucco, was successfully produced and he was acclaimed a new Italian musical genius. He took up with the soprano Giuseppina Strepponi and they lived together, without benefit of clergy, for several years before marrying in 1859. All the while Verdi's reputation grew. In 1869 he received an invitation to write a commemorative opera for the opening of the Suez Canal (and for a newly built theater in Cairo); the result was Aida. Verdi's last two operas, Otello (1887) and Falstaff (1893), were incredible feats for a man of his years. On his death, the entire city of Milan mourned, and public conveyances were shut down in observance of the passing of their local genius. Verdi's operas declined in popularity until the fervor of the Wagnerians waned. His best works are superb in their welding of drama with music. At his worst, Verdi's works can turn a St. Vitus's dance sufferer into a narcoleptic.

Choral

A Requiem Mass (In Memory of Manzoni) (1874)

$ Elisabeth Schwarzkopf, soprano; Christa Ludwig, mezzo–soprano; Nicolai Gedda, tenor; Nicolai Ghiaurov, bass; Philharmonia Chorus and Orchestra; Carlo Maria Giulini, conductor; Angel S–3649 (2 discs), ▤ 4X2S–3649.

Operatic

A Aida (1871)

$ Leontyne Price, soprano; Grace Bumbry, mezzo–soprano; Placido Domingo, tenor; Sherrill Milnes, baritone; Ruggero Raimondi, bass; John Alldis Choir; London Symphony Orchestra; Erich Leinsdorf, conductor; RCA LSC–6198 (3 discs), ▤ ARK3––2544.

B Un Ballo in maschera ("A Masked Ball") (1859)

$ Kathleen Battle, soprano; Margaret Price, soprano; Christa Ludwig, mezzo–soprano; Luciano Pavarotti, tenor; Renato Bruson, baritone; National Philharmonic Chorus and Orchestra, London; Sir George Solti, conductor; London 410210–1 LH3 (3 discs), ▤ 410210–4 LH3.

C Don Carlos (1867, 1884)

* Montserrat Caballé, soprano; Shirley Verrett, mezzo–soprano; Placido Domingo, tenor; Ruggero Raimondi, bass; Ambrosian Singers; Royal Opera Chorus and Orchestra, Covent Garden; Carlo Maria Giulini, conductor; Angel AVC–34060 (3 discs), ▤ AVC–34060.

A Falstaff (1893)

$ Barbara Hendricks, soprano; Katia Ricciarelli, soprano; Lucia Valentini-Terrani, mezzo–soprano; Dalmacio Gonzalez, tenor; Renato Bruson, baritone; Leo Nucci, baritone; Los Angeles Master Chorale; Los Angeles Philharmonic Orchestra; Carlo Maria Giulini, conductor; DG 2741020 (3 discs), ▤ 3382020.

B La Forza del destino ("The Force of Destiny") (1862)

$ Leontyne Price, soprano; Fiorenza Cossotto, mezzo–soprano; Placido Domingo, tenor; Gabriel Bacquier, baritone; Sherrill Milnes, baritone; Bonaldo Giaiotta, bass; London Symphony Chorus and Orchestra; James Levine, conductor; RCA ARL4–1864 (4 discs), ▤ ARK3–2543.

A <u>Macbeth</u> (1865)

$ Shirley Verrett, soprano; Placido Domingo, tenor; Piero Cappuccilli, baritone; Nicolai Ghiaurov, bass; Chorus and Orchestra of La Scala, Milan; Claudio Abbado, conductor; DG 2709062 (3 discs).

A <u>Otello</u> (1887)

$ Renata Scotto, soprano; Placido Domingo, tenor; Sherrill Milnes, baritone; Ambrosian Opera Chorus; National Philharmonic Orchestra, London; James Levine, conductor; RCA CRL3-2951 (3 discs), ▣ CRK3-2951.

A <u>Rigoletto</u> (1851)

$ Dame Joan Sutherland, soprano; Huguette Tourangeau, mezzo-soprano; Luciano Pavarotti, tenor; Sherrill Milnes, baritone; Martti Talvela, bass; Ambrosian Opera Chorus; London Symphony Orchestra; Sir Richard Bonynge, conductor; London 13105 (3 discs), ▣ 5-13105.

A <u>La</u> <u>Traviata</u> (1853)

$ Dame Joan Sutherland, soprano; Luciano Pavarotti, tenor; Matteo Manuguerra, baritone; London Opera Chorus; National Philharmonic Orchestra, London; Sir Richard Bonynge, conductor; London LDR-73002 (3 discs).

A <u>Il</u> <u>Trovatore</u> (1853)

* Leontyne Price, soprano; Rosalind Elias, mezzo-soprano; Richard Tucker, tenor; Leonard Warren, baritone; Giorgio Tozzi, bass; Rome Opera Chorus and Orchestra; Arturo Basile, conductor; RCA AGL3-4146 (3 discs), ▣ AGL3-4146.

$ Leontyne Price, soprano; Florenza Cossotto, mezzo-soprano; Placido Domingo, tenor; Sherrill Milnes, baritone; Bonaldo Gialotti, bass; Ambrosian Opera Chorus; New Philharmonia Orchestra; Zubin Mehta, conductor; RCA LSC-6194 (3 discs).

VIEUTEMPS, HENRI
1820-1881

Belgian Vieutemps was a major violinist and minor composer, particularly works for his instrument. The celebrated violinist, Jenő Hubay, was one of his pupils. His music is strongly Romantic and, with the exception of the piece listed herein, almost never heard.

Concerted

C Concerto for Violin No.5, Op.37, in a--see entry under Bruch, Concerted, Scottish Fantasy for Violin and Orchestra, Op.46, supra.

VILLA—LOBOS, HEITOR
1887-1959

Villa-Lobos is considered preeminent among the composers of Brazilian nationality. He received his musical education from his father (an amateur 'cellist) and at the Instituto Nacional de Música in Rio de Janeiro. After a short time there he left on an expedition to collect folk music in the interior of Brazil and returned not only with folk music, but with his own identity--that of a Brazilian nationalistic composer. Villa-Lobos was, with Telemann, one of the most prolific composers to set pen to paper. Out of his over 2,000 compositions, about 20 or so are worth any attention (look, one out of one hundred isn't bad).

Vocal

C Bachianas Brasileiras No.5 for Soprano and 8 'Celli (1938-1945)--see entry under Canteloube, Vocal, Chants d'Auvergne, supra.

VIVALDI, ANTONIO
1678-1741

Vivaldi is as fine example as one can find of how the long-playing phonograph record's introduction in 1950 brought about a minor revolution in the public's listening tastes. Prior to that time one was fortunate to find any recording of Vivaldi's music, let alone The Four Seasons. Now the various recordings catalogs list pages of his works only because one could record so many Beethoven symphonies, Puccini operas, etc., without exhausting the public's patience and desire for novelty. Back to our subject: Vivaldi was the son of an Italian violinist residing in Venice. Antonio (middle name Lucio) was taught by his father and received additional training from Giovanni Legrenzi, a respected composer of the time. Antonio joined the priesthood in 1693 and was ordained in 1703. Because of his red hair and his tonsure he was easily recognizable, he therefore became known as il prete rosso ("the red priest"). From 1704 to 1740 Vivaldi taught the violin. He was later promoted to maestro de' concerti, at the Ospedale della Pietà in Venice, one of the few famous music schools for girls in Venice. There were probably some breaks in his tenure at the Ospedale, but the times these may have occurred are difficult to identify. His post at the Ospedale afforded Vivaldi the time to write extensively and to experiment as he wrote. About 1740 he travelled to Vienna, probably seeking employment, which he may well have found. Still, once having left the Ospedale, his fortunes declined and interest in him seems to have waned. Vivaldi was a skilled composer, and one of great warmth, energy and wit. Despite J.S. Bach's admiration for his music, Vivaldi's music never approached that of Bach's, and Vivaldi is often overrated now. When "R" numbers are used, they refer to the catalog of Vivaldi's works devised by Peter Ryom.

Concerted

A Il cimento dell' armonia e dell' inventione ("The Contest Between Harmony and Invention") Concerti for Various Instruments (12), (Nos.1-12) Op.8 (Includes the famous "Four Seasons," which are Nos.1-4))

$$ Academy of Ancient Music; Christopher Hogwood, conductor; L'Oiseau Lyre D279D (2 discs), ▤ K279K 22.

Also--for Concerto for Oboe, Op.8 No.9 (or R.454), in D see entry under Marcello, Concerted, Concerto for Oboe and Strings, in d (1716), supra.

A L'Estro armonico ("Harmonic Inspiration"), Op.3
$ I Musici; Philips 412128-1 PH2 (2 discs), ▤ 412128-4.

WAGNER, RICHARD
1813-1883

There is little that anyone can write or say regarding Wilhelm Richard Wagner that will either diminish his musical standing in history or improve the historical view of him as an egomaniacal, bigoted, wretched human being: he was quite literally (and in every sense) a bastard. The determination of the paternity of Wagner is not so muddled that it is any longer a mystery. His nominal father, Karl Friedrich Wilhelm Wagner, was Court Clerk in the Town Council of Leipzig (a more exalted-sounding position than it actually was). Wagner's biological father was the man who became his step-father (Karl Friedrich died when Richard was 6 months old): Ludwig Geyer, a competent singer and actor-playwright. Even Wagner had doubts as to his father's identity, but concerning the matter of his maternity he could be certain. Johanna Rosina Pätz supposedly was the daughter of a miller at Weissenfels. She may have been the illegitimate daughter of either Karl August, Duke of Saxe-Weimar or Prince Friedrich Ferdinand Constantin of Weimar. That Richard was not christened for 3 months after his birth, and that his mother had taken him, shortly after his appearance in this world, to Teplice and harbor with Geyer furthered early speculation regarding Geyer's relationship to the infant Richard. Johanna and Geyer were married in 1814 and 6 months later Richard's sister, Augusta Cacilie, was born. Geyer held a position with the royal court ensemble at Dresden, and there the family lived. As a child Richard was interested in literature and had learned to play the piano. He enjoyed studying Greek and tried his hand at writing in the Shakespearean style. Geyer died in 1821 and the family moved back to Leipzig in 1827. Wagner's musical education was, so far, rudimentary at best, most of it coming from local tutors in the form of piano lessons and a few such on the violin. Regular schooling was a bore to Richard and he was a frequent truant. Wagner's sister, Luise Wagner, had married Friedrich Brockhaus, Schopenhauer's publisher, and it may be this connection which helped shape Richard's philosophical view (which, in scrutinizing some of his behavior, may have been solipsistic). After studying Logier's Method of Thorough-Bass (borrowed, incidentally, from Friedrich Wieck, Mendelssohn's father-in-law), Wagner set about to become a composer, specifically, of operas; this would indulge his love of music and passion for poetry and drama. In 1831 Wagner enrolled at the University of Leipzig and here he lasted a year. He had succeeded in making a friend of Weinleg, erstwhile cantor of St. Thomas' Church, and Weinleg it was who persuaded the prestigious music publishers, Breitkopf and Härtel (Brahms' own), to publish some minor works of Wagner. Until this time Wagner had lived on the generosity of his mother and sister, Rosalie, whose loans were almost never repaid. He finally obtained a job in 1833 as chorus coach at the Würzburg Theater, this through the good offices of his brother, Albert, who was the Theater's stage manager and also a singer. While there Richard composed his first complete opera Die Feen ("The Fairies"). For this, as for all the rest of his works, Wagner wrote his own libretto. In 1834 he was given the post of conductor at the Magdeburg Theater and, while there, he fell in love with the actress, Christine Wilhelmine "Minna" Planer. In the meantime, the great opera singer, Wilhelmine Schröder-Devrient, agreed to sing in Wagner's new (and second completed) opera, Das Liebesverbot ("The Forbidden Love," based on Shakespeare's Measure for Measure). The public stayed away from the production of an opera by an unknown composer, despite Schröder-Devrient's participation. Wagner fled to Leipzig in order to elude his creditors (something at which he would become quite adept) and in November 1836 he returned to Magdeburg and married Minna Planer. After some attempts at composing trivialities, during which time he and Minna quarrelled often, Minna ran off with a merchant to Dresden. Wagner followed her and there was a reconciliation. After additional domestic differences Minna again took off for her merchant, this time to Riga. In Minna's absence, Wagner read Bulwer Lytton's Rienzi and began setting it as an opera. He removed himself to Riga and Minna rejoined him (bringing along her sister), and right behind were the creditors from Magdeburg. In 1842 Rienzi was staged at the Dresden Opera for an appreciative audience. Der fliegende Holländer ("The Flying Dutchman") was Wagner's next opera, also produced at Dresden, and its success led to his appointment as Kapellmeister to the court of Saxony. "The Dutchman" was also performed in Berlin through the assistance of Meyerbeer. Borrowing money hither and yon (and seldom repaying it in fact or in kindness), Wagner travelled extensively (some of his peregrinations were necessitated by creditors but, more importantly, he was also forced into exile for political machinations, the exile lasted from 1849 to 1860), fell in love a few times, found time to write his anti-Semitic tract, Das Judentum in Musik (published under a pseudonym and attacking, in particular, Meyerbeer and Mendelssohn, possibly partly out of jealousy), and was reconciled with Minna often. In 1857 they became residents on the estate of Otto Wesendonck, a wealthy merchant in Zurich. Wagner fell in love with Otto's wife, Mathilde, and set 5 of her poems to music (Die Wesendonck Lieder). In 1861 Minna left him for good and in 1864 he began a relationship with Liszt's daughter, Cosima, who was then married to Wagner's friend, the conductor Hans von Bülow. Wagner and Cosima's daughter, Isolde, was born in 1865 when he was readying Tristan und Isolde for production, and in 1866 Cosima joined him at his retreat in Triebschen, on Lake Lucerne. In 1870 she divorced von Bülow and married Wagner. In 1872 Wagner moved to Bayreuth to begin building the Festspielhaus where his operas could be "properly" performed. Always in debt and now in failing health, Wagner, on his doctor's advice, went to Venice where, true to the adage, he died. His music is among the most original, provocative, colorful and intense ever written for the opera stage. In fine, he did accomplish his aim of fusing music and theater into one new form: "musicdrama," obviously. A note on Der Ring des Nibelungen ("The Ring of the Nibelungs") cycle, it consists of 4 separate operas in the following order: Das Rheingold ("The Rhine Gold"); Die Walküre ("The Valkyries"); Siegfried and Die Gotterdämmerung ("The Twilight of the Gods"). For a full explication of the plots the reader is referred to Anna Russell's lecture on the subject, to be found in her album "Anna Russell Album?" (Columbia MG–31199, 2 discs). Madame Russell makes as much sense out of this thick set of plots as anyone communicating in English ever has.

Operatic

A Der fliegende Holländer ("The Flying Dutchman") (1843)

$ Janis Martin, mezzo–soprano; Réne Kollo, tenor; Werner Krenn, tenor; Norman Bailey, baritone; Martti Talvela, bass; Chicago Symphony Chorus and Orchestra; Sir George Solti, conductor; London 13119 (3 discs), 5-13119.

A Die Gotterdämmerung ("The Twilight of the Gods") (1876)

$ Birgit Nilsson, soprano; Claire Watson, soprano; Christa Ludwig, mezzo–soprano; Wolfgang Windgassen, tenor; Dietrich Fischer–Dieskau, baritone; Gottlob Frick, bass; Vienna State Opera Chorus; Philharmonia Orchestra; Sir George Solti, conductor; London 414115-1 LH5 (5 discs), 414115-4 LH4.

B Lohengrin (1850)

$ Anja Silja; soprano; Astrid Varnay, soprano; Ramon Vinay, tenor; Franz Crass, bass; Bayreuth Festival Chorus and Orchestra, 1962; Wolfgang Sawallisch, conductor; Philips 6747241 (4 discs).

A Die Meistersinger von Nürenberg ("The Master Singers of Nuremberg") (1868)
$ Caterina Ligendza, soprano; Christa Ludwig, mezzo-soprano; Placido Domingo, tenor; Dietrich Fischer-Dieskau, baritone; Roland Hermann, baritone; Peter Lagger, bass; Berlin German Opera Chorus and Orchestra; Eugen Jochum, conductor; DG 2713011 (5 discs), ▤ 3378068.

A Das Rheingold ("The Rhine Gold") (1869)
$ Oralia Dominguez, mezzo-soprano; Josephine Veasey, mezzo-soprano; Gerhard Stolze, tenor; Dietrich Fischer-Dieskau, baritone; Zoltán Kélémén, bass-baritone; Berlin Philharmonic Orchestra; Herbert von Karajan, conductor; DG 2740145 (3 discs).

A Siegfried (1876)
$ Birgit Nilsson, soprano; Dame Joan Sutherland, soprano; Gerhard Stolze, tenor; Wolfgang Windgassen, tenor; Hans Hotter, bass-baritone; Gustav Neidlinger, bass; Vienna Philharmonic Orchestra; Sir George Solti, conductor; London 414110-1 LH4 (4 discs), ▤ 414110-4 LH3.

C Tannhäuser (1845)
* Anja Silja, soprano; Wolfgang Windgassen, tenor; Eberhard Wächter, baritone; Josef Greindl, bass; 1962 Bayreuth Festival Chorus and Orchestra; Wolfgang Sawallisch, conductor; Philips Festivo ▤ 7650026.

B Tristan und Isolde (1865)
$ Birgit Nilsson, soprano; Christa Ludwig, mezzo-soprano; Wolfgang Windgassen, tenor; Eberhard Wächter, baritone; Martti Talvela, bass; 1966 Bayreuth Festival Chorus and Orchestra; Karl Böhm, conductor; DG 2713001 (5 discs), ▤ 3378069.

A Die Walküre ("The Valkyries") (1870)
$ Régine Crespin, soprano; Birgit Nilsson, soprano; Christa Ludwig, mezzo-soprano; James King, tenor; Hans Hotter, bass-baritone; Gottlob

Frick, bass; Vienna State Opera Chorus; Vienna Philharmonic Orchestra; Sir George Solti, conductor; London 414105-1 LH4 (4 discs), ⊞ 414105-4 LH3.

Orchestral

A Overtures: <u>Der fliegende Holländer</u> ("The Flying Dutchman") (1843); <u>Rienzi</u> (1842); <u>Tannhäuser</u> (1845); and Prelude to the First Act of <u>Die Meistersinger</u> von <u>Nürnberg</u> ("The Master Singers of Nuremberg") (1868)

* Philharmonia Orchestra; Otto Klemperer, conductor; Angel AE-34418, ⊞ AE-34418.

A <u>Tristan</u> <u>und</u> <u>Isolde</u> Prelude and <u>Liebestod</u> ("Love Death") (1865)

$ Royal Philharmonic Orchestra; Leopold Stokowski, conductor; RCA ARL1-0498, ⊞ ARL1-0498. Includes selections from <u>Die Meistersinger</u> <u>von Nürnberg</u> ("The Master Singers of Nuremberg") (1868); Overture and Magic Fire Music from <u>Die Walküre</u> ("The Valkyries") (1870), all rated A.

Vocal

B <u>Wesendonck Lieder</u> ("Wesendonck Songs") (5) (1857-1858)--see entry under Brahms, Vocal, Rhapsody for Alto, Chorus and Orchestra, Op.53, <u>supra</u>.

WALTON, SIR WILLIAM
1902-1983

Sir William Turner Walton was born in Oldham, Lancashire and educated at Christ Church College, Oxford (he had attended the Christ Church Cathedral Choir School at Oxford at the age of 10) from 1918 to his expulsion for failing to study anything seriously but music. His sensational <u>Façade</u> Suite was written to poems by Edith Sitwell in 1922. He was knighted in 1951, having written the coronation march (<u>Crown Imperial</u>) for George VI (1937). He also wrote the coronation march (<u>Orb and Sceptre</u>) for Elizabeth II (1953). His music, after <u>Façade</u>, is essentially serious, well-crafted, and may cause ennui in the unwary.

Concerted

B Concerto for Violin and Orchestra (1939)--see entry under Sibelius, Concerted, Concerto for Violin, Op.47, in d, <u>supra</u>.

Orchestral

252

B Crown Imperial March (1937)--see entry under Elgar, Orchestral, Pomp and Circumstance March No.1, Op.39, in D, supra.

C Orb and Sceptre March (1953)--see entry under Elgar, Orchestral, Pomp and Circumstance March No.1, Op.39, in D, supra.

Vocal

A Façade Suite (To Poems by Edith Sitwell) (1922)

! Dame Edith Sitwell, reader; Ensemble; Frederick Prausnitz, conductor; Odyssey Y-32359.

WEBER, CARL MARIA VON
1786-1826

This German composer had more a pedigree than name: Carl Maria Friedrich Ernst, Freiherr von Weber. Mozart's wife, Constanze, was Weber's first cousin by marriage, and Weber's father encouraged his son's musical endeavors. All of Weber's musical education was received during the family's travels, via individual instructors on a rather "on the fly" basis. His first success was the production of his opera Silvana in Frankfurt in 1811. Given his age at his death, Weber's output was quite large. He suffered tuberculosis early on, and that disease was the cause of his death. With his opera Der Freischütz ("The Free Shooter"), Weber opened the epoch of German Romanticism, and his influence has thenceforth been pervasive.

Operatic

B Der Freischütz ("The Free Shooter") (1821)

$ Gundula Janowitz, soprano; Edith Mathis, soprano; Bernd Weikl, baritone; Theo Adam, bass; Franz Crass, bass; Leipzig Radio Chorus; Dresden State Opera Orchestra; Carlos Kleiber, conductor; DG 2709046 (3 discs), 337108.

Orchestral

A Invitation to the Dance (Orchestrated by Berlioz), Op.65.

$ New York Philharmonic Orchestra; Leonard Bernstein, conductor; Columbia M-33585. Includes the Overtures to Euryanthe (1823); Der Freischütz ("The Free Shooter") (1821) and Oberon (1826), all also rated A.

WIENAWSKI, HENRYK
1835-1888

Polish violinist and composer Wienawski was a most precocious child: he entered the Conservatoire de Paris at the age of 8 and graduated 3 years later, not only was he but 11 years old––he had taken first prize in violin. He toured, composed and joined the faculty of the Conservatory at Brussels. Proving himself a full-fledged Romantic, he died in the arms of a prostitute while on tour in Moscow.

Concerted

B Concerto for Violin No.2, Op.22, in d

$ Itzhak Perlman, violin; London Philharmonic Orchestra; Seiji Ozawa, conductor; Angel S-36903, ▣ 4XS-36903. Includes the same composer's Concerto for Violin No.1, Op.14, in f sharp.

Also––see entries under Paganini, Concerted, Concerto for Violin No.1, Op.6, in D and Saint-Saëns, Concerted, Concerto for Violin No.3, Op.61, in b, both supra.

WOLF, HUGO
1860-1903

Along with Schubert, Wolf is one of the three or four greatest exponents of the German Lied. He was born in Windischgraz (then Austria, now Yugoslavia) and christened Hugo Philipp Jakob Wolf. He was the 4th of 8 children and began studying the piano and violin with his father, who was a leather manufacturer. He was later a student at the Vienna Conservatory. He met with, and was encouraged by, Wagner in 1875. He became a music critic in 1883 and was one of the Wagnerites who heaped scorn on the works of Brahms. Wolf had been composing since he was a child (1873) and his output, given that early start, is not immense. His approximately 300 songs are the qua for which he is best known. In this special metier his style is rather Wagnerian in his novel harmonies and counterpoint, but his other attributes are more reminiscent of Schubert and Schumann. After institutionalization in a mental hospital and a couple of suicide attempts, Wolf's death was caused by, you guessed it, syphilis.

Chamber

B <u>Italian</u> Serenade (1893–1894)

* Melos Quartet; Turnabout 37005, ◙ CT–7005. Includes Bruckner's String Quintet, in F (1878–1879).

Vocal

B <u>Italienisches</u> <u>Liederbuch</u> ("Italian Song Book") (1889–1890)

* Elly Ameling, soprano; Tom Krause, baritone; Irwin Gage, piano; Nonesuch 78014 (2 discs), ◙ 78014.

B <u>Spanisches</u> <u>Liederbuch</u> ("Spanish Song Book") Selections (1889–1890)

* Jan De Gaetani, soprano; Gilbert Kalish, piano; Nonesuch 71296.